PRAISE FOR

Blinking Red Light

"Racy."

—*Philadelphia Daily News*

WIFEBEATER

A NOVEL

MISTER MANN FRISBY

RIVERHEAD FREESTYLE
NEW YORK

THE BERKLEY PUBLISHING GROUP
Published by the Penguin Group
Penguin Group (USA) Inc.
375 Hudson Street, New York, New York 10014, USA
Penguin Group (Canada), 10 Alcorn Avenue, Toronto, Ontario M4V 3B2, Canada
(a division of Pearson Penguin Canada Inc.)
Penguin Books Ltd., 80 Strand, London WC2R 0RL, England
Penguin Group Ireland, 25 St Stephen's Green, Dublin 2, Ireland
(a division of Penguin Books Ltd.)
Penguin Group (Australia), 250 Camberwell Road, Camberwell, Victoria 3124,
Australia (a division of Pearson Australia Group Pty. Ltd.)
Penguin Books India Pvt. Ltd., 11 Community Centre, Panchsheel Park,
New Delhi–110 017, India
Penguin Group (NZ), cnr Airborne and Rosedale Roads, Albany, Auckland 1310,
New Zealand (a division of Pearson New Zealand Ltd.)
Penguin Books (South Africa) (Pty.) Ltd., 24 Sturdee Avenue, Rosebank, Johannesburg 2196,
South Africa

Penguin Books Ltd., Registered Offices: 80 Strand, London WC2R 0RL, England

Cover design by Jaimie Keenan and Charles Bjorklund
Cover photos by Tony Barboza
Book design by Tiffany Estreicher

PRINTING HISTORY
First Riverhead Freestyle trade paperback edition: March 2005
Riverhead trade paperback ISBN: 1-59448-072-9

Library of Congress Cataloging-in-Publication Data

Frisby, Mister Mann.
Wifebeater / Mister Mann Frisby. — 1st Riverhead Freestyle trade pbk. ed.
p. cm.
ISBN 1-59448-072-9
1. African American men—Fiction. 2. Custody of children—Fiction. 3. Philadelphia (Pa.)—Fiction. 4. Divorced fathers—Fiction. 5. Rap musicians—Fiction. 6. Extortion—Fiction. I. Title.

PS3606.R575W54 2005
813'.6—dc22

PRINTED IN THE UNITED STATES OF AMERICA 2004061481

10 9 8 7 6 5 4 3 2 1

In memory of the late Steven C. Willoughby Sr. Thank you for being an excellent example of what a father should be. I pray that I live up to your standard.

ACKNOWLEDGMENTS

If you are a member of my family or a real friend and you know me . . . I mean really, really know me the way you tell your co-workers you do . . . the way you tell your neighbors you do . . . the way you tell Meka and 'nem you do . . . then you know that there is no way I can fit you all onto one page. You are so beautifully many, that listing all of your names would be a novel in itself.

I tried that the first time out the blocks and was not successful in showing my genuine appreciation to those who helped me along this eventful literary journey.

To all of my professional contacts and resources, I pray you nothing but excellence, great health, and tremendous fortune. In this business, you are nothing without a force of competent individuals behind you and I recognize that.

To all of the athletes whom I have coached in the last ten years, please know that many of you inspire me more than you'll ever know. I hope that I have made a difference in your lives, because I feel that next to being a father to Skye, coaching is the most important job I'll ever have.

This is only the beginning. By God's grace, many of you will benefit from my long-term vision. Be patient with me and pray for me because writing takes time, and often takes me away from those who I love to be around the most.

I'll leave you with these profound and deep words: "No Roger, No Re-Run, No Rent!"

WIFEBEATER

1. MONDAY, NOVEMBER 10, 2003 (8 A.M.)

I knew it was going to be a hell of a day when me and my daughter looked up to see something so intense it almost burned our eyes out.

It would be a long time before anything on my nineteen-inch RCA would catch me off guard like that again. At two years old, Brie had no idea what her eyes were focused on and would not remember any of it. I was grateful for that because I was two years away from turning thirty and I didn't know if I could handle it myself.

It was a dreary, nasty November day. The weather lady called it "brisk" but from my point of view it felt like the dead of winter in Russia. I remember the weather so well because I dressed Brie in five minutes flat and we went flying out the front door.

People stared but I didn't care. It was rainy and windy and my daughter was being hauled through South Philly in my arms without a hat on and only half her head braided. By the time I reached the corner of 23rd and Christian, at least four women had rolled their eyes at me in disgust.

I hooked her up the best I could, considering my hands were shaking like crazy and I had to piss like a racehorse. Nothing that she was wearing matched. She had on a pair of peach tights, a dark green turtleneck with red polka dots, and a pair of hot pink rain shoes that my aunt gave her as a gift. Brie's hair was only half braided because I started taking it out the night before. My neighbor Jar-u-queesha had taken her time to make my daughter look so pretty when she cornrowed her hair the week before, but at that point she looked like an extra from *The Color Purple*.

Brie's mother and her conniving lawyer would have loved to catch that Kodak moment. Minerva wanted to see me slip up so bad. My ex prayed for the day when I would crumble under the pressure of being a single dad. She wanted full custody, but I knew that Michael Jackson would sooner be Wesley Snipes' complexion before I let that happen.

But that crazy-ass morning changed everything. As flaky and unreliable as Minerva could be, I started to think that her ghetto fabulous rattrap in North Philly would be the safest place for my little princess. I picked up my cordless and hung it up so many times before I left the house because I was tempted to call somebody, anybody, and tell them what we had seen. But I kept stopping myself. It was hardly a conversation to have with anyone, let alone over the phone.

I was instantly paranoid. It wasn't so much the *what* as the *who* that made it so off the damn hook. And that's not saying that the *what* didn't take the cake too.

I have replayed that morning so many times in my head since that day. Brie woke up at about seven that morning, fussing because she wanted to watch a particular *Teletubbies* tape for the umpteenth time. It was cool at first. I used to get a kick out of seeing my baby mesmerized by those four colorful creatures, but after about six months of playing that tape I wanted to go through the TV screen and give Dipsy, Laa-Laa, Po, and Tinky Winky a straight-up rumble. I laughed to myself sometimes just picturing me throwing them off a cliff one at a time.

I was real groggy when she woke me up because I had been up to about five in the morning trying to write a paper for an online course I was taking for like four hundred dollars. I was past the regular deadline and it didn't look like I was going to be finished by the extended deadline either. Being a full-time solo dad with a two-year-old at home was way more off the hook and time consuming than I ever thought it would be.

Brie woke me up the way she does every morning, with one of those wet, sloppy kisses. It did the trick every time. I jumped up right away before I could fall back asleep and Brie wouldn't start bawling out of control. My eyes were barely open while I was looking on the shelf trying to find the VHS case with her favorite characters. Before I could locate the tape, my eyes stopped on a tape that was sitting upright and not in a case. The label had dingy, yellow tape on the side and it read: *Teletubbies (5-Hour Marathon)*.

I knew right away that I hadn't seen the tape before. It made me wake up real quick. I was just standing scratching my braids and trying to figure out where it came from, when it hit me. My mother and her three coworkers took off work a few days before to go to a huge flea market in Norristown. She had definitely mentioned something to me about buying Brie some new tapes, but it went in one ear and out the other.

I was on the phone with the people from the electric company pleading with them to keep my electric on for at least another week when my mom dropped by. PECO was on my back tougher than Verizon and it had me vexed that day. I could hardly remember my mom's visit, let alone her leaving a bag of flea market toys she bought for Brie.

Even though Brie had tapes, dolls, and toys in almost every room of the house, that tape stood out.

Most of the time, it was one big pile of madness. Everything talked. The yellow school bus sang nursery rhymes when she pushed it, her doll baby recited the alphabet, and most annoyingly my baby's Elmo doll sang the *Sesame Street* theme song in Spanish. It could probably do the "Harlem Shake" if you squeezed it the right way.

So, when I saw that one of the tapes had five hours of *Teletubbies* on it, I grabbed it off the shelf with the swiftness of a ninja on crack. Those overstuffed characters kept her glued to the screen and quiet and that's what I was looking for that morning. All I needed was maybe two more hours of sleep and I would have been straight. I wish.

Brie was already settled into her plush little yellow Teletubbies chair when I popped the tape into the VCR and went downstairs to the kitchen to get her something to eat. I was tired as hell so I kept it real simple. I poured her a bowl of Honeycombs. I was too lazy to even put milk in the bowl.

The kitchen was bordering on filthy and I wanted to get in and out. I made my way back into my bedroom, or our bedroom I should say because she never slept in her own room at night.

I handed Brie the bowl of cereal but she never took her eyes off the screen. The Teletubbies had Brie in the zone. I stretched back out across my king-sized bed, our king-sized bed, and dozed off. It was November 10, five days after my baby's birthday. The last thing I remember before our lives took a dramatic turn was Brie leaning back in her chair and watching those four colorful bastards dance around the grassy hills as if they were high on that shit.

I was sleeping hard at first. It was the kind of snooze that you fight somebody for interrupting. About twenty minutes or so into my semi-coma, Brie woke me up tugging on my arms and whining. I was more confused than annoyed because she always, without fail, watched the *Teletubbies* quietly until the credits rolled. Wild Rugrats couldn't drag her from in front of the screen. So even though I was halfway in dreamland, I knew that something had to be wrong. I sat up with a jolt.

It wasn't the normal PBS type of sounds. It was a far cry from Bert and Ernie kickin' it on *Sesame Street.* What I heard that morning was more like the sounds that fill my bedroom when Brie goes to visit her grandmother, and Nia from 33rd Street visits me.

Of course I thought I was still dreaming. I sat up and Brie was standing at the edge of the bed. At first she was blocking my view of the TV, but I could still hear the grunts, moans, and laughter as clear as day. I reached forward and picked my baby up so that I could get a clear look at the screen.

It wasn't so much the *what* as the *who*.

I was stunned. It's not shit else I can say except that I was stuck on stupid. My first reaction was to cover my baby's eyes but it was already too late for that. I realized later that she had already seen about five minutes of the action on screen before I woke up and stopped the tape.

At that moment I vowed that I would never tell Brie about what her precious little eyes had witnessed. That all went out the window when my name, and hers, started to make newspaper headlines. When the smoke cleared, I knew I would have to break it all down for her one day. She was definitely going to have questions and I knew that I would have to do my best to break her off with honest-to-God answers. But in the meantime, what a way to start our week.

2. MONDAY, NOVEMBER 10, 2003 (3 P.M.)

Me and Brie were driving down Broad Street on our way to nowhere in particular. The rain was coming down in buckets at that point and of course the defrost on my '89 Honda Accord was working when it wanted to. I pulled over to the curb at least three times because I could hardly see my hand in front of my face. Tiffany Bacon was on Power 99 telling folks to be careful on the roads because the winds were gusting up to forty-five miles per hour. Brie was extremely grouchy and restless in her car seat and so was I. I tried my best to comfort her by looking in the rearview mirror and singing the Barney song but it wasn't working.

My palms were sweating and my head was spinning because I knew that I had some major shit stashed between Brie's Pampers and sippy cups inside of her purple baby bag. I think I reached over and felt inside of that bag at least three times to make sure it was still there.

I turned the radio off because I couldn't hear myself think with all of the bullshit blaring from the speakers. I couldn't tell Chingy from Nelly or Busta Rhymes from Sean Paul.

As I drove aimlessly through South Philly and Center City, I started to think of who was actually home at that time of the day.

Everyone I knew, except for myself, had a regular nine-to-five gig. Everybody was at work getting it in and I was driving up and down Broad Street trying to figure out who I could trust the most.

There was Nkosi, my boaw from way back. We came up in the projects down South Philly together and basically were like brothers. We went back to kindergarten and fighting at recess and making up by three o'clock. He was one of the few people who I knew growing up that lived under the same roof with their mom and dad. There were so many times when I was a young boaw and my back was up against the wall and he came through without even making a big deal about it. Nkosi fought in the streets like the rest of us living in the projects at 13th and Fitzwater, but I don't think he ever got less than a B when we were coming up. His focus was tight when it needed to be and that's one thing I always respected about him. I hung with him a lot because he pulled a lot of chicks. He looks like a slightly older version of Kobe Bryant and the ladies don't ever let him forget it. Every time we're out together he gets that comparison at least once.

Even though he was always down for a nigga, his line of work made me hesitant about going to him. He had a gig as a news reporter for the *Philadelphia Tribune*. What I was holding would have stopped the presses at any newspaper or magazine in the country, let alone the largest black newspaper in Philly.

Kheli was my next option since she was my closest female friend. In high school she was a bona fide tomboy who handled the rock just like the other boaws we played ball with. She could have easily started at point guard for Tennessee or Duke but by the time she reached her senior year, running ball had played out like *Knots Landing*. She tossed all her sneaks and replaced them with pretty little sandals that laced up her delicious thick calves and showed off every inch of her flawless feet. By the time we were legal, Kheli had totally flipped the script on all the dudes who grew up around the way.

The same cats who used to play dirty against her on the court would stop and stutter when they passed her on the street. Kheli had just the right amount of sexy, cinnamon thickness to make a nigga start offering rent and utility money.

By the time we were legal, Kheli was shutting the whole damn game down every time we went out to the club. She spent hours at the hairdresser and even more time in New York trying to cop whatever the new hot designer pocketbook was. I knew that Kheli was someone that I could trust. She always confided in me with the major drama that was going on in her life and I did the same with her.

She told me more times than I care to remember that I should leave Minerva alone but I ain't listen. They almost came to blows one time because my daughter's mother was jealous of our relationship. Minerva thought that it was more to us, but Kheli was just like one of my dawgs. The only difference is that she wore Louis Vuitton and Prada all the time.

The last person on my short list was Xavier. We met a year ago when I worked a part-time job at AT&T Wireless selling cell phones. We were from two different worlds but we clicked right away. Xavier was a pretty boy who had at least five pairs of the same colored khakis and only wore sneaks to take out the garbage. The boaw spent mad time at the gym when he wasn't getting his hustle on at Home Depot. He was dark skinned, bald, 6'4", and a perfect fill-in for any of them brothas on the *Amistad* slave movie.

He had one kid, a son named Melvin, who lived down in Baltimore with the mom. This jawn gave him major drama when it came time for him to see his son, who was seven or eight years old at the time. If nothing else, we bonded on the strength of talking about the crazy-ass chickenheads in our lives. Even on days when we didn't have to work we would kick it at Dave & Buster's or at one of the hot spots in Old City. Xavier was definitely someone that I could tell some confidential-type shit to.

I never really even considered telling my cousin Shadeed. He was one of my closest friends and definitely my favorite cousin but I ain't think he could handle it. It's crazy when I look back and think just how much he would play in the whole situation.

So, there I was on that crazy-ass Monday morning trying to figure out what to do. Looking back, and I think I might've known it then, I should've just tossed that tape in the Delaware River. As a matter of fact, I should've banged it into a million little pieces, doused it in gasoline, and tossed a match on that bitch.

There are a lot of could've-would've-should'ves but it's too late to talk all that shit now. After cruising around South Philly all day and wasting almost a half of a tank of gas, I decided to drive to Marvine Street and park my car in front of Kheli's house. I said to myself, "If she comes home by five then I'll tell her about the tape." If not, I planned on going to Nkosi's apartment in University City.

It was a few minutes before five when Kheli Stockton, an overworked social worker for the Department of Human Services pulled up behind me in her purple Neon. I guess it was meant for her to be the first one to see it.

She wasn't a minute too soon because Brie was annoyed as hell that I had her strapped in the car seat all day. I took her out when we went to McDonald's and another time when I pulled over to change her Pamper. She had just turned two on November 5 and she wasn't even close to being fully potty trained. I was sick and tired of being in that car, so I know she was too. It's just that I couldn't sit in the house that day for nothing. My energy level was through the roof like one of them overhyped rappers on the MTV awards. How ironic.

The rain had let up a little at that point. Kheli hopped out of her whip and headed toward mine. I rolled down the window real cool and acted like I wasn't about to lose it.

"Wassup? I didn't know you and little Brie-Brie were coming through today."

Kheli was all smiles. It always made her day to see Brie even if we were dropping by unannounced.

"I was around the way and I figured you would be coming home around now so we decided to drop in and check you out. Ain't that right Ka-look-ee?"

"Please stop calling her Ka-look-ee. That's a hot-ass mess. And why are y'all even out in this nasty-ass weather? And what the hell happened to her hair?"

"Oh, we kinda left out the house before I could finish taking it out . . ."

"As a social worker I would have to turn your black ass in for letting her come out of the house looking like this, but as your friend I will finish taking these crazy-looking braids out her head and put in some ponytails."

"I would gladly appreciate that."

Kheli opened the back door and started to unstrap Brie from her car seat. I scooped up the baby bag that was covered in teddy bears and A-B-Cs and got out of the car. We hiked up three stiff-ass flights of steps to get to Kheli's apartment. Like any toddler worth their own salt, Brie went right for the scissors on the oval glass coffee table as soon as we got there.

We spent the first five minutes trying to baby-proof her living room. Kheli was a real neat freak but there was a whole lot of glass and little stuff that Brie could've choked on just laying around in that jawn.

My buddy had her crib laid out. Everything was a different shade of red but it looked decent. The couch, the area rug, and even her chessboard was red. Her kitchen, which was damn near in the living room because her pad was so small, was white though. Pictures of her brothers, all six of them, were hanging in big frames all over the wall. Even at twenty-eight years old Kheli still got a kick out of being the only girl in the Stockton clan. Kheli kept herself occupied with Brie for almost an hour.

She did her hair for me and they played a little before she started rubbing on her eyes and fussing. She fought sleep for a little while but it wasn't anything that a pro dad like myself couldn't handle. My seed was only two years old and I felt like I had been doing the big poppa thing for a minute. Kheli fed her some chicken and broccoli and I poured some apple juice in her sippy cup to polish her off. Brie was down for the count before seven o'clock.

She drifted off to the sounds of cold rain and wind whipping against the windows. After she fell asleep I stood over top of her and stared for a few minutes. Even though she came into my life more than two years ago, I still couldn't believe that I was somebody's father. Every time I looked at Brie it was like staring in the mirror. We had the same high yellow skin and what my mom called "cat eyes." Her complexion was just a tad lighter though. Brie was what they would call a "red-bone" in the hood. Our mouths were shaped totally different but neither one of us really had any eyebrows. She made up for that with all that damn hair on her head. When her hair was wet it dropped well below the middle of her back. My skills only allowed for one ponytail, maybe two if I was feeling patient enough to make a straight part. If you squinted really hard and tilted your head to the side while jumping up and down I guess you could see a little bit of Minerva in her too. At least a little bit is all I wanted to see, because I didn't want my daughter to be anything like her mother.

I turned out the light and went back into the living room with Kheli and just started spilling it.

"Hey yo Kheli, does your VCR work?"

"Yeah man, you know my VCR works. Why you ask me that?"

"Listen man, I have something I need to show you . . . It's crazy."

I stood up and started pacing back and forth because I was trying to find the words to say to Kheli before I popped that jawn in the VCR. I didn't want her to just see it like I did. I wanted her to be warned first, because what was on that tape was some real shit. I handed her the tape and she looked down at it while she was walking across the room to pop it in.

"Oh this daddy day care shit is really getting to you because you want me to sit up here and watch five hours of Teletubbies with you."

"Naw dawg, trust me . . ."

"And stop calling me dawg. I'm a lady, I am not your dawg, or your nigga, or your boaw."

"Whatever man, just put the tape on and make sure the volume is down too. Can your neighbors hear through these walls?"

"Why are you acting so damn paranoid all of a sudden? Oh God, what is this a porno tape . . . ?"

"I wish it was only a smut tape."

The look on her face changed quickly. I think my expression must have told her that it was about to get real up in that piece. Them four colorful nuisances better known as the Teletubbies were dancing around like jerks on the screen, just like when I saw the tape for the first time. I picked up the VCR remote control and fast-forwarded the action with the picture still on the screen. They looked just as goofy going at warp speed.

My heart started beating fast all over again. Kheli was sitting on the edge of the couch with her eyes stuck on her thirty-six-inch Magnavox. She even went into her pocketbook and took out her busted-ass eyeglasses to make sure she didn't miss any details.

I wanted to tell her that it didn't matter. I wanted to tell her that the faces and action were going to jump out at her like a 3-D flick. I didn't say anything else though. I wanted to see what her reaction was going to be.

Just as the Teletubbies were fading from the screen and the fuzzy picture was switching over to the images that had my head messed up all day, me and Kheli got a jolt that almost made both of us jump out of our skin.

There were three loud thuds on her door. I don't know if it seemed loud as hell because I was so on edge, but that shit made me jump off the couch. I dropped the remote and it crashed down on the floor sending both of the triple-A batteries flying in two different directions.

Kheli jumped up and headed to the door while I jetted to the VCR.

"Who is it?"

"Kheli, it's me. Open up."

"Oh Dee-Dee . . ."

By the time Kheli opened up the door and Dee-Dee was barreling into the apartment, I had already hit the stop and rewind buttons on the VCR. She had a laundry hamper gripped in both hands with detergent and fabric softener balanced on top. She was rocking a tight jean set and had a dripping-wet Super Fresh plastic bag covering her head.

"Oh hey. I didn't know you were here. I guess that's your Accord outside?"

"You know it's my whip out there, Dee. Stop acting like you ain't the nosiest chick breathing on the 700 block of south Marvine Street. You probably were peeking through your blinds when I pulled up."

Dee-Dee slammed the door behind her with one of her size twelve Timberland boots and dropped the laundry hamper on the floor.

"Please boy, I ain't thinking about you."

"You're always thinking about me . . ."

Kheli walked back over to the couch and plopped down. She sucked her teeth and let out one of them "I got an attitude" sighs.

"Hey Kheli, you remember you told me that I could wash my clothes tonight right?"

"Oh yeah girl, that's fine with me. You can start whenever you want, I don't have anything in the washer this time."

Dee-Dee looked at me and then back at Kheli like she knew that she had caught us in the middle of something. It was quiet and awkward for a few seconds.

"Am I interrupting something?"

"Girl, no you ain't interrupting nothing. It's just that I forgot you were coming tonight but it's cool."

"If you say so . . ."

The tape stopped and ejected on its own. I bent over and snatched it out of the VCR.

"What were y'all doing?" Dee-Dee asked, as she lifted up her hamper again and walked toward the closet in the kitchen with the washer and dryer.

"We were watching a movie about a nosy neighbor who comes across the street to use her best friend's washing machine and gets hacked into little pieces by a handsome visitor."

She walked by and cut me a nasty look. A few seconds later she was smirking and then she busted out laughing.

"You are not going to worry me, you hear. I ain't paying you no mind up in here tonight."

I loved getting under Dee-Dee's skin and man was it a lot of skin. The funny thing about seeing them two together was how Kheli was the one who used to play ball, while Dee-Dee looked more the part of a power forward.

When we all went around to 10th and Lombard to run ball at Seger's back in the day, cats always thought that Dee was the one coming to play. She was at least 6'1" and stocky as shit. I didn't know too many dudes with shoulders that broad or a jawbone that strong. Ray Lewis would have to come with it to knock her ass over.

Her grill wasn't busted or nothing like that. It's just that she was working with more than enough of everything. Dee-Dee had female bouncer written all over every inch of her 210-pound frame. All that height and brawn and I don't think she ever played a sport a day in her life. In fact, I don't ever recall seeing her break a sweat unless you count all the fights she got in when we were young bucks.

While she started on her clothes I slipped the tape back into the baby bag, on the down low, and zipped it up. Kheli picked up the TV remote and started flipping through channels.

I was pissed because I really wanted her to see the tape and there was no way I could do that with Dee-Dee all up in the mix. Kheli couldn't keep still on the couch after that. I knew the suspense was killing her. If I couldn't watch the tape I at least wanted to be able to tell her about it. Thank God, she was thinking quicker than me.

"Dee-Dee, we are going to run down South Street real quick and get some dessert. Can you watch Brie for a few?"

"Oh yeah, that's no problem. How long has she been sleep?"

"She just went to sleep but we won't be that long. We're just going to run to 5th Street and get something sweet. We'll be back in a half an hour at the most."

"That's fine . . . take your time . . . oh yeah, Netta and Irene said that they were going to drop by with the twins Jonathan and Jason. I wish Brie was woke so that she could play with her little buddies."

"Yeah well don't go waking my baby up to play with Netta's nappy-headed little boys. She had a long day and—"

"Say no more big daddy!"

Kheli put her shoes back on and grabbed her car keys from off the coffee table. I pushed the baby bag up against the side of the couch and threw my sweat jacket back on. It was time for me to put Kheli down.

3. MONDAY, NOVEMBER 10, 2003 (7:30 P.M.)

We made a quick hustle to the Johnny Rockets diner at 5th and South. It was one of them old-fashioned jawns where the waiters and waitresses sang old songs every ten minutes.

Neither one of us was in the mood for Frankie Lymon or Elvis Presley that night. Hard-core hip-hop was more the order of the day.

We ordered milkshakes and cheese fries to justify taking up a booth by the window but neither one of us was hungry. Kheli jumped right to it.

"So what's the deal? What is so damn hot and juicy on that tape?"

I started from the beginning. I told Kheli about how my mother had bought the tape at a flea market and how she had dropped it off for Brie at my crib at least a week ago. Before I moved on I paused to look around. There were people sitting at booths on both sides of us and I was constantly making sure that they weren't listening to our conversation.

The couple that I was facing was dressed in all black with the crazy dark-ass makeup on like vampires. Even though it was ten days after Halloween, it was easy to see that the whole gothic look was their style 365 days of the year. Sitting behind me were three white dudes who all looked to be in their thirties until they opened their mouths. They sounded like a sound byte from a suburban high school conversation.

"Listen Kheli, I thought long and hard about whether or not I should show you the tape or even tell you about this. I have to admit that I still don't know what to do about it but I know you'll be able to give me some feedback."

"What the hell are you talking about? What is on that tape?"

I took a deep breath and then leaned in real close to Kheli across the table. Without coming up for breath I started to run that shit down. I told her about everything that I saw on the tape without getting into too much detail. I knew that she was going to see it for herself.

Her mouth was wide open when I finished telling her what I had seen.

"You need to stop fucking playing with me. Please tell me that you are making this shit up?"

"Why would I lie about something like that? Now you see why I'm so messed up in the head today."

"Are you sure it wasn't somebody who looked a whole lot like them?"

"Kheli, listen to me, there is not a doubt in my mind. I know what I saw, and if Brie could talk in full sentences she would tell you the same damn thing."

I don't know what I was expecting but Kheli definitely didn't react like I thought she would. I thought she would have been more upset but she seemed more intrigued than anything else. Just on the strength that she's a female I figured that she would feel sorry for the woman on the tape.

"You know I love him to death right?"

"Do I know? You're fucking with me right? He's all you talk about. You have all six of his albums and you and Dee-Dee go and see him every time he comes to Philly. That's why I was scared to tell you at first because I didn't know how you would react or if you could keep it to yourself."

Her next statement knocked me off my block for a few seconds.

"I heard about this already . . ."

"What?! What do you mean you heard about this already? You heard about the tape?"

"No I didn't hear about any tape but I was watching MTV the other day and they had it on the news again. And they were talking about it on BET and *Extra* . . . Where have you been, under a rock? The shit happened back in January, it's just that the trial is coming up in a couple of months I guess."

"My cable is cut off."

"They been talking about it on the radio every morning."

"Me and Brie don't get up that early every day and when we do the last thing I do is turn on the radio. What have they been saying?"

"They said that some chick from Philly went to police and pressed rape charges. Did it seem like she was being raped on the tape?"

"With three of them it did, but not with all four of them. The other two I never seen a day in my life. Did they say what her name was?"

"Of course not . . . but damn this is crazy . . . So what are you going to do with it?"

"I don't know, I was hoping you would bless with me some knowledge. I need a female point of view."

We went over a few scenarios at the table. What Kheli said next totally surprised me. Not just because it was coming from someone I knew so well, but because it was coming from a chick.

"I say you get in contact with him and get money from him in exchange for the tape. Don't turn it in so that hoochie can use it to get him locked up."

I just looked at Kheli like, damn, after she said that.

"Are you for real? You want me to blackmail the most popular rapper on the planet?"

Of course the thought had crossed my mind dozens of times during that day, I just didn't expect someone else, especially Kheli, to be on the same page.

"Look what's happened has already happened. Let that trick's attorneys figure out a way to prove that they did it. This is a chance for you to get paid. You got a daughter, remember, and the rent is due and you got a Honda Accord with a defrost that don't work. This is your big meal ticket man! This is like fate or something that you got this tape so you have to run with it."

Kheli was right. My back was up against the wall in a major way. I had three hundred dollars in the bank and most of that was already designated for overdue utility bills. Brie had about five or six Pampers left and it was well past time for me to go food shopping. DHS would drag me away in cuffs if it came down to me giving her potato chips and pretzels for breakfast.

My money situation would've looked a little tighter if I was the type of dude to get in the crack game. There were more than enough offers on the table for me to sell drugs. In those last three weeks alone, two of my boaws from down South Philly were in my face trying to get me to hustle. All I had to do was say the word and I was in, but I ain't want it with the game.

I ain't want to be one of them cats sitting up on State Road depending on somebody on the outside to send me pictures of Brie, or worse, depending on a motherfucker to bring her to see me. I had to be around to protect her and make sure she ain't turn out to be a chickenhead. I felt for them niggas who was locked down when something happened to their kids. When I would see that type of shit on the news it would make me cringe for them because I know they had to feel like a waste of skin sitting in prison.

On the flip side, blackmail was illegal too and could land my ass in hot water just as quick. For some reason I ain't look at it the same way at the time. Standing on the corner selling drugs was a definite dead-end way to get my ass killed or put away. But getting money from the rapper dude ain't seem like it was that dangerous.

I was in a position that I never in a million years expected to be in. You just can't plan on getting a video tape with the largest rapper alive doing something illegal. I fantasized about hitting the Powerball just as much as the next nigga, but I ain't think my first million was going to come to me through hip-hop.

Everything Kheli said made sense, but I really didn't want to hear that from her. I wanted Kheli to talk me out of doing something as insane as blackmailing Snatch-Back. Not that I thought much of him anyway. His rhymes were about as original as a Ricki Lake talk show topic. He wasn't a real thorough emcee in my opinion like Common or Mos Def, but he still had a solid reputation with hip-hop fans.

Snatch-Back came in the game and invaded LL Cool J territory by getting just as many half-naked screaming females on his tip as well as the thugged-out crowd too. His empire was built on spitting rhymes that were not as over the top and raunchy as 2 Live Crew but were still pretty X-rated for when they played on the radio at three in the afternoon. He was far from a thug himself though and you could tell that from a mile away. *People* magazine voted him one of the sexiest people alive too, so it was obvious that he had managed to cross over.

If Snatch-Back ever fell off as a rapper, he could easily find a career as a poster child for one of them gyms. Dude was chiseled, dark skinned, and he had all of his teeth. His rhymes were triple-X but what made him really stand from a lot of other dudes in the game was that he didn't have one tattoo on his body. He always bragged in interviews that he would never mark up his body since he worked so hard to keep it looking tight.

Since I wasn't a hard-core fan like Kheli, I still had to learn more about him, but there were a few things that everybody knew. The drama at hand was not the first time he made headlines for being arrested.

At the end of 2000 he was locked up in L.A. for supposedly forcing this chick to perform oral sex on him. That shit blew up big on the news for a couple of reasons. Not only was the jawn that accused him only seventeen years old, but she also had a sexual assault case pending against an R&B singer in another city.

Her credibility got ripped apart before the main trial even started and the charges eventually got thrown out. Snatch-Back lost some of his sponsors when everything broke but when the smoke cleared he came up like a motherfucker. He bounced right back with a million-dollar ad campaign for a new brand of jeans, so I guess the joke was on everybody who hated him and thought his career was over.

Since beating that case he made two new movies and put out a couple of albums. If anything, getting accused of a sex crime only boosted his career. Before that he was strictly a ghetto superstar but then all of a sudden they were showing him on *Access Hollywood* and *Extra* alongside the white folks.

"Are you just telling me to do this because you don't want to see him go to jail? Or are you really concerned about me getting some cheese to pay my bills?" I asked.

"I mean I love him and all yes! But I am more or less thinking about you feeding Brie and putting clothes on her back. That man sold six million copies of his last album and knocked 50 Cent and Jay-Z off the charts. I don't think he'll have a problem coming off a little bit of them chips to keep his ass out of jail."

"How much would you ask for?"

"I don't know . . . I have no idea . . . how about start with a million and see what happens from there . . ."

"A million . . . are you crazy? That seems like too damn much. Could you imagine if a million bones turned up in my bank account all of a sudden? That would send a red alert to the White House or some shit. I got like three hundred dollars in the bank right now. That's it."

"Exactly. How are you going to pay the rent and buy Brie's Pampers and food with three hundred dollars? You need this cash. And the last thing you need is Minerva finding out that your ass is broke. She would get a lawyer and be all over you if they knew your bank account was on E."

"I know that I need the cash but what would I have done if my mom never bought this tape?"

"You would be evicted and back home with her and with your two-year-old daughter that's what. You're still trying to figure out what you want to do with your life and you ain't nowhere near getting a degree. The fact remains you and Brie have to eat every day, and obviously your case money is wiped out."

"I don't know about this . . ."

Her words made me cringe, but she was right. I knew one way or another Kheli would bring up the fact that I managed to blow almost twenty grand in less than a year with little to show for it. Other than my new leather sectional, a dope new computer, and a name-brand wardrobe for Brie I didn't have much at all to show for winning my case against SEPTA.

I got fucked up real bad when a bus I was on slid on a patch of ice and slammed into a tree. I was banged up for a minute. My shoulder hit this metal pole so hard that I was sore for a month. After a few months of physical therapy and mad visits to my lawyer's office they settled on twenty grand.

I managed to break my landlord off with six months of rent in all of the madness. I was wining and dining and smashing every fine-ass chick south of City Hall. Yet in still, I couldn't tell you where all of the loot went when it was gone. I was spending so fast that I didn't put anything aside for me to get another car or even pay my taxes for that matter. I blew it big-time.

Kheli's words put a lump in my throat. I loved my daughter more than anything on this crazy-ass planet and there wasn't much I wouldn't do to see her happy. And it just so happened that little things like milk, food, and a warm house made her happy.

There was so much stacked against me raising a child by myself, especially a daughter. I think that if Brie was a boy people wouldn't ask me all the time if I could really hack it alone. Like I always said, everyone, no matter how many kids they have, was always a parent for the first time at one point or another. Anybody with kids has to learn as they go and I was no different.

I leaned back in the booth and just stared at Kheli. The wheels inside my head were spinning full speed. Just that quick I could picture me and Brie out in one of them suburbs like Bala Cynwyd in a phat crib where she could actually go outside and play without ducking gunshots.

If I went through with what Kheli was suggesting, I knew it would be a crime and all but it was a chance that I had to take. Having a seed made me think differently. I hadn't been one for making any real major moves up to that point in my life, and it was about time. It was like a billion-to-one chance that I would even get my hands on that tape so I knew it had to be a sign for me to get it crackin'.

"Where do I even begin?" I said.

"You'll figure it out. I mean come on, your best friend works for a newspaper. Nkosi can help you get in contact with him. I know he interviewed him before. I say you get started now because somebody else may have a copy of that tape too."

That was something that I never thought about. Even though I still didn't know at that point how the tape got to my house, it seemed like a total fluke that I had a copy. It had never crossed my mind that there could be another one floating around out there.

Kheli and I were at the diner for more than an hour and a half before we flagged down our waiter and settled the bill. I was in a total different mindset when we got up to leave out. Kheli had convinced me that I had something that was very valuable. I knew that one way or another it would change me and Brie's lives for the better.

Shit, I felt like Superman or Hulk Hogan when we were walking back to Kheli's car. I had the power and it felt good. The most popular rapper on the planet would have to bow down and kiss my feet because I had something that he needed. In my head I saw myself walking right up to him and saying here's my routing number, make it happen beeyotch!

The fantasy in my head and my power trip was fun while it lasted. Looking back I would say that it was all of twelve minutes.

4. MONDAY, NOVEMBER 10, 2003 (8:30 P.M.)

When me and Kheli got back to her apartment, Dee-Dee was laying on the couch watching an episode of *Las Vegas*. Her big-ass feet were draped over the arm of the couch. She had certainly made herself comfortable.

The first thing I did was dip into Kheli's bedroom to check on Brie. She was knocked out. I mean slobber out the corner of the mouth and all. I pulled the sheets up over her legs and kissed her on the cheek.

After that I went straight to the kitchen to get me something to drink because I hardly touched my milkshake when we were at the diner. Kheli and Dee-Dee were yakking it up while I poured a big-ass cup of Pepsi.

"Where were y'all at for so long? Netta stopped by with the twins and Irene had her brother's baby too."

"Aww, I wanted to see Irene's nephew. When did they leave?"

"Y'all just missed them. Jonathan and Jason started acting kind of wild so you know how that goes. Netta scooped them up and they rolled out of here in a hurry."

I almost choked on the soda when she said that because at that very moment I looked up and Brie's baby bag was not on the side of the couch where I left it. My body got numb for a split second and it felt like I was going to shit on myself. It was like spiders were crawling up my arms all of a sudden.

"Yo Dee-Dee, where is Brie's baby bag?"

"It's right where you left it at fool."

Dee-Dee lifted up one of her well-manicured hooves and pointed in the direction of the television. I slammed the cup down on Kheli's miniature kitchen table and took three big steps to get back in the living room.

A zipped-up baby bag was sitting directly in front of the VCR. I rushed over to the bag and picked it up. The spiders started crawling again because it felt like somebody had put a bowling ball up in that jawn.

I knew instantly that something was wrong because Brie's bag was never that heavy. When I packed Brie's bag for the day I didn't pack it like a woman. Minerva would always cram a whole lot of unnecessary bullshit in there, most of it belonging to her. Me and Brie only rolled out with the essentials.

My hand was shaking when I finally unzipped it and Kheli was on her feet at that point. All I could do was curse when I looked in that jawn. It was a purple baby bag covered in teddy bears alright, but it wasn't Brie's.

The tape was nowhere to be seen. There were just two bottles filled with milk, a big-ass jar of hair gel, a hot iron, a pack of batteries, a photo album, and all of these squashed Pampers.

"Yo Dee-Dee, this is not Brie's fucking bag! Where the hell is her bag?"

"What the hell are you talking about? Why ain't it her bag?"

I just started pulling everything out of the bag and throwing it to the floor I was so pissed.

"Because none of this shit belongs to me and my daughter!"

"Oh my God . . . Oh my God . . . Netta or Irene must have taken Brie's baby bag by mistake and that's one of theirs . . ."

"What! You let them walk out of here with my daughter's bag!"

Kheli walked over to me and grabbed me by my wrist. I was so damn mad that if smoke could come out of my ears it would've been thick and black like charcoal.

"You need to keep your voice down before you wake Brie up. Now I'm sure there is a very logical explanation for all of this. Irene or Netta probably picked up Brie's bag by mistake thinking that it was theirs. As soon as they figure it out I'm sure they'll bring it back."

"Kheli, you know I can't fucking wait. I need to get in touch with them. Dee-Dee, do you have their numbers?"

"I have their home numbers but I know they're not all the way up Mt. Airy already because they just left right before y'all got here."

"Do they have cell phones?"

"I think Netta has one but—why are you so pressed? Kheli has extra bottles here and I can run the store to get a bag of Pampers if you need them right away."

"I am so pressed because I want my daughter's baby bag. I don't want Netta's fucking baby bag and I don't want Irene's baby bag. I want the one that belongs to me."

Kheli started sifting through the mess I had made on the floor and figured out pretty quickly that the bag belonged to Netta. The photo album was packed with pictures of Jonathan and Jason, the bad-ass twins. The hair gel was another dead giveaway now that I think about it, because that chick always had a gang of baby hair matted to both sides of her face.

"So now what I am I supposed to do, Kheli?"

"Listen, all you can do is wait. I am sure that she is going straight home with them two monsters in her car. They're a handful when they get grouchy."

I just sat down on the couch and buried my face in my hands. I knew it was going to be a long-ass half an hour. Dee-Dee apologized so many times over the next fifteen minutes or so, but it didn't stop me from wanting to wrap my hands around her thick-ass neck. I wanted to kick myself too for not taking the tape with me but I didn't see the need at the time. I was so pressed to tell Kheli about what was on that thing that I wasn't thinking. And what made me really feel like a dickhead was the fact that the very exact thing almost happened before.

Me and Brie were in line at McDonald's one day when a lady behind me reached down and accidentally picked up our bag. I stopped her before she walked off with her baby and my bag, and we laughed it off. Everybody and their mother had the same purple baby bag with teddy bears and A-B-Cs on it. They gave them out for free at nearly every hospital before you leave with your baby. Brie's bag was pretty dogged because I was too cheap to get another one. It was clean, zipped up most of the time, and it served its purpose so I saw no need to upgrade.

I was starting to sweat in Kheli's apartment because I could see my million dollars slipping away. Snatch-Back didn't even know I existed and I had already started counting the loot in my head. There was a dark orange Hummer with my name written all over it.

The phone rang about twenty minutes after we got back to the apartment and we all made a mad dash to the coffee table where the phone was sitting. Kheli pushed the talk button before one ring could finish. It was some clown from her job at DHS who was trying to get in her panties. I knew it was a dude right away because she started blushing and walked away from me and Dee-Dee into the kitchen. I used the opportunity to put Dee-Dee straight with a little of truth and a little bit of lies.

"Listen Dee, sorry I was acting all crazy and screaming but I really need that baby bag. Brie's medical cards and my custody court papers are in there and I don't have copies."

"Oh I see, I was wondering why you were trippin' out so hard."

"Yeah, I'm sorry it's just that I have to stay up on top of these things when it comes to my baby. I can't give her mother any fuel ya know. She is so pissed that we're not together that she will do anything take her away from me."

"So what's up with Minerva anyway? I heard she was messing with one of the Eagles on the down low."

"It ain't that down low if you know about it."

"True."

I ignored her question because I heard Kheli say hold on. She clicked to the other line and from the look on her face I could tell it was Netta. I ran across the room and stood real close to Kheli so that I could hear what was being said.

"Hey girl, where are you . . . Oh OK, listen, are you going to be there for a minute . . . Oh OK, stay put for a few, I have something very, very juicy to tell you . . . I'll be there in fifteen minutes . . . Yeah don't leave!"

Kheli clicked back over and told boaw that she would call him back and then she hung up. If I would've stood any closer to Kheli we would have been technically making a baby. She looked at me and said, "Let's roll, I know where she is. We need to get that bag."

Dee-Dee looked confused and frustrated.

"Yo Dee-Dee, can you please stay here and watch my baby until we get back. I promise we won't be that long."

"OK, but hurry up because my clothes are done and I have to get up at six in the morning to go to work."

"Aight, bet. We'll be back in like thirty minutes tops."

Me and Kheli flew out her front door and down the steps like two bats out of hell.

5. MONDAY, NOVEMBER 10, 2003 (9 P.M.)

The drive out to Mt. Airy probably took us like twenty minutes but it seemed much longer.

Kheli pushed her whip that night like she was rushing to save her mother from a burning building. Once we got to Lincoln

Drive, one of the most treacherous and winding roads in Philly, Kheli almost banged the Neon against the concrete road divider twice. Both times she blamed it on the wind and the rain.

Now this was the same road where Teddy Pendergrass had the infamous car accident that put him in a wheelchair, so I was on edge like a motherfucker. Her crazy driving was making the hair stand up on the back of my neck.

When we finally pulled up to Netta's crib in the 8300 block of Fayette Street I felt relieved.

"Yo Kheli, when we leave here I'm driving home because you're a crazy bitch behind the wheel."

"You said you wanted to get here fast . . ."

"Yeah but you was on some Mario Andretti shit."

We hopped out the car and hustled to the house quick. Netta's home was a far cry from her fourteenth-floor apartment of our childhood projects. It was a clean block of row houses with trees and no trash on the sidewalks. She married this truck driver dude who used to come down South Philly all the time to holla at her. As soon as they got married he knocked her up with twins. She had them two little monsters like two months before Brie.

Netta used to be a dime, but over the years and especially since she had the twins, she had fallen off big-time. It's not that she was a total mutt, but she had seen better days. She used to be the truth and now she was just average. Nothing to write home about.

Netta swung open the door before we could knock.

"I saw y'all pull up. Come on in."

"Where is your fine-ass husband, girl?"

"Darnell is on the road as usual. He has been working so much lately since Christmas is coming up. You know we always got to buy two of everything with the boys."

I wasn't in the mood for small talk or hearing about her two little monsters. After I put Netta's baby bag on a coffee table, I wiped my feet on the rug and stood at the door to give her a hint that we didn't plan on staying. I should've been more blatant because Netta started offering us everything out of her refrigerator.

"I just made a bangin'-ass sweet potato pie yesterday. Let me get y'all some."

Before I could reject the pie and tell her that I just wanted the damn baby bag, Kheli cut me off and accepted.

"That sounds good, girl."

"OK, I'll get y'all a couple of slices. The baby bag is in the kitchen too. Won't y'all go 'head upstairs and see the twins. I just put their pajamas on and put them in bed. They're probably sleep by now but y'all can still look and see how big they got. I left the night-light on."

Now I hadn't seen Netta's bad-ass twins in almost a year so I had to play it off like I cared. Me and Kheli looked at each other and tried to hold back our laughs. We hiked up to the second floor like we were going to our execution. All we wanted was a baby bag and now we were forced to go and look in on the devil's spawn.

I remember one of them old folks down South Philly saying to me that all children are beautiful. To that I say, once you get old the eyes must be the first to go. Jonathan and Jason are by no stretch of the imagination beautiful. They got the biggest heads I ever seen on any child under the age of eighteen. Maybe, just maybe, if they were good kids then I could see past their huge domes and funny-looking faces. But to top it all off, they are the baddest, craziest two kids that I've ever seen. Once I had to keep myself from body-slamming Jonathan after he knocked Brie to the ground and started to laugh. I knew exactly why their dad was always driving that damn truck. If I was Darnell I'd be on the road twenty-four/seven too.

We crept into the room and tried to be quiet. The last thing we wanted to do was wake either one of them up and start something we didn't want to finish. Me and Kheli whispered back and forth.

"Damn Kheli, their heads got bigger since the last time I saw them."

"Yes, I didn't think they could get any more swole . . ."

"These boaws have faces only a mother could love on graduation day."

"Fuck graduation day, only on payday could I love that grill."

Kheli covered her mouth to keep from laughing out loud. I just looked around the twins' room and shook my head. They had every toy and book known to man. For it to be packed with stuff it was very neat. A stranger would look at the room without the kids and think that it was the space of two normal little boys.

"Yo, we need to get going. I need to get that sex tape out of the baby bag."

"Ya know, I can't wait to see my man in action. Is he packin'?"

"What?"

"Is Snatch-Back packin' like a racehorse or what?"

"Come on Kheli, you think I really sat there with Brie and was checking them niggas out like that."

"I mean . . . I don't know, you don't have to get all homophobic on me. When I look at him on the videos and onstage . . . the way he be moving his hips and shit it just look like he workin' with something."

"Well, you'll see for yourself when we get the tape. We been up here long enough to play that shit off, let's go and get this nasty-ass pie and be out."

If walking up the stairs felt like going to an execution then coming down had to be like going to Judgment Day. As soon as we got to the bottom of the steps and turned to walk through the living room toward the kitchen where Netta was, it was on and crackin'. She came flying out of the kitchen with a butcher knife in one hand and the baby bag in the other.

"Here nigga, take your daughter's bag and get the hell out of my house. You too Kheli!"

She unwrapped the strap of the bag from her wrist and threw it at me hard as shit. I tried to grab it with both hands but I lost my grip and it flipped over and fell on the carpet. Brie's baby wipes, Pampers, and the million-dollar sex tape spilled out.

Kheli jumped away from her and started yelling.

"Netta what the fuck is wrong with you?"

"What's wrong with me? Y'all motherfuckers come up in my house and disrespect me and ask me what's wrong with me?"

She was waving that knife around like she was about to cut both of our heads off. Everything was happening so fast that I don't even remember throwing Brie's stuff back in the bag and standing up.

"OK Netta. How did we disrespect you?"

"Pussy, don't play dumb. I heard you and Kheli talking about my boys. I know they got big heads but they're gon' fill out one day and their heads ain't gon' look so big!"

Me and Kheli ain't have shit to say. We were just standing there looking stupid with no defense. We were talking shit and somehow she knew what we said. Kheli tried to say something first.

"Yo Netta . . . I'm sorry . . . Netta . . . it's not like that. You know I love your boys . . ."

"Whatever bitch! Yeah I said bitch! Now get y'all asses out of my house before I slice one of y'all motherfuckers. And I'm telling Darnell when he come home on Wednesday too."

I grabbed Kheli by the arm and we started walking toward the door backward. It was no way I was going to turn my back on this chick the way she was acting. Netta was heated and I didn't know what she would do. By the time I grabbed the knob and flung open the door she put the knife back down to her side.

We were out the door and walking down the steps when she dropped the bomb on us. Me and Kheli already felt small as hell but then she went and just rubbed more salt in the wounds.

"The next time y'all go over somebody's house and talk shit about their kids make sure they don't have a baby monitor in the kitchen!"

Netta slammed the door so hard I thought it was going to shatter every window in her house.

We were almost totally soaked by the time we got in the car. Kheli got behind the wheel and I didn't even argue it. We just felt so damn stupid there was nothing left to say. About a minute into our ride home, Kheli broke the silence.

"Are you thinking what I'm thinking?"

"What Kheli?"

"What else did we talk about when we were up in that room?"

"Oh shit . . . the tape . . . We said something about the tape."

"Damn, so now Netta knows that we have a tape with Snatch-Back having sex on it."

"Maybe. Maybe she didn't hear exactly what we were talking about."

"She heard what we said about the twins."

"Yeah, you're right but let's hope she was so mad about that, that she didn't pay too much attention to what else we said."

There was silence almost the entire ride back down South Philly. That was a lot to hope for.

6. WEDNESDAY, NOVEMBER 12, 2003 (6 P.M.)

It's like this.

When a doctor gives somebody major news, especially if it's bad, the first thing they do is get a second opinion. And if it's bad news all over again, then some even seek out a third.

I didn't look at getting that tape as bad news but I knew that my scheme had some bad elements that could easily fuck my whole world up if everything didn't go down right.

Kheli was on point with her advice. After she watched the tape about four or five times, she was even more convinced that I should go dig in that boaw's pockets. She claimed she kept watching the tape to make sure that it was Snatch-Back on the tape, but I think it was just an excuse for her to see him naked again.

It was do or die at that point. I knew I had to make big moves to make big things happen. Still, I wanted to run it by my boys to see what they thought about the whole situation. Kheli begged me not to, but I told both Nkosi and Xavier anyway.

Xavier got to my house at about six o'clock. He came straight from his new job at the Home Depot up in Cheltenham. Ever since he put on that little orange apron he thought he was the comedian from *Home Improvement.* I don't recall him even knowing how to change a lightbulb before he got that job. Then, all of a sudden, he was telling me what I needed to do to fix up my crib.

Xavier spent the first twenty minutes blabbing about much of nothing. I told him I wasn't putting money into nobody else's property. Me and Brie had been crashing there since she was about six months old, but I knew that the day when I owned my own house was not far away. I felt at that time like our days on Madison Square were numbered. My lease was up in three months and that was perfect.

Besides, the shit was starting to get too expensive. My neighbor told me that ever since Hollywood came to the hood that the real estate folks went buck wild. They used a house a few blocks over on St. Alban's Place to make *The Sixth Sense.* It was the one where little white dude who saw dead people lived in the flick.

Bruce Willis and crew went back to living the good life in New York or L.A. or wherever and they started hiking up prices in that section of South Philly like the celebrities were flocking to live there.

I let Xavier get off all of his recommendations. After he was finished rambling we grubbed on some spaghetti. Brie made a crazy-ass mess that night. Most of the noodles and sauce never made it to her mouth. It was all smeared in her hair and on her undershirt. I normally would have been pissed but it was all gravy because I was in a good mood.

I didn't tell Xavier specifically about the tape at that point because I wanted to tell him and Nkosi at the same time. I did tell him though that I thought I was maybe going to come into a couple of dollars.

"Yo what is this Chef Boyardee, it taste aight."

"Naw nigga, it ain't no Chef Boyardee. I got skills."

"Yo if this whole deal that you're keeping so hush goes through and you get paid can you hook a brotha up?"

"What you want a Navigator and a platinum iced-out watch?"

"Naw it ain't even like that. I just want you to help me get a two-bedroom crib up in West Philly and maybe hook a brotha up with a couple dollars so that my bank account can look legit."

"Word. If the dice roll in my favor then you know I got you. You need to start seeing your seed again. He'll be eight soon right?"

"Yeah. And I haven't really seen him in the last two years because my BM and the dude she's with now are blocking me big time. They getting money now and they go to court and act like I ain't shit since I ain't driving a Benz and because I still live with my mom."

"They ain't shit for trying to keep you from Melvin but you do need to get it together, man. You'll be thirty in a few months and you still chillin' with your mom. Man, this pad right here is far from Buckingham Palace, but I can do me up in here. Ya heard? I don't have to worry about answering to nobody."

Xavier was a deep cat. From the outside looking in I bet a whole lot of people would never know how bad he was hurting since he couldn't see his son. It was killing him and I knew it was only a few people who he really opened up and talked to about it. I don't know what it was, but sometimes niggas just shut down and act like we ain't care when we really do.

It's crazy but if a chick has a baby in the hood and then a

few years later you never see her with the baby that would be the talk of the town. She wouldn't make it five steps to the Chinese joint without ten people asking her, "Where your baby at?"

With niggas it's the absolute opposite. If a dude has a seed and everyone knows it, you will almost never, ever see anyone asking him about his kid. Everybody gets on the same page and acts like they kid don't exist. The dad is expected to just be another dude paying child support and seeing their kid every other month or so if even that.

Xavier was a prime example of this. That nigga has a mother and three sisters and none of them ever pushed him to try and get custody or to fight to see Melvin more often. Just like everybody else, they just figured that's the way it's supposed to be.

Nkosi showed up right after we finished wolfing down two plates of spaghetti apiece. He sat right down on my couch and started knocking off a chicken cheesesteak and fries that he brought with him. Nkosi hated pork and beef and he ain't let it get nowhere near his lips.

Him and Xavier acted cool toward each other but I got the feeling that it was only because of me. They had nothing in common and I know they would have never even had anything to say to each other if they didn't roll with me like that. After Nkosi wolfed down his grub in like a minute flat he put Brie on his lap and sparked up the meeting.

"What's the deal my good brotha? Tell me why you left four messages at the newspaper telling me to get over here right after work."

"Yeah nigga, I'm dying to know too."

Kheli had me nervous because of what she said about not telling anyone else about the tape. I knew I could trust my boys but her comments made me doubt myself. A lot was on the line, but they were already sitting in my front room waiting to see what I was so hype about so I just went for it.

"This is the deal. What I'm about to show y'all is on some ol' *Mission Impossible* James Bond type shit. That means it's top secret and that's no bullshit. You will be tempted to tell somebody but I'm going to need for y'all to ride with me on this. Especially you Nkosi, you're going to really want to run back down to the paper and tell one of your editors what I'm about to show you."

"Don't tell me you know where Saddam Hussein or Osama Bin Laden is 'cause if you do I don't know . . ."

"Naw nigga, stop playing. I got some real breaking news. I'm talking ghetto fabulous breaking news that black people actually care about way more than the war in Iraq."

Xavier sat up on the edge of the couch.

"What the hell are you talking about man?"

Since I didn't want to torture my boaws with the *Teletubbies,* I already had the tape cued to where the action jumped off. I hit play on the remote and scooped Brie off Nkosi's lap. I took her upstairs so that I could change her Pamper and to clean the spaghetti off of her. Plus, I didn't want her to see or hear that tape again.

I could hear them niggas howling and yelling from all the way upstairs while they watched the tape. Most of the time though they were just quiet. The bulk of the action lasted about fifteen minutes. When Xavier hollered up the steps that the tape switched back over to the *Teletubbies,* I brought Brie back downstairs. Of course she ran right over and plopped in her purple Barney chair to watch.

"Now do y'all see why I said you can't say anything?"

Xavier was speechless at first but like the true reporter, Nkosi was asking me like a million questions before I could sit down.

"How the hell did you get this tape? Is that the woman on there who accused him of rape?"

"That's the thing. I have no idea how I got that specific tape. My mom went to one of them big flea markets on Saturday up in Norristown and brought that tape back for Brie. It says *Teletubbies 5-Hour Marathon* on the label but y'all niggas saw for yourself that it's more than that on there."

"Hell yeah! That shit is off the hook. So what are you going to do? Are you going to turn this tape in to the cops?"

"I don't know yet. That's why y'all are here. I have an idea of what I want to do but I need to see what y'all think first. I was thinking about asking him to buy the tape off me for a mill."

"Got-dayum! A mill? That's a lotta bread. You think he gon' go for that?"

"I have no idea. If I was in his shoes I would cough up the loot if it meant I ain't have to go up north."

Xavier stood up and started pacing real quick back and forth across my living room floor.

"Now I don't agree with Nkosi on going to no cops because I don't trust the cops for shit. You need to do what you're going to do and get money from that boaw. You know he got it."

"Naw, Xavier. He has to go to the authorities with the tape because this woman has filed a criminal charge against Snatch-Back."

"Yeah but ain't nobody put a gun to her head to go up in that room with them niggas."

"So you're saying she deserved what happened to her. That's so damn ignorant."

"Why I gotta be ignorant because I'm keeping it real. Her ass probably got paid already and she trying get broken off even more now."

"Listen, like I said I think you should go to the cops. Man, what if that was Brie on that tape. Wouldn't you want somebody to go to the cops if they had somebody committing a crime against your daughter on tape?"

His comment stopped me in my tracks. I saw where both of them were coming from but when he threw in the Brie factor it made me feel guilty for a minute. I would definitely want somebody to come forward if the script was flipped. But there was a lot of money on the line and I had to think about that too. I had no control of what had already went down. For some crazy reason I had a tape in my possession that could change my life and I had to act on it one way or another.

We went back and forth for about an hour before we all decided that we were getting nowhere. I had to tell them to stop screaming at each other like three times before I said that I wanted them to leave so that I could think on it a little bit more.

After they left I gave Brie a bath and put her to bed. She was out like a rock but that was one of those nights where I could hardly keep still long enough to sleep. I tossed and turned and kicked off the sheets all night. I might've got like two hours total if that.

I thought mostly about what Nkosi said about if Brie was on a tape like that, but I got over that real quick. I convinced myself that I would do such a good job raising her that she would never be the type of girl that would turn into a hip-hop groupie. I figured that as long as I kept her time with Minerva to a minimum, she would stand a fighting chance of not becoming a gold-digging smut.

But that wasn't the biggest problem at the time. My whole squad didn't trust each other.

Kheli said I shouldn't have told Xavier because I didn't know him long enough. She said she didn't get a good feeling from him and that he was an opportunist. Xavier told me that I shouldn't trust Nkosi because he worked for the press. He acknowledged that I had known him since kindergarten but Xavier thought he would be tempted to put a story in the *Tribune* and kill my chances of getting paid.

As a reporter, Nkosi wrote about backstabbing and corruption every day. He ain't trust nobody and he ain't want me to either. He thought Kheli was the last person I should've told since everyone knew how much she was on Snatch-Back's dick. He swore he wasn't a sexist but he also stressed that a woman couldn't be trusted with a secret that big.

We lived through so much shady shit down 13th Street that I really couldn't blame Nkosi for being so paranoid.

At that time, I had been taking a three-credit distance learning writing course through Legette University. I was way past the deadline for the writing course but I still had to read three books and write three papers. The books were boring as hell and the assignments wanted us to focus a lot of our attention on the main plot and subplot.

I started thinking of the scenario with Snatch-Back as the main plot of my life. I was obsessed with the thought of getting in contact with him and getting some cash for that tape. Nothing else mattered so that was definitely the main plot. Man was I wrong.

I would've never guessed in a million years that the subplot of my life would be what really shut the whole game down.

7. THURSDAY, NOVEMBER 13, 2003 (3 P.M.)

Nkosi is the man.

Less than twenty-four hours after I told him about the Snatch-Back sex tape, he was in all-out reporter mode. He was hard-core with his. My man was like one of them reporters on the movies with the long tan trench coat, matching hat, and a tape recorder glued to his hand. But since he was South Philly born and bred he flossed with his own flava.

I don't think Nkosi owned a tie. Dress codes were for lames, he said. I've seen that nigga roll out of the *Tribune* in a Dickie set with some Timbs on and a fitted cap cocked to the side. They had him covering crazy shit like homicides and mafia hits so he figured there was no need to stand out like the other reporters on the scene. If he had to go to a press conference or something on the high-saditty tip, then he would throw on a sweater or a nice button-up. Other than that he was keeping Rocawear and Sean John in business.

It worked most of the time because he always got bangin' interviews and quotes in the paper that the big timers over at the *Daily News* and *Inquirer* missed out on. He got people to talk because he knew how to get down and dirty in the hood.

Nkosi always kept me in the loop on how reporters get information so quick.

He hipped me to the "trick book," which was like a reverse phone book. He could look up a random address and tell you who lived there and for how long. If somebody got shot or stabbed in 123 Mockingbird Lane, he could look up the neighbors at 121 or 125 and get the scoop from them. Even if they were unlisted.

It didn't stop there. If the person who owned the house was behind in their mortgage payment he could find that out too, and even how much cheese they made the year before. Their kids' grades and how many times they were late and absent from school wasn't off limits either.

Brotha man could do all of this in less than an hour if he had to. Since he had a personal interest in me getting paid like a motherfucker, he kicked his journalistic skills into overdrive.

I didn't ever think I would know how that tape found its way to a shelf in my bedroom. I didn't know Snatch-Back, and I didn't know anyone who knew him. That's of course not counting Kheli who was obsessed with the boaw the way I was gone off En Vogue in the early '90s. Nkosi was more of a Salt-N-Pepa freak back then but I couldn't be mad at him.

We met during his lunch break on the corner of 16th and Lombard about a half a block from his job. My aunt Cassie kept Brie for a few hours. It was the worst day to be out on any corner though. The hawk was out and he was madder than a motherfucker. The wind was getting up to like sixty miles per hour in the city, which made it feel like it was like twenty degrees. People could hardly walk up the street because the wind was whipping so damn hard.

Nkosi came strolling up to the corner and gave me nigga dap, the grip-up handshake with a half a hug and a strong pound on the back.

"So what's the deal playboy? Why you want me to meet you on this corner when it's hawking out here?"

"One, I'm on deadline so I can't be away from my desk for too long. Two, a newsroom is the worst place to talk about this kind of stuff. If anyone in there knew what was going down it would be on the AP wire before the ten o'clock news. We gotta keep this on the low."

"Definitely."

"Don't say definitely nigga, you done already told two people too many."

"What? Why you keep coming at Kheli and Xavier like that?"

"I'm not saying you can't trust them, I'm just saying that this is a helluva secret to tell somebody nah mean, and then expect them to keep it under wraps. You know I dig Kheli, we came up together down 13th Street. I don't know Xavier that well but if you say he's cool . . ."

"Naw they're straight. I only told the three of you and I know that all y'all niggas know how critical this shit is. We about to come up crazy."

"True but I'm just telling you because I'm your dawg. We go way back to two-tone jeans and Pumas."

"And fake gold ropes and two finger rings."

"Yeah nigga, so I'm just letting you know for your own good. You know what I want you to do with that tape but I got your back either way."

Nkosi looked me dead in the eyes when he said that shit. I knew he was serious and I took his words to heart.

"Aight with all of that nigga, it's cold as shit out here. What you got?"

Nkosi broke it down and told me how he thought the million-dollar sex tape wound up in my South Philly bedroom. I told him that my mother bought the *Teletubbies* tape from a flea market in Norristown, which was about twenty-five minutes outside of Philly. That's where he began.

He started digging around in his computer and found that the lady in charge of the "Fall Into Giving" charity sale that my mom and her friends go to every year is a woman named Stella Rosenthal. She lived in Gladwyne and was filthy rich like all of the other stay-at-home wives in that suburb. Nkosi pointed out that Patti LaBelle had a crib out in them parts too. The sale was held every year to raise money for breast cancer and some kind of women's shelter. Nkosi found out that they raised more than 10 Gs every year selling all types of shit.

Most of the goods were donated by people who had nothing better to do than go through their closets and garages to find stuff they didn't need or probably had never used. In those parts, all of those cats had money so I'm sure most of their throwaways had some serious value. That's why, we figured, my mom was so pressed to get there every year. She could sniff out a yard sale the way black rappers found hoes to dance in their videos. It was a piece of cake.

The more he dug, the more he found out about Stella the do-gooder. She was quoted in one wire story as saying that she got the bulk of her merchandise from her neighbors. Nkosi started there. On a hunch, he went through the trick book and started to slide his finger down the page where her neighbors were listed.

At first it seemed like a waste of time, when he came across a name that caused him to stop. Three houses up the road on the same side of the street lived one Lucretia Johnson. On Stella Rosenthal's very Jewish block that name stood out like a fully garbed Muslim at a taste test for pork chops.

He entered Lucretia Johnson into a few of his top-secret newspaper search engines and two results popped up. Two was all Nkosi needed to get the connection.

Lucretia Johnson was a fifty-seven-year-old widow who lived in a five-bedroom jawn near the end of Stella's block. There was a pool, Jacuzzi, and built-in grill out back and a silver 2003 CLK Benz and Range Rover in her two-car garage.

She had been living in the crib for the past four years and it was totally paid off within the first six months of her moving in. Not one red cent was owed in property taxes. At first glance, Nkosi knew that Lucretia was gettin' it in one way or another.

He dug deeper and found that she had three children, two sons and a daughter, and seven grandkids. Two of those grandkids were Patrick and Kim, who were five and seven years old. Their pop was one Cephas Johnson. Yes, Cephas Johnson. A country-ass name no doubt, but more important it was the birth name of the hottest rapper alive.

Lucretia Johnson was in fact Snatch-Back's mom. It was crazy because the mom of the rapper-turned-homemade-porn-star was the culprit in all of this. The first question I had was whether or not his mother had seen what was on the tape.

Nkosi doubted that. We couldn't think of anything else except that she gave her good neighbor Stella a copy of what she thought was a *Teletubbies* tape. I could definitely relate to his mom's logic. If I had to donate anything out of my crib to charity the first thing to go in the box would be all of Brie's *Teletubbies* tapes. One way or another the Golden Fleece of all fucking VHS tapes wound up at my crib and I loved it.

After Nkosi finished breaking me off with all of that info I wasn't cold no more. Trash cans were blowing down the street and stray cats were blowing up the sidewalk but I ain't care. I was so hype that my blood was starting to run hot. I got that tape on a bona fide fluke, which made me feel even more like it was meant for me to get paid. It could have popped up anywhere else, but it was meant for me and Brie to get a taste of the good life.

My mom probably paid a dollar for that tape and I was looking at making a million-dollar profit. Now that's a come-up.

"So that's how I think you got your mitts on that tape."

"Man that shit is crazy. I know he would probably want to strangle his mom if he knew how it got out."

"Yeah, but man I have to get back in the newsroom before the shit hits the fan. Make sure you do some research of your own and find out as much as you can on that nigga. He lives in North Jersey now but he's from Philly so there's enough people here who know him and knows what he's about outside of that."

"You interviewed him before though, right?"

"Yeah but that was three years ago and that nigga was so high I know he wouldn't remember me. He gave me a lot of one-word answers so the interview sucked. I had to work a miracle to pull that piece together."

"Word."

"Yeah, but like I said before, plan on learning as much as you can about boaw because this shit you're getting into is serious. Cover all your bases on this one. I want to see you and my god-daughter get paid so it's all good but I don't want you to end up in jail either."

"Aight, bet. Hit me when you get off. I have to go and pick up Brie from my aunt's house in North Philly."

"Aight, peace."

We gave each other dap again and hustled our separate ways out of the brick-ass weather.

While I was running up to 17th Street to get in my car I thought about the comment Nkosi made about Xavier and Kheli. I felt like I could trust all three of them. I truthfully had no doubts.

I followed my gut and I never was wrong. But there was a first time for everything. There weren't three people on the planet that I trusted more.

In the end, I learned that I would have to settle for two.

8. FRIDAY, NOVEMBER 14, 2003 (11 A.M.)

The week had jumped off to a crazy start. My whole world now revolved around a rapper I had never really paid that much attention to before. It was Friday before I realized that I ain't really do much of anything with Brie all week.

I read to Brie and played with her as much as I could but I started turning into one of them dads that sat their kid in front of the television more than anything else. Brie didn't mind overdosing on *Dora the Explorer* and *Blue's Clues* but I knew she needed to get out more often.

With that in mind I got her dressed and told her that we were going to go to Chuck E. Cheese's. I never took her there more than once a month because it did damage to my pockets. Between game tokens and pizza it could set a nigga back.

I loved to see the look on her face when we pulled up though. Her eyes always got wide and she started trying to pry herself out of the car seat before I could stop the car.

There were a couple of Chuck E. Cheese's restaurants in Philly but I liked going to the one at Broad and Snyder in South Philly because there I could kill two birds with one stone.

One, Brie could have fun playing and eating pizza, and two, I could check out the chicks who were in there with their kids. Even on a Friday morning there was always at least one hot jawn for me to crack on.

I picked a table near the play area so that I could chill at a table and eat and still keep an eye on her while she was playing in the balls and running around like a wild monkey. She shook off her coat and dashed away from me like she was in the baby Olympics.

Me and Brie had on matching Penn State sweat suits because that was my team. The only difference is I had on Nike track shoes and she was rocking a pair of patent leather shoes. I know it was ghetto, but her feet were too big for her Nikes and I didn't get a chance to get her a new pair yet.

I always made a killing at that location. Some of the best ass that I ever got in my life came from a trip to Chuck E. Cheese's. I met this chick Abby there, who was an ice-water freak and had no gag reflex. That meant her tonsils could take a pounding all day and I loved it. Her sex game was so tight that she had me blowing up her cell phone whenever Brie was with Minerva.

When I first stepped to her at Chuck E. Cheese's she was there playing with her son, who is about a year older than Brie. At the time she was separated from her husband so it was lovely. She got back with him about six months after I started hittin' it and that shut our whole sex game down.

There were always a lot of women at them kind of places but it was rare to see a dude there, especially on a weekday morning. I think I was the shit to these chicks just because they saw that I was putting in time with my daughter. I could've looked like a silverback gorilla and it still would've been all gravy.

My whole focus was to spend some quality time with Brie, but on the real I knew I had to handle some other important business while I was there.

Right before we left the crib, Nkosi called and gave me a phone number that would change my life. He looked in his Rolodex and found out that Snatch-Back had a manager named Jeffrey Stokes. He was the dude that he had to go through the last and only time he interviewed the rapper.

Nkosi gave me his office and cell number and told me to see about setting up a meeting. He offered to do it for me but I ain't want him getting in deep unless I really needed him. That day would soon come.

So while Brie jumped and played in the colorful balls, I flipped open my cell phone and made the call that set it all off. I dialed the number and got into hardnose business mode. The phone barely rang once.

"This is Jay."

"Is this Jeffrey Stokes?"

"Yeah I said this is Jay. Who is this?"

"Slow down playboy. I know you got people to see and places to go but I want you to chill for a minute."

"Who the hell is this? I ain't got time for no games."

"Listen man let me get right to the point. I have something that you and your man Snatch-Back need to check out."

"Nigga is you trying to pitch me your demo? You need to call my assistant and get the address—"

"Be quiet and listen. I ain't trying to pitch no damn demo tape. What I got just may keep your boy from going to jail."

"What? Who the hell is this? What are you talking about—"

"Listen, I know your man is in hot water because this bitch has accused him of rape. I got something that proves her case. In fact, I got the ultimate proof. What I'm offering you is a chance to get it from me before she does."

"Is this Juan?"

"No this ain't no damn Juan. Are you paying attention? I can save your boy a whole lot of headache and not to mention a trip to the pen."

"I think you're bluffing."

"Really? Would Ryan Wilson and Snatch-Back's two other roadies who were there think I was joking too? This is not a game."

Jeffrey Stokes was completely silent for a few seconds. That mention of Ryan Wilson's name caught him off guard because it wasn't made public in any of the newspaper stories. He was a sitcom star and kind of a household name, but he wasn't as famous as the Snatch-Back. The chick from the tape left him out of it for some reason and only went after Snatch-Back and his boaws.

"You'll have your ass in Philly tomorrow to discuss the details of what I want."

"Naw nigga, I ain't coming to Philly. I want you to meet me here in New York."

"Let's not get it fucked up, you ain't in no position to tell me what you want. I'm in control and I say we meet in Philly tomorrow night."

"Tomorrow night? I can't meet with you tomorrow. Snatch is in the middle of a video shoot and the soonest I can get down there is next Wednesday or Thursday."

"How about this? How about I send what I got to Katie Couric and the whole country sees your client go down on the Today Show *on Monday morning. Have I made it a priority yet?"*

"What kind of evidence do you have?"

"I have enough to make it worth your trip to Philly tomorrow night at six o'clock in the lobby of the Loews hotel. There's a restaurant there called SoleFood. Meet me at the bar and don't be late."

"Man, this is really pushing it. I don't even know your name or whether or not we can trust you."

"You can call me Sticks. And as word of advice, you can't trust anyone. That has nothing to do with whether or not I have something that your client would do anything to get his hands on."

"So how do I contact you in the meantime?"

"The number that came up on your caller ID screen is the best way. 215-476-5071."

"This better be worth it."

"Just don't be late and tell your man to start getting some major funds in order. Holla."

I ended the call on my cellie and took a deep breath. My heart was beating fast and my hands were sweating. I had put myself out there and it was no turning back. Now the waiting began.

I wondered whether or not he would show up and whether or not I would be able to get the kind of cash that I wanted out of him for the tape.

I spent the next hour or so walking around Chuck E. Cheese's with Brie, putting her on different rides and eating pizza. I had just taken Brie off of a merry-go-round horse ride when something shady caught my eye.

The quickest way to stand out in Chuck E. Cheese's is to be a grown-ass man with no kids anywhere around you. A red flag goes up and in my mind it usually says child molester. This dude was standing right over my table with his back turned to me. I couldn't see his whole face but I could tell that he was dark skinned, a little shorter than me, and had a thick-ass neck.

When I picked up Brie and started walking toward him, it hit me that not only was my cell phone on the table but so were our game tokens, and the baby bag, which was stashed underneath our coats.

"Yo . . . can I help you?"

He took a quick glance over his shoulder and then before I could blink he turned and jetted in the other direction. The man almost knocked this one lady down who was walking with her son in her arms as he tried to get to the door. This chubby-ass manager tried his best to catch him but it was like Star Jones versus Marion Jones. It was a joke.

I didn't go after him because my attention was on the table and our stuff. Fortunately he ain't have the chance to get me for my phone or anything else but that shit still had me pissed that the people who worked there ain't notice him lurking around.

After that incident, I knew it was time for us to be out. I ain't even stay to crack on none of them jawns. All of the women in there were all shook up and screaming at the managers anyway for not reacting quick enough to stop the dude. It showed me just how much you have to watch your kid because anything could happen. I put me and Brie's coats on and headed for the door because it was a madhouse.

The drama of that morning was not over though. As I walked across the parking lot up to the car, I saw that the door was slightly cracked open on the driver's side. I noticed right away that my glove compartment was open and all of my papers were scattered all around the front seat.

Brie's car seat was unfastened from the seat belt and flipped upside down in the backseat.

I was mad as shit because I knew that it wasn't a coincidence that the dude was staking out our table inside of the Chuck E. Cheese's. Whoever the hell he was, he wanted something specifically from me. And since I wasn't pushing a Maybach Benz or walking around with a grand in my pocket I knew it wasn't for my valuables. I had a gut feeling that he was after that tape, but I couldn't figure out how the hell he knew about it.

But like my grandmother used to say, time reveals all things.

9. SATURDAY, NOVEMBER 15, 2003 (11:30 A.M.)

If nothing else, my daughter's mother has a lot of balls.

Minerva showed up at my doorstep dressed like she was on her way to the Soul Train awards. The sun was high in the sky and the temperature was somewhere in the high fifties, but she was rocking a red fur coat.

Her skirt was so short that I could barely see it and she was wearing those black stiletto pointy-toe squeezer boots. I wonder how chicks can even put those things on let alone walk in them.

Minerva's fur was open and I could see what looked like a rhinestone handkerchief, but in her case a shirt. Her hair was done of course, and she had on so much lip gloss that it was glistening in the sun and making me squint. To top it all off she had one of them Louis Vuitton bags swinging on her arm.

There I was struggling to get Brie a new winter coat and plotting a million-dollar blackmail plot against the hottest rapper alive and this chick showed up decked out in five thousand dollars worth of gear. Minerva was cleaned up real nice but I could tell that she hadn't been home since the night before. I guessed that she probably woke up in some rapper's suite after a night of getting nailed to the wall, freshened up, and then made her way to my crib.

For a hot second, and I do mean a hot-ass second, I gave her the slow up and down look over. Minerva was light brown skin and was stacked thick like a pile of pancakes on a fat boy's plate. With those heels on she looked to be about 5'6" but in reality she was a few inches shorter. From the day I met her she has always wore her soft black hair short and away from her face. Her lips were sexy and full and her tongue was as thick as a leather belt. I don't think I've ever seen a chick with a fatter ass in my life.

I know that she thought I was gone off of her, but deep down I was furious. My moment of brief lust that morning came and went like a rash. I stood in the screen door with my arms folded and stared at her with a blank expression on my face.

"What you want, Minerva, you know that this ain't your weekend. You get Brie every other weekend and that ain't until next weekend . . ."

"I have a calendar just like you and I'm well aware of what weekend it is. I was just dropping by to say hello and to ask you if I could see Brie for a few minutes. I miss her. Please."

"Really?"

"Yes really. Waiting two weeks to see my own baby is a long time you know."

"No I don't know. I've never been away from her for more than a couple days."

"Please, save the lecture. Please. I just want to say hi and to see how she's doing."

"She's doing fine and she's sleep."

"Brie is still sleep at eleven o'clock?"

"She got up at around quarter to seven this morning and she just went down for a nap a few minutes ago."

"Well can I just see her? I won't be long at all."

"Minerva, there's a restraining order in my kitchen drawer that says you can't come within five hundred feet of me at any given—"

"Yes, I know. But are you really going to call the cops on me for wanting to peek in on my baby for a few minutes."

This chick, who had brought me so much drama in the last six months, was standing at my front door unannounced, wanting me to cooperate with her. This was the same woman who doused my leather coat in lighter fluid and set it on fire at the corner of my block while Brie and all my neighbors watched. She also got her cousin Saadiq to come and rumble me another time, but that all backfired because I whipped his ass like he stole something from the collection plate at church.

Long story short, I went against my gut and let her in that day. I wasn't feeling her or nothing she had to say but I didn't want to keep her from seeing Brie. I figured it would be quick and painless but what do I know.

We were technically supposed to meet at the police station on Point Breeze Avenue when we had to exchange Brie, but that played out quick. After a few months neither one of us felt like keeping up with that part of the court order so we slowly went back to meeting at the corner of my block on 23rd and Madison Square.

My meeting with Snatch-Back's manager was scheduled for later that same day and I wanted to get my head straight for that shit. It ain't every day that you meet a total stranger and demand a million ones from his client on the strength of a scandalous sex tape. I knew I would have to have my game face on big-time.

I stepped back out of the doorway and invited Minerva in. She sat down on my couch while I went upstairs to get Brie. She was knocked out when I handed her to her mother. She didn't try to wake her up, she just laid her across her lap and rubbed her back. It would've been a nice Kodak moment if I gave a fuck.

"You want something to drink?"

"Yes, some fruit juice if you have it."

"I only have a little bit of that left and it's for Brie. You want some iced tea?"

"Yeah, that'll do."

I walked to the kitchen to get her tea and was gritting my teeth the whole time. I could not believe that she was sitting in my living room. I handed her the cup and walked back across my living room and sat on a foldout chair. There was more than enough room on the couch for me to sit but I didn't want to give her the slightest idea that I was trying to be brown with her.

I do remember wishing that my crib was in better shape that morning. It looked like a tsunami blew through that motherfucker. Brie had managed to pull every single one of her toys and books out and spread them all over the hardwood floor. Cheerios were everywhere. It was as if my baby just turned the cereal box upside down and shook until every grain covered our small-ass living room.

There were like seven or eight newspapers and magazines spread out all over the coffee table courtesy of Nkosi. Being the hard-core reporter that he was, my dawg kept stressing me to learn as much about Snatch-Back as I could if I was going to go through with the scheme. I know now that it was the best advice that I would receive in a long time.

I was normally much better at keeping my spot looking tight, but it was just one of those days. And who worse to just drop in out of the clear blue. Minerva definitely peeped the mess all around her but she acted like she didn't notice.

"Do you have an attitude with me?"

I just looked at her and walked to the other side of the room.

"What the hell are you talking about, Minerva?"

"No, I'm just saying if you have beef with me you need to be a man and just get it off your chest right now."

She never ceased to fucking amaze me.

"I don't have beef with you, or chicken or pork for that matter, Minerva. What we had is dead, past tense, over. You had your chance to shine and you blew it by disrespecting me, our baby, and yourself. I have no rap, that's all. We need to just do what we have to do for Brie and leave it at that."

"So what's going to happen when I get married?"

Minerva flashed a real cheesy grin and held up her hand. She started to wiggle her fingers at me like we were back in preschool and she was taunting me with a lollipop. She was rocking a platinum diamond ring on her left finger. It was the first time I noticed it and I don't know how I ain't see it because it was blingin' like crazy.

"What is that supposed to mean?"

"OK, let me help you out a little bit. This ring was given to me by the man that I have been seeing for quite a while now and am going to marry in February."

"Was he sober when he proposed?"

"Ha ha nigga, very funny. He was very sober and he is very much in love with me. So . . . I am telling you all of this because this is definitely going to affect Brie as well."

"How is that?"

"I mean . . . he's going to be my husband, we are going to move in together after we're married, which means Brie will live with us two when she's with me."

"Who is this dude? Where does he live? What he do for a living?"

"You know who he is. Everybody know who he is because he's big-time."

My blood started to boil because the first thing that came to mind was that she was messing around with some drug dealer nigga from around the way who I grew up with.

"How do I know him, Minerva? Ai yo, let me find out this dude is into something shady and he ain't coming nowhere near my baby . . ."

"Shady? I know you ain't talking about shady. I still can't figure out what it is that you do to pay the rent. For your information my fiancé plays for the Eagles."

"Oh, here we go . . ."

"Here we go what? Yes he plays for the Eagles and his name is Eric Brockington."

It caught me off guard when she said dude's name because not only did I know who he was, since I was a big Eagles fan, but I also saw him out at the clubs on the regular. I ain't even going to front, I was definitely a big fan, but talk about going from sixty back to zero at the drop of a dime.

He got props from me because he was the truth as a wide receiver but as far as him coming into my space with my daughter, that was a different thing altogether. He might as well have played for Dallas or New York after she said that.

"He loves her like she was his own daughter."

"You tell that nigga that she has a father already and ain't nothing jumping off."

"Oh is that so? I can see this is just going to add more drama to our lives. Instead of being jealous you should be happy that a real baller's going to be in the picture to help me take care of Brie."

"My daughter don't need a half a man in her life . . ."

"Let me tell you something, he is one hundred percent more man than you'll ever be. Every time he slips out of his silk boxers he makes my jaw drop."

"Well of course your jaw drops, Minerva. That's your natural reaction, to open up wide whenever you see a dizz-nick in your face."

"Fuck you, you just mad—"

"Ai yo, watch your mouth in front of my daughter—"

"You just mad because I found somebody who knows what it is to make a woman's eyes roll in the back of her head. Don't get it fucked up! He gets the good cheese in his grits before he leaves my house in the morning. I don't believe I ever made you more than a bowl of Apple Jacks when we were together."

Our voices were starting to get louder and Brie was starting to toss and turn.

"You can talk all that shit now but I know the deal—"

"Listen nigga, your stroke game was lame. You never wondered why I always had fresh packs of batteries in my top drawer? I can tell you that they wasn't for a Sony Walkman."

"Whatever, listen, you saw Brie, now it's time for you to roll."

"You're so right because the more I stand here the more I feel sorry for you for being such a hater. I am the center of a rich, fine-ass man's world and I'm happy, and you can't stand that."

Minerva was pissing me off and I wanted her to make a quick, clean exit. I walked over to the door, pulled it open with one hand, and made a sweeping move with the other.

"I'm outta here. Just remember that when you see our wedding picture in *Jet* magazine, don't break out in hives or nothing . . ."

She kissed Brie on the forehead and made her way through the doorway. As soon as she sashayed by me I tapped her on the shoulder.

"Yo, if you're going to be a NFL groupie you need to upgrade from just reading *Vibe* and all them hair magazines. I suggest you start a subscription to *Sports Illustrated* or *ESPN* magazine."

"What is you talking 'bout?"

"There are two jawns in two different states that have paternity cases against that clown and one of them also is suing him for giving her a STD. Been to the clinic lately?"

Her face looked like she had just seen her best friend get hit in the face with a bag of nickels. Always one to bounce back, she kept on yapping and making herself look like more of a fool.

"Listen pussy, you can't believe everything you read. Them bitches is just trying to get paid off of my man's blood, sweat, and hard work. He's building a house from the ground up for us in Jersey and all them cluckin'-ass bitches will be outside the gates of our estate begging for crumbs!"

"Minerva what makes you so different from them other chicks? You think you're special to that boaw. What you got going for you that all them other chicks don't. He see bad-ass dime pieces day in and day out."

Minerva stepped back up onto the top step and lowered her voice into what she thought was sophisticated and sexy.

"You know exactly what sets me apart. You ain't senile so I know you remember exactly how these sugar walls feel."

I busted out laughing because she was talking in her porn-star voice trying to get me open but it wasn't working. Minerva could've been butt naked right there on my step and I would've still asked her to leave. Her shot was major, but she was poison.

"You're laughing now but please mark my word. It's not Eric's fame and money that you have to worry about. So don't be threatened by what my man's direct deposit slips are saying. He's more of a threat than you know. Trust me, the joke will be on you."

Then she turned and switched her phat ass down the brick walkway on Madison Square toward 24th Street. She said that the joke would be on me. Looking back, that was the biggest understatement that I ever heard in my life.

10. SATURDAY, NOVEMBER 15, 2003 (5:40 P.M.)

I was at the hotel at least twenty minutes earlier than our meeting time of six o'clock. The lobby of the Loews was pretty busy so I took a seat at the bar inside of the restaurant SoleFood. I was nervous as shit because it started to kick in that I had this man's future in my hands. If that tape found its way to the police it would be over for Snatch-Back.

Instead of spitting rhymes with Tigga in the basement on BET he would be headlining the meat-beater tour on the yard at Graterford prison. The jury wouldn't waste a minute finding his ass guilty.

The more I thought about it the more I knew why his people were meeting with me so quickly. If he got busted that meant a whole lot of other people wouldn't be getting paid either.

At one point, I said to myself, "Just get up and walk out of here and never call them people again," but I couldn't get up from that bar. Any chance of me giving up on this mission ended when Minerva told me she was about to get hitched to a millionaire. Even if she was talking shit, and for some reason I believed her, I couldn't take the chance of some other man coming into the picture trying to outshine me in front of my daughter.

It was a male ego thing. I ain't even want no other nigga buying sneaks for my daughter. So the thought of her potential stepdad being a NFL baller was enough to make me want to rob a bank.

Eric Brockington was a multimillionaire but if I got some major coins from Snatch-Back, then I could at least get Brie out of South Philly. I ain't want to be like my deadbeat dad. I was having problems figuring out what I wanted to do with my life but I knew more than anything else that I wanted to make a difference in my daughter's.

I was jobless, and this dude coming into the picture was going to surely make me look like a lame. Kheli told me stories all the time about fathers who lost custody to the moms after they got their shit together. Judges loved to see little girls with their mothers even if they were chickenheads.

The Eagle boaw had me vexed and he ain't do nothing to me except dive headfirst into my leftovers. I respected his game on the field but he must ain't have all his marbles if he was going to marry Minerva. She had a tight game, but after a while most boaws saw right through it. I guess she just put it on him something mean. Oh well, I had business to take care of so I shook all that shit off and tried to focus on the matter at hand.

Nkosi asked me if I wanted him to come but I passed. If I needed him he would be right on speed dial in the cellie. I wanted to meet the manager boaw face-to-face and get right to the point. I ain't have time for no games or a whole lot of back and forth. I wanted the cash straight up with no bullshit and then they would get the tape. It was as simple as that to me, but I would find out that the rapper who *The Source* magazine called "the new millennium hip-hop porn star" saw things differently.

Jeffrey Stokes looked totally different in person than what I pictured from our phone conversation. He had one of them gruff, deep, Barry White voices that gave the impression that he had no neck and was ripped with muscles from head to toe. His heavy New York accent made it seem like he was gangsta too, but that wasn't the case at all.

When he strolled through the lobby toward me I thought to myself, "no way." This brotha was about 5'5" and round like a basketball. He wasn't outright fat, but dude could stand to take a few more trips to the gym.

He was much lighter than me, and his hairline was starting to take that hike to the back of his head where it eventually jumped off the cliff. He was rocking blue slacks, not jeans or khakis but slacks, and a brown jacket that barely buttoned over his gut. It didn't match at all, but from the looks of his gear he paid a couple dollars for that shit.

I almost lost it when I noticed his mustache because it looked like he drew it on with a pencil. My first impression was that this man had major cash but he ain't have no style. He sounded like Brooklyn's finest on the phone, but he was far from being a thug. This dude's image was so far from the rapper he represented that it was like they were living in two different worlds.

"Sticks?"

He said my nickname with a whole lot of hesitation as if I didn't look like what he pictured either.

"Yeah. It's me."

"Jeffrey Stokes."

He reached out his hand and I grabbed it firm and strong, the way I was taught to shake a hand. The boaw on the other hand shook my hand like a bitch. He hopped up on the barstool and flagged down the barmaid.

"Yo, what's the deal sweetheart? Let me get a Corona and my man here wants a—"

"Make it two."

Our fine-ass barmaid went to get our beers and we both looked her up and down like we were about to put an inspection sticker on her butt cheek. After he took in the view he turned to me and got right down to business.

"So what you got my friend?" he said, rubbing his hands together. He was trying to act like we were brown like that but he was coming off faker than a pair of titties at the MTV awards.

"I got a tape with your boy on there and his squad, and they're getting it in."

"What do you mean 'gettin' it in'? Can you tell that it's him on the tape? Is he fucking on the tape?"

"Ray Charles could tell it's him, and yes he's fucking. All of them are. Now that's if you want to call it fucking because it don't seem like the chick is with it at all."

"What do you mean?"

"I mean after the one boaw hit it, the other three including your man, started beating up her guts, she didn't look like she was down."

"That's for a jury to decide."

"Well if they see this tape I'm sure they'll decide to send your Grammy Award–winning client upstate."

He looked over his shoulder to make sure no one was listening and then he leaned in close to me and lowered his tone.

"How did you get this tape?"

"Man, all of that ain't important. All you need to know is that I got the tape and that the shit is legit."

"I disagree! I think it's very important that I know where you got it from, because I don't want to have to make another trip to Philly to give your ass another million dollars when you pop up with another tape of my client having sex with another bitch on a beach in Hawaii."

He realized how loud he was getting and he sat back up and acted casual.

"Dude, I ain't down with the paparazzi. I ain't stalking Snatch-Back. This is it. I have no more tapes. Once I get paid off of this shit you won't ever have to see my face again. I guarantee you that I only made one copy of this tape."

He paused for a while because the barmaid walked up and put our Coronas down in front of us.

"Like I said on the phone, this is blackmail. You gettin' into some serious shit with this. Snatch is pissed as shit that you're trying to get up in his pockets."

"Yo, I don't care. I told you what I'm working with so you either want to make a deal or not—"

"One hundred grand and a new truck. A Tahoe."

I took a swig of my beer and laughed at that clown-ass nigga. Then I started bullshitting like I was big-time.

"That wouldn't even cover the note on my Hummer or my debt. Like I said one million, not a dime less. And don't worry about getting me no whip. I got that."

"I'm being honest with you, he is not going to pay you a million dollars. That's way overboard. I think I can get him in the neighborhood of two hundred grand but that's pushing it."

"Listen playboy, I read the paper, and I watch BET. That nigga sold six million copies of that last CD alone so I know he can get back at me with the mill no problem. He been in two movies and I heard he about to make another one real soon. Don't insult my intelligence with no bullshit-ass hundred grand like I'm supposed to jump through hoops or something. I ain't one of them corner boys y'all used to dealing with who ain't ever been nowhere, don't know nothing, and don't want nothing for themselves. What I'm saying is that I ain't that easily impressed, duke. Ya feel me?"

He didn't blink. Jeff Stokes took a sip of his beer and looked at me like I was speaking another language. That nigga was used to negotiating million-dollar contracts and record deals so this was nothing to him. For me though, my life was on the line.

My heart was beating like crazy because he just got real quiet. He was looking at me like he was trying to read my mind, but I wasn't going to give him an inch. I knew I wasn't cut out to play record industry hardball, but I knew that I wanted that cash.

"So what if I got Snatch-Back to take a trip down to Philly? Would you demand that kind of loot from him to his face?"

I leaned close to him and gritted on him like he had just spit in my face.

"What you think, I'm supposed to be scared because that nigga is a rapper and he drives a Bentley? That don't faze me dawg. I'm from South Philly. It take a lot more to knock me off my block than a fake-ass Casanova slash rapist. Call that nigga now and tell him to make it happen."

He pulled a twenty out his wallet and put it under an ashtray.

"Did you bring a copy of the tape with you?"

"Of course."

"Let's take a walk."

He jumped off the stool, and I do mean jump because his stubby little legs were so far off the ground. He motioned for me to follow him with his head and he headed toward the Market Street entrance. Once we were out on the sidewalk a black 2004 Expedition with tinted windows pulled up to the curb.

"Yo, where we going?"

"Just get in, I want to take a look at what you got."

He held open the back door and waited for me to make my move. I jumped in the truck and slid over to the driver's side. The chauffeur had dreads down his back and a pair of dark-ass shades on. He was rocking a blue Sean John sweat suit and way too much cologne.

I had been in trucks with DVD players before, but never one with a VCR and flat-screen monitor in the backseat. This nigga came prepared. I took the copy of the tape out of my inside pocket and handed it to Jeff. He handed it to the driver who popped it right in the VCR. There was a screen on the floor of the passenger side in the front seat too.

Laa-Laa, Dipsy, Po, and Tinky Winky were nowhere to be seen on this version. Nkosi hooked it up so that the Teletubbies were edited out. It jumped straight to the action.

The tape opened with the back of Ryan Wilson's head moving up and down. The screen was fuzzy at first but as it started to clear up you could see dude standing there butt-ass naked. The camera was behind him and he was hittin' it doggy style on top of a bangin'-ass pool table with a red top.

From the view on the tape the woman was a winner. Puberty was a long-ago faded memory for this chick. I thought Minerva's ass was classic but this chick took donkey to a whole 'nother level. It looked like she got stung in her cheeks by about a thousand bees, because her shit was swollen. It was the kind of ass that you had to just sit and stare at for about five or ten minutes before you even thought about making a move. Her legs were thick and smooth too so that made her even more of a dime. You couldn't really see her face that well on the tape because of her long blond braids. She definitely wasn't underage though. That chick was legit, a grown-ass woman no doubt.

At one point she was working her ass so fierce on that nigga that I thought his head was going to spin off. Snatch-Back and the other two boaws were hooting and screaming while she did her thing. She flipped the script on Ryan Wilson because she was fucking "him" simple and plain. This chick was no amateur.

Snatch-Back and his squad were all around her on their knees with their meat hanging out waiting for her to step up to they mics.

The one boaw, I'll call "Uno," had to be about 6'5" but he was all skin and bones. He was light skinned and had cornrows and a goatee. His throwback jersey was pulled up over his head and around his neck the way young boaws do in the street when they want to show off their chest without taking their shirt all the way off. Dude was putting her tonsils to the test because his dick was bigger than her forearm. He never took off his boxers but the body part he wanted her to see most was out there, way out there.

His partner, I'll call "Deuce," was the exact opposite. He was dark skinned, about the same complexion as Snatch-Back. He wasn't that tall but he was diesel like he lived in the gym on some twenty-four-hour workout shit. His stomach was like a six-pack on a toy action figure.

Between throwing her ass at Ryan Wilson, the chick would pull back her braids and give one of the three a quick chewie. She wasn't trying to win a deep-throat contest or nothing, it was just enough to make all of them want more.

The chick was working them like a pro on top of that pool table but you could tell that she didn't know she was being taped. The camera was probably sitting on top of a dresser or under the infamous pile of clothes. Wherever it was positioned, it was dead center in front of the action and Snatch-Back knew it was there. He looked at the camera more than once and winked as if he was performing for a sell-out crowd at the Garden.

He was in the zone and loving every minute of it. Every now and then he would take a swig from the bottle of Cristal champagne in his right hand and grab the back of her head with the other.

Ryan Wilson jumped up and threw his head back and started to nut all over her ass and back. Dude was moaning and screaming like a gorilla. After he got his self together, he jumped up off the pool table and started picking his clothes up off the floor. He disappeared off the screen right away.

Wherever they were bonin' at, it looked tight as hell. It was cream carpet on the floor and the light fixture over top of the pool table looked like something out of a hotel lobby. What stood out the most was a monster-sized painting of Marvin Gaye on the wall.

"Yo, get this bitch a towel."

Ryan Wilson came back on the screen wearing boxers and a black tank top. He handed a towel to Deuce and he started wiping the jizz off of her. At this point in the tape it seemed like the session was over and she was about to get up off the pool table. Out of nowhere, Uno flipped her over onto her back and mounted her. His boxers were still on and his jersey was still up over his neck.

The chick was laughing at first but it was uncomfortable laughter like she ain't know what else to do. I could tell that the "elephant cock," as Kheli called it, coming at her made her a little bit intimidated.

They were all laughing at first but the woman on her back was starting to see that the joke was on her. You could see her start to struggle a little with Uno. She put both of her hands on his chest and started to push but that nigga wouldn't budge.

"Yo, you buggin' dude, get off me!"

"Oh, I can't get no ass? I know you ain't think you was leaving here without giving me some ass—"

"Nigga, you buggin, get off me. Ai yo, Snatch tell your boy to chill."

Snatch-Back just smiled and shook his head.

"Oh you can suck my dick but I can't get no ass. What I don't got no album out so I ain't good enough?"

"Nigga you trippin'. Get off me!"

Snatch-Back grabbed Uno by both of his skinny-ass arms and lifted him from off top of the chick. He faked her out real good because she let her guard down. She relaxed for a hot second and Snatch-Back was on top of her before she could blink. He held her down with his forearm and slid his boxers off with his free hand.

She was struggling a little but not nearly as much as when Uno tried to push up.

"Yo wassup Snatch, I thought I was just fucking Ryan tonight."

"Yeah I know but I changed my mind. It's my turn to get up in that ass."

"Well you know I gotta get paid more for this."

"Come on bitch I pay you good money. Stop acting like I don't be lacin' your ass on the regular."

Snatch-Back was butt naked at this point and she had stopped struggling.

He got down on all fours and started to eat her out. That shit shocked me every time I saw the tape and at that point I had watched it more than a few times. That nigga started going to town on her coochie like it was fresh, virgin twat that wasn't just smashed by one of his homeys a few minutes before.

That didn't last long. Before she could really get out a decent amount of fake moans, he jumped up and got on top of her. Once again he had my head messed up because he just started nailing her with no rubber on. I'm thinking, is this dude fucking crazy? HIV was on the rise like a yeast infection and this boaw was hittin' a freak jawn raw like it was sweet like that. He pushed her legs back so far that her knees sandwiched her head.

Snatch was smashing her hard on the homemade triple-X video, and fast as hell like a teenager who was in a rush to nut before his peeps came home. I'm sure that the chick in the tape nailed him before, but this time it was obvious that she ain't want no part of him then and there. The boaw was drilling in and out of her pussy walls like a machine while Uno and Deuce took turns sucking on her titties and trying to stuff their Johnsons in her mouth.

Jeff Stokes was starting to get real uncomfortable at that point. Watching his prize-winning client was giving him a major headache and it was written all over his face. I was just trying to figure out how much tax I would have to pay on my first million dollars.

The dread who was driving kept looking down on the floor of the passenger side in the front at a small screen on the floor. He almost crashed the truck a few times because he kept taking his eyes off the road. Jeff sat up on the edge of the seat and looked up at the screen. I don't think he blinked once.

The second time out, the jawn wasn't so willing to dish out BJs. She started gagging and it looked like she was trying to lift herself up. Every time she tried to move or turn her head away from one of two cocks that were flying at her head, she was pushed back down on the pool table.

"Take this dick like a champ. You wanted to be down with ballers and now you got. You gon' take this dick . . ."

The rapper was on a mission to get his nut and he didn't care that she was trying to push him off after every stroke. Snatch-Back, the sex king who could allegedly work it all night long—to the break of dawn—'til the cops came knocking—'til the walls caved in—lost his load in a little under two minutes. It was almost comical how his body started shaking and how he was making crazy faces like Jim Carrey in *Ace Ventura*. That nigga was Hollywood all the way to the end. He pulled out of her and dumped his babies all over her stomach.

Kheli said I was hatin' but dude ain't have no hang time below the belt. I think because she loved that nigga so much she was seeing something that wasn't there. If she thought he was packin' then she would have to call me Mandingo Goodthrust.

Before she could gather herself from the thrashing that Snatch gave her, Uno and Deuce got at her like hyenas on the carcass of a zebra after the lion has taken all it wanted.

Deuce, the short diesel one, stood over top of her and jizzed all over her face and in her braids. Uno wasn't far behind. He stood in front of her and faced the camera. If his dick was a pen then he wrote his name on her face—in cursive. The chick just laid still while they all jumped up off the pool table and walked out of the picture. You could still hear them boaws talking and laughing though.

She actually laid there for a while. Even though you couldn't see any tears rolling down her face from the angle that she was laying, you could tell by the way her body was heaving up and down and shaking that she was bawling.

Jeff Stokes was rubbing both sides of his face real slow and hard at this point in the tape. He was pissed because it was starting to become clear to him how hard it was going to be to get over on me with a bitch-ass two hundred grand. Not only could this tape land that nigga in jail but it could also cause some serious drama on the home front.

Snatch was married for seven years to his high school sweetheart, a chick named Lori who modeled for Phat Farm and a couple of other urban designers. They had a son and a daughter and they were always doing interviews together talking about how strong their marriage was.

Nkosi pointed out to me that Snatch took her to 106th and Park on BET and told AJ and Free that he was more in love with Lori than he had ever been. He also said that he was looking forward to retiring at thirty and spending all of his time with her and their kids. We did the math and figured that the interview was taped about three days before him and his boaws went buck wild on the pool table.

"Where the—how the hell did you get this tape?"

"I already told you, I ain't giving up no info. All I want to talk about is the cheese. Trust me, I want to get rid of this tape just as bad as you want to get it off me."

The driver slammed on the brakes, making me and Jeff jerk forward and slam into the back of the front seats.

Stokes screamed out, "Fuck, what the hell are you doing?"

I looked up to see a little girl on her bike in front of the truck. We were all the way down at 10th and South in front of the Super Fresh. The girl scrambled out of the street and onto the sidewalk before the driver peeled off to cross the intersection before the light changed.

At that point Jeff Stokes' cell phone rang. He was on the phone screaming at somebody about a video shoot for a few seconds before my cellie rang too.

I unclipped my phone and lifted it up to see Kheli's face on my screen. My cellie had a few pictures programmed in it so when a certain few people called their faces popped up. I used the phone to take a picture of a red cartoon devil from a magazine and I programmed that image under Minerva's name and number.

Kheli sent me and Dee-Dee a fly picture of her chilling on the couch with a pair of Daisy Duke shorts and a wifebeater on with no bra. We always teased her because she didn't realize when she sent it to us that you could see her nipples through the shirt. It was the best damn feature on my AT&T cell phone. I flipped it open, turned away from Jeff Stokes, and lowered my head so that he couldn't hear our conversation.

"Wassup, where you at . . . ?"

"Yo let me hit you back. I'm in the middle of something—"

"I just wanted to let you know that they were just talking about Snatch-Back on MTV—"

"For real . . . yo let me get right back—"

"They said he didn't show up for his video shoot today in NYC and that they can't find him—"

"Word . . . let me hit you back in like fifteen minutes."

"Aight, bet."

I closed the phone and turned back to face Jeff Stokes. I can count on less than one hand how many times pure ice water ran through my veins. That day, that instant I should say, was one of those times.

When I turned around I was staring straight into the eyes of the man of the hour. Snatch-Back was turned around in the driver's seat. In his right hand he was holding the realest looking dreadlock wig that I'd ever seen, but that's not what made my blood turn into floating popsicles. That nigga had a hammer aimed right at my face.

"Tell me why I shouldn't kill you right now."

11. SATURDAY, AUGUST 27, 1989 (8 P.M.)

That was the second time I had a burner aimed right at my head.

You remember little details when your life flashes before your eyes. I saw my mom's face, the crayons on the desk in my kindergarten class, my yellow and black ten-speed bike with one broke pedal, and when Brie was born. I even smelled the lotion that I used to jerk off with when I was in eighth grade. It was that serious.

Things that I thought I forgot smacked me in the face like a cast-iron frying pan. For so much to be rushing through my brain there was one event that clearly stood out. Considering the circumstances that I was under, it made it easy for my brain to dredge up that memory.

Me and Nkosi were both fourteen years old when it all went down.

We both lived in the 1311 building, which was the tallest of the four in our projects at fifteen stories. The two girls who we went with at the time lived right across the street in 1312. Nobody called it that though. It was just known as Saigon. Later on I would understand the significance of that nickname. There was definitely a war going on inside of them walls at the Martin Luther King Plaza.

I went with Gale, and Nkosi's boo was Angela.

It was a big deal for Angela's mother to go out so we had been looking forward to that night for a long time. It was a Saturday night in the summer of 1989 and her mom and the rest of her friends were somewhere screaming their heads off at a Luther Vandross concert. Angela's big brother Benjamin went to a house party in the 1241 building so everything was all set.

We were fresh to death. I was sporting a Boston Celtics short set with a pair of white Pumas and Nkosi had on the Sixers set with a pair of red K-Swiss. Except for the sneaks, it was all knockoff from a stand on Chestnut Street.

There was a boaw named Tim who lived right next door to us who was about seventeen at the time. He overheard us talking about our big night and pulled us into his apartment to give us some tips. He gave me and Nkosi one rubber apiece and told us to make sure that we used it the right way. After that he hooked us up with some cologne from his collection.

He told us to dab a little on our neck, but we were so hype about losing our virginity that we splashed a little more than we probably should've. I knew we did for a fact because Gale said she could smell us coming up to the door before we knocked. It was all good though because they were happy to see us and it was on and poppin'.

First we sat out on the couch for a little while and watched television. Angela gave us some pretzels and some flat Pepsi. I wanted to make a move but I didn't have the heart. It's not like I wasn't ready because I remember that my dick was rock hard before the elevator door opened up on the eighth floor where her apartment was.

Of course me and Nkosi both lied and said that we had sex before. Nkosi even went so far as to tell Angela that he knew how to give girls orgasms. I thought an orgasm was something that you got in your back if you lifted something off the ground too quick. All I knew is that I wanted some coochie.

Angela was probably the cuter one. She was brown skinned and skinny and had nice-sized titties. Her mom always kept her laced with the hottest new sneakers and clothes so she was popular. Everyone knew her name. And if you didn't all you had to do was read her big gold earrings that you could see from half a block away. My mom used to call them ghetto door knockers but we still thought they were doper than dope.

Gale was a little thicker and much lighter. She had a real major acne problem when we were in seventh grade but by the time I got with her it had cleared up. She had braces too but her hair was always done and she dressed fly. She had a lot of jewelry too but her earrings weren't nearly as big as Angela's. They were much smaller and I think they were called figure-eights.

We all had just graduated from Palumbo about a month before and were all headed to different high schools. So, we figured it was no better time to start acting grown like the older cats. Neither one of them were virgins.

Out of nowhere, Nkosi just started tongue-kissing Angela and rubbing all over her titties. Both of the girls had on different color Coca-Cola shirts and acid-wash jeans. Gale's Reeboks were red and Angela's were pink. I remember because they were known down 13th Street for having every color.

After Nkosi made his move, you couldn't tell me nothing. I had a rubber in my back pocket and I smelled like a grown-ass man. I turned to Gale and started tonguing her down too. It was one of them long old-school couches that still had the hard plastic on it. At one point in time the plastic was actually clean and see-through but that night it was smudged and almost beige.

The couch was almost long enough for all of us to lie down on it but not quite. We were dry-humping, rubbing, and kissing damn near on top of each other for a minute. And then I guess Angela couldn't take it no more. She said the words that every teenage boy lives to hear, and the words that every father hopes his daughter won't say until after her wedding reception.

"Let's go in the room and fuck."

What! Me and Nkosi jumped up like somebody set fire underneath our asses. I ran track at the Ridgeway rec center at the time so I was doing high-knee lifts down that hall toward her room. Me and Gale would've got busy right there in the living room if it was up to me but the girls insisted that they didn't want to be separated.

Hey, if they liked it, we loved it. As long as we were getting some coochie it was cool with us. I could tell when we walked in her room that she had cleaned up real good just for us. It smelled sweet and she only had one little lamp on in the corner.

We got right to it because the clock was ticking. Luther Vandross might've had women throwing panties at him down at the Spectrum, but me and my boy were ready to get some panties of our own.

I never took my Celtics shorts all the way off. I just slid them down my legs all the way until they were wrapped around my new sneakers. I had on tighty-whities so my dick was bulging out like I had a gasoline nozzle between my legs.

Gale looked at it and then looked at me and started shaking her head.

"Your dick look kind of big. I don't know about this."

"Come on girl, stop tripping, it ain't that big. It's gon' feel good."

"I don't know—"

"Listen, well let me just put the head in and I'll work my way in little by little. If it starts to hurt just tell me to stop and I will."

"I don't know—"

"Pleeease!"

"All right but be careful. Hmph, I heard light-skinned guys were supposed to have little ones."

"What? Where the hell you hear that from? That's some ol' nut shit. I'm high yellow to the core baby but you can see that I'm handling."

I kissed her on the cheek and yanked her shirt over top of her head. There was no way I was going to figure out how to get her bra off too so she just stood up and took it off herself.

Both of her earrings fell off on the floor but we didn't stop. She stood up and took off her bra and pulled down her panties on her own. Nkosi and Angela obviously ain't have as much to talk about as me and Gale. They were both butt naked and under the sheets before the light from the lamp could go out.

Since it was kind of dark I couldn't really see but it seemed like he was tearing it up. Angela was moaning real loud like the girls we had seen on the porno tapes and screaming Nkosi's name. He was going up and down so damn fast that I thought he was going to have a seizure.

I couldn't be outdone. I mounted Gale with the intention of giving her one of them orgasms I was hearing so much about. I was hyped. But I was having a little trouble maneuvering my way around the twin bed because my shorts were wrapped around my ankles and I still had my sneakers on. I whipped the condom out and pulled the wrapper off. It wasn't as simple as I thought it would be.

My hands were shaking because I was nervous and I didn't know how to roll that bad boy down. I took heed to what KRS-1 said in his song "Jimmy" about using protection, but I wish he would've added a verse where he said how to put it on. Eventually I got it rolled all the way down, but I was sweating bullets before I even got off one stroke.

Gale was getting impatient but I could tell she was just as nervous as I was. I spread her legs apart and got on top of her. I didn't grab my jawn with my hand, I just got on top and aimed and prayed that it found its way to the coochie.

Once the head was in she started digging in my arms and started breathing heavy.

I put about half of it in before she started pushing back hard on my chest. Since she wasn't going to let me get all the way up in it I just started giving her half strokes. You couldn't have told me that I wasn't doing major work. I felt like I was on top of the world that night. Before I was done I had already had the list of niggas in my head who I was going to brag to about finally getting some ass.

Nkosi clowned me for years for what happened next.

We were about a good minute into the action, when all of a sudden the tip of the condom broke. It went from being the best damn feeling I ever felt in my life to one million times that feeling in one second flat. I knew Gale ain't know that the jimmy hat broke because she started grabbing my ass and pulling me into her even more. I thought that was a sure sign that she was on her way to getting the big O.

I could handle myself with the rubber, but when it broke all bets were off. It felt so good that I lost control of my manhood and before I could take a deep breath and think positive thoughts I busted like crazy. My mouth never made it anywhere near a nipple. In fact it would be the summer before twelfth grade before I knew what that was all about.

Nkosi said I sounded like one of the monsters from the *He-Man* cartoon. Angela said I sounded like a whale making a mating call. Gale just said I sounded stupid.

I was done in less than two minutes. Gale was already pissed at the quickness of our episode but she was really fuming when she figured out that the rubber broke.

We got dressed real quick and just sat there on the other bed while Angela and Nkosi were still going at it. I was already embarrassed as hell and Nkosi wasn't making it no better. He was working that girl over like he had the world championship belt in getting skins, and it was only his first time. For a minute there, I was starting to think he had lied to me and he had been having sex since sixth grade or some shit.

The fact that he lasted way longer than me wasn't enough. He added insult to injury when he flipped her over and said that he was going to hit it from the back. The back! It would at least be three years after that before I got any more coochie, let alone even know how to get to it from the back. He might've clowned me for years because of how quick I was, but he was the one who almost pissed on himself that night.

My sex game might've been weak as hell but at least I can say that I got a nut my first time out. Nkosi can't say the same.

Right after he started humping Angela from the back, her brother Benjamin kicked in the bedroom door and turned on the light. He was with this dude Merk and these two older chicks whose names I can't remember for shit.

I was so scared that I jumped straight up off the bed. I don't know if this is a scientific fact or nothing but the quickest way to make a dude go limp is to put a gun to his face. Nkosi was at full attention one minute and shriveled like a raisin the next.

Benjamin went into his waist and pulled out a gun. Nkosi jumped off his sister and held his hands straight up in the air.

"Pussy what the fuck are you doing with my sister?"

"Please don't shoot me! Please don't shoot me!"

Benjamin aimed the gun back and forth between me and Nkosi with this crazed look in his eyes. We could tell that him and his crew had been smoking reefer because you could smell it all in their clothes.

"I should blow your little ass nuts off."

"Please don't blow my nuts off, please, please, please!"

The two chicks that he was with pushed their way into the room and started to point at Nkosi and laugh. They are probably what saved our lives that day because after a while Merk and Benjamin started laughing too. They were all cracking the hell up like it was the funniest thing they had ever seen.

"Nigga get your clothes on and stay your little bitch ass away from my sister."

He decided not to shoot Nkosi but it ain't end there. Benjamin put the gun back in his waistband and then out of nowhere just slapped the cowboy shit out of him. The sound of the smack made everybody in the room jump, including Angela who was crying and trying to get her clothes on with everybody watching.

We all jumped because the slap sounded so loud. Nkosi fought back the tears and just started to put his clothes on.

"Every time I see your ass outside I'm going to slap the shit out of you so I suggest you run every time you see me. You got that?"

"Yeah."

Nkosi would later interview him while he sat on death row.

I just stood there and ain't say shit because I didn't want it with Benjamin. I knew that his knuckle game was mean because he left a lot of dudes down 13th Street stretched on the sidewalk. And I knew that he had a burner in his waist.

"And you pussy. You lucky I don't crack your jaw. The only reason I won't is 'cause the ho you with ain't my sister so I don't care what you do with her."

Nkosi was dressed before I could blink. He had one K-Swiss on and the other was in his hand. We laughed about it later but his Fruit of the Looms were still somewhere under the sheets because he ain't have them on when he got home.

Benjamin told us to get out but he purposely blocked the doorway with most of his body.

"And if either one of y'all touch me I'm gon' whip both of y'all ass."

We twisted our bodies and ducked underneath his extended arm like we were playing a mix between limbo and Russian roulette. Neither one of us touched him but he still mugged us in the back of our heads and kicked us as we went out the door.

Nkosi told me later when we were flying down those eight flights of steps that his face was still numb from the slap.

That was the first time I had a gun in my face and I escaped without a scratch.

Now my life had stopped flashing before my eyes, and the reality of my situation in 2003 started to set in live and in living color. I had one mad rapper to deal with.

12. SATURDAY, NOVEMBER 15, 2003 (7:05 P.M.)

I remember a special on Court TV about why eyewitnesses of crimes were always so damn wrong when it came to identifying people who stuck them up. The expert on the show said something about when a gun is in your face, how your attention is rarely on the perpetrator. The lawyer said that all of your attention turns right to the barrel of the hammer.

He ain't ever fucking lied.

Snatch-Back could've had worms crawling all over his face and I wouldn't been able to tell anybody one way or another. My body tensed up and just didn't want to move. I didn't want that nigga to think I was reaching for nothing because I knew that just that quick my brains could've been splattered all over that cream butter leather interior.

Nkosi warned me that there would be resistance to my plan but I ain't think he was going to resist like that. I couldn't even talk.

"Are you deaf nigga? Tell me why I shouldn't kill you right now!"

"Yo Snatch, put the gun down. Let's not make this any worse than it already is."

"It's going to get worse for him, not for me. Who the fuck are you nigga, how did you get this tape?"

"Give me the gun, Cephas!"

Horns were honking like crazy at that point because Snatch-Back had crossed Bainbridge Street and parked with the butt of the truck out blocking most of 10th Street. At first he refused to acknowledge the other cars. Every bit of his attention was on me. I felt like if I blinked he was going to bury a slug in my forehead.

The first words to come out of my mouth made me sound like a major bitch.

"Please, don't do this man . . . let's talk—"

"Oh so now you want to talk. I ain't got shit to talk about with you because I don't know you nigga and you trying to get me for my paper and take me under. I should just smoke your ass right now."

"Listen man, you can smoke me but there's no guarantee that this tape still won't get out to the public. I told my people that if anything happens to me then you are the first nigga for them to look into. I have one other copy of this tape stashed and only one other person knows where it is."

He paused for a long time but he was still giving me the ice-grill like he wanted to slap the shit out of me.

Then, the sound that I had so dreaded all of my teenage years was like sweet, hot sex in my ears. A police siren. Jeff Stokes was about to have a stroke when he saw them flashing lights and heard the boys in blue coming.

"Oh shit! Snatch, stash the heat! Stash the fucking heat!"

Snatch-Back snapped out of his blood-thirsty trance long enough to turn around and put the burner underneath the driver's seat. He tossed the dreadlock wig on top of the screen that was on the floor and sat up straight.

Just then, the cop walked up to the driver's-side window. Officer Ford was built like a brick wall at the end of a dead-end street. He was just as tall as he was wide, and he had that look on his face that said, "I will yank your ass out of this truck and beat you into a coma." He was so dark that he made Bernie Mack and Whoopi Goldberg look like Donny and Marie Osmond.

"Yes, officer?"

"Yes, officer? Who taught you how to park, Stevie Wonder?"

"No sir, but he's a good friend of the family."

Snatch-Back tried to flash a phony smile but Officer Ford wasn't feeling him or the Stevie Wonder comment.

"I'm so sorry but what had happened was, I was driving down the street and got a painful charley horse in my leg. I just hurried up and pulled over to the curb because it hurt so bad."

"Is that so? A charley horse."

The cop glanced into the backseat at me and Jeff Stokes and then turned his attention back to Snatch-Back.

"Yes, and it came out of nowhere. I'm so sorry I was blocking traffic."

"You look very familiar young man. Is my partner going to run this New York tag and find out you're wanted for armed robbery? Or for not paying child support?"

"No, sir. I ain't no thief. I'm married and I take care of my kids."

"Then why it seem like I know you from somewhere?"

"A lot of people recognize me."

"And why is that?"

"I'm an entertainer."

"Is that so?"

Officer Ford stepped back and squinted his eyes a little and kind of cocked his head to the side as if it was going to help. He folded his arms and leaned back in toward the truck.

"Are you sure I ain't lock you up on Fitzwater Street last week?"

"No sir, I'm positive."

"Well to me it look like you're the chauffeur and these two young men in the back are the stars. So what kind of entertainer?"

"A rapper."

"A rapper? You consider that entertainment. When I think of entertainers I think of James Brown and Tina Turner. Hell, even MC Hammer."

"Well you may not consider me one, but millions of other people around this country do."

"License and registration please."

Snatch-Back handed him the items and then started to lay it on thick. He grabbed at his calf and groaned like the pain from a charley horse was shooting back and forth up his leg. For dude to have been on all of those movies and TV shows he was the worst actor I've seen since Ray Allen in *He Got Game.*

Officer Ford looked at the license and then looked back at the rapper who kept a straight face and was trying not to lose his cool.

"Cephas Johnson. Is that your stage name?"

"No sir. That's my birth name."

"So what do you go by, MC Cephas or Ceph-Diddy?"

"No, you're confusing me with P. Diddy and I sell way more records than him."

"Is that so? So if I called up my seventeen-year-old daughter right now and told her your name she would know who you were?"

"Unless your daughter lives under a rock, she would definitely know who I am."

And then, as if a lightbulb turned on and smashed against his forehead, Officer Ford started to get it.

"Hey wait a minute, I think my daughter has your poster on her wall. You go by Strike Back!"

"No but you're close."

"What is it then, Fat Back?"

"Naw, it's Snatch-Back."

"Yes! Yes! That's it. She listens to that madness every day and every night."

"Madness?"

"Have you ever met a curse word that you didn't like or a woman that you didn't sleep with? Y'all young folks leave nothing to the imagination in the music nowadays. It's either A or Z. It ain't no in between."

"Word."

"You got so many young people listening and you don't even take the time out to say anything positive like stay in school or don't do drugs."

"I'm sure you tell her that every day?"

"Of course I do."

"Then she'll be cool right?"

"She'll be cool because she's being raised up the right way. All these young girls who listen to that mess ain't so blessed to have somebody like me who's there to put a foot in their ass when need be."

Me and Jeff Stokes were absolutely silent while they went back and forth. I know that he was thinking about the gun as much as me but I was also thinking about how I was going to get my ass out of that truck.

After he realized who Snatch-Back was, the cop started giving him a lecture about what kind of songs he should make. He came off as a cross between Bill Cosby and a retired NFL linebacker. He was kickin' a lot of wisdom but he was hard-core with it at the same time.

"Well I ain't gon' stand out here and talk a hole in your head about what you need to be saying on them records you putting out so let's make a deal. If you sign an autograph for my daughter Radeen I'll just let you off with a warning."

"Where do you want me to sign?"

"Hold tight, let me get something from my squad car. I know just what I want you to write it on."

As soon as he walked away, Snatch-Back rolled up the tinted window and turned his attention to the backseat. Jeff Stokes put his face in both of his hands and shook his head from side to side. He let out a loud-ass groan and then dropped his hands back to his lap. He was pissed and I got the impression that it wasn't the first or last time that his client would have him stressed the hell out.

"Don't think I'm done with you yet. Sticks is it? You lucky I don't snap your bones in half like sticks tryin' to fuck with my money. And what kind of name is Sticks anyway?"

"Are you serious? This is coming from a nigga whose rap name is after a type of hair roller that chicks curl their hair with."

"Are you trying to clown?"

"You came at my neck first nigga. What?"

"Oh I see how you play. You one of them dudes who like to act like they got a lot of heart when they really soft and sweet."

"Ain't shit sweet about me dude. And if you ain't have that hammer at your foot you'd see what the deal was."

Officer Ford came back to the window but this time his partner was with him. Officer Ayala was tall, skinny, and Puerto Rican. He looked like he was closer to my age.

"Yo wassup kid. I got all of your albums. You're the truth man."

"I appreciate that Officer Ayala. I appreciate the love. You want me to sign something too."

"Yeah, you can just sign the back of this Dunkin' Donuts napkin. I'm going to put in a frame and hang it up in my house."

"Word."

Snatch-Back signed the napkin and handed it back to him. Officer Ayala shook his hand like he didn't want to let it go and then backed away from the window so that Officer Ford could approach.

"Well young man I may not appreciate your kind of music but my daughter does and I know she would never forgive me if I told her that I met you and didn't bring her an autograph."

He then reached through the window and handed Snatch-Back a balled up white shirt. He shook it out and held it up in front of him.

"You want me to sign your wifebeater?"

"Are you trying to be funny boy? I couldn't fit that thing if I greased my body up with Crisco and had three people pull it over my head. I bought a three-pack of them things for my daughter this afternoon."

"Are you sure you want me to write on this?"

"Yes I'm sure. You're acting like I'm asking you to sign a five-hundred-dollar silk shirt. It's only a white tank top young man."

"I know. I probably got like fifty of them back at the crib but I don't even like the slightest bit of dirt to get on mine."

"Let me guess, you consider this to be a piece of fancy dress clothes? I can't figure it out anyway. I just bought a pack for my nephew last week and now my daughter wants some. It's that rap music that got boys and girls wearing what used to be underwear on top for everybody to see."

"I'm not surprised at all, Officer Ford. Men and women are all motivated by the same things both good and bad, nah mean, so it's only right that they rock the wifebeaters together too. You might see it as only a white tank top but to your daughter and her crew it's much more."

"So you're the type to show up at a formal party, a wedding maybe, dressed in a smooth pair of shoes, some black tuxedo pants, and then you top it off with a wifebeater. You know it's the wrong thing to do but you do it anyway just to push the envelope and just for the sake of rebelling. But the crazy thing is you young folks are rebelling in all the wrong ways and for stuff that don't matter. If y'all black rappers read more than the back of the cereal box and expanded your minds then . . . but who am I to judge. Sign the shirt please, and Officer Ayala and myself will see that you get on your way."

Snatch-Back laid the shirt out on the passenger seat and took the cap off of the black Sharpie marker. As soon as he started to scribble his autograph, I seized the opportunity and reached for the door handle.

"You know what, Cephas? I'm just going to hop out right here. You got me close enough to my crib."

Snatch-Back spun around in the front seat so fast that I thought he was going to catch whiplash. He was irked, one, because I was calling him by his country-ass real name, and two, because I was making a sweet escape and it wasn't shit he could do about it.

"I'll take you home just hold tight."

"Naw, it's cool. I need to run in the Super Fresh anyway so it's all good. Besides, I don't trust you behind the wheel catching all of them charley horses. I already been in one accident too many and I don't need another. Holla."

I shook Jeff Stokes' hand and pushed the door open. Both of the cops looked at me funny when I slammed the door and stepped up onto the sidewalk.

Snatch-Back played it off real smooth in front of the cops like we were really tight like that. If they only knew, that right before they got there he had a gun cocked and aimed at my head.

"You're a funny dude. I'll holla at you soon."

"Call me tonight and we'll hook up later on next week. I already gave you one wifebeater for free but if you want the other one, you can get it off me for a cool million."

"Is that so. A wifebeater for one million, dollars? We'll see."

I winked at the two cops as I backed away from the truck.

"Trust me the one I have is worth a million, Officer Ford. It would be the showstopper at any wedding. Y'all have a good night now."

I turned around and hustled up 10th Street toward South. My car was parked in a garage downtown near the Loews hotel so I had like a twenty-five-minute walk ahead of me. It would've been much quicker than that but I made sure to crisscross streets and take a lot of small side streets in case they were trying to follow me.

My adrenaline was racing and my heart was pounding but it wasn't because I was walking fast as hell. I saw my life flash before my eyes but it was all gravy. Snatch-Back drove all the way to Philly to chump me and shut my game down, but he ain't do nothing but set it off.

13.

I knew that I was going to die two days after Thanksgiving.

Not only did I know I was going to die, but I knew it would be a horrible, painful death. The worst part of it all was that it was happening right before my daughter's eyes. I ain't want Brie to witness any of it but it was too late for making wishes.

I had got us into some real nasty shit.

Nothing could be a worse distraction when you're fighting for your life than hearing the person you care about the most on the planet crying out. Brie was already helpless being as she was only two years old, but hearing her cry for me and scream out "DADDY!" over and over just tore me apart.

She was hysterical at what she was seeing. I never had any intention of bringing so much pain and confusion into our lives but that's what it was. My ribs were weak from the blows I had taken and my legs were like rubber.

I was in the craziest straight-up rumble of my life and it was no turning back. It started out straight up, but of course it wasn't long before I was put at a disadvantage. A one-on-one quickly turned to a three-on-one but that way I felt, they would need a fucking army to put me down.

My ribs were stinging and I was covered from head to toe in white paint that was dotted with drops of blood from my nose. The same chicks who always told me that I looked good enough to be a model would've thrown up on the spot if they saw me like that.

I was leaking and the right side of my face was numb. My right eye was twitching and it felt like it was closing on me.

Christmas Day was less than a month away and I ain't know if I would make it to see Brie rip the paper off her toys.

They were bold as hell coming at me like the way they did. I knew deep down that I probably deserved it because of what I had done but they could never justify putting my baby through that torture.

For that alone, I would not stop until I got the last word. Death would be too easy, too much of a cakewalk. I wanted motherfuckers to suffer beyond all of that.

What stands out the most about that night was when everything started to move in slow motion for me. There were a lot of unanswered questions but one thing was fucking for sure, someone very close to me had stabbed me in the back. That very same person looked on as my body was pummeled and my baby hollered at the top of her lungs for me. That very same person had not only twisted the dagger against my spine but threw salt in my wounds too.

There was a lot of regret on the face of my personal Judas but it was too late for all that shit. They had set it off in the worst possible way, all in the name of greed. There was no turning back. No apology would ever be good enough.

I would never be able to look at those eyes, that face, for as long as I lived without my blood starting to boil. Yes, that face. The eyes of the traitor were on me like a hawk.

The last time I really paid attention to them eyes I immediately had my suspicions.

It was at a diner on a Sunday night, the day after my first encounter with Snatch-Back.

14. SUNDAY, NOVEMBER 16, 2003 (8:30 P.M.)

Our wings and cheese fries were getting cold.

It hadn't been twenty-four hours since Snatch-Back came at my neck, and there I was with three sets of eyes burning a hole in my face. I looked at them one at a time to see if I could read what they were really thinking.

Xavier, Kheli, Nkosi were sitting with me at the diner at 40th and Walnut on Penn's campus right next to the Cinemagic movie theater. The grub was good but we had more on our minds than club sandwiches and watered-down milkshakes.

Even though I asked all of them to be there I was too wrapped up inside of my own thoughts to really talk. Xavier had the raps however.

"Listen dawg, I say you should just ask dude to give you five hundred grand and call it a day. This shit is getting crazy."

"Fuck no. He's going to pay me a mill. If he has enough balls to ambush me and put a burner to my face, then he gon' have to pay up."

"How do you know that it was his idea to do that? Someone else could've put him up to that shit."

"Are you serious? You sound like you're working for him man?"

Kheli and Nkosi looked at him like they thought the same thing. Xavier was starting to get to me.

"Naw man, come on. It ain't even like that. You real deep in this shit now and I just want you to get what's yours and get out. I'm on your side, not his."

We were there for about two hours at that point, and nothing was coming out of the meeting. They were all scared for me and I could feel it. Kheli signaled for the waiter to come and clear our table off. After he left, she leaned in and asked the million-dollar question.

"So where is the other tape? You said that Nkosi made a copy and then you gave that copy to them so where is the original?"

Nkosi slammed his hand on the table.

"Hold up, hold up. Why you need to know all of that?"

"Why I need to know all of that? Nigga why you coming at my neck like I'm the enemy? I was just asking to make sure he had it in a secure place so that nobody could get to it."

"If he tells you then it won't be so secure now will it?"

"What the hell do you mean by that Nkosi? You better go 'head with all of that paranoid newspaper reporter shit. The way I look at it we're all in this together."

"Oh yeah, we're all in it together. So you mean to tell me that when the police roll through Marvine Street asking folks about blackmail and conspiracy, you're going to jump your black ass up and admit to being a part of this."

"Ain't no cops gon' be coming to my fucking door Nkosi because Snatch-Back don't want it with no cops right now. That nigga will go to jail for a minute if that tape gets out so he'd be a fool to go to the cops and say something."

"All I know is this. You, Xavier, or myself for that matter don't need to know where the tape is at."

"That's easy for you to say. You probably already know where it's at. Or better yet you probably made a copy for yourself already."

Xavier was chewing on a straw and leaning back in his chair with his fingers locked behind his head. He yanked the straw out of his mouth and pulled his chair back up to the table.

"Yo, I'm with Kheli. I just think that if we going to be in this we need to know what's going on. What if something happens to you? We couldn't even go to the cops to tell them about the tape with no proof."

I was taking it all in, every single word. Xavier's words made my stomach turn. In my head I was still thinking that everything was going to go down smoothly. I ain't even want to think about the possibility of anything happening to me.

"Well I still say there ain't no need for none of us to know where the tape is at. We just have to see what that clown is going to do next and play it by ear."

I spoke up before they started ripping each other's heads off.

"Listen, I don't have no problem telling any of y'all where the tape is. I gave Snatch-Back the version that Nkosi made and the original is stashed in a good hiding place at my crib."

It was silence.

"I stashed it where no one will find it but in case something does happen, all of you know me well enough that I know you'll be able to figure out where I put it. And that's all I'll say about that. Now my question is this. Do the both of you agree with Xavier that I should just take what I can get and just be done with this shit?"

In a rare move Kheli looked at Nkosi and signaled with a head nod for him to speak first.

"Listen brother, you know how I feel about it. I told you from the gate that this whole plan was kind of crazy but you went through with it so I got your back. Having said all that, I still think you should get his ass for the mill."

Kheli sucked her teeth and sat up in her chair.

"Listen, five hundred grand is more money than you got right now and all of this gun action is making me nervous. I was all gung ho for you to get him for everything but now I would just ask for half a mill, or whatever you can get, and then take it from there."

I was taking it all in but I was still pissed over the stunt he pulled in the truck. I felt like if I backed down and just took whatever crumbs Snatch-Back threw my way, then it would be like he chumped me or something.

That nigga's freedom was on the line and he was trying to play tough with me like his balls were the size of grapefruits. I told the crew that I didn't want to make up my mind right then and there because I wanted to think about it some more.

Kheli made a good point. Five hundred grand would look real nice on my ATM receipt. Especially since me and Brie were about to be eating ramen noodles for breakfast, lunch, and dinner. And that was especially fucked up since the holidays were rolling up on me like a freight train.

I could've went to my mom or some of my family for some loot but I was tired of leaning on everybody else. I was too damn stubborn for that even though I know they wouldn't mind helping. It was time to make major moves for me and my baby and this is where I would start.

"This is what I should do. I should get that nigga for the mill and then demand that he make me the star of his next video."

They all busted out laughing. Nkosi jumped right on it.

"Yeah, y'all can be the 2003 version of Kid 'N Play like back in the day. You can take out your cornrows and get a high-top fade and you'll be the high yellow one Kid, and he can learn how to do the kick step and he'll be Play," said Nkosi.

"Imagine that."

"Man y'all wouldn't sell too much because these rappers don't dance no more. They too damn mad to dance. They mad 'cause they got six baby mothers, mad 'cause they on more than one prescription for their VDs and mad because they signed their contracts after they got blunted and now they realize they got screwed," said Nkosi.

Xavier jumped up from his chair and threw his napkin on the table.

"Word! If I was making the kind of bread they pulling in I would be dancing so damn hard every time y'all saw me," said Xavier.

He proceeded to do this spastic-ass dance so hard that it looked like his arms were going to fly off of his body. What made it so hysterical was that Xavier is cog-diesel, 6'4", and has no coordination. It looked like he was doing the cabbage patch, the chickenhead, and rowing a boat at the same time.

We lost it. We ain't even care that we were up in the diner making that much noise.

For a minute, all of the stress that I was feeling over the Snatch-Back situation just left me. It was nothing like a gut-busting laugh to make you forget all of the bullshit and just let go. It was all good. We were choking with laughter when I heard the deep voice behind me.

Kheli's eyes almost popped out of her head.

"Y'all motherfuckers know y'all disrespected me right?"

I whipped around in my chair to see one of the maddest niggas I seen in a minute.

And that's saying some shit considering a rapper had a gun to my face the day before. It was Netta's husband, Darnell, and from the look on his grill, his wife had definitely passed on what me and Kheli said about his twins.

He was rocking a pair of jeans and a dark-colored Miskeen hoodie with the splotches of paint all over the front. Dude was much shorter than I was but he was huskier than a motherfucker. If I looked hard enough I probably would've seen steam rising off of his bald-ass head.

I figured he was just coming out of the movies since he had this big red plastic Coke cup in one hand. The other was balled into a fist.

I've talked my way out of some pretty sticky situations but I was tongue-tied that day. He was pissed and I couldn't say that I blamed him. I know I would've been the same way if I found out somebody that I was cool with was talking shit on Brie in my house.

People in the diner were already staring at us because of the scene Xavier made with his 2003 version of the Hammer dance. Darnell standing over me like he wanted to knock my head off made them stare even more.

"Yo wassup D, listen it wasn't even like that—"

"So you saying my wife is a fucking liar?"

"No I'm not saying that, it's just that I think she kind of misunderstood what was said. Me and Kheli were joking and I think she kind of took it to heart."

He totally ignored what I said and looked over at Kheli in disgust.

"So you ain't say shit about my boys either, huh?"

"Darnell, you know that we're cool. I apologized, we apologized to Netta, and I'm so sorry if you thought we were making fun of your boys. You know I got love for your family."

"Do I, Kheli? Do I know? I think you need to save all that shit because I'm going to believe my wife over y'all snake-ass niggas any day."

That's when he turned his attention back to me.

"I should whip your punk ass right now."

I just choked on my spit at that point because I knew Darnell was seriously ready to rumble. He had perfectly good vision so I know he saw my squad sitting right there and he was still calling me out. I'm thinking, either he had a Mack-10 under that hoodie or he was just that damn bold that he ain't give a fuck. Nkosi jumped up and held out his hand.

"Wait, wait, wait! Listen man, it don't even have to go there D. We can settle this some other kind of way."

"Man . . . Nkosi, I know he your boy and shit, but I ain't trying to hear that. Netta is fucked up over this. They was up in my crib dawg."

"I know, I know but y'all can't be fighting up in here over a misunderstanding. We can talk about this and work this shit out."

While Nkosi was talking I slowly started to twist my chair around because I didn't want to be caught off guard if Darnell decided to sucker punch me. He was one step ahead of me though.

"Wassup partner! What you trying to set this shit off?"

"Naw man, chill. Listen, we said we were sorry. I don't know what else to say. What the fuck you want me to say?"

"What I want you to say? Pussy I want you to meet me in the middle of the street so I can get this off my chest. You done fucked up man!"

Now Xavier was back on his feet again.

"Ai yo, here come the manager, you need to chill."

"Nigga who the fuck is you and what I care about a manager?"

The manager looked vexed as hell. He had on the tightest little cheap black suit known to man and he was moving quickly. From his expression, I could tell that he would rather be dismantling a bomb on a moving truck than getting in the middle of our mess. He ain't want no part of that shit.

"Please, please, people you have to keep it down or take this outside. Please."

Darnell stepped back a few feet and threw both of his hands up in the air over his head.

"You heard the man. Let's take this outside."

I didn't want to fight Darnell. Me and Kheli knew that we were dead wrong so I couldn't even be too mad at him for coming at us like that. But he was making me look like a bitch in front of all of those people and I was starting to get annoyed. Still, my plan was to ride it out and let him vent.

That all flew out the window when he started to play dirty.

"Why you still sitting there pussy? Huh? You would be ready to go to war if I said something about your funny-looking-ass, lightbulb-head daughter. She look like a Snork on crack."

The shit was on and poppin' after that.

"What? What did you say?"

"You heard me nigga. I ain't stutter!"

"Ai yo Darnell, you need to make your way to the door real quick before it gets ugly up in this bitch."

"It can't get no uglier than that funny-looking daughter of yours."

That was it. I don't think the small Pakistani manager ever stood a chance. I hopped up so quick and lunged at Darnell that I knocked him into another table and he spun around and hit the floor.

Darnell jumped back and threw up his hands to fight, but Nkosi grabbed me from behind.

"Oh you want it! You want it! Let him go, Nkosi, let him go!"

It was crazy after that because Xavier gripped me up too and then Nkosi let go and went after Darnell to try and calm him down. A lot of the people who were in the diner jumped up to get a better view of the action. The diner has a big glass window that looked out onto the walkway leading from the movie theater, so even people outside could see the chaos. A few of them started running into the diner making shit even more hectic.

Kheli jumped in front of me too and started screaming at me.

"Yo, calm down! He's trying to get you to fight him. Just ignore it man and let Nkosi talk to him. Calm the hell down!"

Nkosi put his arm around Darnell's neck and started walking him out of the diner. I was surprised that he went with him so willingly and didn't put up a fight.

Just as that was happening the manager got up off the floor and started screaming like a madman.

"Get the hell out! All of you get out! You knock me down on my own floor, you're crazy. I'm calling the police!"

I didn't want it with the cops so we made our way to the door real quick. Kheli slipped the manager a twenty-dollar bill on top of the tip we left at the table. He was still pissy mad, but the gesture made him bring it down a notch.

When we got outside Nkosi was standing on Walnut Street about three car lengths away from us. He still had his arm around Darnell and from the looks of things had calmed him down some. Dude still had the look of a starved pitbull in his eyes but he was much less animated than when he was in the diner. There was a crowd of nosy-ass onlookers between us.

Even though Nkosi's car was parked right around the corner on 40th Street in front of McDonald's, Xavier and Kheli grabbed my arm and led me in the opposite direction toward 39th Street so Darnell and I wouldn't cross paths.

I didn't even argue. I just went along with the plan because I knew if I had to walk right past him then we would probably have to lock that shit up. When I looked over my shoulder I noticed that Darnell was standing in front of Netta's minivan and that his wife was leaning out of the passenger-side window.

The look on her face spoke volumes. She was pissed with both of us. I don't even know if Kheli was paying any attention but I was. Netta's eyes were like hellfire that night and I noticed.

15. THURSDAY, NOVEMBER 20, 2003 (11 A.M.)

Snatch-Back was knocked off the radar for a minute.

His rape trial was scheduled to start in January but just as his drama was starting to blow up on the news, bigger fish started to fry. A lot of stuff was going down in a major way and it worked to his advantage.

A few days after my unexpected meeting with Snatch-Back, Michael Jackson was arrested because they said he molested a twelve- or thirteen-year-old boy at his house. The King of Pop took over the media spotlight that week. I know that Snatch-Back was sitting somewhere happy that MJ liked spending time with little boys because it took the heat off of him big-time. He was the largest rapper alive, but no one had more juice than crazy-ass MJ.

One news anchor mentioned that MJ's first single from his new album was produced by R.Kelly, who was also knee-deep in his own scandal. He was waiting for his trial to come up on accusations that he smutted out a young jawn in Chicago. He was charged with twenty-one counts of possessing child pornography. It was the first time I heard his name in a minute. R.Kelly was avoiding heavy media attention too because of all of the other shit that was going down.

You couldn't tell from how he was carrying on though. Ever since the day he was arrested and charged, his videos and songs were even more X-rated and off the hook. It was like he was thumbing his nose at all of his haters every time you saw him on television. I was one of his biggest fans but if he was messing with young jawns like they said, he lost me big-time. There were too many bad-ass dime chicks out there who were of age and ready to get it in for a grown man to even bother.

During that same time, Mr. Los Angeles himself, Kobe Bryant, was also in the middle of hearings for an upcoming rape trial in Colorado. I saw less and less of him on the TV screen after the MJ shit broke, but Kobe had to know that the cameras would be right back in his face when his day in court rolled around.

The chick he was accused of raping worked for a resort in Colorado. For that alone I wanted to pimp-slap the shit outta that nigga. She made beds for a living. If he was going to creep on his wife he was supposed to do it with somebody like Jada Pinkett or Angela Bassett, chicks with just as much to lose as him.

It was a crazy time to be a celebrity. While I was surfing for information on Snatch-Back, I typed in "celebrity sex scandal" on an Internet search engine and so much came up. The more I searched and read the entertainment magazines, the more I saw just how much he needed me. That tape was a major piece of evidence and it could definitely throw a monkey wrench in his flashy lifestyle.

I always laughed to myself when he told the press that he was from Philly, because he was actually from Chester, which is well outside the city. It was more convenient though for him to attach himself to a place that people had heard of.

It didn't matter though because as soon as he started to blow up he migrated up the turnpike to New York like so many others before him.

The case from back in 2000 with the seventeen-year-old who accused him of forcing oral sex on her popped up the most on the search engine, but there was so much more to Cephas Johnson.

I already knew that he used to mess with Debbie Dutch, one of the most popular female rappers out. I also knew that he was an all-state running back with potential to play Division One ball until he dropped out of school to pursue his music.

But then there was stuff that I didn't know. Right before Snatch-Back got his first record deal he was actually trying to get his freak on for a living. One of the fan Web sites said that he was about to start doing porn movies and then he got the call that changed his life. A copy of his triple-X audition tape sold on eBay for ten grand. The girl he used for that tape, Cindy Banx, went on to be a popular on-air radio personality in New York. Of course nailing Snatch-Back will forever be her claim to fame.

In a fitness story that ran in *Us Weekly*, the boaw actually told them that he had sex with somewhere around a hundred women before he settled down with his wife. He was quite a character.

Jeff Stokes and his gun-toting client were both blowing up my cell all day on Monday, but I ignored the calls. I wanted them bastards to sweat a little bit. I wanted them to think that I was about to do something crazy like show up on Barbara Walters with a smile on my face and the tape in my hand.

He picked the wrong nigga to fuck with. The stunt he pulled in the truck only made me hungrier. I ain't going to front like I was a gun-slingin' boaw or nothing like that but I ain't no nut either. If nothing else they were going to respect me before it was all said and done. They could save all of that Hollywood shit for the next nigga.

Jeff Stokes was all on my dick when I called him back on Tuesday afternoon. I acted real casual and laid-back.

"What's the deal?"

"Sticks! Good Lord, where have you been?"

"I been around."

"Man, I didn't know what to think. We been calling you all week."

"I got the messages. Why you so pressed to speak with me after you set me up like that?"

"Listen, I had no idea he was going to pull that stunt. Trust me, we had it out over that incident all the way back to New York. He was way out of line and I apologize."

"I'm supposed to believe that?"

"Yes . . . man you have no idea how pissed I was when he did what he did."

"Well this is the deal. From here on out I want to deal strictly with Snatch."

"Whatever you need to discuss I can work it—"

"You're not listening. I don't want any more dealings with you. From here on out I deal with that nigga strictly. That's what it is. There's no negotiation on that. If he don't want to spend the next ten to twenty taking back shots from some horse-hung nigga named T-Bone then he better recognize."

Jeff Stokes paused for a few seconds. He let out a loud sigh and then he started talking again real slow.

"OK, here's the deal . . . he's in a meeting right now with the record company, but when he gets out I'm going to have him call you right away. Will you be available at this number?"

"You know it. Holla."

I hung up the cellie before he could say anything else. I was in control and I wanted to keep the ball in my court. It was time to get paid.

Snatch-Back obviously knew I wasn't playing, because he was blowing up the horn less than ten minutes after I hung up with Jeff Stokes. He had much less venom in his voice this time around. As crazy as it may sound, he sounded like he was happy to speak to me.

"Wassup Sticks."

"Yo."

"Listen, first off I just wanted to apologize for what went down the other day. I just snapped and I lost it. I been under so much pressure with all of this bullshit, nah mean, that it's like all of it just came out that day."

"Word."

"Yeah, yeah. I know you probably ain't trying to hear all that shit but that's the truth. When can we hook up? I'm trying to sit down and talk about some things."

"What is there to talk about? Either you are going to give me the loot or I'm dropping this tape in the nearest mailbox and it's going to be addressed to the DA's office."

"Naw dude it don't even have to go there."

"You're right it don't. It's all up to you. I know you got the cheddar."

"Man, it's not that simple. People always think we got more than what we got, nah mean? You ever see the VH1 special on TLC."

"Yeah I saw that shit."

"Exactly. Everyone thought they were balling out of control and they had to file for bankruptcy because of bad business issues. There's more to it than the fans know."

"Listen man, I know a little about contracts and the record industry so I don't need a lecture on how y'all clowns don't know how to handle y'all business. What's the deal on my paper?"

"Listen, I can give you some of it this week. Can you come to New York?"

"It's not going to happen. I want you to meet me in Philly, by yourself."

"What! You think I'm crazy. Why would I come down there by myself after what happened. How do I know you ain't gon' have me merked."

"How much sense would that make for me? It's in my best interest nigga to see that not one hair on your black-ass head is harmed. I need you in one piece to get mine so you don't have to worry about that. When I get paid, I don't want nothing else to do with you. Period."

"Dawg, that's asking a lot . . ."

"I know but if you think it's worth it you'll be there."

We went back and forth for a few minutes before he finally agreed to meet me in Philly on Thursday morning. He asked to pick a low-key location where we could discuss some things. Before we hung up I also gave him the name of my bank and checking account number, which was holding up at about a hundred bucks.

I refused to give him my real name and after a while he said fuck it. He said he could make things happen with just the account number and the name of the bank.

I told Snatch-Back to meet me on 3rd and South at John's, one of my favorite burger joints in the city. I figured it was a pretty low-key place for a meeting on a Thursday morning but what the hell do I know.

Under any other circumstances it would have been a cool place to connect on the low, but as luck would have it another superstar changed all of that. Just as I sat down at a window table looking out on South Street, who should roll up but the Sixers' star point guard. Allen Iverson parked his big black Bentley right in front of the restaurant. He jumped out of his whip with a few of his boaws and headed next door to City Blue. I guess it was time for him to restock his arsenal with another dozen sweat suits.

It was no big deal at first because it wasn't that crowded down there and people just stared a little and kept walking like it was nothing. After about ten minutes though it started to get thick out that piece. People were pulling out camcorders and getting on their cell phones like he was about to have a press conference.

AI was my nigga and all but I wasn't that pressed because if you went out to the club on any given night you would see him. I gucss most of the people who were getting so excited have never been out in Philly after dark.

From where I was sitting I could tell that City Blue had shut down the store while he shopped because the crowd was getting deep on the sidewalk. It was turning into something serious real quick.

Snatch-Back was already five minutes late at that point. He was on some ol' Hollywood shit and it was his career and future on the line. Just as I flipped open my phone to call him and switch the location he strolled up to the table. I never saw him come through the front door.

It was a cloudy-ass day but this dude was rocking these huge dark shades that almost covered his whole face. He had on a fitted Yankees cap that was pulled so low it didn't look he could see and a beige velour sweat suit. He had a cellie in his hand his jewels was blingin' from a mile away.

He was mean-muggin' from the gate but I wasn't impressed. That nigga wasn't tough. He hung around a whole lot of people who were tough but he wasn't. That boaw was soft as cotton candy underneath the tight jaw.

Snatch plopped in the seat across from me and started bitching right away.

"Yo, I said somewhere low-key and you set up our meeting next door to the AI circus."

"Look nigga, I ain't know he was going to be down here. If you want to go somewhere else we can bounce. I just wanted to be the one to pick the place because I didn't trust you to do it."

"Why you don't trust me?"

"Because less than a week ago you had a toaster in my face."

"Desperate times call for desperate measures. Like I said I'm sorry."

"So do you want to go somewhere else?"

"Is your bank near here?"

"There's a branch around the corner on 2nd and Lombard. Why?"

"Cool, let's take a walk there."

I didn't know what he was up to but for some reason I ain't feel paranoid. It was broad daylight and I didn't think he had the balls to try something again. If nothing else, I knew I wasn't getting my dumb ass back in a truck with him.

We hustled out of John's and walked down 3rd Street toward Lombard. This Asian boaw recognized him while we were crossing South Street but he ain't say nothing. He just did a double take and then acknowledged him with the infamous head nod. No one else paid us too much mind considering AI was in the vicinity.

It was awkward as hell at first. I wasn't used to walking down the streets with a famous rapper so I was constantly looking over my shoulder to see if anyone knew who he was.

He was playing it real cool though. At one point his cell phone vibrated and he answered it but he told whoever it was that he would call them back in ten minutes. My phone was on vibrate too and it was going off too but I wasn't answering it. I just looked down at the caller ID to see the number or picture if I had a photo programmed in there to come up instead.

Between South Street and the bank, my mom, Kheli, Xavier, and my neighbor who always braided me and Brie's hair called. She took a picture of my hair once after she braided it so whenever I saw the back of my braided head on my cellie screen I knew it was Jar-u-queesha.

Me and Snatch-Back weren't saying too much to each other at first. Because I was so self-conscious about walking down the street with him, I wasn't paying attention the way I should've been.

Nkosi and Xavier clowned me for days about what happened next.

Just as we were turning the corner onto Lombard Street a Chinese girl came speeding at us on one of them old-fashioned bikes with the big-ass basket on the front. There was no time to think so I dipped real hard to my right. Problem was that Snatch-Back also decided to dip but he went to his left even harder.

We collided and I screamed like a bitch because the Chinese girl steered the bike toward me and the tire slammed right into my leg. It was crazy as shit because all three of us fell to the sidewalk.

Snatch-Back didn't go down as hard as us because I was on my back and the bike was practically on top of me. My cell phone went flying one way and I remember seeing Snatch-Back's keys and glasses hit the ground too. The Chinese chick was so traumatized that I thought she was going to have a seizure.

She was crying hysterically and she kept apologizing. He did a good job of calming her down.

"Listen . . . listen . . . we're fine, it was an accident. Are you OK?"

"Yes . . . yes . . . I am fine. I'm so sorry. I'm so sorry."

"Don't worry about it. We're fine."

By the time he calmed her down, I had gotten up off the ground, picked up the cellie, and dusted myself off. Snatch-Back picked up his shit off the ground, because everything went flying out of his hands too, and then we went on our way.

It was awkward as hell because we walked down Lombard without once looking at each other while we talked.

"So is blackmailing rappers how you make a living, Sticks?"

"Naw, it ain't even like that. This is a one-time thing."

"Oh yeah?"

"Yup. It just so happens that it was you for my one and only time. It has nothing to do with you specifically, it's just the way the ball bounced."

"So you're telling me of all the rappers in the world, you just happened to get your hands on a tape with me fucking. One of the richest dudes in the game."

"I know it sounds bad, but I guess I got lucky."

"Lucky? Is that what you call taking food out of my kids' mouths?"

"Spare me aight. Your iced out platinum watch and that chain is worth enough to feed a small African village. You spend your loot with motherfuckers that don't give two shits about your community, so you have to come better than that."

"Do you have any children?"

"Yes I do."

"So how would you feel if somebody, nah mean, was coming at you for cash that you planned on giving to your kids."

"Well I only have one kid and if I had the kind of cake you have, I would've made sure that my kid was set for life. Even if I ain't sell another record."

"That's easier said than done when you have to pay damn there everything you make on lawyers because motherfuckers is always coming at your neck."

"Listen dude, remember I saw the tape so you can save the sad song for the next nigga. I know you did exactly what that chick said you did, so you having to cough up bread for a lawyer . . . I mean you brought that on yourself."

Even though I didn't look at Snatch-Back to see his reaction I can tell that my comment pissed him off. My phone vibrated again. I glanced down real quick and saw Kheli's familiar face on my screen sitting on her couch in a black wifebeater. I laughed to myself because I know she would've fell out laughing if she saw how we got nailed by an out-of-control Asian biker.

Snatch-Back just stopped talking to me after that until we were in the lobby area of Commerce Bank. He strolled up to one of the ATM machines and signaled for me to come and stand next to him.

"This is the deal. Do you have your bank card with you?"

"Of course."

"Aight, bet. I want you to get me twenty dollars out of your account."

"What? You want me to give you twenty bucks?"

"Yeah dude. I don't have any cash on me and I need it for cab fare to get back to where I have to go."

"What the hell that got to do—"

"Listen man, just do it. Please."

"Aight stand back."

I set my phone and keys down on the counter right next to the ATM and pulled my wallet out of my pocket. I laughed to myself because as I was punching in my pass code, I covered the pad with my other hand and glanced over my shoulder to make sure that he couldn't see. Like he really was pressed to get a piece of my fortune. Imagine those headlines. Millionaire rapper arrested for stealing eighty dollars from an unknown, broke nigga in Philly.

I handed him the twenty after it spit out and pressed the button to get my card back and a receipt. Snatch-Back was standing so close to me that I could feel him breathing on my neck. He set his stuff down on the counter too and grabbed for the receipt as soon as it came out. I snatched it back and pushed him back with one hand.

Talk about an adrenaline rush. When I flipped it over my knees almost buckled. My balance was one hundred thousand and eighty-four dollars. There was no playing off my excitement. I took a deep breath and let it out like I just got picked to be the next contestant on *The Price Is Right.*

"I see you were almost on E there. You got to me right in the nick of time."

I balled up the receipt real quick and stuffed it in my pocket. I was kind of embarrassed for a second because he knew how much I had in my account before he made the deposit. I got over it real quick though because my plan was starting to come together and I was getting paid.

We left the bank and headed down 2nd Street toward South. All the while I was wondering where his people were because I knew that nigga ain't really roll out by himself. If I had eyes on us then I know he did as well.

Once we got in front of the Wawa, he stopped walking and turned to me. He took off his big-ass shades and looked me dead in the eye this time. I guess he wanted me to know he was serious as a heart attack.

"Now I know this ain't all that you're asking for but I wanted you to see that I'm serious, nah mean, about giving you what you want. It's just that getting that kind of money is going to take some time."

"How much time?"

"It could be a couple of weeks or more before I'm able to move that kind of money your way. But I'll keep you posted every few days or so. So we straight?"

"We'll be straight when I get the rest of my loot but in the meantime you can rest assured that not a soul is going to see that tape."

"Word. I ain't happy that you coming at me like this but I just want to handle this shit and be done with it."

"Aight, bet. So what are we doing now?"

"Well I'm going to hop in one of these cabs right quick and I'll talk to you in a few days."

I could see that Snatch-Back was doing the best he could not to pimp-slap the shit out of me. His jaw was tight and he was fidgety but he was really trying to keep his cool. The whole situation was making him be humble and I could tell that he wasn't used to that.

"OK, cool. I'm going to walk back toward South Street. Call me and keep me updated on the status of the balance aight."

We actually shook hands before we headed in different directions. He hailed a cab and hopped in it before I could get to the corner. As soon as it turned on South Street toward Front I whipped out my cell phone and called Nkosi.

"Where you at?"

"I'm right behind you on the other side of the street."

I turned around to see Nkosi waving his hands between two parked cars on Second Street. He was wearing a dark blue short-sleeve Dickies shirt with a white thermal shirt on underneath and the matching Dickies pants. Not too many people would look at him from his Timbs to his fitted Sixers hat and think, "news reporter." He signaled for me to follow him, and I crossed the street.

Nkosi's black Explorer was parked at a meter on the other side of the divider. He jumped right into it as soon as I got in the car.

"So what happened? What did he say?"

"He said that it was going to take a little time to move that much bread into my account. It may take a few weeks, maybe even more."

"Word. Did he agree to pay the whole mill?"

"He didn't say, but get this. I went and checked my balance at the ATM and look at this."

I reached into the pocket of my jeans and pulled out the balled-up receipt. Nkosi didn't even let me unfold it all the way before he pulled it out of my hands. His eyes almost popped out of his head after he saw the balance at the bottom.

"Damn! He put a hundred Gs in your checking account! Damn man, this shit is crazy."

"Yeah, I was like whoa! This shit is off the hook. That's major paper and the sweet thing is that this ain't it. This is only the beginning."

Nkosi didn't want to let go of the receipt. Those numbers at the bottom had him mesmerized. For someone who didn't want me to go through with the plan at first he was mighty hype.

"Yo dude, what are you going to say to justify this much money being in your account? You're out of work right now and you have no verifiable source of income."

"Man I ain't even think about all of that."

"Well you better because this shit could come back to bite you in your ass if you don't dot them Is and cross them Ts."

"Maybe I can say that I wrote some songs on his album and that this was my payment."

"That's a good idea but with this much money changing hands you're still going to need something in writing to say that."

"You might be right."

"Getting him to do that is going to be hard as hell, but you're going to have to try. In the meantime, you can transfer most of this cash to my account if you want."

"Huh? Why would I do that? I mean I trust you and all but why would I put the money in your account? Then you would be in the same boat almost."

"True, but I'm a reporter and I freelance for magazines and I write bios for celebrities and politicians. I could justify having that kind of change. It's a long shot but I have more of a chance of pulling it off."

"I don't know . . ."

"Listen, you don't have to make up your mind now, I just wanted you to know it's an option."

"Oh OK."

Nkosi looked at me real for a few seconds like he was starting to get offended.

"What you think I'm going to stick you for your green, nigga?"

"Naw, that's not it at all, you know we cool. I've never had this much money get dumped on me in one lump sum like that so I guess my head is still spinning."

"Well think about it. I just wanted you to know that you had an option. In the meantime, where to now?"

I leaned the passenger seat back as far as it could go and laid back with my hands behind my head like I was the original Don Dada. I had a mission to go on the next day and I needed to look pretty.

"Take me to 15th and Walnut. I need to pay my good friend Kenneth Cole a visit. It's been a long time."

16. THURSDAY, NOVEMBER 20, 2003 (10 P.M.)

I had a hundred Gs sitting in my checking account and one of the baddest chicks in Philly sitting on my face.

Less than twelve hours after I made a come up with Snatch-Back's cash, it was time to get my nail on. After me and Nkosi left the Kenneth Cole store on Walnut Street, I hollered at Nia to see what was up for the night.

I first met her back in June at the Odunde street festival at 23rd and South. She was walking with like three of her girlfriends when I cracked on her. At first she acted like she wasn't feeling me, and then she told her roadies to keep walking and that she would catch up with them.

I knew I had her after that. There was always thousands and thousands of people at Odunde so once you lost contact with whoever you came with, it was a wrap. You had a better chance of getting Star Jones to put down a piece of cake than finding them again. When she told them to keep going I knew she wanted to kick it with me for a while.

Nia was about 5'4" and tough, a bona fide dime-piece coming and going. Her legs were toned and sexy and smooth just the way I like them. She was slightly bowlegged but it didn't jump out at you right away. Her smooth brown skin was my favorite part of her but her sexy-ass brown eyes were right up there too.

There were a lot of chicks out at Odunde that day but she stood out from the rest because she was sexy as hell without being half naked. She rocked a skirt that came a little bit past her knees, but it was fitting so right that it made a nigga want to light a match and sway to music that wasn't even playing. For her to be so petite she had a nice little donkey.

Her white tank top showed just enough to make me want to look further. Nia wasn't handling in the titty department the way I like, but it was still all good. An old head chick I used to mess with always told me that more than a mouthful is too much anyway so it was all right.

I bought us a couple of mango water ices and we made our way to the stage on Grays Ferry Avenue to watch a group of kids perform African dance. After that was over she got in line to get an autographed book from an author who was selling books off the side of the stage. The name of the book was *Blinking Red Light* or *Red Light District* or something like that.

He looked so damn familiar but I couldn't place where I knew him from. Nia was all geeked to be getting a signed book. I was so pressed to impress her that I slapped the fifteen dollars down on the table when it was her turn at the front of the line.

I knew I was feeling her then, because I ain't never put up cash that early in the game. When the author boaw signed the book and told her to e-mail him when she was finished I felt some kind of way. I ain't even know her last name at that point, and I was tripping on the inside because of how he was flirting with her on the low.

I gave him the ice-grill as we were walking away and he ice-grilled me right back like he wanted to rumble. I figured then that he must be from South Philly too.

After she got her book, we left that crowded scene and walked around the corner to my house. She didn't come in at all on the first day, but we learned a lot about each other sitting on my steps just people watching.

I told her from the gate that I had a daughter because I ain't play no games that way. Chicks always assumed that I had more than one kid so when I told them I only had Brie, it normally didn't make them run off right away.

Nia was a fifth-year prelaw student at Temple. She said she wanted to move out to California and work as a talent agent when she was done school. She knew all the ins and outs of Hollywood like the back of her hand. Talking to her was like watching an episode of *Entertainment Tonight*. She was up on the drama that was going down in hip-hop and R&B but she was just as hip to the happenings with white Hollywood actors. She turned me on, period.

She made me wait a minute before I hit it the first time. Odunde was always the second Sunday in June so I would have to say that it was around Labor Day when I finally poked.

We had enough in common to get down, but I ain't know if I wanted to make her wifey. Honestly, my lack of focus when it came to getting a career made her have doubts about me too. But in the meantime, we ain't have a problem smashing every now and then. I had to give her props because her sex game was like that.

I stop short of saying she had me whipped because I'll never admit that but her shit was murder. She had the snapper that a nigga looks high and low for, so on the day I got paid it was on and crackin'.

Just to be on some different shit, I rented out a suite at the DoubleTree at Broad and Locust. We had fucked in every room of my crib so it was time for something different. I dropped Brie off at Kheli's apartment and went back downtown. It felt good as hell to be balling out of control after being broke for a minute.

I got to the 'tellie about an hour before her so that I could set up the suite. I felt corny as hell breaking up rose petals and putting them all over the floor and in the bed but I knew that chicks loved that kind of shit. If she was a smut jawn then I definitely wouldn't have gone through all the trouble, but she was worth it. She was going to be big-time one day so I played my cards right.

When Nia got to the suite, she was dressed in a real laid-back casual hookup but it was still sexy as hell. My jaw dropped when she took off her leather coat. She had on these skintight jeans that were so low that I could see her lacy blue thong every time she bent over. The black shirt she had on was long-sleeve, but it was tight and the shoulders were cut out.

She couldn't stop smiling when she peeped the rose petals and the bowl of chocolate-covered strawberries on the table next to the bed. Since she didn't drink alcohol I had two bottles of sparkling peach cider chilling in a bucket of ice on the other nightstand.

"I underestimated you. I didn't know South Philly guys got it in like this."

"Well if you're going to be a celebrity agent one day then you should know to never judge a book by its cover, nah mean. You never know what you'll miss out on."

"Is that so?"

"Yeah, they ain't kicking knowledge like that to you down at Temple are they? You need to be paying me that tuition."

Before she could respond I just gripped her up and started

kissing her like my life depended on it. We were standing right there in the middle of the floor, wrestling tongues and feeling each other up.

After I pulled her shirt over her head and ripped it off, I rubbed the chocolate strawberries all over her nipples and then sucked every drop of it off slowly. Nia was so open after that. Absolutely open. When all of the chocolate was gone, she told me that she wanted to take a shower with me. I was game because that was something that we never did at my crib. We were all over each other again as soon as we hopped in the jawn.

Nia started handling her business right from the gate. We weren't in there even a minute before the hot water was running down my back and my dick was in her mouth. Her head game was always A-1, top of the line, classic. She kept good rhythm and she didn't try to take more in her jaws than she could handle.

She squatted down in front of me and started doing major justice to the hammer. And just when I thought it couldn't get no better she upped her game. It was already vicious and then she pulled her neck back until just the head of my Johnson was in her mouth. Then she just put all of her attention on the tip. I came so hard that I had to hold on to the shower curtain rod with both hands.

There was no way I was going to let her outdo me. After we got out of the shower and dried off I returned the favor big-time. I hiked her up onto the bathroom sink and then pushed the back of her head against the fogged-up mirror. I told her to close her eyes and relax. I put both of her legs over my shoulders and ate her pussy so good that she was plucking skin from my back out of her nails days later.

She was so short that I could handle her just about any way I wanted. That made it all the more better when I threw her up there and twisted her body. She was moaning loud as hell and out of control every time I flicked my tongue on her clit. I reached up and grabbed her titties real rough and squeezed on them while her legs were up in the air. I tried to put my whole face in it.

She was shaking so much after about five minutes that I went in for the kill. I picked her up and took her into the bedroom and I laid her down across the king-sized mattress. I grabbed her and sat her up on my face and went back to licking and sucking on her pussy until she was whimpering like a baby.

In the next few hours we fucked three times in every position we could think of.

Nia's favorite was when I pushed her legs back all the way and then sat on her thighs with my back to her and entered her that way. I loved it too because I had to slide her hips all the way to the edge of the bed, plant my feet on the floor and squat up and down to get deep in her coochie. I loved how she would scream and moan but I hated that I was facing away from her and so I couldn't see the look on her face while I was smashing it.

It was tight as hell to be in a phat hotel downtown with a chick that I was really feeling. I had smashed at a hotel before but never anywhere that nice. It beat the Motel 6 hands-down.

I didn't feel like the money made me because I always got chicks before that. With cash though it was like living to the tenth power. With that hefty deposit, Snatch-Back gave me a taste of the good life. I was ready for more, but what I wasn't totally prepared for everything that came along with it. I wanted it bad but not enough to go out the back door on anybody close to me.

What a shame that everybody ain't like me.

17. FRIDAY, NOVEMBER 21, 2003 (6 P.M.)

It was time to get down and dirty with Eric Brockington.

Since the minute Minerva told me that she was going to marry that boaw, I knew I had to get the scoop on him. He played for the Eagles and all but that ain't mean shit to me. I needed more.

He was going to be under the same roof as my baby girl and that was serious.

Every day on the news it was a different story of how another young girl was killed or raped. What pissed me off the most was when it was the mom's fiancé or ex-boyfriend. These bitches were too quick to let down their guards and let these niggas in.

I'm a grown-ass man with my own spot and it's different but I still ain't want Brie around a lot of different women just because. If I dug a bitch out at my crib I always made sure that their ass hit the bricks before Brie woke up. I ain't need her seeing a whole lot of chicks laying around the crib in my T-shirts with thongs on.

Xavier said I was drawing since she was only two years old but I figured before I knew it that she would be fourteen and think that it's cool to lay up in some nigga's house. I ain't no saint and I ain't a rocket scientist either, but I have a little bit of common sense.

So all in all, chicks who I fucked with knew the deal. I dicked 'em down real good and they bounced before Brie could rub the sleep out of her eyes.

As for Eric Brockington, I followed my gut, and then followed his ass to the Marriott hotel downtown. Having a reporter as a homey went a long way. Nkosi got a press release at the *Tribune* about a celebrity pool tournament that was sponsored by a news reporter named Arthur Fennell and Kenny Gamble, the music legend who set off the Sound of Philadelphia back in the day.

There were about sixty people signed up to play for the charity, and one of them was Brockington. Nkosi couldn't make it because he had to cover another event but I knew I was definitely going to be up in the spot.

I got to the hotel at about six o'clock. These two honeys at the bottom of the escalator greeted me and directed me to the fifth floor where the tournament was taking place. One was dark chocolate with high cheekbones and a sneaky look to her. She couldn't stop staring at my eyes. My mother always told me to beware of women who liked me just because I had "cat eyes" as she called them.

While she was stuck on my eyes, her vanilla partner was looking me up and down like she was an army inspector. I peeped that she had major gravy. Her ass was almost as phat as Minerva's but not quite.

I glanced back as I was going up the escalator and of course they were both still staring and smiling from ear to ear. They looked like they were inhaling and trying to hold on to the scent of the Dolce & Gabbana I was wearing. Like I said, I killed them coming and going.

Comedians joke that light-skinned brothas had played out, but I knew that wasn't true. I was on point that night thanks to my sexy new friend from the Kenneth Cole store.

The sexy saleswoman at Kenneth Cole helped me pick out the most murder hookup I had seen in a minute. Her name was Sanya and she was so fine that I was stalling while I was shopping just to spend more time with her.

After I tried on the suit, I opened the door to the dressing room on purpose while I got dressed. I wanted sexy Sanya to see what I was working with in my boxers and she definitely noticed. Her eyes went right down too but then she caught herself and looked away real quick.

I spent more than seven hundred dollars on one outfit. I figured it was worth it because the suit was so classic that I could rock it for the rest of my life. It was a black pinstripe jawn that looked like something out of a *GQ* photo shoot. I copped a pair of black dress shoes that set me back about two hundred and a gold-colored shirt for about a bean that matched the stripes in the suit exactly.

Sanya picked out a simple black leather belt. I already had one that looked similar at home but I wanted to impress her like money wasn't a thing. Her digits were mine before we made it to the register. She said she was a student at Penn and that she was so single that it hurt.

On top of the new gear from KC, Jar-u-queesha had hooked me up earlier that day with some fresh cornrows. It was on and poppin' that night and it had to be for the mission I was on. I wanted to be the prettiest nigga in there and from the way them bitches melted at the bottom of the escalator I knew I was on point.

It was a necessary mission but not one that I ever want to set out on again. There's a first and last time for everything.

At first I thought I was in the wrong place because when I got to the top of the first escalator there were a lot of middle-aged white people dressed in capes and all types of crazy-ass costumes.

It was off the hook. I looked one way and saw a man dressed like a pirate and another and there were three overweight dudes coming at me dressed in all black leather suits like they were in the *Matrix*.

The lady at the bottom of the next escalator explained to me that there was some type of sci-fi convention going on. Just as she was explaining it to me, a white guy who was about forty-five years old and pushing four hundred pounds came up and started waving his hand back and forth in front of her.

He stopped for a few seconds, glanced down into a book he was holding, and started up again. I figured out that the nut job was actually trying to levitate her off the ground with his super powers. There's a loon born every day.

Once I made it up to the fifth floor I paid the forty dollars at the registration table. I was given a red all-access wristband and sent on my way. It was packed up in that jawn. I ain't know anybody up in there but it was cool with me. I wanted to stay under the radar until it was time for me to show my face.

They had a few chefs up in that jawn making pasta and carving turkey and roast beef so I got my grub on first. For forty ones I should have brought some aluminum foil so I could make a plate and take it with me. I had a couple dollars in the bank, but I still wasn't out of the woods yet. The change I spent at the Marriott that night was truly an investment.

After I ate, I hustled into the ballroom where the tournament was being held. There were four pool tables on the floor where the competition took place with bleachers surrounding the floor. I think it was being taped for television because there were bright lights and cameras everywhere.

I played it real low in the background like a fly on the wall. I actually shouldn't say fly on the wall, because a fly on the wall doesn't want to be seen. I did.

It couldn't have been ten minutes after I grabbed a seat that the man of the hour walked in. The tournament had already started but nobody seemed to mind that Eric Brockington had strolled up in the place almost an hour late.

He was with another dude that I didn't recognize. Maybe he was an Eagle too but I doubted it. There were a lot of rookies that rode the bench but I knew the team and I had never seen that boaw before.

Eric Brockington was decked out in cream suede pants with a matching button-up shirt. The flashy wide receiver topped it off with a pair of caramel-colored gators. Normally when I see him out he's thugged out in jeans and Timbs or a sweat suit. He's usually dipped in ice, but this time he only had on a platinum and diamond watch.

Cameras were flashing all over the place. This one chick, who I think lived in the middle of my block, was pushing up so hard on the brotha that I thought she was going to mount him right there on the spot. She leaned into him and wrapped one of her long skinny legs around him while her friends snapped pictures with their cheap throwaway cameras.

He was eating up the attention like a vulture, especially from the chicks, because he had his pick of the pussy. They were eating so hard out of the palm of his hand that if he snapped his fingers most of them would have been butt naked.

One of the event organizers pulled Eric Brockington away from the mob of fans so that she could hook him up with his partner for the night. From a distance it ain't seem like they knew each other. The partner was a white-haired black guy who looked like he played pool all night and all day. I saw that he had his own pool stick on his back and that he refused the free stick that everyone else was given.

When they were finally up to play it was obvious that Eric Brockington wasn't no pool shark. Now I remembered seeing his crib on MTV and I remember it being a bangin'-ass pool table in his den. It was obviously just for show. He was knocked out of the competition quick as shit.

I made my way toward where he was standing. There were a lot of his teammates in the house and he was standing off to the side rapping to a few of them. Once I got close enough I stood where he could see me. He was so gone in his conversation at first but then he looked up and I caught his eye.

I gave him the head nod and he acknowledged by doing the same.

He went back to his conversation and never looked back up. I turned my back to him and just stood in that same spot. A few minutes later he walked up and stood right next to me so that we were shoulder to shoulder.

If I didn't know that he was in the NFL his body wouldn't have given it away. I read an article in *ESPN* magazine where they took him out in Times Square and asked random women what they thought he did for a living. Not one of them said football player.

He wasn't flat-out bony, but he was about 6' even and smaller than any other player that I ever remember seeing in the league. He wore braids too but he was just a little bit darker than me. It was obvious what Minerva's type was because if not brothers we could have at least been first cousins. I played it real cool and sparked up a conversation.

"Wassup Eric Brockington. Y'all got the Dolphins on Monday. You ready to come with it?"

We shook hands and I patted him on the back.

"Oh yeah. We definitely ready."

"Well good luck man. I been a fan of the birds ever since I was a young boaw."

"Is that right? I heard you said boaw so you must be from Philly."

"North side born and raised."

"Yeah when I first got here my teammates had to hip me to some of the Philly slang."

"What, like 'jawn' and 'boaw'?"

"Yeah and y'all say 'sneakers,' and in Baltimore we say 'tennis shoes.'"

"Yeah but everything ain't a tennis shoe. When we say sneaker that includes a whole lot."

"I guess that's true."

There was a brief uncomfortable silence. He just stopped talking for some reason but he was still staring at me.

"You look so familiar."

"Well I be out at the club all the time with my niggas and I always see you and some of the other dudes from the Eagles out."

"Maybe that's it."

I changed the subject real quick.

"So listen, what's jumping after this pool tournament is over?"

"What you mean?"

"Like is there an after-party or something?"

"Yeah, you have the red wristband so you can go downstairs to the VIP after-party on the third floor when this is done."

"Word."

"I never caught your name."

The lies were rolling off my tongue like wildfire.

"Reggie. Reggie Kenyatta."

"Well it's good to meet you Reggie Kenyatta. You're a smooth dude. You seem like the type that likes to hang out and wild out."

I didn't know what the hell he meant by "hang out" and "wild out" but I had a feeling I was halfway to accomplishing my mission.

"Naw I just chill. I'm real low-key."

"For real. What you do for a living?"

The lies kept coming.

"I work for SEPTA. I drive the 17 bus."

"I bet you see some crazy stuff every day. What you use on your face yo, you have beautiful skin."

"Thanks yo. I just use lotion that's all."

Silence again, but this time it wasn't so awkward. He signed like three autographs here and there but he never took his attention off of me. I had the feeling that if I tried to walk away he would've tackled me.

"Give me your number, Reggie."

"You want my phone number?"

"Yeah, I want to put you on my guest list for next week's game at the Linc. You said you were a big fan so that's the least I can do. I'm going to leave you two tickets at will call."

"Aw . . . that's wassup. I appreciate that man."

"Yeah plus I always have events and my guest list and the chicks and the niggas are always off the hook. I only invite the sexiest people in Philly to my shit so you know you're in there."

Bingo. That's what I was there for. I knew he was going to say something to seal the deal and there it was. Nkosi throws that hot shit on when it's time to go out and I would even venture to say that Xavier is handsome but never on any given day would I ever describe another nigga as sexy.

That threw up the red flag for me right away. My amazon informant Dee-Dee was on point with her hunch. I made a mental note that I was going to treat her to a catfish platter at Ms. Tootsie's on South Street.

I gave Eric Brockington a fake number, actually my old house number, and we said peace to each other. When I turned to walk away the boaw he came in with gritted on me so hard that if looks could kill I would've been ashes in the bottom of an urn by the time I reached the door. When I left the Marriott that night I felt like my mission was accomplished.

It was just like Dee-Dee said. Minerva was getting ready to marry a bona fide homo-thug.

18. FRIDAY, NOVEMBER 21, 2003 (MIDNIGHT)

Shit hit the fan and started flying back at my face at warp speed later that night.

Since I found out what I needed to know about sugarboy much quicker than I anticipated, I jumped on the expressway and went to pick Brie up. My mom said that it was fine if she stayed until the morning as long as I picked her up by seven o'clock. I figured I would just get her then because I knew I wouldn't feel like getting up that early.

For a split second my gut instinct told me to let her stay with my mom all day, and I should've trusted it. I could have spared myself from almost having a heart attack.

Right before we got back to the crib I stopped around the corner at the twenty-four-hour McDonald's on Grays Ferry Avenue to get a Happy Meal. It wasn't so much for the nuggets as for the free toy. I spent about a good $150 at K-B on Brie's last birthday and she spends most of her time playing with the free shit from Mickey-Dee's and Burger King.

By the time I got her undressed and laid her out in the bed she was knocked out. I checked my e-mail, which was mostly junk mail and forwards from my friend Alexis who I worked with at the Mattress Giant a few years ago. Once, her claim to fame was selling more twin beds than anyone in that store's history. Now she had simply become a mass sender of Internet spam.

Once Brie was down I cleaned up my bathroom because it was filthy and then hopped in the shower. I did all of my thinking and planning in the shower. It was always where I cleared my head and figured out what my next move was going to be. After that night, it would be a very long time before I let down my guard long enough to even enjoy a five-minute shower.

Now that Dee-Dee's tip turned out to be true, I had to figure if that information really mattered. I knew deep down that Eric Brockington was a switch-hitter, but I honestly didn't think that he was any real threat to Brie. I was just going off of instinct but the boaw seemed cool. Minerva was going to have a whole different set of issues once she figured out what that freak was into.

He was one of them "down-low" thugs that they talked about on Fox Undercover, but he ain't seem like the type to bring no drama into my daughter's life.

Kheli had already warned me that even if he messed with niggas that it wouldn't affect how the judge would rule on whether Minerva was entitled to have more time with Brie. It didn't matter one way or another with the system as long as their home was suitable and Minerva had her shit together.

The wheels in my head were in motion until suddenly they came to a screeching halt. I slid open the shower door real slow and poked out my head because it sounded like Brie was out of the bed. Every now and then she would get out of bed and go looking for me if I wasn't in bed next to her. One time I was in the shower and she almost fell down the steps trying to see if I was in the living room.

I left the bathroom door wide open because it was tight as shit in there and it always steamed up real quick. Plus, if she started crying or got out the bed I could hear better. There was a framed mirror on the wall in my bedroom to the right of the bathroom door. The television was on mute but it didn't give that much light.

I listened for a few seconds and just when I decided to duck my head back in the shower. My heart almost jumped out of my fucking chest.

It happened real quick but I know my eyes weren't playing tricks on me. Something moved in my bedroom and it wasn't Brie. Even if she stood up on the bed and jumped as high as she could, the mirror was so high up on the wall that I still wouldn't be able to see her in it.

I slid the door open real slow and stepped out onto the cold floor. I never turned the shower off. I crept on my tippy-toes butt naked and dripping wet toward the doorway with my eyes locked on the mirror. As soon as I got a few feet from the door I saw the motion again. This time I almost shit on myself because I could tell without a doubt that it was a person.

In a situation like that you don't even think, you just go, and that's what I did. I sprinted out of the bathroom and ran in the direction of bed where Brie was laying. It all happened so quickly, but as I was running I turned to my left and saw that it was a man. This nigga was standing at the foot of my bed staring at my daughter.

He was a little bit taller than I was and he had on a red do-rag with one of them black winter masks that covers your face from the nose down. All that was showing was his eyes and his forehead.

I only had the TV light to see by but it was enough. I scared the shit out of him because he must've thought I was still in the shower. He lunged toward me and swung a wild-ass right that missed but I made sure I didn't on the return. I hit that nigga with a two-piece and it made his knees buckle long enough for me to turn and go toward my bed.

I kept a cast-iron shovel from my fake chimney set right underneath my bed on the side I slept on. I dove on the floor and reached for it. Once I hit the floor my arms flailed out and I knocked it a little bit out of my reach under the bed.

Before I could react the dude dove on my back and wrapped his arm around my neck. He had me in a choke hold and I was stuck underneath his weight. I couldn't breathe right away and I started to panic. I was kicking my legs but the way he was pinned on top of me I couldn't move.

I felt the air leaving my body. All I could do was reach out my left arm and reach as hard as I could. Inch by inch I was getting closer. He was so occupied with trying to squeeze the air out of my lungs that dude didn't notice that I was reaching for the shovel. He put his mouth real close to my ear and spoke for the first time.

"You ready to die motherfucker?"

He jerked my neck back real hard and slammed me down on the floor again and that little motion gave me the few more inches that I needed.

I gripped the handle of the shovel with the tips of my left hand and switched it to my right as quick as I could. When he saw what I was doing he let up a little so that he could try to get it from me. I reached back and cracked him in the head as hard as I could. I ain't get him the way I wanted to but the blow was enough to make him take his weight off of me and get on his knees.

I rolled over and kicked the shit out of him. He fell back on his ass but he popped right up on his feet. I didn't hit him as hard as I wanted to the first time but I knew that if I had a second chance I was going to try to knock his fucking block off.

He ain't think twice about it, he just turned around and jetted toward my bedroom door. I reacted with him and lunged at him across the bed. I leaped over Brie who was right smack in the middle of the bed and out like a rock. She would sometimes wake up out of a dead sleep if I dropped a brush on the floor or if I was talking too loud on the phone. As crazy as it seems, she ain't even stir a little bit.

When I got to the top of the steps he was about halfway down the flight. I didn't think about it, I just lunged forward like I was

Wolverine in *X-Men.* When I collided with him I gripped on the back of his shoulders with both of my hands and we just started rolling over top of each other to the bottom of the landing in front of the door.

We crashed hard as hell on the wood floor. He rolled one way and I rolled another but we were both hurting. My stomach was turning into knots because I had hit my nuts somewhere during the fall. I think that I blacked out for a split second because I don't remember getting off my back and moving toward the coffee table. I just remember crawling across the floor with my mind on getting that shovel back in my hand. It spun to the right of the staircase and stopped between the couch and the coffee table.

That nigga was stunned too because it took him a while to get to his feet.

Everything was in slow motion at that point. When I got up off the floor and turned around he was coming at me across the dark living room with a blade in his hand. I got a good grip on the chimney shovel and jumped back at him. I wasn't ready to back down one inch to that pussy because all I could think about was Brie.

If I let him slice me up or worse, he would be left alone with my baby to do whatever he wanted. That right there was enough motivation for me to take on Tyson and Holyfield with one hand tied behind my back.

Whoever he was, I figured he must ain't have no kids. If he did he would know that he would have been better off going off to the zoo and trying to walk off with a bear cub.

Better than that, it's like an unspoken ghetto rule that if you come rolling up in somebody's crib with beef you had better be ready to do battle. I probably seemed at a disadvantage to him since I was wet, butt naked, and caught off guard, but it was cool.

Even though it was dark, I could tell that it was a knife in his right hand, but as he got closer I saw that he was working with way more than a switchblade. It looked like a butcher knife and it was big enough to slash a first-grader in half.

I got a good grip on the shovel and held it up in a defensive position so that he could see it. He looked me up and down and started to snicker.

"Is that all you're working with short stuff?"

"Take one more step and you'll feel what I'm working with right on your forehead."

"I ain't talking about that shovel pussy, I'm talking about your small-ass Johnson."

"If your mother was here to put her mouth on it like she did last night you would see that it's bigger than you think."

"Oh yeah pussy. Is that right?"

"Yeah pussy, let's get it!"

We lunged at each other and he swung the knife. I whacked the shit out of him on his left arm near his shoulder and that made him wince and jump back. He got me too though with a quick little slice right underneath my belly button. I never looked down at it to check it out but I could feel that shit.

He was working with a nice piece of steel but I could tell by how wild he swung at me that he ain't have no real knife game. He thought he was a ghetto samurai but that one slice he got off was pure luck.

He was backed up against the banister of the steps and breathing real heavy.

My stomach was burning a little but I was getting more heated inside than anything. That shit was too close for comfort because I was naked and that low-ass cut made it seem like he was going for the jewels.

He wasn't done though because the motherfucker came back at me swinging wild as shit like he was trying to dice me from head to toe. I kept moving around the coffee table and throwing the shovel up at him. A few times the knife clanked against the shovel but that was about as close as I let him get to me. I was letting him swing his heart out because I knew he was getting tired. We were probably getting it in for a short amount of time but it seemed like an eternity when I finally caught that bastard the way I wanted to.

I kept it moving right until that one millisecond when he swung the knife a little too high for a little too long. He swung his arm up so high with the knife that he looked like the shadow on the wall in the *Psycho* movie. Dude was trying to seriously take me out of here but he fucked up.

I jabbed him in his ribs with the shovel and when he bent over and grabbed his side I cracked the shit out of him on the left side of his head. He crumbled to the floor and fell flat out on his back.

The knife hit the floor right next to his hand. I jumped over the coffee table and grabbed it off the floor. He was stretched out on the floor and he was groggy as shit. I don't even know if he knew where he was because he was stunned. The mask was still there but it had slid down just enough for me to see his face. My heart started racing because I knew exactly who it was.

I was so fucking mad that I stood over top of him and put my bare foot to his throat. I had switched the shovel to my left hand and the knife was in my right. I had every intention of disfiguring that pussy. I wanted to stab him in the head and then work my way down his body. That motherfucker had the gall to break into my crib and come that close to my baby. I figured that he deserved to lose an eye or at the least a couple of fingers.

I put my knee in his chest and started running the tip of the blade across his forehead. I came down the bridge of his nose and then stopped in the middle. I paused only because I was trying to decide which eye I was going to pluck out.

And then came the luckiest break of his life. Or maybe it was simply divine intervention.

"Daddy . . . Daddy . . ."

I snapped out of my homicidal trance and jumped up from on top of him.

When I got to the bottom of the stairs I could see Brie standing there in her oversized Teletubbies nightgown rubbing her eyes. I skipped up the steps two at a time until I was at the top of the landing with my baby. I dropped the shovel and scooped her up into my arms. I reached over right away and turned on the hall light.

When I looked back down the steps all I saw was my door fly open and his punk ass flying out of there like a bat out of hell. The next few minutes are a blur but I remember calling Nkosi to tell him what went down and to not call the cops.

I wanted street justice for that pussy simple and plain.

Nkosi was on my doorstep in less than fifteen minutes and he was furious. I knew that after what happened there was no way in hell that I was going to be able to sleep. He insisted that I pack up as much as I could and come to his crib in West Philly.

I didn't argue with him because I knew that we had to get out of there.

"Who would do this? Who the fuck would break in here and try to come at you like that with Brie in the crib?"

After we were packed and ready to roll I finally answered his question.

"I know exactly who it was."

19. SATURDAY, NOVEMBER 22, 2003 (10 A.M.)

I've had my own crib since I was nineteen years old.

That's almost ten years of coming and going as I pleased and basically just doing my own thing. I knew that I would never be the poster child for holding down a career. If there was a gig to be worked though, I worked it.

I got my hustle on at Boston Market, AT&T Wireless, Acme, and even the electric company once for about two years. I still hadn't figured out what I wanted to be when I grew up, but I knew that whatever it was I had to get paid big-time.

In the meantime, I tried not to depend too much on any one person for anything. Before Brie was born I lived in a one-room efficiency in North Philly that specialized in roaches, and an overpriced studio apartment in West Philly.

There were times that I could've went back to stay with my mom in Mt. Airy, but I loved my freedom. Nkosi always made it known that he was an option but he was way too caught up in the newspaper life and too damn neat for me to even consider. Besides, he was my boaw from way back and I figured the quickest way for us to end our friendship was to move in with each other.

After the break-in, Kheli also made the offer for me and Brie to come stay with her, but that wasn't going to work. There would hardly be room for my luggage or space for a two-year-old to run around in at her crib since it was so small.

Nkosi had a huge three-bedroom apartment off of 46th and Spruce in West Philly and it was just him. He used the middle room as his office and the third room at the end of the hall across from the bathroom was his guest room. It was nothing for Martha Stewart to do cartwheels over though.

The mattress and box spring was on the floor without a frame or headboard. The only dresser in the room was this worn-out little jawn that he had since college. All the knobs were missing and you had to jam it real hard to close it. There were coats and clothes that I ain't seen that nigga wear in years stacked up in the small closet.

It wasn't home but I had no room to complain. I was stressed the hell out that somebody was able to get up in my crib and get that close to my baby. Nkosi gave us a place to stay so I was grateful. I just knew it wouldn't be easy.

The good thing was that at least I had some cash to look for another apartment in the meantime. My lease wasn't up for a little while in South Philly but I'm sure my landlord would have to understand that I couldn't stay there with my baby after what happened.

Me and Brie got settled in as best we could considering the circumstances. With all that was happening I had totally forgotten that it was Minerva's day to come and pick up Brie. When I answered my cell I could tell that she was in one of her bitchy moods. She was screaming into the phone that I was throwing her schedule off by not being at my crib when she came to pick Brie up.

I told her to come and get Brie from Nkosi's but I never mentioned the intruder because I ain't want to give her no ammunition to use against me later. Minerva got to Nkosi's crib in like fifteen minutes. I didn't invite her in, I just got Brie's clothes and shit together and met her outside at the corner.

Brie was happy to see her mom but she started fussing a little bit when she realized that I wasn't going with them. I could hardly pay attention to any of that though because the whip caught me off guard.

Minerva was pushing a 2003 three hundred series cranberry BMW.

"Hold up let me get her car seat out of—"

"We're straight. My fiancé went out and got a brand-new one yesterday . . . you know to go with my brand-new BMW."

"Oh, aight."

"He wants to meet you by the way."

"What he want to meet me for?"

"Well, like I said before, he is going to be my husband and he's going to be around Brie. We just basically have to sit down to discuss some very important stuff."

"Where does he want to meet?"

"When you come to pick up Brie tomorrow. Can you meet us at the Chuck E. Cheese on the Boulevard? It's very important."

"What time?"

"Around one."

"That's cool."

She loaded Brie into the Beamer and sashayed her phat ass around the car and hopped into the driver's seat. She was stuntin' something serious and she knew it. She was flossing but I wasn't fazed because I knew it was only a matter of time before I dropped something sickening on her too. My time to shine was right around the corner.

I watched them pull off before I came back into Nkosi's apartment. I don't know why but all I could think about was what would happen if dude got traded to another team. That would mean Minerva would have to move and expect that Brie would stay with them too. I couldn't wrap my brain around the thought of Brie leaving Philly with Minerva, even if it was to go across the river into Jersey for an hour.

Once I was back in the apartment, me and Nkosi talked for a while about what went down the night before. The obvious burning question was whether or not Snatch-Back had anything to do with it.

The stranger, who me and Nkosi started calling Darkman, was obviously trying to get to the tape. The question was how did he know about it and how the hell did he know where I lived?

Nkosi was worried about whether or not the dude got his hands on the tape, but I assured him that Darkman was way off. We walked through my house after he got there on Friday night and noticed all the places where that masked dickhead looked.

He hit all of the obvious places where you see people hiding shit on TV. Of course he ransacked my freezer, the kitchen cabinets, my dresser, and the shoe boxes in my room closet. That fool practically tore the pillows on my couch apart trying to find my million-dollar tape. I guessed that he was contemplating looking under my mattress but since Brie was in the bed he was standing there trying to figure out how he could do that without waking her up.

When we were young we played a game called "Come and Get Your Supper" where you had to look for something like a football or a deck of cards. If you were close, someone screamed "hot," if you were far off they screamed "cold." Darkman was in "Antarctica." The tape was in my house all right, but he wasn't even close.

Even though he caught me way off guard I still felt like I was one step ahead of that clown. Nkosi told me in the very beginning to brace myself for the worst so I figured I was ready. As long as I got my cash everything would work itself out and me and Brie would be sitting pretty.

"So are you sure it was him?"

"Man, I'm positive. The dude who I was fighting last night was the same motherfucker who was lurking around me and Brie at the Chuck E. Cheese down South Philly. I am sure of that beyond a shadow of a doubt."

"And you say you never saw him before?"

"Never! You know how even if you don't know somebody that if you saw them before you still might at least remember seeing them? Well his face don't even ring a bell."

Kheli stopped by that afternoon too. We filled her in on what we had discussed and how we thought Darkman was able to track me down. She agreed that Snatch-Back had something to do with it but we were all confused as to why he would do something so foolish.

I guess all bets were off since his livelihood was on the line. All he did was made me stay on my toes more after that. I had a mission and I was sticking to it because me and Brie were moving out of the hood. My first preference was a condo, but it had to have security after what had happened.

Kheli was kind of quiet when she first got there, and when she started to talk her focus seemed to be right back where it was less than a week before.

"So you took the tape out of the house didn't you?"

"Here she go, she's right back on that tape."

"Don't start Nkosi. I just was asking because—"

"Why, so you could make sure it's in a 'secure place'?"

Nkosi threw up air quotes with his fingers and Kheli rolled her eyes at him. He busted out laughing and hit her with one of the pillows from his couch.

"I'm just messing with you, Kheli. You always take everything so personal."

"'Cause you play too much, Nkosi. You keep acting like I'm so pressed over the tape when I just don't want nobody else to get it."

"I know what it is. You just want to see your boy on there getting it in. I remember you had a big crush on Snatch-Back a few years back. You want to see that tape so you can get your rocks off, ain't that right?"

"Man, I am so over him. Matter fact I was kind of getting over him before I saw the tape and that just did it for me. It killed the fantasy, ya know, seeing the man I loved all those years raping a defenseless woman underneath a picture of Teddy Pendergrass."

"You sound more and more like a social worker every time I see you."

"Whatever man. I'm just keeping it real."

Xavier was missing in action that Saturday afternoon. I had talked to him in the middle of the night after the fight with Darkman. He didn't call once on Saturday to see if me and Brie were straight and that was unlike him. That struck me as odd at first but then I didn't think much of it.

We spent the rest of the afternoon going back and forth in a rented U-Haul van getting the shit that I really needed from down South Philly. It mostly amounted to Brie's clothes and toys and some of my paperwork. Nkosi called a storage company and made a reservation for them to come and get my couch and bedroom furniture. I planned on leaving a lot of shit in there, just to make room for the fresh new shit wherever I was moving.

When I told Kheli that I was going to meet with Minerva and Eric Brockington, she suggested that I take a picture to capture the look on his face when he realized who I really was. We agreed that his face would crack into a thousand pieces when he realized that I was the same dude he tried to crack on at the Marriott.

I had no plans on exposing him to Minerva for the homothug that he was. I just wanted him to know that I knew so that

I could hold it over his head. He was rich and famous and that was all good, but now he was trying to invade my space with my daughter and I wasn't feeling that shit at all.

But like Minerva said when she popped up at my house to tell me she was engaged, the joke would be on me. The meeting made that Sunday the second worst day of my life.

The worst would soon follow.

20. SUNDAY, NOVEMBER 23, 2003 (12:45 P.M.)

It was supposed to be sweet.

It was supposed to be the day when I looked Eric Brockington's punk ass dead in the eyes and laughed because I knew what his trick-ass fiancée didn't.

Minerva said she wanted us to meet face-to-face. She went into the same song and dance about how she wanted us all to be on the same page for the sake of Brie. Yada yada yada. I knew what it really was.

Minerva was so hell-bent on impressing that dude that she put on the ultimate front of acting like a concerned, good mother. I wouldn't have been surprised if she showed up dressed in an ankle-length flower dress with a bun on top of her head like one of them suburban housewives.

I could always tell when she called me and Eric Brockington was around, because her whole tone changed. She was pleasant, she never cursed, and the most obvious thing was that she never cracked gum in my ear.

She was a self-centered smut who was so materialistic that she could quicker tell you when the new Louis Vuitton pocketbook was coming out before she could any of Brie's doctor appointments. And now she was fronting like she was Clair Huxtable or the Brady mom.

Minerva only saw Brie every other weekend for two days and there have been times when I heard that she got her little sister to babysit so she could run the streets. That kind of shit burned me up, but after two years nothing she said or did surprised me.

She was a good piece of ass and fun to roll out with when we were together, but the older I got the more I saw how superficial and empty she was. I was hell-bent on making sure that Brie knew that there were more important things in life than copping a pair of Seven jeans and some Gucci boots.

Minerva is slick all the way down to the tips of her fingernails. She set the meeting up at the Chuck E. Cheese's out on Roosevelt Boulevard in the Northeast. It was clear across town from where either one of us lived but I figured she was trying to make it convenient for him. The Tacony-Palmyra bridge was up there and ran right across to south Jersey where a lot of the pro-ballers who played in Philly lived.

After a while, I knew exactly why they picked a public place with lots of kids. They figured that I wouldn't tear shit up in the midst of a bunch of toddlers. They tried to play it safe, but where they were trying to take it, there wasn't a place on the face of the earth where they should feel safe.

It was Minerva's weekend to have Brie so my baby was already with her and Eric Brockington that day. I got to the restaurant about fifteen minutes early because I wanted to get an order of buffalo wings and a salad.

It was different on that end of the city. The Chuck E. Cheese's in South Philly was overrun with mostly black kids on any given day. The Northeast location was dominated by white and Puerto Rican kids from the likes of Kensington and Fishtown. They were off the hook and wild just the same though.

I sat at the last booth and waited for the waiter to bring me my grub. I called Kheli on my cell to kill the time until they arrived.

"What the deal?"

"Hey wassup, have you met with them yet?"

"Naw. I'm sitting up here waiting for them to come now. I got a feeling she's going to say something to piss me off."

"Don't she always?"

"Yeah but like I told you she gets real new when Mr. NFL is around."

"The DL brotha?"

"Yeah, sweetcakes the wide receiver."

"That's what that bitch gets though. She went right ahead and played herself trying to be Ms. It and she don't even know it."

"Word."

"I told you what she gon' say. She is going to ask if she can get partial custody. She think 'cause she fuck with somebody on the Eagles that a judge just gon' be like here you go take your daughter for half the week when you ain't been shit since she was born. I see it in court every day. Mark my word."

"We'll see. I'm going to call you as soon as I leave out of here. The waiter is bringing me my food."

"Aight, don't forget to call me as soon as you leave."

"OK."

Looking back, Kheli was kind of right. She knew what Minerva was going to go after but she could have never known what else she had up her sleeve. I went through them twelve wings like it was a couple of Tic Tacs on that plate. Who knew that my appetite would be wiped out altogether so soon afterward? Just as I was wiping the sauce off my hands, I looked up to see them walking toward the table.

Minerva wasn't as Clair Huxtable as I thought she was going to be. She was rockin' skintight, so tight that I could see the lips of her coochie if I looked hard enough, jeans with a pink-and-green-striped sweater that showed both of her shoulders. She was sporting a white fur jacket, a huge pink pocketbook, and a pair of pink roach-killer boots with the pointy toe. Brie was draped over her shoulder and it looked like she was sleep.

I don't know how I would've handled it if he was the one holding her when they strolled in there.

In the end, it didn't matter though. They gave me much more to worry about.

Eric Brockington had on a Sixers throwback sweat suit with a white do-rag and a fitted Sixers hat pulled real low over his eyes. His wrist was covered with ice, a platinum watch and a bracelet on his left arm.

A few of the adults recognized him right away but nobody approached. He wouldn't have noticed anyway. His eyes were locked on mine like a heat-seeking missile on its target.

I only wish I would've took Kheli's advice and brought a camera to take a picture of his face. It was like slow motion in a music video or some shit. He looked like he wanted to die right there between the horse carousel ride and the hungry hippo game. Eric Brockington's grill was twisted with the saltiest expression I had ever seen.

Minerva sat down in the booth first and slid over across from me. Her platinum diamond ring could have stopped a truck it was blingin' so hard. Brie woke up almost right away. Instead of sitting next to her, Eric Brockington walked toward me and extended his hand. I shook his hand but I didn't stand up. I didn't see the need to act that damn phony like I cared. His grip was firm but his palm was soaking wet. We had business to handle and I wanted to get to it.

He sat down and slid over real close to Minerva and put his arm around the back of the booth. I was instantly disgusted because it seemed like he was trying too hard to look like a happy family.

You always hear the expression, "You could cut the tension in the air with a knife." Well it was so damn thick at that booth that it would've taken three chainsaws to get through that shit.

Eric Brockington was trying his damnedest to look cool and collected. He probably thought that at any minute I was going to blurt out that he was as sweet as two honey-dipped Pop-Tarts but that wasn't my mission. It was just fun watching him sweat.

Looking back, they had every reason to look like they were being led to a pit of ravenous alligators. They had every damn reason.

When Brie turned around and saw me she almost leapt out of Minerva's arms. She still had her coat when she walked across the table to me. I gave her a big exaggerated hug and an even bigger kiss.

"Daddy! Daddy!"

"Hey Ka-look-ee! You miss your daddy?"

She wrapped her arms around my neck and kissed my cheek over and over again. Brie was cheesin' and jumping up and down in my lap like I hadn't just given her to Minerva the day before.

I noticed right away that she was sporting a new fur coat and a new outfit but I didn't outwardly acknowledge it. If they were holding their breath for me to say something, they would've both died painful, slow deaths at Chuck E. Cheese's that day.

I had bought most of Brie's gear since she was born so they would have to come a lot better. Minerva cleared her throat and made the lame-ass introductions. I nodded at the boaw and he did the same.

"OK, you know I invited you here because we had to discuss some very, very important matters."

"So you picked Chuck E. Cheese?"

"Well, we wanted to pick a neutral spot where Brie could have some fun."

"Word."

I was paying attention to Minerva but I made it a point to keep my eyes on Eric Brockington. The harder I stared at him the more he went out of his way to turn his attention back to Minerva. That boaw was nervous as hell. He kept fiddling with his hands and looking around the room like somebody was about to jump out on him and stick him up. I figured he was going to be a bitch and let Minerva do all the talking but he surprised me when he spoke up.

"It's like this dawg. Even though I never met you before, I heard a lot of good things about you from Minerva. Like I know you handle your business when it comes to Brie and that you do the best you can to be a decent father—"

"Yeah I know I'm a thorough dad. And—"

"If we're going to move forward as a family unit, nah mean, we have to put everything on the table right now. We gotta just be adults and put it all on the table."

"Now what kind of table would that be, a coffee table or say a pool table because I love playing pool. What about you?"

He almost choked on the toothpick that he was twirling back and forth in his mouth. Minerva sucked her teeth and let out a sigh because she could see that I wasn't taking either one of them too seriously. She didn't get my smart-ass comment but Eric Brockington got it loud and clear.

"Come on with all of that. We're serious now."

"I'm serious too, I just want y'all to get to the point. So what's the deal? Say what's on your mind, Minerva. Or wait a minute, let me say it for you. You and this man right here want to get partial custody of Brie. Is that it?"

They both looked at each other like I'd hit the nail right on its head. For a few moments they just stared at me and Brie, who had started pulling napkins out of the dispenser.

Sugarboy spoke first.

"Well that's part of what we wanted to talk to you about. We do want to get partial custody, nah mean, but it's deeper than that."

"Oh yeah. Tell me exactly how deep it is my good brotha. Tell me how you plan on trying to get partial custody of my daughter when you're playing ball from August to January and you're on the road most of the time. Is this about you wanting a family or is Minerva using the fact that you in the league to try and get Brie more often? Huh? Tell me what's on your mind man. I'm all ears."

Of course Minerva interrupted.

"Please. Let's not go there. We came here today to discuss some very important issues with you and we're not trying to get all ghetto up in here. First of all, I don't need to use nobody's money or fame to get more access to my child. It has nothing to do with me getting engaged to Eric or any of that. I am at the point in my life where I am ready to be a more dedicated, responsible parent."

I was knee deep in Minerva's bullshit and it was starting to stink like rotten raw fish covered in maggots. My stomach was starting to knot up, so I knew it was time for me to be out.

"Listen, I don't have time for this shit. If this is all y'all wanted to talk about, we'll just see each other in court and let a judge decide."

I stood up and stepped out of the booth. Just when I started to put Brie's coat back on Minerva plopped her ugly pink pocketbook on the table and started rooting through it real quick. She pulled out yellow sheet of paper that was folded in half.

"Please, sit back down."

"Why should I?"

"Trust me, please sit down for this."

I sat back down but I continued to get Brie ready to roll out. He started talking again.

"Dawg, this ain't gon' be a smooth ride but it's a ride we have to take."

"Yes. I guess what Eric is trying to say is that we need to see past all the drama and hold it down for Brie no matter what."

I put Brie's hat on and buttoned the top button on her coat.

"Listen, there ain't no other way for me to say this but to say it you know."

Eric grabbed her hand with his right hand and used the other to rub her back. I could tell that she was getting choked up. For a split second I thought she was about to tell me that she was dying of cancer or something.

I knew it was serious and for a half of that split second, I even felt sorry for her, because her face started to break up and I could see that cold, hard ghetto fabulous Minerva was trying her best not to break down and cry.

She didn't tell me that she was dying but the words that crept across her lips were equivalent to her telling me that. One way or another she had instantly called for her own death when she opened up the paper and slid it across the table.

"This is so hard to say but I have to tell you the truth. We had a blood test done and you're not Brie's biological father. Eric is."

21. SUNDAY, NOVEMBER 23, 2003 (3:15 P.M.)

From the look on his face, I thought Nkosi was going to faint when he opened up his apartment door.

My baby looked like somebody stood over top of her and splashed cherry Kool-Aid all over her white fur coat. The snot and caked-up boogies were blocking her nostrils so bad that it looked like she couldn't breathe. It got like that when she cried a lot.

Her two ponytails were pretty much in place but both of her shoes were missing from her feet. They probably came off somewhere between Chuck E. Cheese's and the parking lot.

I walked inside of the apartment and put Brie down on the carpet. Nkosi slammed the door behind us and put on both locks at the same time.

"What did you do man? Where is this blood from? Is Brie OK? What the hell happened? Please tell me you ain't kill nobody! Please tell me you ain't fucking kill nobody!"

My head was spinning and throbbing like a pair of linebackers had jumped up and down on my temples. I walked over to his couch, the white leather couch that he was so anal about getting the slightest bit of dirt on, and just collapsed into the seat.

On any other day Nkosi would have had my head for putting one grain of dirt on that thing.

I had on my oversized beige Woolrich with the fur on the collar and it was ripped in like three places. There was blood on the front of my coat too but it was mostly on the front of my sweats. Nkosi didn't bitch about me sitting on his couch. I think he was in shock at what he was seeing.

I was physically exhausted from winning the battle, and mentally devastated because I felt like I was going to lose the war. There was nothing else for me to do but sit there and cry. My hands were shaking and I couldn't stop bawling. I had never in my life been filled with so much rage.

Nkosi took the messy coat off of Brie and tossed it on the floor by the door.

"Talk to me man, what the hell happened!?"

Brie started fussing and I couldn't even be mad at her. After what she had been through that afternoon, I should've let her cry for an entire day if she wanted to. She ran to where I was sitting on the couch and wrapped her arms around my leg.

Nkosi was bouncing off the walls and I could hardly put together a sentence.

I couldn't talk at first. I just sat on his couch and broke down crying. I was so fucking mad. Snot and blood were running out of my nose down my lip and I ain't even care. I had cuts on both hands but my right one was the worse. It was already starting to swell up and it felt numb too. Being as my skin was so light it made them look even worse than they felt.

"What the hell is going on with you man? You done rumbled more in the past two days than you have in the past ten years. Is it that damn tape? I knew you should've left that shit alone—"

"It don't have shit to do with that . . . Minerva . . . she . . . that bitch . . ."

"What happened with Minerva? Please don't tell me you did nothing to her man. Where the hell did this blood come from?"

Before I could answer him there was a frantic knock at the

door. A few seconds passed before it started up again. Nkosi was so paranoid that he tiptoed to the door. His shoulders relaxed a little bit after he looked through the peephole.

"It's Kheli . . ."

"I called her from the car. Let her in."

Nkosi had hardly taken off the locks before Kheli was forcing her way in.

"What the hell happened? Oh my God Brie! Is she hurt?"

"No she's fine. None of this blood is hers. It got on her though. She's straight."

"She don't look fine. What the hell happened?"

Nkosi came and stood right next to her and folded his arms. They started talking about me like I wasn't sitting right there in front of them.

"That's what the hell I'm trying to figure out. He won't say nothing."

"He called me from his cell phone rambling about the cops and Minerva and wanting to kill somebody. He said he was coming here so I jumped in my car and drove over to West Philly."

I stood up and took off my coat. Kheli dropped to her knees and just hugged Brie who had at least stopped whining at that point. I didn't think I would be able to bring myself to talk about it. Every time I tried to tell them what happened, the words got caught in my throat and wouldn't come out my mouth.

I was starting to see what it was when the people on Court TV said they were temporarily insane. That was a real thing and not just some Hollywood bullshit. I lost control of myself that day and there was no turning back.

Out of the blue I just spit it out.

"That bitch said Brie ain't my daughter."

"What!? What the hell are you talking about?"

"She said I ain't her father."

"Come on man. She just fucking with you. You know how she is. Minerva lives to fuck with you."

"Naw she showed me a blood test and everything. She said that motherfucker she about to marry is her real dad."

Kheli and Nkosi were stunned. They looked at each other then turned their attention back to me.

"Eric Brockington . . . but that can't be. That just can't be. You and Brie are damn near twins."

"Have you ever taken a good fucking look at Eric Brockington? Me and him are damn near twins!"

Nkosi was pounding his fist in his hand at that point.

"Wait, wait, wait, hold the fuck up. Is she trying to say the boaw from the Eagles is Brie's real father? That's impossible!"

"All things are possible when you're dealing with a smut-ass bitch like Minerva. I hate that fucking whore! She's going to burn in hell for this."

"Why in the hell would she say Brie is not your baby?"

"Dude came to Philly in like 2000 right?'

"Yeah. He was traded from the Ravens in 2000, I remember."

"Well she must've met his sweet ass some time around then because she was fucking with both of us at the same time. Of course she got pregnant and ain't say shit since he had just proposed to some other chick."

"So what the hell happened to her if he's engaged to Minerva now?"

"Man, how the fuck should I know!? All I know is that the pussy knew all along it was a chance that Brie was his baby and he never asked for a blood test or tried to see what the deal was until he started messing with Minerva again."

Kheli had picked Brie up at that point. She was rubbing her back and trying to keep her calm.

"Oh I see. They started kickin' it again and he lookin' at it like if the baby is mine, we got ourselves a ready-made family."

"That's what he think but I'll strangle both of them motherfuckers and watch them die slowly before I let them get her. That's my word! I will erase both of them bastards from the face of this earth before I let them get to my daughter!"

It was quiet for a moment. Kheli and Nkosi were struggling to digest what I had told them and I ain't even get down to the nitty-gritty of what happened at Chuck E. Cheese's. I know they wanted to know what went down but I really ain't think I would be able to go through the whole thing again since I had just lived it.

At that point I remember wishing that someone else could tell them what happened so I wouldn't have to talk about the shit no more. As crazy as it seems, my wish partly came true.

Just as I was about to tell them what went down at the Chuck E. Cheese's, Nkosi's phone started ringing. He ignored it and let the answering machine pick up. Xavier was on the other end screaming like a hundred words per minute. He ran across his living room and picked up the phone.

"Yo Xavier . . . slow down man . . . what's the deal . . . what . . . are you serious . . . Jesus Christ . . . aight, bet . . . yeah he's here . . . you coming now . . . aight, bet."

Nkosi hung up the phone and turned to face both of us. Kheli was on pins and needles.

"What he say, what he say?"

Nkosi looked me dead in the eye.

"Xavier said that you and Eric Brockington are going to be on the news at five. Jesus Christ! What happened!?"

22. SUNDAY, NOVEMBER 23, 2003 (1:20 P.M.)

It was like one of those 70s revenge flicks where the loud, crazy-ass music plays and the screen gets red. You see the face of the person hell-bent on getting even and then all hell breaks loose.

That was me up in Chuck E. Cheese's.

I couldn't see or hear straight because of the noise in my head. Even if no one else heard it, I could. I was seeing red, bloodred, and there was nothing anyone could've done to shut down the rage.

The alarm was ringing in my head for a few seconds and then just as suddenly there was silence. I ain't hear the kids ripping and running back and forth. I ain't even hear the noise from the video games.

Minerva was shaking and crying and Eric Brockington was rubbing her on her back and hugging her like she was in mourning at a funeral. I was about to give her something to be sad about all right.

It seemed like an eternity before I could get my brain to send the signal to my lips to talk but when it happened it jumped off in a major way.

"What did you just fucking say to me?"

"I . . . I been trying to tell you but . . . I was scared you was going to be mad. I don't know."

"What the fuck are you talking about Minerva!? You done met a NFL player and sucked on his dick a few times and now you talking like you bumped your fucking head."

Eric Brockington held out his hand in front of him and motioned for me to sit back down.

"Pussy, don't say shit to me because I know that you put her up to this bullshit!"

"Naw man, it ain't even like that. Please sit back down."

"If you ask me to sit down one more time I'm going to crack your fucking head open. Do you understand that?"

I snatched up the yellow paper from the table and skimmed through it. I don't know why I was looking at it, because I didn't believe it. Jesus of Nazareth could've signed it and I still wouldn't have believed it. My hands were shaking and Brie was fussing because I was ignoring her. My eyes were scanning that paper like I was a robot trying to find anything that verified what Minerva had said.

"What the fuck is this? Y'all are on some bullshit today."

"It's true man. Please sit down so that we can explain."

"Explain what!? How you went to one of your fancy doctor friends and had them forge this bullshit-ass document . . . fuck outta here!"

Minerva wiped her nose with one of the napkins from the dispenser on the table and cleared her throat.

"It's true. You can go take Brie to get a blood test yourself and they will tell you the same thing. I'm so sorry I didn't know until Eric came back into my life. I'm so sorry."

"Hold up, hold up. Why the hell you think you're her father?"

He sat up in the booth and looked around. I was getting loud and people were starting to stare. The boaw was extremely uncomfortable but I ain't give a fuck.

"Listen man. The possibility of Brie being mine has been pressing on my mind for some time now. I should've followed my gut instinct from the beginning and just did the blood test a long time ago."

"Whoa, what do you mean? Let's go back. I thought y'all motherfuckers just met."

"No. We met a few years ago at 8th Street Lounge where Club Beyond is at now. One thing led to another and we hooked up . . ."

"So basically you fucked him while we were still together. Just say it for what it is Minerva. You got smutted out by this nigga and then he played you and ain't call you no more. Is that it?"

"It wasn't even like that. Eric was engaged to be married at the time but it didn't work out."

"So what you're saying bitch is that your his backup plan."

I can't figure out why they decided to tell me some major shit like that at Chuck E. Cheese's. The only thing they could've done that would have been worse was to take me to Sesame Place and tell me I was dying of cancer.

So many people were looking us. I knew it was getting bad because the person inside of the Chuck E. Cheese costume stopped playing with the kids and started walking toward us to see what was going on. One of the managers, this tall skinny white guy, started running in our direction too.

"Excuse me, can you please keep it down. You're cursing and you're loud and I can hear you all the way at the register.

You're going to have to take this outside. There are kids in here."

I must've had the heat of hell coming from my eyes because he looked at me and I swear his knees buckled and he stepped back a little bit. Dude slowed his roll real quick after he saw that I was in the zone.

Eric Brockington started talking again and it turned my attention back to them.

"I didn't think you would take this as good news but I at least thought you'd be happy that we came to you before she got older."

"Before she got older! Are you fucking serious!? Are you fucking serious!?"

I couldn't believe that he said that. If they had told me that shit when Brie was sliding out of Minerva's pussy I still would've been pissed. If they had told me when she was eighteen years old and walking across the stage to get her high school diploma, I still would've wanted to rip their heads off. There was no appropriate time, period.

They thought that telling me while Brie was two years old made it better but I was still ready to snap. She was all I had.

"Listen man, look at it this way. This is a good thing because at least Brie won't have to worry about money no more. She'll be straight for life now that . . ."

I didn't even let the rest of that sentence roll off of his cocksucking tongue. In one quick motion, I snatched the metal napkin dispenser from the table and smashed it right across Eric Brockington's face. I followed it up with the hardest jab I've ever thrown in my life straight to the bridge of his nose.

By the time he reacted I practically dropped Brie back into the seat. Eric Brockington put his hand up to his face and it was instantly candy apple red. Blood was gushing out like someone turned a faucet on inside of his head. He charged at me raging mad, swinging wild haymakers and screaming.

I took two steps back to get my balance and threw my hands

up. Minerva was screaming and trying to hold him back but he shoved her back down in the booth and came at me with everything he had. I caught that nigga with a two-piece and grabbed the collar of his Sixers jacket.

Eric Brockington made the mistake of dropping his head and throwing blows to my body. He caught me real good a couple of times, but my adrenaline was rushing so hard that it was like throwing pumpkin seeds at a fucking rhino.

I literally wanted to murder him right there in front of all of those screaming kids and their parents. If I had a gun, at least six bullets would've been dumped right into the middle of his forehead. But since I didn't, I set out to tear him apart with my bare hands.

After I yanked him to the ground by his collar he was down on one knee but he was still swinging. I was just drilling that nigga in his face when the manager and the person in the Chuck E. Cheese costume came up from behind me and tried to pull me off of him.

The few seconds that it took for me to turn my attention away from Eric Brockington and push them back, he got up off the floor and charged at me while my back was turned. My thighs slammed into the table where Brie and Minerva were sitting and I lost my balance. I doubled over so my face was almost smack-dab on the table.

My baby was crying hysterically at that point and Minerva was reaching across the table to try and scoop her from the other side of the booth. Eric Brockington was behind me, with one hand gripped on the back of my neck waling away at the back of my head with the other. He was strong as hell for a skinny dude but that shit ain't faze me. All I could think was, "No way is this nigga going to get the best of me after what they just told me."

In the process of Minerva picking Brie up, she dropped her keys in the middle of the table. It was all I needed to make that motherfucker really feel the pain because along with her keys on the ring was a container of pepper spray. I flipped the nozzle with my finger and when I gathered enough momentum to turn around I pushed my finger down on that bitch and let it go right in his eyes and his mouth.

Eric Brockington grabbed his face with his hands and turned away screaming. He was hollering like a bitch and bumping into all of the games since he couldn't see where he was going.

That was when shit really got off the hook because people started scooping up their kids and running toward the door. It was major chaos in that jawn after I sprayed the pepper spray because nobody, including myself, wanted it to get anywhere near their kids. I turned my attention back to Brie and Minerva.

"Get her out of here now!"

"Gimme my keys!"

"Fuck these keys, get her out of here before this shit gets in her eyes!"

Minerva stood up with Brie and hauled ass toward the cash register and the exit.

Kids were crying and screaming but I ain't give a fuck. It was just me and the wide receiver and if I had it my way he would never catch another touchdown pass again.

I ran up behind his monkey ass and grabbed him by the neck. When I got a good grip on his neck I smashed his head into the hard plastic bubble that covered the hungry hippo game. He hit the floor like a bag of rocks but he started scrambling away from me on his knees up the aisle and toward the cash register.

I stood over top of him and kicked the shit out of him in his back and watched him collapse onto his stomach. His head was turned so that the right side of his face was up. Without thinking twice, I lifted my foot and stomped the right side of his face. I ain't ever in my life been so happy I wore a pair of Timbs.

That's when I paused and started looking around for something to choke him with. A jump rope, a jacket, whatever, as long as it was something long enough for me to get around his neck and squeeze.

But God had a different plan. It was definitely a good thing because that slight pause was all I needed to snap back into reality. For all of his victory on the gridiron, Eric Brockington took an L that day.

"Please, please, please! I can't see . . . my eyes . . . my eyes . . . they're burning . . . I can't fucking see!"

I don't know why, but I just stopped. I was off in a zone that I ain't think nothing could bring me back but I just stopped. A lot was going through my mind but thank God I still had enough sense to just chill at that moment.

He rolled over onto his back but both of his hands were still up to his face. He was rubbing his eyes like crazy and coughing extremely hard. I thought one of his lungs was going to fly out of his mouth he was hacking so much.

There was a big pitcher of water sitting on a table that he had crawled next to. Somewhere deep inside of me there has to be mercy, because I grabbed the pitcher before I could even think about it and I just poured it all over his face. There was another one on the next table so I did the same thing again.

Eric Brockington's blood was running off his cheeks, down his neck, and onto the floor. I think the water helped but he still was fucked up. I got down on one knee and pulled him off of his back and out my mouth right up to his ear. He was gagging and hawk-spitting everywhere.

"Listen to me pussy, maybe you can't see but you can hear! Listen! I know they called the cops already, so if you press charges on me I will tell Minerva the truth about you and I will tell it to every got-damn newspaper and TV station in Philly! You understand me?"

"Yeah dude, yeah, I won't press charges. Please get me some more water! Please!"

I stood up and left him sitting right there in the middle of the floor. As I was walking toward the exit to find Minerva and Brie, two workers and the skinny manager came running toward me.

"Yo, he needs some more water. Get him some water!"

They looked at me like I was crazy because they couldn't believe I was insisting they help him after what I had just done. One of the boaws turned right around and went flying toward the kitchen. The other two ran around me and went to attend to him.

"Oh shit, this is Eric Brockington! Oh shit! Yo dude, don't go nowhere, the cops are on their way."

But I just kept walking and never turned around.

"He'll be all right. I have to get to my baby."

It was chaos outside the entrance too. The parents, mostly women, were hugging their kids close to them like I was a child molester on a kid-snatching rampage. I felt bad because some of the kids were crying. They were petrified of me. If they only knew what really went down. One of the little boys screamed at me as I walked by him and his mom looking for Brie.

"He beat up one of the Eagles! He's bad!"

They were nowhere to be seen outside of the entrance, so I just started running. As soon as I got to the top of the curvy ramp that led to the parking lot I saw them. Minerva was hustling fast as hell across the parking lot holding Brie in her arms.

I started sprinting toward them without even thinking. This chick in a green Subaru slammed on her brakes and swerved to avoid hitting me. She was calling me all kinds of names out of her window but I ain't care. My eyes were locked on the back of Minerva's head like a heat-seeking missile.

She had just got to that nigga's black Hummer when I ran up behind them. Minerva put Brie down and started digging in her pocketbook. My baby was crying at the top of her lungs. I scared the hell out of Minerva because she jumped and let out a bitch-ass squeal when I ran up on her.

"Where you going with my fucking daughter?"

"You need to calm down first. You are acting crazy as shit. Where is Eric?"

"He's in the fucking Chuck E. Cheese on his ass where he should be."

Minerva pulled Brie closer to her.

"You know them people called the cops don't you?"

"Yeah I know, I ain't worried about that shit."

"You ain't worried?"

"Naw, like I said, I'm cool. That nigga ain't sweatin' it either."

"Is he OK?"

"Go in there and check on him and see."

"Oh my God, I can't believe this shit!"

"Why can't you? It's all your fault. You the one sparked all this Minerva. You to blame for all this shit!"

"Listen, even though she ain't your real daughter we still planned on letting her go with you today. We wasn't gon' just take her or nothing like that—"

"Minerva, don't act like you doing me no fucking favors aight! I want my daughter and I want her now. This is my weekend to have her and ain't nothing changed."

"Yeah I know but—"

"There are no buts. Come on Ka-look-ee."

Brie looked traumatized. For a few moments she didn't move from where she was standing in between the Hummer and a blue Chevy Cavalier. Then she just yanked her hand away from Minerva and ran toward me.

"Daddy!"

"That's it mommy. I got you. Let's roll."

I picked Brie up off the ground and I was out. She was still crying but she had calmed down a little.

"I'll call you, don't call me."

I headed back across the parking lot toward the Chuck E. Cheese's where my car was parked. Minerva went flying by us in the Hummer and parked near the curb. A cop car pulled up behind her just as she was hopping out of the whip.

I was almost to my Honda when I realized that I got blood from my hands all over Brie's coat. Both of her shoes were gone too but she had on stockings. My car was in the first parking space near the top of the ramp that led to the entrance of Chuck E. Cheese's.

The white lady whose son screamed at me was all up in the black cop's face as soon as he got out of his patrol car. When she caught my eye, she didn't waste a hot second before she pointed at me.

"There he is right there! That's him with the little girl."

The black cop started walking toward me just as I opened the car door and sat Brie down in the back next to her car seat. Officer Syres was about my height and complexion and he seemed young as hell.

"Hello sir, can I speak to you for a minute?"

"Yeah you can speak to me but I'm kind of in a rush."

"What happened in there? The woman over there says you were in there fighting a football player."

"Yeah we got into a minor altercation."

"Who is the football player?"

As soon as he said that, Eric Brockington walked around the Hummer and he looked like death on a shit stick. He had taken off his jacket and was using it to rub his eyes out along with this huge-ass wad of wet paper towels. His face was tomato red, especially on the side where I kicked him. Minerva was right by his side with her arm around his waist.

Officer Syres was obviously a football fan like me, because he knew who Eric Brockington was right away.

"Oh snap, is this who you were in there fighting?"

"Yeah but he started it and he said he ain't pressing charges."

"Oh really. Don't you move one muscle. I'll see about that."

He jogged over to Eric Brockington but kept looking over his shoulder to make sure I wasn't going to try to make a run for it. By that time his white partner and the skinny manager were standing in front of Eric Brockington too. I couldn't hear what they were saying but I could see that nigga was just shaking his head from side to side.

After about five minutes or so, all of them started walking toward me. Minerva looked extremely irked and confused.

"So . . . Mr. Brockington says that you and him got into an

altercation inside of this establishment and he admits to starting the said altercation. Is this true?"

"Yes, it's true. He started it."

"Are you and your daughter OK? Would you like to press charges?"

I paused for a little bit to make them think I was considering it. Minerva was holding her breath and it looked like she was about to faint.

"Naw I'm straight. I don't want to press no kind of charges."

"Are you sure now?"

"Yeah, I'm positive. He already got what he deserved for messing with me."

Eric Brockington was still coughing but it wasn't as bad as when he was inside. His eyes were barely opened. He still managed to speak up though.

"Listen, I already explained to the manager here Mr. Jacob that I would pay for any damage and I offered to pay for any kid's birthday party in there that was ruined today. I also admit that it was my pepper spray that he used on me after I tried to use it on him."

The manager frowned his face and looked even more confused than Minerva because he knew it ain't happen that way. Officer Syres turned back toward me and looked over my shoulder and through the back window at Brie.

"You and your daughter are free to go then. Mr. Brockington, you need to get to a hospital. Follow me and my partner and we'll escort you there."

I strapped Brie into her car seat and then jumped my ass in the driver's seat before anyone could change their mind. Before all of them could even get in their cars I was pulling out of the parking lot. I ain't even turn the radio on.

After I turned left onto Roosevelt Boulevard and started driving I just lost it. I was fucking devastated and I just lost it. I started crying hysterically and I couldn't think clearly enough to drive in a straight line.

I wasn't on the road for a whole minute before I turned into the parking lot of Red Lobster. The first handicap spot was empty so I just pulled in and put the car into park. That's when I just broke the hell down. I just fucking lost it.

I don't know how long me and Brie was sitting there in the parking lot of Red Lobster, but I do know this. Neither one of us could stop crying.

23. SUNDAY, NOVEMBER 23, 2003 (4:45 P.M.)

I was about to shit a brick by the time Xavier got to Nkosi's apartment.

All of our cell phones were blowing up. The only two calls that I accepted were from my mom and Nia. My mother was hysterical because so many people had been calling her and telling her that I was going to be on the news for having a fight with one of the Eagles. Within the next few days after that I would have to say she called my cell at least twenty times.

I had been waiting to see her in person to tell her about the break-in at my crib. After I rumbled Eric Brockington I decided not to tell my mom about it at all because I knew she would really be stressed the hell out. Nia was ready to jump in her whip and come to see me but I told her to chill. I really didn't want to be around too many people at that moment in time. To be honest, I wasn't exactly feeling like I could trust anyone.

Before I hung up, I told her that I would come and see her the next day.

Everyone else ignored their phones too mostly because all eyes were on me. Nkosi turned the television to channel six but he left it on mute.

"Listen, no matter what that blood test say, Brie is your daughter."

"You think I need you to tell me that Kheli? Is that the kind of lame-ass shit people are going to start saying to me now, huh? I don't need for you or nobody else to tell me that she will still be my daughter because that's all she ever has been. Get the fuck outta here—"

"I know but I was just saying—"

"You ain't saying shit Kheli cause I don't want to hear it. I don't want to hear shit about her not being or being my daughter because of what some fucking doctor say. I been taking care of her since day one."

"You're right—"

"I know I'm right! The only thing Minerva ever did for Brie was give birth to her and she ain't done shit for my daughter since then!"

"Please calm down and lower your voice. I don't want you to upset Brie. It's going to be all right."

"How the hell do you know that Kheli? Huh? Tell me how you know it's going to be all right? If that test is in his favor what the hell is a judge going to say to me? Is a judge going to say oh well he's been raising her all along so he gets to keep her? Or is he going to give her to the rich football player sperm donor who's ready to fucking play daddy now?"

Xavier went to the kitchen and put fruit punch in Brie's sippy cup and got me some iced tea. He handed me the glass and stood right over me.

"Listen bruh, I can't even begin to imagine what you're going through right now but we got your back. Trust me, you'll be OK."

"Man, I don't think I'm ever going to be OK. If this shit is true I ain't ever gon' get over it."

"Word, but just know that I got your back no matter what if these niggas start trippin'. That's all you need to know."

"You talking about his boaws?"

"Naw I mean the niggas in Philly!"

"What you mean?"

"What do I mean? Does the name Steve Bartman ring a bell?"

"No, should it?"

Xavier sat down on the couch right next to me.

"He's the dickhead who reached out and touched the foul ball that probably would've been caught by the boaw Moises Alou when the Cubs were playing the Marlins in a national championship game last month."

"Oh yeah, I remember that."

"Yes, well do you remember that he had to have police protection at his house twenty-four/seven because they thought somebody was going to merk his ass."

"You think I'm going to need the cops following me around because I was rumbling Eric Brockington?"

"Man, these Eagles fans are fucking crazy when they want to be. Donovan McNabb is throwing bombs, they're undefeated, and the city is getting all hype again hoping that the Super Bowl is within reach."

"He deserves to be in the morgue."

"Word, but get this. Do you think that's going to go down smoothly? You have to brace yourself for some backlash from all of this shit is what I'm saying."

"Well the way I feel right now is I don't give a fuck. I dare one fucking person to say something to me about Eric Brockington. One fucking person! I'll rip off their fucking head if they even mention his name and I mean that shit."

The conversation was interrupted when Nkosi grabbed the remote control and pressed the volume button until the little green lines almost ran across his entire thirty-six-inch screen.

We were like statues as the theme music for *Action News* played.

When it first came on, the reporter Rick Williams made it seem like he was going to talk about three other things but then he switched it up.

". . . but the big story on Action News *tonight . . ."*

My heart jumped when I saw myself on the screen. The first thing to pop up was a shot of me standing over top of Eric

Brockington and kicking him in the face. Even though you could hardly see him on the screen, they showed at least two fuzzy, herky-jerky close-up shots of me.

One of those people in the Chuck E. Cheese's had used a camcorder to tape us fighting from a distance but they were zooming in and out really fast. From the awkward angle, it seemed like the person behind the camera was standing somewhere near the entrance.

Whoever gave the tape to *Action News* apparently didn't capture the whole rumble because they kept showing the part where I smashed his face into the hippo game and then kicked him in his face. The footage outside of the Chuck E. Cheese's was of Eric Brockington walking up the ramp toward the parking lot rubbing his face with his jacket. They showed his face up close and it looked nasty as hell. There was also a quick shot of me getting inside of the Honda and pulling out of the parking lot.

Between showing the same exact clips over and over again, they would flash Eric Brockington's Eagles team photo on the television screen and clips of him catching passes in the end zone. They kept referring to me as "an unidentified man."

The tall, skinny Chuck E. Cheese's manager whose name is Stanley Jacobs was interviewed first. He basically just repeated what Eric Brockington had told the cops in front of me even though he knows the shit ain't go down that way.

A little Hispanic girl who looked like she was about eight years old said that she never wanted to come back to Chuck E. Cheese's again because she was scared that there was going to be another fight. They showed her a close-up of her face and it looked like she was about to break down and cry.

Rick Williams described it as an alleged altercation over a woman. They also said that police filed no charges and that reps from the Philadelphia Eagles had no comment on whether he would be fined by the team because of the incident. The last thing they said was that Eric Brockington had been admitted into a local hospital to be treated for minor injuries and released the same day. There was no mention of Brie at all.

And just like that, *Action News* was on to the next story.

Nkosi muted the television and everyone turned their attention back to me.

"You won't be an unidentified man for long."

"What you mean?"

"Now that everybody seen that shit on the news they're going to get bombarded with calls from people who recognize you, and they're going to be telling them who you are and where you live."

"But don't nobody know where I live now."

"True, but give them time and they'll find out. I track people down every day, day in and day out."

There was a lot of nervous energy between us all because it seemed like they were all starting to feel sorry for me and it's the last thing I wanted. Xavier and Kheli promised that they wouldn't tell anyone what really went down at the Chuck E. Cheese's before they went on their way a little before nine o'clock.

My head was thumping. Brie had settled down and gone to sleep but I was still raw and on edge. I was popping way more Tylenol than I should've and soaking my hands in a big bowl of ice water.

Nkosi was right on the money because by the time the eleven o'clock news came on I was no longer the "unidentified man." In six hours they not only found out my name but they had somehow managed to get a picture of me, find my address, and snag an interview with the neighbor who braided my hair.

Jar-u-queesha basically told *Action News* that I was a good person and that I kept to myself. She started laying it on a little thick by the end when she said that I was a big brother to a lot of the little kids in the hood. She was being extra, but I had to give her props for trying to make me look good.

Nkosi was down for the count by one in the morning but I was still wired. I didn't think I would ever go to sleep again because there was too much going through my head. I laid in the bed next to Brie and took the balls and barrettes out of her hair while she was sleep.

It was a habit for me to stare at her while she slept but now I was looking harder and with a different purpose. Her lips, her complexion, and her eyebrows were so much like mine. For every hundred times that I convinced myself that she was my flesh and blood, I would doubt myself once and that would put me back at square one. And that's all it took for my head to start throbbing again. There were so many damn questions and it felt like my brain was going to shut down.

Was she really Eric Brockington's baby? Did it make a difference? Did I stand any chance of keeping Brie if she wasn't mine? Could I get away with slitting Minerva's throat and dumping her in the Schuylkill River?

By the time I took the barrettes out of Brie's hair I was crying again but it was far from being tears of sadness. The tears that came from my eyes were hotter than acid. I was so furious and wrapped up in the matter at hand that I almost forgot about the other drama that was centered around me.

There was still the issue of a platinum-selling rapper sending a thug to my crib. Snatch-Back picked the wrong time to fuck with me. He too was going to be on the receiving end of my fury.

24. MONDAY, NOVEMBER 24, 2004 (6:30 A.M.)

Three hours of sleep didn't take off the edge one fucking bit.

By the time Brie and Nkosi got up that morning I had already paced back and forth through the apartment at least a dozen times. I wasn't hungry or thirsty, I was just up.

Channel 6 was still showing my fight Eric Brockington during the morning news updates. The news cameras caught him and Minerva as they were dipping out of a back entrance of the hospital. They got a quick close-up of his face and even though he had on shades you could see a clear mark of my handiwork. There was a perfect imprint from the bottom of my Timberland boot on the side of his face. It was the only thing that made me smile that morning.

Since I was up so early, I had plenty of time to start chipping away at the block. My first order of business was to figure out how to go about getting a blood test done. Kheli mentioned before she left the night before that she would help with that, but it was too early to call and wake her up. I didn't want to bother her just yet, but I could give a rat's ass about waking Snatch-Back's monkey ass up.

I went into Nkosi's bathroom and shut the door because it was the only room in the house to get decent reception on my cellie. It was about a quarter to seven when I dialed his number. The voice mail message came on twice and both times I hung up and called right back. When Snatch-Back finally picked up the phone he sounded groggy and annoyed but I ain't give a fuck.

"Who the hell is this?"

"It's me pussy."

"What? Who the fuck?"

"It's Sticks, now wake your punk ass up."

"Hold on . . . hold up . . . yo it's six-thirty in the morning. What the hell do you want?"

"I want to know why you sent that nigga to my house?"

"What? What the hell are you talking about?"

"Don't play dumb pussy! You sent that sucker to my house to try and find that tape didn't you?"

"Man you're losing it because I don't know what the fuck you're talking about."

"You sent the boaw to my house while I was in there with my seed. So that's how you're playing now. You think I'm supposed to feel intimidated and threatened now pussy."

"Huh?"

"Well get this, when you put my kid in the middle of this, you're asking to get your shit blown up. Do you understand that if any one of your goons even thinks about coming anywhere near me and my baby again you'll be watching yourself on Access Hollywood*."*

"Look man, I ain't send nobody to your crib. I'm holding up my end ain't I? I gave you a hundred Gs already and I told you I'm going to give you more soon."

"Listen man, I don't care about that. I could've gone to the fucking tabloids and got paid off that tape but I came to you straight up so that you could get it and save your ass. And this is how you do me?"

"Man, I don't know what you're talking about. I don't get down like that."

"Oh yeah, like I'm really going to trust a lying rapist. Well peep this, like I said if anybody else comes at me over this shit it's over for you. I'm going to get paid one way or another."

"Naw it ain't even like that listen . . ."

I hung up the phone and turned the power off. I knew that nigga would be calling right back and when I checked the phone later that afternoon I saw that he did like five times in a row.

I felt like a totally different person from the second I woke up that day. There was a lot of life-changing stuff staring me in the face. On one end I was on the come-up because I was about to be a millionaire. On the other, I was looking at the possibility that the person I loved more than anything in the world might not even be mine to love.

I tried to remember how I felt about things in my life before that afternoon in Chuck E. Cheese's, but it was so hard. It felt in a lot of ways like my life didn't start until that day. That's how much things had changed.

Kheli actually called me from her cell phone while she was on her way to work that morning. As a social worker she always ran into that paternity bullshit so she knew what to do. She told me from the gate that it would cost a couple of dollars if I wanted the results back within a week or two. I would've gave every dime in my bank account to know right then and there what the deal was, so that ain't bother me.

Me and Nkosi rapped for a while before he went off to work. I told him about my conversation with Snatch-Back earlier that morning and he agreed that I had to make him see that I was not to be fucked with.

He offered to take off work and stay with us at the crib but I told him no. If ever there was a day where I wanted to spend one-on-one time with Brie, that was it. Time crept along so slowly. The funny thing about babies is that the sky could be falling all around them and they still don't have a care in the world. One day she would learn about all of the mess that Minerva caused, but in the meantime it was business as usual with Brie. *Teletubbies*, apple sauce, and *Dora the Explorer*.

I was flipping through channels after Brie went down for her nap, and ironically the topic of *Maury Povich* that afternoon was paternity testing. But then again that seemed to be the topic of his show every afternoon. There were about five chicks on there and all of them were extra confident that they knew who their kid's father was.

Maury brought them onstage one at a time, and one by one all of their faces cracked when he told him that a particular dude was not their sperm donor. Donita, Rebecca, Sharquita, and Rondella all stormed off the stage salty as hell. It was the third appearance and fourth guy tested for Rondella on the *Maury* show, and she still had no idea who her daughter's pop was.

Sharday was the only chick up there who got the result she was looking for. Tiago, this greasy, country-ass nigga who rocked a Paco jean set and had mouth full of gold teeth, was in fact her baby's daddy. She was clapping and dancing across the stage after Maury read the results, but I wasn't sure if she should've been so happy.

I wondered how in the hell these people could go on national television to get that kind of news. I was embarrassed enough at the triangle I was in, so there was no way I could see putting Brie out there like that. The only upside I guess was that they ain't have to pay for the test.

Kheli called back at about one and said that she had set up an appointment with one of her contacts who did blood work at Jefferson Hospital. She told me to go to this one site on the Internet and order the kit, which was about four hundred dollars. For another four hundred they would get back the results within one week.

After I paid the eight hundred dollars with my debit card a customer service person e-mailed me and said that the kit would be sent in two days to Nkosi's crib. Once our blood samples were taken by Kheli's contact, they would send it back to the company and then they would mail me the results.

That was the hand I was dealt I guess and I had to work with it. Until then I had to find a way to keep that shit from destroying me. I had a bank account full of bread and I couldn't really enjoy myself the way I wanted to. There was just too much going on.

In the one motherfucking moment when my mind wandered away from Minerva and all of her bullshit, the inevitable happened. When I looked at the cell phone screen and saw the picture of Satan I knew it was about to be on. I started not to answer at first but I changed my mind real quick. I had to see what she had to say.

"What the fuck do you want bitch?"

"Listen, let's not get off on a bad foot today."

"Bad foot? My bad foot about to be up your ass!"

"Can you just listen to me for one second. I know you're pissed the hell off and you have every right to be but we need to deal with this!"

"No, Minerva you need to deal with this because if this test comes back and says that pussy is Brie's dad then you are going to have to go in hiding."

"Look, threatening me is not going to help. Don't you want to talk about what we're going to do next?"

"I know what I want to do next, but it'll get me twenty to life."

"You have every right to be bitter and I'm the first to admit that. I messed up I really did—"

"Yeah I know—"

"Let me finish. I really fucked up on this but we have to keep Brie in mind. Even though Eric is her real dad, you will always play a major part in her life. I mean you have her all the time, she don't know no other dad but you."

"And that would be because I'm her only father. And once I get my own blood test results back, both you will see that too."

"I know you have to do what you have to do for your own peace of mind and all but I promise you to God that those results that we showed you are legit."

"And those words spoken from a child of God. We'll see about that."

"OK, so when will I be able to see Brie again?"

"I don't know."

"Come on, I am her mother. No matter who the father is I have the right to see my baby."

"You also had the right to tell the truth and nothing but the truth and you didn't so what's your point?"

"Listen, I can't change the past, nah mean, but that is my daughter and I really want to see her. Especially after what happened yesterday."

"I gotta think about it."

"That's fine, just let me know aight. Can you call me tomorrow?"

"I said I'll think about it."

"OK, OK, fine. Hit me up."

I just hung up without saying another word, mad at myself for not coming at her harder. The phone started ringing right away and I thought it was Minerva calling back again but it was Kheli in the wifebeater on the screen.

I let the call go to voice mail because I was too pissed to talk. Especially to Kheli, since she was the reason that me and Minerva hooked up in the first place.

It wasn't love at first sight or no bullshit like that because them two had instant beef. It was one of them heat wave days where the weatherman kept reminding people to check on the old folks because they might be dead.

Our boaw Hasan, who grew up with me and Kheli down 13th Street, had invited us to come and kick it with him and his wife Tami at a block party on Tasker Street. That nigga ain't have one air conditioner in the whole damn two-story house. It was just big metal fans blowing hot air on top of hot air.

Because it was hotter inside the house than on the street we sat on the porch and killed off his bushel of crabs and barbecue chicken. We were sitting there playing cards when Kheli noticed Minerva across the street standing on somebody's steps. She pointed at her and said that she seemed like she was my type. I made some kind of comment about her only saying that because she had a donkey butt and a pretty face and Kheli busted out laughing.

It was a good observation on Kheli's behalf because I knew I was going to holla before the day was out. I was just waiting for the right moment because I ain't want to seem all Joe in front of them niggas out there.

In the meantime, a couple of these chickenheads who ain't have shit better to do told Minerva that they saw Kheli pointing and laughing at her. It ain't take Minerva but a minute to get enough heart to strut her fine ass across the street to where we were. The two chicks she was with were right on her heels.

I guess they figured since Kheli wasn't from that part of South Philly that she was going to be played sweet but it ain't go down like that at all. Minerva got real loud from jump and started drawing attention.

"Do you know me from somewhere?"

"Excuse me?"

"I said, do you know me from somewhere."

"No what are you talking about?"

"Then why are you sitting over here pointing and laughing at me. Do I fucking amuse you?"

"Oh hold up I don't even know you bitch and you coming at my neck."

"Bitch!? Bitch!? Who the fuck is you calling a bitch?"

Minerva tossed her Prada bag to one of them cluckers and just as quick as she did that Kheli threw her crab claw down and started making her way around the card table. My future baby momma was at the bottom of the steps with her fist balled up and her ice-grill on.

"Bring your ass off that porch ho and I'm going show you what a bitch is!"

Me and Hasan jumped up and grabbed Kheli from behind by her arms. She was tussling and pulling away trying to get away from us but we wasn't having it. Hasan's wife Tami was heated at that point so she made her way in front of us to the top of the steps.

"Listen, you need to take all that ghetto shit from in front of my door. Wasn't nobody over here laughing at you. We're out here trying to enjoy ourselves like adults and here y'all come with this madness. Please people, go ahead with all of that."

Fight plus two chicks from different sides of the tracks equal crowd when you're down South Philly, so it got thick out there real quick. It was like a sauna outside too, so everybody was already irritable as hell and restless.

The funny thing is neither one of them were from that block so people were really watching just because it was something to do. Kheli and Minerva were out there trying to rumble and they ain't even know each other's names.

This one dude came out of the crowd and started to pull Minerva back too and just as quickly as they sparked that shit it was over. Of course they called each other a few more names as

Minerva was being led back across the street but other than that it was squashed pretty quickly.

After a while we went back to playing cards like nothing ever happened. After a couple of hours, right before it was about to get dark, Kheli went in the house to use the bathroom.

I used that time to make my move. I wonder if I would've stayed my ass right there on the porch how my life would've turned out. I strolled across the street on some ol' pimp shit to holla at Minerva for the first time.

She told me that she was at the block party with her friend Tracy whose brother lived on the block. At first she ain't seem too interested because of the whole Kheli connection. I guess it was guilt by association. But after I laid the charm on her and convinced her that Kheli really was giving her a compliment she softened up a little bit.

I would say a week passed before she actually used my number and a week after that we were out on our first date. We went to get seafood at O'hara's on 39th and Chestnut and that was the beginning of me and Minerva. Kheli wasn't too thrilled that we were talking but she got over it.

That was how we set it off. It was hot and heavy and off the chain in the beginning and now years later Minerva had me wanting to strangle her with my bare hands.

Being as though Thursday was Thanksgiving I would have to wait until Friday morning to get the blood test done. I didn't know how I would make it that long not knowing, but as fate would have it, enough happened in the meantime to keep me occupied.

25. TUESDAY, NOVEMBER 25, 2003 (6:15 P.M.)

I went from being just another boaw from South Philly to the hottest news story overnight.

Just like that, my face was in newspapers and on all the news stations. The photo that all of them kept using was my lame high school yearbook picture. I guess since I wasn't a celebrity and didn't have a mug shot on file, that was the most recent photo they could get their hands on. I was so desperate to see them stop using that wack-ass picture that I wanted to anonymously send in one of me that wasn't ten years old. I had a stupid expression on my face and a high round fade that made me look like a backup dancer for MC Lyte.

My cellie was blowing up so much that I just turned it off after a while. It was nonstop madness.

One sports reporter from the *Daily News,* Chaz Willoughby, found out that I was staying with Nkosi and started calling him out of the clear blue. They were cool, but they weren't all that tight, so Nkosi knew what the deal was. Chaz figured that he could get a scoop but the shit wasn't going down. I wasn't feeling the dude at all because he wrote an article that day that claimed I packed up and moved out of my house in South Philly because I was scared for me and my daughter.

The boaw had no idea that I moved out of the crib two days before the fight at Chuck E. Cheese's. I was pissed that he was screwing up all the details but at the end of the day I was grateful that the whole truth wasn't making it out there. I ain't need nobody knowing that there was a possibility that Brie wasn't my biological daughter.

Chaz wasn't the only one fucking up. A chick from the *Inquirer* wrote that me and Eric Brockington were brawling because I said the Eagles sucked and then spit on him. That hurt, but what stung the most was when she reported that the incident happened while he was out at Chuck E. Cheese's with his girlfriend and daughter.

Nkosi told me to ignore it but that one was a tough pill to swallow.

The whole situation was causing major drama for Nkosi with his editors too. Everybody down at the *Tribune* knew that I was his boaw and that put him in a sticky situation. He was jammed up because he refused to write anything on the incident since our friendship made it a conflict of interest. On top of that, Nkosi wouldn't give any of his coworkers access to me either. No matter how hard they tried to squeeze him, he held his ground.

Even though he was in the business, Nkosi talked all the time about how the media exploited cats who ain't know no better. He worked for a newspaper and all, but he knew that sometimes they were just dead wrong. Nkosi wasn't about to let me get played especially since all of my beef with Eric Brockington revolved around his goddaughter.

It was rough because I couldn't get one landlord to give me the time of day. Mostly everyone I called in reference to getting a crib for me and Brie started talking slow when I gave them my name. I guess those are the breaks when your last name has fifteen letters and it's impossible to forget. They knew right away that I was the one who had beef with one of the Eagles.

Life for me and Brie was supposed to be sweet, but everything had started going downhill ever since Snatch Back broke me off a hundred Gs.

I wanted to hold a damn press conference so the truth could be told, but Nkosi told me to just lay low and let it blow over. He said it would've been much worse had dude decided to press charges.

There were criminal charges so the media really had nothing to go on but rumors and gossip. I heard what Nkosi was saying but it was tough for me. That shit ain't cool, having a whole bunch of motherfuckers talking about you and there's nothing you can do about it.

My mom was being harassed by her coworkers day in and day out because they all wanted to know why I beat Eric Brockington's ass at Chuck E. Cheese's. She said one dude even went so far to accuse me of being a Dallas Cowboys fan who was hatin' on the Eagles wide receiver just because.

My mother let me listen to her voice mail messages so that I could hear all of the prank calls that she was getting, and it made me even more upset. I had so many thoughts of just being out. I had a nice chunk of change in my account and I knew that I could make it for a while. Shit, if I could get by on next to nothing for as long as I did I knew that me and Brie would be all right.

I was so close to packing up our shit and just rolling but then I started thinking about Minerva and Eric Brockington. They would have a field day in the media bashing me and making me seem like I was a monster for keeping the baby away from her mother.

Those days tested me, so having a trio like Xavier, Kheli, and Nkosi around made a lot of shit easier. That's why what went down with Nkosi later that day made me question his loyalty. He was always down for a brotha, and then suddenly out of nowhere I felt like I couldn't trust him beyond an absolute shadow of a doubt.

Me and Brie hadn't even been there for a week when it happened. I was surfing the Internet for apartment listings and searching for more articles on the Eric Brockington incident. It was the Tuesday before turkey day and I was in a fucked-up mood.

I had never really made the newspaper except for one time when a reporter stopped me on the street when I was in high school and asked me what I thought about the war in Iraq. My quote was a quick sentence and the lady spelled my name wrong so it was no big deal. There it was, ten years later and we had a new George Bush in office and a new war in Iraq, and I was getting ink again.

This time I was more than a quick, silly quote. All types of shit popped up when I put my name in the Internet search engines. I had just started reading a little blurb on the *ESPN* magazine site when an instant message popped up from one of Nkosi's boaws named Khary. He had his computer set up so that it automatically signed him on every time he logged on the computer.

> *"Wassup Nigga . . . you still coming to run ball with us at Marian Anderson tonight?"*

I typed him back a quick message letting him know that it wasn't Nkosi on the computer. He said peace and that was that. The next IM message to pop up was from a chick named Nikki who sounded like she was trying to come and kick it with him.

> *"Hey sexy Nkosi, what are you gettin' into tonight?"*
> *"Yo wassup Nikki. This ain't Nkosi . . ."*
> *"What? Who is this?"*
> *"It's his best friend."*
> *"Oh, I'm so sorry, tell him to call Nikki when he gets in."*
> *"Aight, bet."*

I was almost tempted to keep a conversation going with her to see what she was all about but I didn't. About ten minutes later my boredom got the best of me and I decided that I would have a chat with the next chick who dropped a line to him. Brie was sleep and I had nothing better to do.

The next message to pop up on the screen came from a user who went by Lilly. It not only caught my attention but it made me sit up straight in the computer chair and stare at the screen. It took me a few seconds to get it together.

"Wassup Nkosi? Have U had any luck finding that tape? You have to get your hands on it or else it's your ass . . ."

I had to read that message at least a dozen times in a very short amount of time before I reacted. After denial started to fade away, I realized there was a possibility that my ace had told somebody else about the tape. I replied, and on a humbug I acted like I was Nkosi.

"Yo, what are you talking about?"

"Stop acting retarded Nkosi, U know what I'm talking about. The tape with all the action on it . . . have U found it yet?"

"Oh yeah that tape. I haven't been able to find it."

"What! This has gone on too long. I'm starting to think that U weren't joking about putting it on the Internet to make some cash."

"Maybe I will put it on there."

"What! Are you fucking kidding me? You would really do that?

"Yeah, why not?"

"Why not? I think you have really bumped your head."

"Yeah and . . ."

"Yeah and . . . that's easy for you to say when you're not the one on there getting your brains fucked out. You promised that you would try your best to find it and now you're talking crazy . . ."

"Listen, I'll get it when I get it."

"Look, that wasn't part of our deal. You need to make some shit happen fast because I'm really losing my cool here."

"Be easy aight."

"Be easy? That don't even sound like you . . . wait a minute is this really Nkosi?"

"Yeah it's me, why you trippin . . . ?"

"Then what's my name nigga. . . . Tell me who you're talking to."

"Come on why you acting crazy?"

"Tell me who you're talking to! This ain't Nkosi. I know this ain't you."

"Girl, you're tripping."

"No U R trippin. Who is this?"

I just stopped typing after that. The chick had already realized that it wasn't Nkosi, and I'd already had the wind knocked out of me like darts through cheap balloons. I was sitting there thinking, could this really be the chick who Snatch-Back and his crew were nailing on the pool table? She wrote the next three messages in a row because I didn't respond at all.

"Are you bullshitting me Nkosi? Is this you? You play too much. I need to know wassup right now!"

"Are you there? Fucking answer me!"

"OK, I can see you're playing games motherfucker. Just know this, if I see anything from that tape on the Net, I am calling the cops. Your sneaky ass ain't keeping all the money to yourself. Trust me this ain't over . . ."

I think Nkosi came home maybe like an hour after I turned off the computer but it seemed much longer. I called his cell like five times and he ain't answer so I was getting more vexed sitting there waiting.

After I made the calls I realized that he left his cell home by mistake because it was vibrating across the kitchen table. I looked on the screen of his cell to see who else had been calling and three calls from someone named Stephanie came in about the time I logged off the computer.

Brie woke up so that took my mind off of the IM conversation for a little while. When you have a hyper two-year-old in your face, there's not much you can do but give her all of your attention.

I read her the *Lion King* book for the hundredth time and then heated up a can of Beefaroni. Chef Boyardee always set it off and that night was no different. By the time she was finished eating, Chef Boyardee's recipe was all over the place. It was even caked inside the barrettes in her hair.

When Nkosi got home that night, I had already put Brie in the tub. I kept her in longer than normal because I wanted her to be worn out so she'd sleep like a rock. She splashed around and played with her rubber ducky for about twenty minutes before I took her out and threw her pajamas on. I gave her some apple juice in a sippy cup and she was down for the count in about ten minutes.

Nkosi was sitting on the couch flipping through the channels on cable when I came in the living room. My blood was boiling and I ain't even know where to begin, so I just blurted out the first thing that came to my mind.

"Yo dawg, we gotta talk, right now."

When he looked up from the television screen I could tell that he knew I wasn't playing. I sat on the couch and I looked him dead in the eye.

"Yo, did you tell anybody about the tape?"

"What tape?"

"Nigga, what tape? What tape do you think I'm talking about? The Snatch-Back tape."

"Hell no. Why would you ask me that?"

"Man, I have a very good reason to ask you. I just want you to be absolutely honest with me."

"Nigga what are you talking about, honest? You think I'm lying? Why would I tell somebody about that tape?"

"I don't know, you tell me? So you're telling me that you ain't keeping nothing from me."

"Come on bruh, you know me better than anyone else. Why you acting like a bitch all of a sudden?"

"Oh I'm acting like a bitch now? OK, well tell me this. I was on the computer today looking for an apartment and guess what popped up? A message from a special friend of yours."

"Special friend, nigga what are you talking about?"

"Does the name Lilly ring a bell?"

Nkosi's face dropped instantly and he looked salty as hell. He dropped the remote on the coffee table and started stammering and stuttering right away.

"Wait, wait, wait a minute. Who?"

"Nigga you heard what I said. Lilly. Now you tell me who."

Nkosi stood up and started pacing back and forth in front of the couch. I knew him like the back of my hand. I could tell by his body language and by the way he was talking that he was, one, lying and, two, hiding something from me.

"Listen man, I don't want you to think I was being slimy or nothing but I hooked up with her about two months ago and we been messing around ever since."

"You fucked her?"

"Yeah man, I hit it but it ain't even all like that. I saw her at the Pathmark on Grays Ferry one night and I got her number. We talked a few times after that and then she came over and I poked. I been fucking her ever since but I ain't even think it was a big deal all like that."

"So wassup with the tape? She asked on the IM if you had found the tape yet and she said you said you were going to put it on the Internet for cash."

"She said what!?"

"Yeah nigga, she asked if you found the sex tape yet and what were your plans. Now I don't know what that sounds like to you but to me it sounds you been running your fucking mouth."

"Whoa, hold up. You gotta be kidding me. I ain't tell her shit about no fucking Snatch-Back tape."

"Then how she know about it then?"

Nkosi stopped pacing and started pounding his fist in his hand.

"Oh shit! She was talking about the tape that we made here at my crib. She let me tape it one time when I was fucking her and she been buggin' me ever since to give her the copy of the tape. I was messing with her one day and told her I was going to put it on the Internet."

"What!?"

"Yeah nigga. She was talking about the tape I made of us nailing. I lied and told her that I lost it and that I can't find it and she keeps sweatin' me. I ain't really lose it I just don't want her to have it."

"Wait, wait, hold up. Are we talking about the same chick? Is this the chick that Snatch-Back and his squad ran a train on on the tape?"

Nkosi's face screwed up like I asked him he hardest question known to man. He looked mad and confused as shit.

"Dude, what are you talking about?"

"Did you nail the jawn from the tape?"

"I don't even know who the chick is on that tape. You know that. Why would you ask me that?"

"If that's not her then who is it?"

"Huh? You're confusing me now. You don't know who that is you were talking to?"

"No nigga that's what I'm asking."

"Aww man. The one who wrote you on the IM is Stephanie. Remember Stephanie? She's the jawn we met at Beyond at the end of the summer and you cracked on her and got her number. Remember you were kickin' it to her and you said she ain't never call you back."

"What?"

"Yes! Remember the one you kept calling and you said she was playing you. I knew you was feeling her that's why when I hooked up with her and I hit it I ain't even say nothing. I ain't think it was going to get like this. I felt bad that I started messing with her and I know you was trying to holla."

I just stopped talking for a few seconds to get my head together. Nkosi was fucking a chick that I tried to crack on and it was all coming out. I really didn't give a fuck because our friendship was more important to me than a bitch, but all of a sudden

I felt some kind of way. He was my best friend and I ain't keep nothing from him. Then all of a sudden something like that happened and it made me question some things. I tried to let it go but it made me start thinking about whether other shit had gone down in the past that I ain't know about either.

"So wait a minute, you've been messing with this chick Stephanie for only a couple of months and she already letting you tape it? I thought she was talking about the other tape."

"You thought she was talking about the Snatch-Back tape?"

"Yeah nigga."

"Aww shit. Did you say anything to her about it? Did you mention him by name."

"Of course not. I was just trying to see how much she knew."

"So you really thought I would sell you out like that? That's fucked up man."

"Is it? You act like you ain't been nailing a jawn that you knew I was trying to holla at like that."

There was one of them awkward silences because Nkosi knew he was wrong. It was like an unspoken rule when it came to messing around with them chicks to get permission first. It was all gravy with me, I just wanted to know what the deal was so that we wasn't breaking our necks chasing the same wings.

"You believe me right?"

"Yeah I believe you man. If you say she was talking about a tape that y'all made then so be it. I believe you."

"Naw man, I hope you really mean that because it's true. You know what? Watch this."

Me and Nkosi shook hands and left it at that. He ran back into his bedroom and came back into the living room cheesin' like a little kid that just broke into a toy store.

"I'm going to do better than just tell you about it. I'm going to let you see your boy in action."

"You really got her on tape."

"Yeah man. Watch this."

Nkosi popped the tape in the VCR and hit play. They still had their clothes on when the tape came on. It was definitely the chick Stephanie. She was dark skinned with long thick legs and perfect titties. Her hair might've been a weave, I could never really tell, but it looked like it was growing right out of her scalp. She was a dime-piece and Nkosi was smashing it like a champ.

I told him that we ain't have to watch the whole thing. He had proven his point.

Just as Nkosi was pulling his home porno out of the VCR, Xavier started knocking on the apartment door like the cops were chasing him.

When he came in the apartment he was breathing hard and he was smiling like he had the key to Fort Knox. He made a beeline to West Philly straight from his job at Home Depot up in King of Prussia. Besides working that regular nine-to-five gig, Xavier also had a nice little side hustle going. He had managed to book at least two outside jobs a week laying bathroom tile, installing appliances, or whatever other home-repair-type shit that needed to be done. That day, his side gig opened a major door for me.

"I got us in."

"Got us in where? What's the deal?"

"I got a work order to install three ceiling fans tomorrow in a mansion in Gladwyne."

"So what does that have to do with us?"

Nkosi jumped up from the couch.

"Get the hell out of here! Don't tell me—"

"Yes. I have to install three ceiling fans for one Lucretia Johnson of Gladwyne!"

"You gotta be kidding me."

My homey had got the ultimate hookup. Snatch-Back's mom was about to get a visit.

26. WEDNESDAY, NOVEMBER 26, 2003 (12:45 P.M.)

My heart was pounding real damn fast after Nkosi rang the doorbell.

The time had come for us to put my plan into full effect. There was no room to fuck up for a couple of reasons.

One, Nkosi was putting his professional career on the line by being down with the plan. If what we planned got out, the *Tribune* and all the other magazines he wrote for would definitely be done with him.

Two, there was the criminal aspect of it that could land us in hot water. We were fronting like we were private contractors and that was a sure enough way to get the law on our backs. Xavier was trying to get his shit in order so that he could try to see his son more often so he didn't need a record either.

All of that was gnawing at the back of my mind the whole time because I know how hard Nkosi worked to get where he was in life. There were times when he could hardly pay the rent because the newspaper wasn't paying him that much. Eventually, he busted his ass and landed big-time magazine articles that paid him a couple grand or more every time out, but it had taken a lot of work.

Even though I was out for blood, I ain't want to fuck my boaw's life up in the process. We went too far back for that.

There was more than enough on my mind at the time. I was still raw as hell since it was only three days since Minerva and Eric Brockington came at me with their bullshit. I was losing my mind waiting for Friday to roll around so that we could get our blood drawn and shipped off. The trip out to Gladwyne took my mind off of that situation for a minute.

Me, Xavier, and Nkosi set out on the day before Thanksgiving to get up inside of Lucretia Johnson's crib. The whole purpose of our trip was to get Snatch-Back to feel the heat too. I wanted him to know what it was to see a loved one in a vulnerable situation. I wanted that nigga to break into a cold sweat and get the chills just like I did when Darkman broke into my crib and stood over top of my baby.

Nkosi and Xavier were pretty much anonymous faces in all of this, but because of the Eric Brockington fiasco I was in the newspapers and on television. Just to be on the safe side, I added a little disguise to the mix. I wore a pair of bifocal spectacles and I pulled the fitted baseball cap so low that you could barely see my eyes. We all had on khaki Dickie sets and Timbs.

I didn't know how much Lucretia Johnson kept up with current events, but I ain't want to take the slightest chance that she would recognize me.

A small middle-aged Puerto Rican woman answered the door. She had to be in her late fifties, maybe older, but she was fine and very pleasant. We told her that we were there to install the ceiling fans and she stepped aside and let us in.

Just like that, we waltzed right up into the home of the mom of the rapper who was behind the million-dollar sex tape.

The crib was tight. The black marble floors were sparkling clean and it looked like they went on for days. There was no expense spared in hooking the pad up. The furniture was top of the line and everything looked brand-spanking-new. It was tight from the outside, but the inside of that jawn took it to another level.

The aroma of stuffing and turkey slapped us right in the mouth as soon as we rolled up in there. It smelled so damn good, like dinner was about to be served right then and there. My stomach started growling right away because all I had that morning was a Snapple iced tea.

Not long after we came in, Lucretia Johnson made her ghetto fabulous entrance down the grand staircase. She had a Newport in one hand and a can of Pepsi in the other. Her head was covered in different colored hair rollers and she was walking on the back of an old pair of black leather shoes. The red tights that she wore had small holes in both knees but that's not what set it off. Her nightgown, which came right above her knees, had a huge picture of New Edition on the front. It wasn't an adult picture of the group, but an old one with precrack Bobby Brown front and center.

Snatch-Back's mom had to be pushing sixty but she was rocking that jawn proudly.

She was sitting on a mint and living the good life, but she was still straight ghetto. My aunt Cassie always used to say, "You can dress 'em up but you can't take 'em out." I guess meaning that no matter how much a nigga came up in the game, they were always going to show their true colors at the end of the day.

I found it hard to picture her interacting with those other rich women up in Gladwyne. Maybe she cleaned up real nice and acted more hoity-toity when they were around, but I doubted it. I'm sure them women all stayed behind to talk shit about her whenever she left any of those rich folk gatherings. Especially since most of them chicks were born filthy rich and she was just the mom of a black rapper. She was the best of new money and it took everything within me not to bust out laughing.

One thing for sure was that Snatch-Back looked just like his mother. If you put a wig on the nigga he could play her in the TV movie about his life. She came at our necks from the door.

"I just know y'all niggas is going to take them boots off. I just had these floors cleaned. Take 'em off and leave 'em by the door!"

All three of us stepped back toward the entrance and did as we were told. We ain't want to ruffle her feathers. Xavier was carrying this supersized ladder so he made an attempt to lean it on the wall so he could take off his boots.

"Is you crazy, don't put that ladder on my wall! Have one of them hold it while you do that. And another thing, y'all niggas is late. I said I wanted y'all here by noon and it's almost one o'clock."

Xavier passed the ladder off to me and then spoke up.

"We got lost ma'am. It won't happen again."

"I don't want to hear that shit. Y'all need to invest in a map or some shit. I got twenty people coming over tomorrow to eat and I need for this place to look nice."

She looked us all up and down as if we weren't good enough to be in her crib. This woman had the grill of a silverback gorilla and she was giving us the house nigger treatment. Lucretia Johnson acted as if we just came over in a boat and were in the street begging for crumbs.

We all played it cool though. Xavier looked at Nkosi and he looked at me and we just understood that we were going to ignore her and make it happen. If she wanted to ego-trip then so be it. I knew what I was there for and nothing was going to keep me from getting what I needed.

After she got to the bottom of the Hollywood staircase, she flicked some cigarette ashes in the palm of her hand and motioned for us to follow her. The first thing I noticed when I walked across the living room was this huge oil painting of Snatch-Back over top of the fireplace. It was almost life-sized and so detailed that it looked like a photograph.

In the painting he is standing onstage holding a microphone up to his mouth with the other hand raised up over his head in the peace sign. He's rocking a pair of jeans and a wifebeater and there are a few sets of women's arms and hands grabbing at his legs at the bottom of the painting.

I'm sure whoever painted that picture of his monkey ass got a lot of loot for it because it looked like something that should be in a museum. I played totally dumb.

"Wow, you must be Snatch-Back's biggest fan."

Lucretia Johnson whipped her head around and looked at me like I was retarded.

"What you say about Snatch-Back?"

"I said you must be a big fan. That's a really nice portrait."

When I pointed to the picture she looked at it like she was seeing it for the first time. She flicked some more ashes in her hand took another puff of her Newport.

"You can say that. I gave birth to him."

She kind of rolled her eyes and looked me up and down as if she was offended that I didn't know. Nkosi piggybacked on our conversation real quick.

"Wow, are you serious? He's like the best rapper out right now. I have all of his albums."

"Is that so? Well you helped pay for all of these wonderful acres of land I'm living on, now didn't you?"

"Now that you mention it you do look just like him."

"No baby, he looks like me and if you don't mind I really need for y'all to go in the dining room and get them fans so that I can get back to cooking. I ain't even cut up the cheese for my macaroni yet."

Xavier kicked it into full brownnose mode.

"Hey you're Snatch-Back's mom, you shouldn't be cooking. He's one of the largest rappers alive and you're a beautiful black queen. Somebody else should be in here cooking for you."

For the first time she actually cracked a smile. That smile soon turned into a soft giggle. A soft giggle coming from a hard face. What a day.

"Aww, honey ain't you sweet. I know your mother is proud of you. You want something to drink?"

She slowly looked Xavier up and down like she wanted to devour his diesel, 6'4" body right on the spot.

"I would love something to drink."

"Well come on into the kitchen so that I can get you a glass of Pepsi and then I'll show you where the fans need to be put up."

She walked off shoulder to shoulder with Xavier like me and Nkosi weren't even standing there. It was cool with me though because it gave me just enough time to accomplish goal number one.

The whole point of us going to Lucretia Johnson's house was so that we could get some flicks of the inside of her crib. Neither of us bothered to bring along cameras. Thanks to technology, all of us had cameras right at the tips of our fingers on our Nokia cell phones.

I remembered from when we dropped our phones on Lombard Street that me and Snatch-Back had the same exact phone.

It would be simple as pie for me to send them to his cellie when I was ready.

There was no better way to get his attention than to show him that I could get close to his people too. He was on some other shit, sending a thug to break in to my crib while Brie was there. I was hell-bent on showing that fool he wasn't messing with an amateur.

As they were walking out of the room, Nkosi grabbed me by the arm and pointed to the painting without saying a word. I pulled the cellie out of my pocket and got a clean shot of the portrait within a few seconds. For icing on the cake, I also snapped one of the grand piano across the room in the corner.

We hustled quickly into the kitchen. The Puerto Rican maid was in her own world, washing off greens in the sink and humming an unfamiliar tune.

"Do y'all want something to drink too?"

"No ma'am I'm just fine. I would like to use the restroom if I could."

"Walk out this door and go to the end of the hall. The powder room is on the right."

I dropped Xavier's bag of tools on the kitchen floor and headed down the hallway, which had framed black art on the walls from the floor to the ceiling. As soon as I got inside the bathroom I locked the door behind me and went to work. It was a small, simple bathroom but it still had enough shit in there for me to get some flicks that Snatch-Back would recognize as being in his mom's crib.

The sink was one of those big white ceramic bowls that sat on top of a dark brown wooden countertop. This was strictly a powder room as she said because there was nowhere to even put a toothbrush or a can of cleanser. The mirror on the wall was in a big fancy silver frame and was just as big as that side of the wall.

On the opposite wall over top of the toilet was a framed piece of artwork. It was a rear view of a female tennis player scratching her ass on the court. Her skirt was hiked up so that you could see one of her butt cheeks. I snapped a picture of the mirror, the bowl sink, and the artwork, and then flushed the toilet to play it off like I took a piss.

When I rejoined them in the kitchen, Lucretia Johnson was breaking down exactly what she wanted done. She had already purchased the ceiling fans and had the old ones taken down so all we had to do was put up the new ones.

I shouldn't say all "we" had to do because I wasn't the handyman type at all. Xavier thought he was Bob Vila so he was definitely game. Nkosi's dad always took him along on fix-it jobs when we were young so he was familiar with the task of mounting a ceiling fan too. I on the other hand planned on being filthy rich so that I could pay other people to do that type of shit just like Lucretia Johnson was doing.

Xavier was basking in all of his Home Depot glory that day. He was really being extra with it after Snatch-Back's mom started to flirt with him. Somewhere between her calling him a "tall glass of chocolate somethin'" and smacking him on the ass, he ordered me and Nkosi around like we were on his payroll. He was playing it up to the hilt but I couldn't be mad at him.

The ceiling fans were to be put up in her master bedroom, the guest room, and in the game room which was in the back of the house on the ground floor.

"Y'all should be done in no time since it's three of y'all and three fans to be put up. I'll take you upstairs Xavier so that you can see my bedroom. Y'all two figure out who is doing the other two rooms and get it done. The fans are still in the boxes on the floor in the dining room."

Xavier looked over his shoulder and winked at us as we were leaving the kitchen and heading up the steps. I went and got the ladder and followed everyone up the back stairs where the steps were marble too but with a with a strip of plush, bright red carpet going right up the middle. It was something straight out of MTV *Cribs*.

Lucretia Johnson's bedroom was much more tastefully decorated than I thought it would be. It was mostly beige and cream. The king-sized bed was big and dramatic with at least a dozen pillows on there. I couldn't figure out how she fit in the bed with all of them damn pillows, but it was all good.

Once we got up to her room and saw how high the ceiling was we realized that having one ladder meant we would have to mount the fans one at a time. In all of that palace there was not one ladder. Lucretia Johnson wasn't happy at first but then she turned her attention back to Xavier who she was obviously very smitten with.

Lucretia's cordless started ringing just as she was halfway through undressing X-Man with her eyes. She pushed the talk button without taking her eyes off him, or the grin off her face.

"Hello . . . hey now . . . what you say, you're breaking up . . . is that so . . . oh that's wonderful . . . well call me back when the reception is better I can't hear a damn thing you're saying . . . oh, OK . . . that sounds good . . . I'll be here."

She clicked off the phone and tossed it on the bed.

"This is y'all lucky day I guess. That was my son. Him and his wife are stuck in all of that holiday traffic on 76 but he's on his way. They'll be here soon."

Lucretia dropped a bomb on us.

After she told us that her superstar son was on his way to the crib, we all looked at each other and faked like we were pleased with the news. My insides tightened up like a balled-up fist because that wasn't supposed to be part of the game.

Nkosi had put on his reporter hat and called Jeff Stokes to see if his client was doing anything special for the holidays. He confirmed that he would be headed up to a Brooklyn shelter to feed the homeless on turkey day. That's when we decided that we had the green light to go to her crib because Snatch-Back wouldn't be out of Dodge. Just that quick, things had changed.

One way or another he was headed to his mother's suburban mansion. That shit threw a major monkey wrench in our plans and we knew that we had to get out of there pronto.

Xavier set up the ladder underneath the hole in the ceiling like he didn't hear what she just said. He was giving Lucretia Johnson way too much attention. It was almost like he was kicking game to a chick at a club.

Snatch-Back was headed back to home base and it was time to make some moves. Me and Nkosi excused ourselves and left the room. We went to the middle of the grand staircase and started whispering.

"Yo, I gotta get the fuck out of here before he gets here."

"Yes! That nigga can't see me either because I don't know if he'll recognize me from when I interviewed him. It was a while ago but I don't want to risk that he'll put two and two together."

"I'm with you. We gotta get some more pics and raise the hell up outta here. Have you been snapping any?"

"Yeah I got a few in her room while she was talking to Xavier and one or two in the kitchen."

"Yo, we can take Xavier's Jeep and be out. It don't matter if he stay because he's the only one who really knows how to put them damn ceiling fans up anyway."

"Yeah. I'll go in there and let him know on the DL when I get a chance. You go downstairs to the game room and get a few more pics and we'll be straight."

"Aight, bet, we just have to come up with an excuse to get the fuck out of here within the next five to ten minutes."

"Aight, bet, go and handle that."

We shook hands and Nkosi ran back up the steps, skipping them two at a time.

I went to the kitchen and asked the Puerto Rican maid to show me how to get to the game room. She obliged after wasting about three minutes rinsing off more greens and then washing her hands.

When we got to the room she stepped aside and held out her arm for me to go in first. I thought she was going to come in with me but she turned around just as quick and disappeared through the maze of hallways that led to that part of the house.

I literally held my breath when I walked in there because it caught me off guard in a major way. What a revelation. If I had paid closer attention when I went up in there, I would've known sooner which one of my friends was shady as hell and not to be trusted. Like my mom said, it was all about black and white.

Up until that point I had always assumed that Snatch-Back's infamous tape was made somewhere in New York or North Jersey where a lot of rappers and their roadies lived. I never gave any thought to the possibility that him and his crew was putting it down right underneath momma's roof.

Maybe I should've assumed that, being as she was the one who gave the tape to the charity sale in the first place. Whatever the case, it changed the whole game.

I had watched the tape so many times that it felt like I had been in that room already. Lucretia Johnson was definitely a fan of soul music. On the right side of the room was the familiar, huge painting of Marvin Gaye. Directly across the room on the opposite wall was an old painting of Teddy Pendergrass that looked like the same artist did it. It had to be old because in the picture he was standing up singing.

I was standing just a few feet from where the rape took place. It made the hair on the back of my neck stand up. I couldn't stop staring at the pool table. It seemed smaller in person so I was having a hard time imagining four people on top of it, but I had witnessed with my own eyes that it was possible.

In the far left-hand corner of the room was a small bar area. I walked behind it and just stared at the view of the room from that angle. Bingo. It had to be the spot where Snatch-Back set up the camcorder because it was the exact angle that I saw the action on the tape from.

I whipped the phone out and went to work in that room too. I snapped a picture of both of the paintings, the pool table, and the bar area. I walked back to the doorway so that I could get a picture of the room from another angle altogether. A few arcade games, Ms. PacMan, Donkey Kong, and Frogger, lined the wall next to the bar and I wanted to be sure to get a picture of them as well.

The moment after I took the picture I could feel somebody walk up on me and put their hand on my shoulder. I almost jumped out of my skin. I was so preoccupied with getting the flicks that I ain't hear Lucretia come right up on me.

"It's hard to hear in this house on them cell phones."

"Oh . . . yeah I see . . . I can hardly get any reception bars in here."

"Why you so jumpy? Who you trying to call anyway, you supposed to be putting that fan over top of that pool table."

"I was trying to check on my son. The day care called when we were on our way here and said he was throwing up. I'm getting kind of worried."

She stared at me for a few seconds like she knew I was bullshitting and then her face softened.

"So wassup with you getting this ceiling fan up?"

There was a hole in the ceiling with wires hanging out over top of the pool table. This was obviously the spot where the fan was going but I ain't have a clue where to begin.

"Yeah I wanted to ask you about that. People normally don't put ceiling fans over top of their pool tables. Don't you think a simple stained glass droplight would look better."

"Am I paying you to give suggestions? I know what normally goes over a pool table but I don't want that. I want something different. Trust me that ceiling fan costs a lot of money and it's going to look sharp as shit up there. Just put it up!"

"OK, you're the boss. Are they almost done with the ladder upstairs?"

"Boy, you don't need that ladder in this room you can just stand up on top of the pool table and do it."

"Will do. Let me get this bad boy out of the box and get to it then."

"OK, let me know if you need anything."

"Thanks."

"By the way my baby just called and said that the traffic on 76 cleared up. An accident with a truck and a SEPTA bus had everything all backed up. Anyway, he'll be here in a few."

I let out a deep breath when she walked out of the room. The good news was that she didn't realize that that my cell phone was a camera. The bad news was that Snatch-Back would be there any minute.

I stood there for a few moments and thought out my next move. The lie had already been set up, I just had to follow through. When I got upstairs to the second floor, Lucretia had her attention all on Xavier again.

He was up on the ladder fiddling around with the wires and talking in Home Depot jargon like he was the president of the national coalition of electricians. Nkosi was on his way out of the room as I came in. I signaled for him to stand there and wait.

"Listen, I'm sorry Ms. Johnson but I'm going to have to leave. The day care said that my son is really getting sick so I want to go and take him to the hospital. Nkosi, you come with me so that you can drive me there and then you can come back and pick Xavier up later. I really have to go."

"He's going to have to do all three fans by his self?"

Xavier jumped off the ladder and walked over to Lucretia.

"Naw, naw, Ms. Johnson it won't be a problem at all. In fact, it'll be a piece of cake. I'll call y'all to come back and get me after I get these bad boys up. Aight?"

"Yeah that's cool. OK, we gotta roll."

"Y'all go ahead and handle your business. I know you need to go and look after little Bartholomew."

Me and Nkosi looked at him like he was crazy. Bartholomew? He was really pushing it with that crazy-ass name but we still kept up the act like we were pressed to leave.

"Aww, I wish you didn't have to run off so fast. My son will be here any minute."

"You know what, we'll be back to pick up Xavier so we'll meet him later on."

"If you say . . ."

She hardly completed her sentence and we were out. Nkosi grabbed the car keys from Xavier and we headed for the door like runaway slaves. We got tripped up for a few more minutes when we got to the bottom of the steps because our Timbs were gone.

I panicked but Nkosi just ran into the kitchen and asked the maid if she moved our boots. She nodded yes but continued to rinse the greens until she was good and ready to stop. Once again she lathered up and washed her hands real slow like she was in a dishwashing liquid commercial. At that moment I wished I knew how to say "Hurry up bitch" in Spanish.

She indicated for us to wait there in the kitchen and then she disappeared down the hall toward the powder room. After what seemed like a whole minute, she came back with all three pairs of boots.

Me and Nkosi snatched the Timbs out of her hands and put them on so damn fast that she looked at us like we were on crack. We left Xavier's by the front door again as we were running out of the house.

We hustled out of the house and to the curve on the horseshoe driveway where Xavier's Jeep was parked. Lucretia's car must've been out back because there was nothing parked in front of us. Just as we approached the Jeep, a shiny black Lincoln Navigator with bangin'-ass rims came flying around the bend and up the driveway. Snatch-Back pulled right up behind the Jeep.

I kept my head low and flung open the passenger-side door and hopped in the truck while Nkosi ran around the car and did the same on the driver's side. We could see Snatch-Back and his wife getting out of the truck in the side mirrors. His wife went straight to the back doors of the Navigator, I guess to help the kids get out, but he took off his sunglasses and headed right toward the Jeep.

We were stressed as hell. Nkosi was cursing and screaming and fumbling with the car keys.

"Fuck, fuck, fuck!"

It was like a got-damn white-girl scary-movie moment for one good reason. In the excitement of getting out of the house we both forgot one very crucial thing.

It wasn't a problem for me that Xavier's candy apple red 1994 Jeep Cherokee was a stick shift. Nkosi, on the other hand, ain't have a clue how to drive that bitch.

27.

When I was a young boaw, my mother always kept her foot in my ass because she said I didn't pay attention. She stressed that I should always be aware of my surroundings and to stay on my toes.

She constantly worried out loud that I would be the kid who spent all of the grocery money on seeds for a magic beanstalk. It seemed like she doubted my street smarts and common sense, even after I became a teenager and thought I'd learned the ropes of the ghetto. Every decision I made, she would always make me doubt myself and point out what I could've done differently.

It hurt my feelings at first but as I grew older I understood what she was talking about. I really did need to be extra sharp in order to survive the madness of living in the projects down South Philly. It was crucial that I stay one step up on them niggas just on the strength of who she was . . . and what that made me.

Of all the thousands of people living in the 13th Street projects, my mother, Sarah, was the only white person. My dad, God bless his soul, was the absolute opposite. Lamont Fox was midnight black with a bald shiny head. He reminded me a lot of Michael Jordan but wasn't a champion at anything.

He was gone most of the time, according to my mother in

another South Philly project apartment with his other chick and her daughter. My father was actually the one who gave me the nickname Sticks after he saw me run at a track meet during my sophomore year in high school. "Sticks" is slang for hurdles and that was the event I was really good at. I was thinking a lot of my dad throughout the Snatch-Back drama since that was what he and Jeff Stokes knew me as.

In the scheme of things, I owed my mother big-time. When shit started really getting crazy with the sex tape and the paternity bullshit I thought a lot about what she always used to say to me.

"Pay attention to the little things. Take your blinders off and look around you for God's sake! Everybody ain't your damn friend and no matter what anyone says, everything revolves around black and white."

Her words were ringing in my head constantly for some reason ever since the day I first saw that damn sex tape. One day, out of the blue, it jumped up and bit me on the tip of my nose like a poisonous snake.

I was overwhelmed, dumbfounded, and crushed all at the same time.

I ain't have it in my bones to fuck over nobody who I was tight with. It almost killed me to think that I should've known all along which one of my compadres didn't mean me no good. Somewhere along the way, the cash became more important than our friendship.

My mom always said that everything revolves around black and white. Black and white, she said. It all went back to the wifebeater . . .

28. WEDNESDAY, NOVEMBER 26, 2003 (1:30 P.M.)

The last time Nkosi interviewed Snatch-Back face-to-face was back when the *Sex Master* album dropped in the beginning of 2001. At the time the CD had already sold more than two million copies and he was on damn near every magazine cover and talk show.

Getting that interview was a big scoop back then, especially since Nkosi was a no-name reporter working for a small Philly newspaper. I remember him telling me when he went to interview the boaw at a hotel in Center City that there were bad-ass jawns all over the suite. He said that every last one of the chicks were off the hook.

Halfway through their conversation, Snatch-Back left the living room and went into the bathroom with one who looked like a young Janet Jackson. About ten minutes later he came strolling out of the bathroom with a grin on his face and his chest all poked out.

Nkosi asked him what was up with that and his response was that he just had the urge to get some head all of a sudden. Snatch-Back told him to leave that out of the article and Nkosi did. He regretted not writing that in his story because he pulled the same stunt with a reporter from *Vibe* magazine and that reporter broke it all down in his story.

Compared to early 2001, Nkosi looked basically the same except that he'd gone from a dark fade to a nappy little blowout. I could see that sometimes, especially when he was dressed up in a suit and tie. He had gained a little bit of weight since then too but there was definitely a chance that Snatch-Back could recognize him.

There were no options at that point. Nkosi turned the key in the ignition and pushed the button to roll down the window. Him and Snatch-Back were face-to-face and I was losing it in the passenger seat. The first thing that came to mind was to fake like I was coughing up a lung. I rolled down the window, turned my face away from both of them, and started hacking.

"Hey how's it going? It's so nice to meet you man. Your mom was just talking about you."

"Wassup dude. What are y'all here for?"

"We were hired to install the ceiling fans in there. My partner is still inside but we have to make a run to the hospital."

"Is he all right?"

"Yeah he'll be fine, he just has these bad coughing spells every now and then. We're actually going to take his son to the hospital though."

"Word."

Nkosi told me that the whole time I was coughing that Snatch-Back was looking at me with this half-crazy look on his face. He craned his neck a couple of times to try and get a better look at me but Nkosi would lean forward on the steering wheel to throw interference.

"Yeah, but we'll be back to pick up my man Xavier in a few. He's in there but we'll be back aight."

"Aight cool. Nice meeting you, I'll see you when y'all get back."

"Peace."

For added effect, I opened the passenger door and started hawk-spitting in the driveway. Somebody should've sent a tape of my performance to the Oscar people because I was acting my ass off. Morgan Freeman ain't have shit on me.

Snatch-Back's wife was on the passenger side of the Jeep and she looked me right in the face before I pulled the door closed. That made me 'noid at first but then I figured it ain't matter if she knew what I looked like. I'm sure that nigga ain't tell his wife to be on the lookout for a light-skinned boaw with green eyes and braids because he's blackmailing me with a sex tape. I would kill to see that conversation while they were busting a grub at breakfast.

"Baby come and get these bags."

As soon as Nkosi's window was rolled up all the way, we locked the doors and climbed over each other. I put the car into gear and we pulled out of the driveway while Snatch-Back and his fam made their way up the walkway toward the front door.

Nkosi took me to pick up Brie and then we rolled back to his crib. After he dropped us off and chilled for a little bit, he was about to head back to Gladwyne. It was kind of odd but Xavier called and insisted that Nkosi didn't come back out there to pick him up. He said that he would get back to University City on his own to pick up his truck in a few hours.

Xavier came to get the keys to his Jeep a little before seven that night and really didn't have too much to say. Me and Nkosi were trying to pick his brain for information but he just acted like it was another day at the office. He just told us that he installed the fans and that nothing else happened. Xavier claimed he only met Snatch-Back for a quick second because him and his family were off in a separate part of the house for most of the time that he was there. I don't remember him ever saying how he got back to Nkosi's spot to get the keys to his Jeep.

We were kind of annoyed with him that night because we were expecting him to come back with something, anything, to give us more of an edge on Snatch-Back. Xavier only stayed about fifteen minutes and then he was out.

It wasn't the first time that Xavier acted shady so I didn't even sweat it. Nkosi on the other hand was vexed as hell. He kept bringing up how familiar he was acting with Snatch-Back's mom and he wondered how he even got the gig in the first place. Of all of the contractors everywhere, Xavier, who happened to have a friend who was blackmailing this lady's son, gets a job to do work in her house.

Being a reporter made Nkosi instantly suspicious of almost everyone. It was a given that he ain't put shit past bitches, but niggas was high up on that list too.

I brushed it off as a coincidence. If he said that Lucretia Johnson rolled up in Home Depot and copped three ceiling fans and asked him to come put them up then so be it. He ain't ever give me no real reason to think I couldn't trust him, not if you count the shit that went down in AC in the beginning of the year.

I never mentioned to Nkosi or Kheli for that matter how Xavier kind of played me on one of our little quick runs to Atlantic City. We were broke as hell and still trying to be on some ol' pimp shit with these two jawns. He was messing with the one chick Jade first and then she introduced me to her cousin Wanda. They both looked good as shit but they wasn't wife material or nothing like that.

I drove us down in my Honda and slipped Xavier eighty dollars since he was leaking. We ain't have no real cash to floss with all like that but one of Xavier's uncles hooked us up with a room at Trump Plaza. His uncle, who we called Big Bill, went down AC so much that different casinos always gave him vouchers for free rooms.

Of course we ain't let the jawns know that because we wanted to seem like we were balling a little bit. I looked back and laugh at how lame we must've looked because if our shit was really tight we would've had our own rooms. It was all gravy though because them chicks ain't want to be separated from each other no way.

It was January or February because I remember that the hawk was out. The wind was coming up off that motherfucking water like "nigga what." Since it was so cold we played it real close to the Trump.

First we hit up the buffet because in order to bust a good nut you got to bust a good grub.

That ain't go down too well for me because somewhere between wolfing down the crab cakes and the chocolate mousse pie my stomach was on some other shit. I had started to feel sick so I swigged down some ginger ale right away and it seemed to help.

We gambled for a few hours but only one of us really got paid. The chick Wanda, who I was with, came up like eight hundred dollars on this slot machine after only playing about twenty dollars. She hooted and hollered like she had just won a house and new car but I couldn't be mad at her. Eight bones goes a long way when you got PECO and PGW both coming at your neck with shutoff notices.

Wanda was smart and stopped while she was ahead so we all headed up to the room. I was hoping since she had some more cash to deal with that she would get us our own room but she ain't even hint at it. She probably had already made plans for that cash in her head at that point, and they didn't involve me.

It was a little bit before midnight once we got to the room. We were all just chilling and talking with the television on mute. Xavier went real old school on them and pulled out a deck of Uno cards. Nothing broke the ice like a game of strip Uno so he got points for that.

Now before this night I had never fucked Wanda or even got head. We had been out on a couple dates and kissed and messed around a little but that was it. She was making me work to even get close enough to smell it. Xavier had already nailed Jade to the wall like a picture frame.

Whoever lost the hand had to take a shot of vodka too, so as the night went on we were all getting pretty bent. Jade was the first to be almost naked. She was down to a red thong and bra and even though I wasn't there for her I wanted to rip that shit off with teeth and just go at it.

Me and Xavier were down to boxers, socks, and wifebeaters. Wanda was hardly losing so she was almost still fully dressed. Somewhere after the sixth or seventh hand I started getting real sick. My stomach had settled a little after the ginger ale but the liquor made it worse I guess.

When I came back in the room, Xavier had on just a wifebeater and sweat socks with no drawls. That nigga was just chilling with his balls and cock swinging low like a porn star. Jade's bra was gone and she was just down to her thong. I can't remember but I must've been in the bathroom for a minute.

As soon as Wanda started to finally come up off of some of her clothes, my head started spinning and my stomach was bubbling again. I made a dash back to the bowl but it was a false alarm. Just that quick though, they had definitely fucking started without me. Or should I say they started fucking without me.

Xavier was ten inches deep in Wanda, the chick I was there to fuck, with a mouth full of Jade's titty. They had started a good ol'-fashioned menage à trois while I was in the bathroom puking my brains out. The crazy thing is that I was so twisted that I couldn't say shit right then and there. I was done.

I ran back into the bathroom for round two and just lost it again. Talk about bad timing. It felt like I was pulling muscles in my stomach I was vomiting so hard. In a nutshell, when I finally got myself together to come back in the room they were still going at it. Jade was riding Xavier at that point while Wanda sucked on his nipples.

I just laid out on my stomach across one of the beds while they carried on like they were making a *Booty Talk* porno on the other. Everything after that is a blur because I was out of it.

That's why I say he "kind of played me." I don't know that if the shoe was on the other foot I wouldn't have pulled double dick duty on both of them jawns too. I was just salty that I left AC the next day assless and with a nasty hangover.

The real salt in the wound came when Wanda bought Xavier a fresh pair of Timbs from a sneaker store near the casinos the next morning. I never got out of the car since they all were acting so shady.

Wanda ain't even offer me a stick of chewing gum and I had taken her ass out to eat twice before then. Xavier thought that shit was so funny but I ain't see no humor in none of that bullshit at the time.

It wasn't the shadiest thing that I ever heard a nigga doing to one of his boaws, but I ain't expect that from him. When I brought it up after I dropped off Jade and Wanda he blamed it all on the liquor and told me to stop sweating it. That was easy for him to say after I drove his ass to AC and him broke him off with spending money. He got a fresh pair of boots out the deal, ass from two chicks, and he ain't even offer to cough up no gas money.

That was that. I let it slide and chalked it up as a L. I didn't see Xavier as being shady on a grand scale or no shit like that. I just let it go.

So on the day before Thanksgiving, even though it got a little tense at times, we accomplished the mission that we set out on. I had some good flicks from the inside of Lucretia's house and I knew that I was going to use them to my advantage. But if I was paying closer attention I would've left that house armed with a little more than a few cell phone flicks.

They say knowledge is power. If that's the case I should've felt like the Incredible Hulk.

Kheli stopped by with Dee-Dee later that night to bring us some of the food that she had just cooked for her family's Thanksgiving dinner. She hooked us up with some turkey wings, rice and gravy, string beans, and a whole sweet potato pie. When we were coming up, she was such a tomboy and never went anywhere near a kitchen. Somewhere between fighting in the street and running ball all day she learned how to cook real damn good.

Of course Kheli invited me and Brie to come have dinner with her peeps the next day but I ain't really want to be around nobody all like that. I had no intention of leaving Nkosi's crib the next day. It would be just another Thursday on the calendar as far as I was concerned.

But in the end, fate got me off my ass and across town.

If the theme of our day at Lucretia's house was *Mission Impossible* or *Unlawful Entry*, then turkey day at my mom's would also go down in history for having a movie title as a theme:

Guess Who's Coming to Dinner.

29. THURSDAY, NOVEMBER 27, 2003 (5 P.M.)

My mom was as white as a hospital pillowcase but she cooked like she was raised in the back of a soul food kitchen.

Her collard greens, potato salad, fried chicken, and baked macaroni were off the hook. But it was the candied yams that everybody looked forward to on turkey day.

My pop wasn't shit but his side of the family was always around. I had a couple uncles and three aunts on his side and they always looked out for us. Me and most of my cousins on his side were really tight growing up, but as time went on most of them ended up dead or in jail.

Somehow it turned into a little tradition for all of my peeps on my dad's side to come over my mom's house on Thanksgiving. They were way more accepting of her being a white woman from a small town in Pennsylvania than her family was of my dad.

My mom's side of the family was very small and something different all together. Of the little fam she did have, not many of them spoke to her on the strength that she moved to the South Philly projects to live with a black man. When I came along in 1975, it sealed the deal. They really ain't want nothing to do with her after a little Oreo baby popped up on the scene.

Nkosi had to practically beg me to go over there for Thanksgiving. After what went down on Sunday I didn't want to be around people, even family. I was dealing with the whole paternity situation the best way I knew how but that shit was getting to me.

Thoughts of murdering Minerva ran through my head all of the time. I don't care how she or anyone else looked at it but, if what they said was true, it was the ultimate act of betrayal.

Cheating is one thing. A nigga can get over that in time, no matter how scandalous a ho is. But telling a nigga that a seed is his when you're not absolutely sure is despicable. Bitches should be thrown in a pit of lions for that kind of shit.

It was maddening just thinking about it. I was popping Tylenol constantly that week. So the last thing I really wanted to do was go to my mom's house to be around all of those people.

I ain't tell nobody in my family the real reason that me and Eric Brockington were rumbling at Chuck E. Cheese's. All of them had been blowing up my phone that week trying to see what the deal was but I ain't return none of them calls.

Everybody assumed I was fighting him because of Minerva, and if that's what they wanted to think then so be it. I wasn't giving them one bit of information because I ain't want nothing to wind up in the newspapers.

I made up my mind that me and Brie were going to spend Thanksgiving alone, but then the growls kicked in. I was hungry as hell and Nkosi ain't have shit to eat at his crib. Him and his family went over to Jersey to have dinner at his uncle's new town house so that left me and Brie to fend for ourselves.

There were all kinds of good-ass smells floating underneath his apartment door. The folks in his building were getting it in on them stoves and it was making my mouth water and my stomach hurt. For Brie, it was just another day and another episode of *Teletubbies* so I know just about anything would've hit the spot for her. I, on the other hand, couldn't take it no more.

I made up my mind to go and bust me a good-ass grub. If my family started sweatin' me to death over that Eric Brockington shit then I would just make a plate and roll out. After I made up my mind to go, me and Brie were dressed and out the door in no time.

But before I wrapped my mouth around one noodle of macaroni, I had unfinished business. I was in a real fucked-up mood that week and I wanted everybody who was coming at my neck to be in one too.

The first on my shit list was Snatch-Back himself. The bombshell that Eric Brockington and Minerva dropped on me put the incident with Darkman on the back burner for a little bit but I worked my way back around to it real quick. Sending that motherfucker to break in my house was a dummy move.

Our trip to his mom's house the day before served its purpose to the fullest. I waited until after me and Brie were in the car and she was strapped in before I made the call. He answered his cell after one ring.

"What the deal?"

"Listen to me Cephas, you really fucked up when you sent that nigga to my crib while me and my seed were in there."

"What, who is this?"

"You know exactly who the hell this is."

"Sticks?"

"Yeah nigga Sticks. Why you send that motherfucker to break into my house?"

"Dude, I already told you I have no idea what you're talking about one, and two I'm about to sit down to have dinner with my family. Can I holla at you in a few hours?"

"Naw dude, we're going to handle this right now. You fucked up my holiday so now I'm going to return the favor."

"Hold up y'all, this is an emergency. Give me a couple of minutes."

I could hear Lucretia cursing in the background as he excused himself to take my call.

"Dude, what is your fucking problem? It's Thanksgiving and you're calling me with this bullshit about somebody breaking into your house while you and your daughter was there?"

"I never said I had a daughter."

"Yes you did."

"Naw bruh, I specifically said 'my seed' and I never told you

I had a daughter on purpose. You got that information from somebody else."

"Man, I don't have time for this. I know what you said. So why you think I had something to do with this?"

"Who else would have any reason to send a thug to my crib to look for that tape?"

"What?"

"Who else would do that?"

"Listen, I don't even know your real name let alone where you live so how could I do that?"

"You got money nigga, anything is possible."

"Naw son, you buggin' now."

"Am I? I'll let you know when I'm buggin'. I want you to take a walk right now."

"What? Where to?"

"I want you to take a walk to the bathroom near the kitchen inside of your mom's house."

"Huh?"

"Just do it."

"How do you know she has a bathroom near the kitchen?"

"Move your ass nigga—"

"Aight, aight, chill."

"When you get there go inside and close the door."

"OK, I'm in here now what."

"Hang up the phone and wait. I'm sending you something. Call me back after you receive it."

I was still parked in front of Nkosi's crib when I sent the first two pictures from my cell phone to his. I pulled away from the curb and started heading down Spruce to get toward the expressway. As expected, my phone started ringing before I even made it to the Wawa at 38th Street. I knew what he saw on his cell phone screen made him want to piss on himself.

"Yo, how the fuck did you get these pictures of my mom's house?"

"Wouldn't you like to know?"

"Listen pussy, I don't know what the hell you're up to but if you come anywhere near my mom, I'll break your fucking neck!"

"So now we're in the same boat. Now you know how it feels to be violated don't you? You fucked with my baby, I fucked with your mother. And what?"

"I didn't fuck with your baby! And you still ain't tell me how you got these pictures."

"Hang up I have to send you something else."

The first two flicks that I sent him were of the inside of his mom's bathroom and the painting of him on her living room wall. On the second go round I sent two pictures of the game room taken at different angles. He called back immediately.

"How the fuck did you get in here?"

"Why did you send that nigga to my house? I thought we had a deal."

"We do have a deal. I gave you a hundred grand last week and told you the rest would be coming soon. Why would I do some crazy shit like break into your house when you got that tape?"

"Because you were trying to get your hands on that tape. I'm trying to figure that one out too."

"Why would I do that?"

"I think you're bullshitting and I hate being played. So, because you tried to be slick I'm going to demand that you give me another four hundred grand by the end of the day tomorrow."

"I can't get that kind of cash to you that quick. It's almost impossible—"

"I don't care about none of that shit. Make it happen."

I banged on him again right before I turned off the South Street bridge to get on the expressway. My life was like a fucking marble rolling off a three-legged table, and I wanted Snatch-Back to feel the same way.

I thought about Darnell, Netta, and their alien twins when I got to my mom's because her crib was on the 8200 block of Willliams Avenue, about two blocks away from where they lived.

She was so damn happy that I decided to come. My mom grabbed me and Brie and hugged us so tight before we could even get all the way through the front door. I knew that I had been stressing her the hell out but she was holding up well.

She was two years away from fifty and she looked like she was coming up on the big four-zero. I think she dyed her hair though so there was no signs of gray anywhere. It was strictly blond.

Me and my mom had the same color eyes and we were only about an inch or so apart. She was 5'11" and still thin just like when I was little. Sarah is as lily white as they come from the outside, but deep down she always has had a lot of soul.

It wasn't as bad as I expected when I got there. My family didn't bum-rush me as soon as I walked in the door like I thought they would. There were about fifteen people there including the kids and everybody played it real cool.

Brie was getting a lot of attention since a lot of my family hadn't seen her since she was a few weeks old in 2001. It was smooth sailing for the most part but I would cringe on the inside every time someone said, "She looks just like you."

Slowly, my aunts and a few of my cousins got around to asking me about what happened. I dismissed it as beef over something between me and him over Minerva and just left it at that. I ain't tell the whole truth but it's not like I was lying.

Our Thanksgiving dinner was nothing like the family gatherings you see on TV. It was all about family and all about love but we were ghetto with ours. My aunt Cassie always remixed the grace until it went on for about three or four minutes and included a prayer for all the sick and shut-ins and the little orphans in Africa. After the mini sermon everybody just went for what they knew.

My mother had a dining room table but it could only seat about six people. Eight, if everybody squeezed real close to each other. Mostly niggas just sat on the carpet with their paper plates, ate standing up in the kitchen, or sat in foldout chairs in the living room. Some of the kids even took their grub upstairs so that they could eat in front of the television in my mom's bedroom.

Some people might call it informal dining, but I just called it ghetto. It was all good though because it was less hassle. Just get your grub on and chill.

I was working on my third plate and second Corona when my mom gave me some good news.

"That was your cousin Shadeed that just called. He's on his way over here. He's running a little late because he went to his new girlfriend's house first."

He was one of my favorite cousins growing up because we were only about three months apart in age and we had a lot in common. His mother, Barbara, was my father's sister and we were the only two boys out of the cousins with Muslim names. Since I had decided not to put him down with the tape, I hadn't talked to him in a minute. That obviously had my attention twenty-four/seven.

He always used to tease me about that too since I had my mother's last name. One day I overheard my fifth-grade teacher at Palumbo, Mrs. Jackson, say that my name was an oxymoron. I made the mistake of telling Shadeed what she said, and he laughed and then proceeded to call me "Ox-Head-Moron" the whole summer.

My mother wasn't amused at all when she got wind of it. I ain't even know what an oxymoron was at the time but my mom broke it down for me with examples like bittersweet and pretty ugly. I figured Mrs. Jackson made the comment since my first name sounded black and my last name was so super white.

Luckily I had just chewed and swallowed a big-ass piece of catfish when Shadeed rolled up in the spot with his new jawn. I think if I hadn't, I would've choked right on the spot. Being around my family that day had finally started to get my mind off all of the shit going down in my life. And then, just like that, a reminder of everything that was swirling around me walked right through the front door.

I was in the kitchen eating off of my aunt Beverly's plate when the volume in the living room went up because everybody was speaking to Shadeed. As I was coming out of the kitchen, my favorite cousin was walking toward me through the dining room with his chick one step behind him. He's husky as hell and about 6'3", but the jawn was much smaller so I couldn't see her face right away.

When Shadeed gripped me into a big bear hug and hoisted me up off the floor, I looked over his shoulder and right into her eyes. She smiled at me politely and just stood there waiting for us to be properly introduced. I just stared at first but I can't remember if my jaw dropped open.

"Yo fam this is my girl Desiree. And Desiree this is my cousin, well you know his name already. Everybody know his damn name since he been all in the news and shit. I been calling you nigga, wassup with that, man?"

I heard Shadeed talking but I ain't respond right away. I was stuck on stupid and stuck on his girl. I was blown away because we had one crazy-ass thing in common.

She had never met me before, but she knew what I looked like because of the infamous Chuck E. Cheese home video. It was ditto for me.

30. THURSDAY, NOVEMBER 27, 2003 (8:45 P.M.)

It was time for me and my cousin to have a little talk.

Shadeed had already eaten dinner with Desiree's family so they were straight on the grub tip. He went in the kitchen to get her a piece of cake and he introduced her to my mom and the rest of the fam. I told him that I needed to talk with him about something so after about fifteen minutes he told her that we'd be right back.

I ain't have no idea how much I would or wouldn't tell Shadeed about this chick, I just knew that we had to rap. He had always been a mack when it came to the honeys so I knew it wouldn't be that big a deal if he had to drop her like a bad habit.

On the flip side, he did have her up at Thanksgiving dinner with our family. It was like blasphemy or something to waste good candied sweets and greens on a smut. So she had to be something special to him.

Once we were outside he asked me right away what was up. Obviously he thought that I wanted to talk with him about the Eric Brockington fiasco so he jumped right into it.

"So what's the deal cousin, you need me to go find that clown-ass Eagle boaw and kick his ass? I know where they be hanging at, so just say the word and me and my niggas is there."

"Naw, it ain't even like that. He mess with Minerva now so you know how that go."

"Word. What he trying to act like he don't want you to talk to your BM?"

"It ain't that, and it don't got nothing to do with him being an Eagle, it's just that I don't like the way he came at me, nah mean. We handled our business and it just so happens that it was cameras there and the shit made the news."

"Yeah that shit was crazy. All my boaws and chicks from down South Philly who know that we cousins was blowing up my cell after that happened. Yo, why you ain't call me back?"

"I'm sorry about that Deed. It's just that this week has been hectic because of that. Newspaper people been trying to get at me and motherfuckers I ain't speak to in years. I just turned my phone off and laid low, nah mean?"

"I can dig it. But you know I'll hold you down if you need me right?"

"Oh I know nigga, you ain't even got to say that."

We walked to the corner of my mom's block and stood next to the stop sign. It wasn't that windy but it was dark outside and the hawk was starting to come out. My nose and hands started getting numb real quick.

"So you straight on that tip so wassup?"

"I'm cool . . . Yo wassup with the jawn Desiree? How long y'all been kicking it?"

"I met Des back in May but we ain't really start getting serious until like the end of the summer. She wasn't feeling me at first since I used to talk to one of her girlfriends but then I guess she got over it."

"Word. So she your main jawn now?"

"You can say that. I damn near moved in with her."

"Where she live?"

"Near 5th and Olney. Why?"

"I was just asking."

Shadeed paused and cut his eye at me like he knew I had to be getting at something else. It was too damn cold outside just to be on the corner shooting the breeze about the new chick he was with.

"Why you ask me that, what you know her from somewhere? Don't tell me you hit it?"

I just looked down at the ground when he said that. If only he knew. I think me nailing her would be a slow walk in the park compared to what the deal really was.

"Naw, I ain't hit it but let me ask you this. Are y'all nailing without rubbers?"

"What you mean nigga?"

"Have you hit it raw?"

"Hell yeah nigga, she on them BC pills?"

"Damn. Aight we need to walk, I'm getting cold."

We headed up Williams toward Wadsworth Avenue walking real slow. I was really shaky on whether or not I wanted to tell Shadeed about her and it wasn't because I ain't trust him. I wasn't sure if I wanted to drag somebody else into dealing with Snatch-Back and all the bullshit that came along with that. At the same time I knew what kind of a freak she was and I ain't want him to catch the dreaded four letters that no nigga can shake. If he met her in May, that was well after she was gang-banged by Snatch-Back and crew. The newspaper articles that I read said that the rape happened back in January.

Me and Shadeed were family and all but I knew that he would never stop messing with her just because I said so. He trusted me but he would need more than just my word if I told him I thought he should step off. It was going to be hard either way because there he was already living with her.

"Listen man, there's something I have to tell you about Desiree."

"Y'all know each other?"

"Naw man, I ain't never met that chick a day in my life until fifteen minutes ago."

"So what's the deal?"

I asked him what she did for a living and he told me that she worked for UPS at night and went to hair school during the day. She had her own whip, a Pontiac Grand Am, and a two-bedroom apartment.

"Deed, has she ever danced?"

"You mean *dance* dance, like at the club?"

"Yeah."

"Not that I know of. Aaawww shit. Don't tell me she a fucking stripper? You seen her at the club?"

"Naw dude. I ain't been to the club in a minute, probably since before Brie was born."

"Then what are you getting at?"

"Do you know if she has a case going right now against anybody?"

Shadeed stopped walking and stared at me with this crazy-ass shocked expression on his face. He was dumbfounded and he just started stuttering like ten things at once.

"Hold up . . . w-w-wait . . . hold up. How do you know about that? Are you talking about the rape case with Snatch-Back?"

"She told you about it?"

"Yeah! How you know about that shit?"

"It's all over the news man. He's the hottest rapper out right now."

"Yeah but they ain't never put her name or what she looked like in the paper because they don't do that when chicks get raped."

"I know, I know but . . ."

"But what? Dawg, how did you know it was her."

I had never seen my cousin with such a desperate-ass look in his eyes. He would've probably wrung my neck right there on the spot if I backed off so I knew I had to go all the way and break it down. I offered him a deal.

"OK, check it. You tell me what you know and I'll tell you how I knew Desiree is the one who accused him of rape."

"Dawg, I promised her I wouldn't say shit. It's legal shit, nah mean, and it's all like strictly on the hush."

"I know man, but you gotta trust me on this. I have a feeling that I probably know a little bit more about this case than you right now."

Shadeed turned away from me and let out a loud-ass grunt. It was cold enough out there for me to see his breath in the air. He turned back with a serious straight face.

"Dawg, I'll tell you everything I know but you gotta keep this shit under your hat aight?"

"Of course."

"Naw for real, this is my girl. I told her I would keep this shit low so you gotta be real with me on this, nah mean."

"I got you Deed . . . I got you."

Shadeed spilled his guts right there on the spot. He took me all the way back to the beginning and told me about when they first met. Desiree played that ol' innocent game and talked a hole in his head about all of the shit that she didn't do. She claimed that she ain't like giving head all like that and that in the past she only had sex in like two or three positions. Sex, Desiree also claimed, was not that big a deal in a relationship.

He might've been open but Shadeed knew game when he saw it. When he finally got a chance to hit it, he said Desiree Perry was a motherfucking cannon. He said he ain't know if he was coming or going after the first time because she came with her A game and left him on his back with his mouth wide open. By the third or fourth time they nailed she tossed his salad, ate the gun, and swallowed all his babies.

He ain't really have to tell me because I saw her in action and I knew she had skills. There wasn't shit amateur about Desiree and I think we both knew that.

Shadeed said he started to figure out something was wrong around Labor Day when she started sleeping less and always seemed depressed. She was losing weight and could hardly concentrate on her work for hair school.

He knew she had a lawyer but he ain't know the reason. Desiree lied at first and said that the lawyer was for a personal family matter involving her mother and her uncle. After a while she just broke down and told him that Snatch-Back and two of his boaws raped her.

Shadeed didn't say a word to nobody about the case until he talked to me. He just kept it under wraps and stuck with her. He went with her to a preliminary hearing for the trial on Halloween to show his support. My cousin said he was heated because Snatch Back and his roadies ain't seem pressed about the case at all. They were laughing and joking with each other before the judge came in the courtroom and at one point Snatch-Back even blew her a kiss when no one was paying attention.

He was on some real cocky shit that day and it burned Desiree up too. Shadeed said she was even more fucked up in the head after that because she figured that pressing charges was all in vein. She ain't think she had a chance in hell of proving that they were guilty.

When my cousin told me that I figured him and his squad was acting cocky since they thought they were all going to get off. I ain't get my hands on the tape until November 10th so he had every reason to be feeling himself at the end of October.

Shadeed asked if she and Snatch-Back had sex at any other time before the rape and she admitted that they did. Desiree said that the first time he hit it he randomly picked her and another chick that she ain't know after one of his concerts. They all went back to his hotel room and Snatch-Back told them that it was a fantasy of his to have a menage à trois with two women who ain't know each other. That was how they set it off.

Just as I expected, Desiree's version of what went down back in January was a little different than what actually happened. For one, she never mentioned to Shadeed anything about the sitcom boaw Ryan Wilson. She only told him about Snatch-Back and his two boaws, who I called Uno and Deuce. I wondered why she ain't never press charges against him too. There had to be something to that.

Shadeed was floored when I told him that she also got nailed by the sitcom boaw before Snatch-Back even hit it. He really wasn't ready for the fact that Snatch-Back had not only been with her before but that he paid her in the past for sex.

I ain't want to be the one to bring bad news but he was my family and he needed to know. I told my cousin that in that entire tape not one of them dudes wore a rubber. His face wrinkled up something vicious like he had just sucked on ten lemons when I said that. And in a nutshell that was the only reason I told him anything at all. With all of the STDs out there, it would've been crazy not to.

I told one lie that night while we were walking around my mom's neighborhood. I never said anything to him about how I was getting Snatch-Back for his loot in exchange for the tape. I told him that I watched the tape once and then destroyed it because I ain't want no part of that shit.

If Shadeed knew that I had still had it, then I know he would've asked me to give it to Desiree so that she could use it for evidence. Snatch-Back was shit on the bottom of a shoe to me but we had a deal and I wasn't going back on it. I was close to getting a cool mill and nothing was going to get in the way of that.

Before we got back in the house. I told him that it was up to him whether or not he dumped Desiree or not. I just ain't want my name in it in no way, shape, or form. He ain't know at the time what he was going to do as far as dumping her or not but he promised that he wouldn't tell her what I said. Shadeed also said that he was going to go and get an AIDS test because it had been a minute since the last time he got one.

I stayed for about another hour after we went back in the house. Shadeed was going out of his way to act like everything was normal but I could tell that shit was going to be way different between him and his jawn after that night. Nobody else might have noticed but I could see that he was salty as hell. I felt bad in some ways but I knew deep down that I did the right thing. I would want somebody to tell me if I was sharing a mattress with a smut jawn every night.

I got Brie dressed to leave and said good-bye to all my fam who was still there. As we were leaving, I slipped my mother a check on the low.

"I know you're going out tomorrow morning to do the Black Friday shopping thing so this should help some. Enjoy yourself."

It was made out for five grand and had "Merry X-mas" written on the memo line.

Her mouth dropped open and she kept staring at it.

"Where did you get this kind of money?"

"Mom, trust me. I ain't sell no drugs to get it or kill nobody to get it so it's all good. I can't get into it right now but trust me on this one."

"Are you pulling my leg? Can I really cash this?"

I picked Brie up and walked toward the front door. Before we walked out of the crib, I turned around and gave her a kiss on the cheek.

"Mom, you have my word. Every penny of that money is there or my name ain't Akbar Saludeen Schraudenbacher."

31. FRIDAY, NOVEMBER 28, 2003 (7 A.M.)

It felt like I was waking up to go to a funeral.

My stomach was already in knots from the disgusting cherry pie that my aunt Cassie made for Thanksgiving. And just thinking about what I had to do that morning made it even worse.

I got in the bed with Brie at about eleven o'clock on Thanksgiving night but I never really went to sleep. Every now and then I would doze off, and just that quick my eyes would pop open and my head would start hurting all over again.

I don't think I got in one solid hour of sleep. Brie on the other hand was knocked out the entire night and snored like a grown-ass man. She looked so peaceful, like she ain't have a care in the world because when you're two years old that's just what it is. Kids live life real simple. It's the adults who always fuck things up.

My brain was overloading that morning when I got up to get dressed. I fucking hated myself so much. I felt guilty as hell, because the thought actually crossed my mind of whether or not I would still raise Brie as my own if she wasn't my blood daughter. I never admitted it to nobody, but that's the honest-to-God truth what I was thinking.

My thing was if she wasn't mine and I let Eric Brockington and Minerva take her right away then I would get over it quicker. But just as soon as I would think that I knew that there was no way in hell I could just let go like that. I needed to know.

There was no way I would make it from day to day without knowing.

If I raised Brie and Eric Brockington was her real dad what would happen when she got older and found out the truth? It would crush me if she got to be a teenager and picked that bastard over me. What would I do? That's why I thought that whatever the truth was I needed to deal with it then and there in 2003.

Deep down I knew that her picking him over me was a major possibility on the strength that he was a popular football player with major bank. My father might've looked like the basketball legend, but if given the choice as a kid I would've picked the real Michael Jordan to be my pop in a heartbeat.

My mom always said that there was a silver lining to every cloud but I was having a hard time finding it in my situation. And I felt like I would die if I didn't find it.

Nkosi was still sleep after I got Brie washed and dressed. I made her some scrambled eggs and grits and she knocked it off in no time. She was at the age where she was starting to imitate everything she heard and that was real funny to me. It actually took my mind off our problems for a minute.

She also got a kick out of pointing people out in the pictures that were in the photo album. That morning when my cell phone started vibrating on the coffee table she scooped it up and looked at the screen.

"Kel-leee . . . yaaaaa . . . kel-leee."

I took the phone out of her hand and looked at the screen and it was sure enough Kheli, cheesin' on her couch with a wifebeater on. She offered to drive that morning so she met us outside of Nkosi's apartment. Kheli did her best to keep my spirits up on the way to Jefferson Hospital. She never once said anything about the blood test or asked me how I was feeling. I guess the whole situation was so damn awkward. She mostly just talked about how crazy the dinner was at her mom's house on Thanksgiving.

It was a little after nine when we arrived in the waiting area. Kheli had pulled some strings to get this woman to squeeze us into her schedule. I ain't have no health insurance so Kheli asked if she could do the test for me and Brie. When the smoke cleared I think I paid close to one grand to have everything done.

The lady who did our blood work was named Pauline. She was dark skinned and in her late fifties or early sixties and Brie took to her right away. Her hair was short and dyed fire-engine red like one of the young jawns from around the way. Even though she was an old head it fit her personality. She was like Gladys Knight mixed with a little bit of Eve.

Pauline got right to work after she tucked the two Benjamins that I slipped her into her bra. Kheli told me before we got there that I had to hook her up and I was fine with that. It was important for the test to be done discreetly and professionally and she was up for the job.

One of the hardest things in life for me is watching my daughter in pain. Brie was terrified of needles. Pauline asked me to hold her down while she did it.

It made me feel like shit because she had this look on her face like, "Daddy, I can't believe you're in on this." If nothing else came out of that experience, I learned that Brie had the potential to be the next Patti LaBelle. She screamed so damn loud that it made my chest tighten up.

And just when I was to the point where I wanted to grab the needle out of Pauline's hands and stab her with it, it was over. I slammed a Blow Pop in Brie's mouth and she quieted down pretty quick. Lollipop or not, she still gave me and Kheli the stare of death when we were rolling up out of there.

After Pauline drew my blood, she put the samples inside of the kit and sealed it. I was putting Brie's coat on when I looked up and caught her staring at me. She kind of cocked her head to the side a little and smiled before she asked the burning question.

"Are you the young man who was fighting one of the Eagles on the news?"

I winked at her and said, "No comment."

"I don't care or nothing. I'm from California so my team is the Raiders anyway."

Pauline winked back at me and left the room.

Me and Kheli made a beeline to the post office. I had totally forgot that the day after Thanksgiving was always hectic. Black Friday or not I didn't get out of that long-ass line at the post office because I needed them results like yesterday.

On the way back to Nkosi's, I had the urge to tell Kheli about my chance encounter with Desiree, but for some reason I just let it ride. I actually didn't tell Xavier or Nkosi right away either.

Kheli dropped us off and then went on about her business. It was a national holiday for chicks like her, who liked to spend money on clothes just because.

The year before when I was struggling to rub two nickels together, I wished that I could go out on the day after Thanksgiving to take advantage of the sales. Now that I had stacks in the bank, I ain't really feel like being in the hustle and bustle all like that. The thought of finding parking, standing in long-ass lines, and ignorant salespeople made me just chill.

It was the best decision that I'd made in a minute because the time alone really allowed me to get in the zone and reflect on the situation at hand. I played with Brie for a while before I read her *Barney Goes to the Zoo* and *The Berenstain Bears*. She fell asleep at around two and I plopped down in front of the television with the remote in my hand ready to zone out in front of an episode of *Three's Company*.

My cell phone rang at that moment. I looked on the screen and it was Shadeed.

"Yo Deed, you not gon' believe this, I was just sitting here thinking about how we used to watch Jack Tripper and them—"

"Yo Saludeen, I got some crazy shit to tell you—"

"What's wrong?"

His breathing was heavy as hell and was whispering which wasn't like him at all. Shadeed always talked loud like he was giving a speech so I knew something was up. There was a long pause on his end.

"Yo, do this got something to do with Desiree? Nigga, you ain't tell her did you?"

"Naw Ak, chill. Listen to me man, I ain't tell her shit that you said. It's what she told me."

From that point on he was still breathing hard and I had stopped breathing all together.

What he said next knocked the wind out of my lungs and fired me up all at the same time.

That Black Friday was the beginning of the end of a very good friendship.

32. FRIDAY, NOVEMBER 28, 2003 (8 P.M.)

When Brie woke up I got her dressed and we rolled out to my mom's house. I packed her a bag so that she could stay the night because I ain't want her around when the shit went down.

My mom wasn't mad at all that I dropped Brie off out of the blue. She was actually happy to see her granddaughter two days in a row. I put the *Lion King* DVD on so that she wouldn't notice me leaving and I was right back out the door.

I was steaming mad and on the verge of tears as I drove back down to West Philly. There was so much traffic on the road that there were accidents on almost every corner and it was slowing me down. Niggas was acting like they ain't know how to drive that night.

Straight runs like Washington Lane had pileups as well as the crazy, winding roads like Lincoln Drive. How ironic that I was stuck sitting in traffic on Lincoln Drive near the actual spot where Teddy Pendergrass had the accident that put him in a wheelchair.

While I was on my way, I called Xavier, Kheli, and Nkosi on their cell phones to tell them I needed for them to meet me at the Chili's on 38th and Chestnut at eight o'clock. I stressed to all three of them that it was an absolute emergency.

If nothing else I knew that all three of them had to be there. I was mad enough to do something stupid, so I definitely needed people there to keep me in check. I sat across the street from the Chili's in my Honda and watched them arrive one at a time. Kheli got there first, followed about five minutes later by Xavier, and then Nkosi.

In all of the excitement I had almost forgotten one very important thing. Before I got out of the car I called the toll free number of my bank to check my balance. I punched in my account number and waited to get the scoop. Goose bumps crawled all over my arms when the computerized voice said that I had a little under five hundred grand in my account. It was crazy but I needed that bit of good news before going into a very bad meeting.

Kheli spoke up first when I walked up to the table. She was the only one looking through the menu.

"Man, I've been out all day shopping and my dogs are barking. You lucky, I'm hungry."

Xavier and Nkosi were both on their cell phones. Xavier sounded like he was talking to a chick while Nkosi seemed to be checking voice mail messages. Kheli and Nkosi were sitting on the same side of the booth together so I slid in next to Xavier. I ain't even bother to take my leather jacket off.

"Listen . . . this is major."

That's all I could get out at first because a lump formed in my throat from the gate. I thought that I would come in there like a gorilla but the thought of being betrayed by a person I trusted with my life had started to get to me.

I purposely wanted all three of them there because if I confronted the traitor alone I don't know what I would've done. The last thing I needed was to catch a case for assault or worse, attempted murder.

Xavier hung up his phone and then nudged me with his elbow.

"Wassup dude, it look like you about to have a breakdown."

"Maybe I am."

They all looked at each other then turned their attention back to me.

"It's like this, ever since I got my hands on that tape, I have had a nagging feeling that somehow, somebody close to me was going to betray me to get to some of that cash. Now, at first I dismissed it as me just being paranoid but now I have more than enough reasons to believe that's not the case."

It was silence at the table.

"That someone . . . that backstabber is sitting at this table."

As soon as I said that our waitress came over and asked if we wanted to order any appetizers. I told her to come back in about ten minutes. They didn't know it but I was fucking positive that nobody would have an appetite after I was done.

Nkosi took a big gulp of the water that was in front of him and cleared his throat.

"What the hell are you talking about man? Are you still on me hooking up with that chick because I'll call her right now and—"

"Naw Nkosi, I'm over that."

Once I got going I wasn't tongue-tied at all.

I started with Darkman, the intruder at my crib in South Philly. The first time I ever laid eyes on that nigga was on the day that me and Brie went to the Chuck E. Cheese's in South Philly. That was also the same day that I called Jeff Stokes for the first time to set up a meeting about the tape.

Within an hour or so of me making the call to Stokes, dude was up in my face. It hit me that one didn't have anything to do with the other. I still believed that Darkman was sent by Snatch-Back but I realized that he knew about me and that tape before I even made the first call.

The only way that could've happened was if one of my crew told Snatch-Back. I only told three people about the tape so that narrowed it down real easy. One of them bastards gave him a heads-up.

Second, there was the whole issue of the game room where they ganged up on Desiree Perry. I never paid attention to the small details until I was standing in the room. The camera that taped all of the action was mounted in the far corner of the room and it never moved.

Keeping that in mind there was only so much of the room that could be seen in the frame. Of course the sex was on the tape clear as day. That's not what had me all fucked up in the head. It was a certain R&B legend who witnessed all the action from up high.

Kheli made a comment about her being turned off by Snatch-Back because he took advantage of the victim underneath a picture of Teddy Pendergrass. That much was true. Teddy was damn sure up on the wall in that room.

But there was no way in hell Kheli would've known that a picture of Teddy Pendergrass was hanging on the wall in Lucretia Johnson's game room unless she had been in there at least once. The only picture you can see on the tape since the motherfucking camera was in one place was one of Marvin Gaye. Kheli had definitely made a motherfucking trip out to the Gladwyne mansion.

The third and final thing that bugged me to death happened on the day that I met with Snatch-Back on South Street. When we turned the corner of Lombard Street our shit was knocked out of our hands by the Asian chick on the bike.

It occurred to me much later that when we dropped our phones, which are identical, I picked up his phone and he picked up mine. I know this to be true for one very simple fucking reason. The picture that comes up on my screen every time Kheli calls my cell phone is of her sitting on her couch in a tight wifebeater.

When the phone vibrated as I was walking down Lombard with Snatch-Back, I looked down to see her in an identical pose but the only difference was the color of her shirt. It was black. The same type of shirt but it was black. So I guess instead of it being a wifebeater it was just a plain ol' black tank top.

For some fucking reason or another, there was a picture of Kheli Stockton in Snatch-Back's cell phone. She claimed that she had never met him and I had figured out that this was not true. I sat down the phone that was in my hand when I used the ATM to get him the twenty dollars. When I picked it up I must've grabbed the right phone.

This chick was my closest female friend on the planet. If she had met the rapper that she obsessed about for years, I would've known. Not the next day or even the next hour but the very moment she left his company I would've known every detail.

So in a nutshell, he was hip to my game before I even knew I had a game. I was sure that Snatch-Back knew more about me than he should've known. Kheli put him onto the tape before I even put in the first call to Jeffrey Stokes. They were expecting my call and I'm sure that Snatch-Back must have then commissioned Darkman to follow me and get the tape back.

Tears just started rolling down Kheli's face while I was talking. They weren't sad tears though because she looked furious. For the first time in a long time, I couldn't read her face. I normally knew where she was coming and what she was thinking since we were so tight, but on that night it was blank. It was like instantly from the moment that I confronted her about that bullshit, our bond was broken. Just like that, she was garbage in the street to me. Fuck that, she was spit on the sidewalk underneath the garbage.

Through all of it, I was surprised at how calm I was. Xavier and Nkosi were in shock. We must've all looked gone because the waitress started to approach our table again and then she just turned around and walked away. It was that serious.

"Why Kheli? Why would you put Brie in danger like that?"

She just stared straight ahead with this stupid-ass look on her face and cried. Nkosi, who was sitting on the aisle side of the booth next to her, turned and looked at her but she ain't return the stare.

"Yo Kheli, is that true?"

She used the napkin that her silverware was wrapped in to blow her nose and to wipe her face.

Kheli was subdued and shocked at first and then she just snapped.

"I can't fucking believe that you would sit here and even put your lips together to say some nut shit like that to me. We go too far back for you to come at my neck with this bullshit. You know I would never do anything to hurt Brie."

"Is that so? You knew that nigga was going to come to my house to look for that tape didn't you?"

"What the fuck are you talking about Saludeen? Huh? I have no fucking idea what you are talking about. I don't have shit to do with Snatch-Back or that nigga that came to your house and I am fucking pissed that you even think that!"

People in the restaurant were starting to stare but I ain't give a fuck. I already had a rep for turning shit out public places so I ain't care. Kheli was pissing me off because she was lying and on top of that she had the balls to get hype back with me like she ain't play no part in all of that madness.

"Yeah, but Brie wasn't supposed to be home that night, remember! You said she was staying over your mom's house the night you went to the pool tournament and then you changed your mind and you went and picked her up!"

She denied having anything to do with it at first and then just like that she was spilling the beans. It was like I was sitting across from someone with a split personality.

"Yeah and . . ."

"She wasn't supposed to be there in the house. I would've never told him to go if I knew Brie was going to be there."

"But it was cool for that nigga to break in while I'm in there. So it's cool for me to get fucked up just so long as Snatch-Back gets that tape back."

"No. I thought you would've still been out too. You never go home when you have a babysitter, and you had a couple dollars so I figured . . . well, bottom line I didn't send nobody to your house to hurt you, it's not even like that—"

"Then what the fuck is it like then Kheli. Tell me huh?"

I picked up the butter knife in front of me and started banging it on the table hard as hell. Xavier reached over and took it out of my hand. Kheli stopped talking and took a deep breath. She looked like she ain't ever expect in a million years that I would figure that shit out. That's when it jumped off between her and Nkosi.

"You don't understand."

"OK Kheli, make us understand."

"Nkosi this ain't got shit to do with you so mind your business right now."

"Nothing to do with me? You really must be on that shit. That's my goddaughter we talking about. You knew that motherfucker was going there. Do you know what could have happened? Is this rapper boaw that damn important to you? Are you that obsessed with that nigga? Was it worth it?"

"First of all I ain't obsessed with no fucking body."

"So tell me why if you're not obsessed that you sold one of your closest friends out for somebody you don't even know all like that."

"That ain't true. I know him better than you think."

"Oh yeah, how so?"

"Look Nkosi, I don't have to answer all of your questions. I ain't one of your interviews. Save that shit for the newspaper!"

I picked up the salt shaker and slammed it down on the table hard has hell. Everybody jumped but Kheli flinched the hardest.

"Well you might don't have to tell him shit but I want to know right now what the fuck is going on. I want to know when you met that motherfucker and why you on his dick so hard that you would sell me and my daughter out?"

"I'm not working against you. He told me if I got the tape then he was going to break me off with a lot of money. I planned on giving you half."

"So why couldn't you just wait until I got paid. You know I was going to hook you up. I planned on hooking all of y'all up."

"I felt bad after I told you to blackmail him and I called him and told him about the tape. And then he said if I got it back he would give me half a million. Plus I ain't want you to get too deep in this shit and killed or something. I figured I could keep him at bay. It seemed much simpler to me if I just handled it with Snatch one on one."

"What? So y'all are tight like that?"

"Something like that."

"How come you never told me you met him?"

Kheli looked up at the ceiling and took one of them dramatic soap opera pauses. I wasn't feeling her at all. Every bone in my body wanted to reach across the table and smack the shit out of her. It was like aliens invaded her body, because she wasn't acting like herself.

"I just met him not too long ago and we started messing around and he told me to keep it on the low."

"Another lie."

"What? Why you think I'm lying?"

"I don't think you're lying Kheli, I know it. Tell me does this sound closer to the fucking truth. You're backstage at one of his concerts with a bunch of other cluckers just dying to get his attention. He picks you and one other chick to come back to his hotel room. Then to top the night off he tells both of you that it's his fantasy to have a menage à trois with two women who never met each other . . ."

"What . . . what are you talking about . . . ?"

"No wait there's more. Then after he smutted both of y'all out he started calling the other chick more and giving her money and you were salty as hell when you found out since he only called you every once in a blue when he wanted some ass. Then you started feeling like shit because you thought you was his main side jawn, his mistress, nah mean, but when the deal is you ain't really much more than a trick-ass bitch on the side!"

Kheli's face cracked into ten million pieces right in front of all three of us. At first she was speechless because there was no way in hell I was supposed to know that much about her and Snatch-Back. I was in the dark for a long fucking time, but now the high beams were on.

"Did he tell you all of that?"

"It don't matter. All you need to know is that I know and you should feel like a used tampon for being so fucking conniving and sneaky. That shit ain't right! I would've never did nothing like that that to you or any of my friends."

"I need to know what else he told you!"

"Why, so you can go back and run it all down for him what I know? It's over Kheli, you ain't shit to me now. Do you understand that because of you a nigga who I don't even know broke into my crib and was standing over top of my baby. You don't exist to me right now. I want you to get up and walk out of here and I don't want you to say shit else to me."

"But—"

"Yo Nkosi, stand up and let her out right now. I got no more rap."

Nkosi got up out of the booth and stepped to the side. Kheli sat there and just stared at me across the booth. She was trying her best to put her lips together to say something else but the words didn't come. They were stuck in the back of her throat like Snatch-Back's jizz. There was really nothing she could say to me. I was disgusted and she knew it.

Xavier ain't say nothing the whole time but he spoke up as soon as she started to put her coat on. "Kheli, you need to leave that pussy alone. He used you and he just caused you to lose one of your best friends. Stop while you're ahead."

Kheli didn't respond to what Xavier said. She was too damn salty at that point. She just buttoned up her coat and looked down at me.

"I know you don't want to hear this but I'm sorry. I was wrong for being motivated by that money, true, but you're just as bad as me because you're blackmailing him for having sex with some trick who deserved exactly what she got."

"Now you would know all about that now wouldn't you,

being one of Snatch-Back's tricks that is? In fact, I would say you're the motherfucking poster girl. Wouldn't you say?"

Kheli ain't say shit else to me after that. She stormed out of Chili's all Hollywood, grunting and sucking her teeth like I gave a rat's ass. She was so zoned out that she almost knocked a tray of food out of this waiter's hands. He looked so pissed that I thought he was going to throw the hot-ass plate of fajitas at the back of her head. If he did I wouldn't have blinked. Kheli Stockton was no longer a concern of mine.

After she left, Nkosi and Xavier started consoling me the way niggas do at a funeral. It was appropriate in a way because in my eyes Kheli was dead. Her heart was still pumping blood and her lungs were still going, but she might as well have been in a box with worms digging through her.

When somebody dicks you that hard it's no way in hell that you could be friends with them again.

It's crazy because this was the same chick that I played "King Ball" with in front of the projects, way before I had hair on my dick. The same motherfucker who I considered to be like a sister. Kheli was so caught up in a fantasy with this rich rapper dude and she basically chose him over me.

I thought that she was smarter than that but I was wrong. There were a whole lot of chicks that I expected to fall for the bling-bling game but not Kheli.

The crazy thing is that she was the one who always talked shit on women who slept with married folks. She talked a good game, but I guess rappers don't count.

"Yo man, how did you know all of that stuff?"

"Nkosi, put it this way, it's a small world. Kheli ain't never think in her wildest dreams that I'd meet the jawn from that tape."

"You talked to her face-to-face?"

"Once, but she told me about Kheli over the phone. I didn't tell her I have the tape but on some real shit I'm thinking about letting her have it."

"What? You gotta be kidding me."

"Yeah dawg, I already got five hundred grand from that clown and I got this feeling that I should just take what I got and roll, nah mean?

Xavier and Nkosi were both stunned at what I was telling them. They didn't really say much else to me that night, I guess because they were still trippin' off of Kheli. It was going to take a minute for all of us to get over that. She had all of our heads fucked up in the game.

I stood up from the table because I ain't never had no intention of eating.

"It's like this fellas, Kheli and that nigga tried to get me but it ain't work, so now the ball is in my court. Payback's a bitch."

33. SATURDAY, NOVEMBER 29, 2003 (10 A.M.)

I had the day all planned out in my head.

For the first time since I got paid, I was looking forward to spending some serious cash. I wasn't really ready to ball out of control on myself just yet. I decided that the day would be all about Brie.

That Kheli shit had me fucked up big-time but I wasn't going to let it knock me off my block. There was already enough going on and if I let that backstabbing shit add to the weight on my shoulders I would've had a nervous breakdown.

As strange as it seems, I slept pretty well the night before. Me and Nkosi talked about what went down at Chili's for a little bit but then that was it. Brie was still with my mother so I went in the room and just passed out. I guess I was still in denial about Kheli, because I just kept it moving.

Me and Kheli had been friends for so long that if I thought about the situation too much and let it get to me then I would've snapped. She betrayed me in a major way but nothing could ever compare to Minerva's stunt. Anything after that just rolled off me like water off a duck's back. That was the ultimate.

The only thing that brought me happiness and made me forget about all of the bullshit was Brie, so I planned a whole day around her. I knew the malls and shit were going to be crowded as hell since it was one of the busiest shopping weekends of the year, but I decided to just suck it up and go. I'm glad that I did too, because it would be the last time I could let down my guard for a long time.

She needed a whole new wardrobe from top to bottom. My plan was just to go through her closet and toss everything to make room for the new gear. Some of her clothes were starting to look a little young on her and she only really had two pair of shoes. The black patent leather jawns were scuffed and ashy-looking and her boots were getting tighter on her feet every day.

I didn't plan on taking her with me to do the clothes shopping because that always made it twice as hard. Brie would get irritable and restless sometimes from all of that store hopping so I let her stay with my mom. The plan was to rack up on winter gear and shoes and then be done with it. As far as her toys, books, and games went, I planned on just getting that stuff off the Internet. There were just as many Christmas sales on the computer as there were in the crowded stores.

I called the jawn Nia, who I messed with every now and then, to see if she wanted to help me shop for Brie that morning. At first she was acting like she didn't want to wake her ass up but when I said that I would cop her something too she hopped, skipped, and jumped her ass out of the bed like an Olympic triple jumper. All you had to say was "free" to most of them chicks in college and they were with it. Fifth-year prelaw students were no exception.

I scooped Nia from her apartment near Broad and Diamond at about ten o'clock and then we hit the ground running. She was in a good mood that day so that helped me get my mind off the troubles at hand. Nia always had good conversation and managed to be so damn classy and sexy at the same time. Some of them chicks you just fucked and ain't never allow yourself to be seen with in public, but Nia was the one you took to fancy dinners and big-time shit.

All three of her roommates had gone home for the holiday break so she was actually happy that I came and got her. Even though she was from Philly she ain't feel like going to her mom's crib and being bothered with all her family drama, especially since she had her own spot.

First we went and copped Brie three pairs of shoes and boots from Hollywood Shoes off 4th and South. While I was down that way I went over to Rodeo Kids, as in Rodeo Drive in Beverly Hills, and got her a few outfits. This powder blue leather jawn had real fur around the collar and was three hundred bucks alone.

Once I had almost spent a grand down there, we headed over to Walnut Street so that I could hit up the Gap. It was hell finding parking around but once we got in it was all out. I got Brie damn near all of the new winter shit that was in a size 3T.

Nia helped me to pick out some pretty girlie stuff for Brie since she said everything I picked out looked like it was something a boy would wear. Kheli felt the same way which is why she always went out of her way to buy Brie pocketbooks and feminine little side items all the time. I was all for pink and flowers too but Brie needed stuff that she could get rough in every now and then.

We hiked a few blocks up and hit up Children's Place too. Once again I got almost all of the new stuff that was in Brie's size and called it a day. It was fun having paper like that where I could just dip in and out of them stores and grab whatever I wanted.

There was a branch of Commerce Bank right next to that store so we went in there so that I could get some more cash. I was balling real tough for Brie and I could tell that it was turning Nia on. Along the way I let her grab some skirts and jeans here and some boots and shoes there.

One of the sales ladies in the shoe store recognized me from the news. She never asked me outright since she was just trying to get that commission, but I caught her whispering and pointing with the chick at the register.

Nia was loving the star treatment but I knew that sooner or later that she would hit me with the *Law & Order* interrogation treatment. It started on the ride home.

"So Saludeen, wassup with all of the green all of a sudden. Did you hit the lottery or what?"

"Yeah I hit the Powerball for a mill."

"Is that right? So why didn't I hear nothing about this on the news?"

"Because I told them I ain't want niggas knowing I hit."

"Really? So when did you hit?"

"You sound like you don't believe me."

"I don't know . . ."

"Listen, all you need to know is I ain't selling no drugs and I ain't stick nobody up. Put it this way, if the cops pulled us over right now they ain't gon' find nothing in this Honda that'll put your lawyer shit in jeopardy. Got me?"

"I guess. It just seemed like all of a sudden you getting money and you know I hate to generalize or clump all men of color into the same ball of clay but—"

"But you thought I was hustling."

"No, not that. Well I don't know what I thought. I know you love your daughter and you ain't the type to do nothing to put her in harm's way so . . . I don't know."

"Well like I said, just know that it's legal and it was money that was due to me."

"OK I trust you. We don't have to talk about it no more."

Nia switched the topic and started asking me if Minerva had been giving me any new drama. I definitely ain't want to take it there so I just changed the subject back to Brie. I ain't give her too many details at that point but I told her that we would be moving out of South Philly real soon. She seemed happy for us.

As soon as we got into Nia's apartment, she ran off into her bedroom to try on her gear again. After she got dressed she came strutting back into the living room with the new knee-high leather boots that I bought her, a short pleated miniskirt and a tight-ass white button-up shirt that I could almost see through.

Her legs were bronze and sexy and I could tell right off she ain't have no bra on. It was something about when chicks wore short skirts and knee-high boots that shut the whole game down for me. She had to know that she was going to get it.

"Yo, don't you wanna dance for me and take some of them clothes off."

"What? I am a law student thank you. You're going to have to take a trip up to Night on Broadway if you want to see women stripping."

"I don't want to see them tricks. I want to see you. I want you to dance for me."

"And what am I going to get for all of my hard work?"

"What do you think?"

"Well the girls at the club get paid. I hope you at least got some ones on you."

"I can do better than that."

When she said that I went into my pocket and pulled out a knot. I had mostly hundreds and fifties so I took out all of the twenties, which amounted to a little under two hundred dollars, and put the rest back in my pockets.

It was broad daylight on a Saturday afternoon and we were about to get it in. Nia went over to her stereo and put a CD on. Of all the songs she decided to play a slow jam called "Pussy Beater" that a R&B singer named Lorenzo Upshaw and none other than Snatch-Back did together. It was on his third album and I can't even front, I used to think it was hot. We had actually fucked to it before but under the circumstances that nigga wasn't on my playlist.

"Yo, put something else on. I don't want to hear Snatch-Back. That nigga played out."

"Are you for real? This used to be our shit."

"I know, I know but I'm over dude. Put on that Dave Hollister or some Musiq."

"Aight, cool."

She put on this Dave Hollister jawn that I liked called "Pleased Tonight" and it was right on time even though the sun was still up. Nia worked it like a bona fide pro. From the outside looking in, somebody would've been hard-pressed to believe she was going to be a lawyer in a few years and not the next feature on HBO's *G-String Divas.*

I just sat back and enjoyed the show. Every now and then I would throw a twenty on the floor or tuck one in her thong to keep her going. She had me rock hard in less than two minutes. It was a good thing her roommates weren't there and that most of her neighbors were gone for the holiday because I had her hitting high notes like a police siren.

Once all of my twenties were gone and she was almost naked I told her to keep the knee boots on and to turn around. She leaned her elbows on the arm of her couch and bent over. I kicked her feet even further apart with my foot and then spanked her ass real hard a few times. After that I just dropped to my knees and started to eat her pussy from the back.

She was moaning crazy and squirming to get away from me. I was taking it easy at first, just flicking my tongue through all that thickness and mashing it against her clit. She was wet as hell and loving every second of it.

My face was all the way in her ass by the time she crawled over the arm of the cheap plaid couch. I flipped Nia on her back and pulled all that junk to the edge of the cushion.

She started getting loud as hell after that because as soon as I started going licking and on her pussy again I took it to the next level. While one of my hands had her right titty gripped up I slowly started to put my middle finger in the booty.

She jerked away at first and slapped my hand but after a few more tries she relaxed and let me slide it in all the way up to my knuckle. The more she let in the harder I sucked on her pussy. She was shaking and vibrating like somebody put batteries up in that ass and I was loving it.

Just when it seemed like her head was about to spin off, I pulled her up from the couch and flipped her upside down. It was time for me to get some head too and there was nothing like an upside down sixty-nine to set it off.

I was standing up in the middle of her living room floor holding Nia upside down while she juggled my man from jaw to jaw. My arms were wrapped real tight around her back and my face was buried in her twat.

I made sure that I had a really good grip on her because one of my boaws actually dropped his girl on a hardwood floor while they were doing the same thing. He told me that he lost his grip and she slid straight down his legs, head first into the floor like a WWF wrestling move. That would be a mood killer and I wasn't having it. I was ready to tear fire to some pussy.

Nia was still upside down and bobbing for apples when I decided it was time to take it to the room. I walked to her bedroom and neither one of us missed a beat. We were still giving each other good-ass head every step that I took towards her twin mattress.

Once we got in the room I turned her around and started hammering it from the back. She arched her back and threw it back at me with every stroke and that just made me want to nail it even more.

It was hard-core smashing from then on out. No chocolate, no strawberries, no music. I had a lot of pent-up frustration and Nia was ready to get it in too so we just went at it. Nia had two strong-ass orgasms that afternoon and that was saying something because she was one of them chicks who had a hard time getting there.

My day went from pure relaxation and ecstasy to hell on earth with one ten-second phone call.

After I got dressed, me and Nia made plans to hook up at the end of the next week. Before I left her apartment, I decided to call my mom to make sure that Brie had at least taken her bath. I already had the outfit I wanted her to wear in the trunk of the car.

My plan was to take Brie to get something to eat and then to go to the movies.

I was still floating off of Nia's company and the bangin'-ass sex when my mom answered the phone and deflated my whole spirit.

"Hey mom. How you doing today?"

"I'm fine. Where are you?"

"I had to go shopping and get Brie a few things but I'll be there soon. Is she washed yet?"

"Washed yet? What are you talking about?"

"Has she had her bath yet today?"

"Saludeen, Kheli came and got Brie this morning at like nine o'clock. She said that—"

"What! What the fuck did you say?"

"Watch your mouth boy. I said Kheli came and got her. She said that you asked her to come and pick Brie up."

"No I didn't mom. No I fucking didn't! Shit!"

"Calm down. What's the matter?"

Nia was begging me to tell her what was wrong but I ain't have time to think straight let alone explain any of that shit to her. I hung up the phone with my mom and went flying out of her apartment without saying a word.

34. SATURDAY, NOVEMBER 29, 2003 (3:05 P.M.)

I don't remember much of the ride from Nia's apartment to my mom's crib.

A lot of that shit is a straight-up blur. I do remember feeling like I wanted to jump out of my skin because I was so scared. It was almost wintertime and I was steaming hot and sweating like I just ran a marathon in July.

I tried so damn hard to stay cool but it wasn't working. How do you stay calm when you find out that the friend who has just fucked you over just came and scooped your baby?

Kheli might've been a slimy bitch but I didn't think she had it in her to do any physical harm to Brie. Or could she? Only a few days before then I would've cut out a nigga's tongue for even suggesting that Kheli was playing me. At that point I was thinking and fearing the worse. Why the hell did she come and get my baby and where the fuck were they at?

I almost banged out at least three times while I was driving down Broad Street. Red meant nothing to me. It was just another color on the traffic light because I wasn't stopping. I weaved in and out of cars at Lehigh Avenue and near Wyoming but I never got stopped by the cops. They could've rolled up on me with sirens blaring and lights flashing and all that would've done was make me go faster. I was not stopping until I got to my mom's.

Ironically I almost ran over this dude who was crossing the street with his daughter near Broad and Lindley. I slammed on the brakes so hard that my tires made this loud-ass Starsky and Hutch screeching noise. The boaw snatched up his daughter who looked to be about Brie's age and jumped back on the curb. He was screaming and cursing me out but I couldn't even be mad because that nigga was protecting his seed the way he was supposed to. I couldn't say the same.

I peeled off again and didn't think about it again. The whole time I was speeding toward Mt. Airy I was dialing Kheli on my cell phone. She had to have her shit turned off because it was going straight to voice mail. I called that phone at least fifteen times in a row and all I got was her fucking greeting. The sound of her voice was making me sick. In between blowing up her cell, I was also calling Snatch-Back but his bitch ass wasn't answering either. Them motherfuckers must've thought it was a game.

I knocked at least ten minutes off the twenty-five minute trip to my mom's. When I got there I jumped out of the Honda and stormed through the door without knocking. My mom and her neighbor Mrs. Spriggs were sitting on the couch drinking glasses of eggnog. I scared the shit out of both of them.

"Saludeen, what the hell is wrong with you?"

"Mom, why did you let Kheli take Brie?"

"Why, what do you mean why? She always watches Brie, what the hell is the matter with you?"

I snatched up her cordless and started dialing again. My thinking was that if Kheli saw my mom's number on her caller ID that she would pick up. Straight to voice mail.

"Mom, me and Kheli ain't brown no fucking more. That bitch shouldn't have my baby right now!"

"What do you mean y'all are not cool? Watch your mouth."

Mrs. Spriggs was looking at me like I was crazy because she had never heard me curse or even seen me get hype before. It was obvious that I was making her uncomfortable because she put her glass down on the coffee table and stood up.

"Girl, let me go and check on my pies. I'll be back over later."

She hopped up from the couch and broke for the door. My mom grabbed my hand and pulled me down onto the couch with her and started to rub my back. Her face was getting red and she was starting to look as paranoid as I was. She was all dressed up in her purple pantsuit like she was about to go out on a date or a job interview.

"We had a really nasty beef last night and I basically told her I ain't ever want to see her again."

"Come on Deen, you and Kheli have had arguments since you all were children. What makes this any different?"

"About a million dollars makes the difference. I found out that Kheli is conniving and sneaky and I can't fuck with her no more."

"What? What are you talking about a million dollars? Who has a million dollars?"

"I can't get into all of that now mom, I just want Brie back right now."

"Have you called her house? Why didn't you go down there to Marvine Street to her house?"

"Yes! I called her house and her cell phone a hundred times and she ain't answering! And I know she ain't home. I know her well enough that she ain't down South Philly."

"Well you know Brie is fine, she is not going to do anything to harm any child, especially Brie."

"Mom, I thought I knew Kheli better than anyone else on this planet and she sold me out so I don't know what she would or would not do at this point. We talking major fucking coins here and on top of that she think she in love."

"This has something to do with a man she is seeing?"

"A man she think she seeing. He don't give a fuck about her."

I knew I was stressed because I was cursing in front of my mother like she was a chick at the bar and I ain't even care. I kept dialing between Snatch-Back's and Kheli's cell phones the whole time that we were sitting there talking. The tears were welling up in my eyes but I never cried. They were there though, just like the lump in my throat and that nasty feeling in my gut.

I didn't think that there was any way I could make it another minute without knowing exactly where Brie was. My insides were boiling and my head was pounding.

I didn't plan on it at all but at that point I really had no choice. My mom was confused as hell and she deserved to be put down with what was going on. Especially since Brie had been basically kidnapped.

Kidnapped. Every time the K word ran through my head it made me feel like I was living in a fucking made-for-TV movie. I was about to snap but I knew that calling the cops wasn't an option. The situation between me and Kheli and Snatch-Back was too messy for me to try to explain it all to some cops when all I really wanted was my daughter back.

I just broke it down as best I could considering the state of mind I was in.

All of the color in her face just disappeared when I told her about the Snatch-Back tape. Just when it looked like she was about to faint, I dropped the real bomb on her.

"How did you get that tape Deen?"

"That's the crazy part mom, I got it from you."

"What? From me—"

"Yes, it was on one of those tapes you brought for Brie at that flea market."

"What? Saludeen what are you saying?"

"It was on one of them *Teletubbies* tapes. Snatch-Back's mom donated it to that flea market that y'all go to by accident. She ain't know that it was on there I guess."

"Oh my God! Oh my God!"

"Yes."

My mother was having a breakdown and I was so amped that I felt like kicking a hole in the wall. It hit me then that I hadn't called Nkosi yet to tell him what Kheli had done. As soon as I picked up my cell to dial his number, Kheli's picture popped up on the screen.

"Kheli where the fuck are you? Where is Brie!?"

"Whoa, slow your roll partner. This ain't Kheli."

"Snatch-Back! Where the hell is my daughter at?!"

"Daughter? From what I heard you don't even know if she yours or not playboy. You fucking sucker, you been raising some other nigga's seed. Yeah, I wasn't the only one caught on tape."

Then he laughed this sarcastic, anal laugh into the phone like he was trying his hardest to get under my skin. I was fuming fucking mad.

"Fuck you pussy! Where is my daughter at?"

"Like I said nigga, slow your roll. I'm doing the talking right now. Do you understand that?"

"I don't hear shit you're saying right now. Where are you?"

"I could tell you where I am but it ain't gon' get you no closer to this pretty little girl."

I ain't know where Snatch-Back was at but he might as well have been right there in my mother's living room ripping my heart out.

"This is what I want you to do nigga. Are you listening?"

"Yes!"

"Just wanted to make sure. I want you to bring me that tape right now. No tape, no Brie. Got that?"

"Yeah I got it. Where is she at? Let me speak to her!"

There was a quick pause and a lot of loud clatter like the phone dropped on the floor.

"Daddy!"

"Hey Ka-look-ee. How you doing Brie?"

"Daddy I saw the doggy."

"Yeah, you saw the doggy."

"A doggy and I saw the kitty cat."

"Aws, that's so nice Brie. Are you OK?"

"Daddy I went bye-bye. I saw the doggy and I ate my apple sauce—"

Snatch-Back came back on the line before I could say anything else to Brie.

"Yeah enough of that, get your ass moving right now."

"Where the hell is Kheli? Where are y'all at?"

"Kheli is a little busy right now and can't get on the line but that doesn't concern you. Get your monkey ass down here and don't even think about bringing nobody with you. And that includes them niggas you was up in my mom's crib with. Trust me, if you fuck with me I'll do something that you'll live to regret."

Snatch-Back told me to just get in my car and start driving toward Center City and that he would call me back on my cell.

"Mom I gotta roll, I gotta go and get Brie—"

"Where is she at? Let me get my coat so I can come with you—"

"No Mom, he said that I can't bring nobody with me or he'll hurt Brie. I gotta handle this by myself. Did Kheli take all of Brie's stuff with her?"

"Yeah she took everything, but wait, at least tell me where you're going Deen?"

"I don't even know where I'm going but I have to go and get my baby."

I hugged and kissed my mom and then I jetted. I had one foot out of the door when my phone rang again. All of my problems magnified a hundred times over. The face of Satan popped up on the screen."

"Yes Minerva."

"Where do you want me to meet you to pick up Brie?"

"Uh, I'll have to get back to you on that."

"What do you mean get back to me? We agreed on four o'clock."

"Yeah I know Minerva, but she's still out with my mother and they're not back yet."

"Well give me your mom's cell number so I can hook up with her to get Brie."

"Listen Minerva, I'll have to call you back with that."

"Why, just give me the number real quick."

"I said I will fucking call you back!"

I just banged on her. There was no way in hell I was telling Minerva what was going on. That would have made the situation worse, especially since she hated Kheli so much.

Minerva was Brie's mother and all but I felt like I had to handle the situation by myself. I got myself into all that bullshit and for the sake of Brie I was going to have to step up and get us out of it.

I had the battle of my life ahead of me.

35. SATURDAY, NOVEMBER 29, 2003 (3:40 P.M.)

I was passing Girls High at Broad and Olney when Snatch-Back hit me back on the cell. I could tell from the way he was talking and from the background noise that he wasn't in the same place as when we first talked.

He seemed distracted but the only thing on the planet that mattered to me was getting my baby back safely. I didn't think I would ever live to feel that feeling again. I felt hopeless and scared. I swore to myself that when I got Brie back I would never let her out of my sight.

"Yo! Wassup nigga, where you at with my baby?"

"Huh . . . oh yeah . . . chill motherfucker, I told you I got this—"

"You got what? You ain't telling me shit and I need to know where my daughter at nigga!"

"Check this out my man, I want you to come to the corner of 38th and Walnut. Be there in like fifteen minutes. If you're one minute late, I'm outta here."

"You're there already?"

"Nigga don't worry about where I'm at. Just get your yellow ass there now!"

"Aight man, aight . . . I may be a little late because I'm all the way on the other side of Philly and this traffic is crazy."

"Whatever man, if you want your daughter back today make it happen."

As soon as he banged on me, my foot slammed on the gas and I turned into a speed demon again. I got on the expressway at the entrance near Hunting Park Avenue and basically dipped and dodged through traffic until I got to the South Street exit. I banged a right at the top of the off-ramp and sped past Franklin Field into University City.

Since the place where he told me to meet him was so close to Nkosi's crib, it reminded me to call him and let him know what was going down. As soon as I reached for the cell, the picture of Satan's face popped up again. It was actually like the tenth time that Minerva had called since I left my mom's crib. I tossed the cellie back into the passenger seat and just let it vibrate.

The corner where Snatch-Back told me to meet him was dead smack in the middle of Penn's campus. Why the hell did he want me to meet him at the University of Penn? I had a feeling he was up to something nasty, so I was down for whatever.

I just wanted to get at him because my mind was playing tricks on me. Even though I was trying my fucking hardest, the worst possible thoughts kept popping in my head. I guess I watched the news too much, because every terrible thing that has ever happened to a kid I pictured happening to Brie on that drive down to 38th and Walnut.

I would be salty for at least a day whenever Brie would come back from her mom's with a scratch on her face or the slightest little nick on her knee or elbow. It wasn't even a question of whether or not I could handle something serious happening to her, because I knew that I couldn't.

I parked the Honda at a meter and hopped out. The second time that Snatch-Back called me it was from a blocked number so I had no way of contacting him. Of course, he wasn't answering his own cell phone. I tried Kheli's phone again. It didn't go straight to voice mail like before but it eventually did after a few rings.

There was no need to leave a message though. I had a feeling that Snatch-Back was somewhere nearby, tracking my every move like a sneaky-ass hawk.

Right after I dropped three quarters in the parking meter, my cell started to vibrate. I looked down and it was a blocked number again.

"Yo wassup, I'm on the corner of 38th and Walnut where you at—"

"Nigga where is my baby at?"

It was fucking Minerva. Shit!

"Yo Minerva, I'm trying to handle something right quick I'm gon' hit you back—"

"You better not hang up on me again! Who the hell are you at 38th and Walnut with? You driving around the city with some bitch ain't you? I'm coming to get my fucking daughter! I'll be there in five minutes."

"Naw Minerva, chill—"

It was no use. She hung up on me and I could tell from the rage in her voice that she wasn't bullshitting. I had no idea where Snatch-Back was or why he told me to come to that corner. Where I was standing was only a block from the Chili's where we met the night before. That made me wonder if he picked that location on purpose since Kheli probably told him about everything that went down between us.

The phone went off again with another blocked number on the screen. The second time I just said hello. My heart started racing right away.

"Hello Daddy. I'm sleepy."
"Hey Ka-look-ee. Daddy is on his way."
"I love you daddy."
"I love you too Brie. Where is Auntie Kheli?"
"Kheli is sleepy Daddy. Kheli go night-night."
"Night-night? Is Kheli okay Brie?"
"Kheli sleepy . . . I want Daddy."
"I want you too Brie. Daddy is coming okay?"

I had a nasty feeling in the pit of my stomach. Why would Kheli be sleep in the middle of the afternoon on a Saturday. That made me feel so creeped the hell out when she said Kheli was sleep. The first thing I thought was that she was dead but then that thought jumped out my mind right away.

As much as I didn't want to fuck with Kheli like that, I needed her to be alive for Brie. The thought of my baby being anywhere near a dead body made chills run up and down my whole motherfucking body. It was crazy.

Snatch-Back got on the horn before my thoughts could go anywhere else. He was cool, calm, and collected like he just smoked a blunt or something.

"Listen up my man. I hear that you're out there at 38th and Walnut pacing back and forth like you're about to go to the electric chair."

"Where the hell you at?"

"Listen man, I'm wherever I want to be at this point. I'm rich, famous, and I can get any bitch I want anywhere, anytime. Basically, I'm everything you're not."

"Stop fucking with me yo, where are you?!"

"Don't worry about where I'm at, just know that I got eyes all over the place. Now walk into the parking garage on 38th Street. The one you're parked right in front of."

"Huh?"

"You don't understand English now? Walk your ass into the parking garage."

"Aight . . . aight . . . where do I got once I get in there?"
"Too many questions. Just walk."

I followed his directions and started walking. Actually I was doing more of a quick jog at that point because I was anxious. As soon as I was almost to the entrance of the garage, a beige minivan pulled up right behind me and honked its horn. The loud-ass noise made me jump since I was on edge. I stood to the side and let it pull up to where I was standing.

I fully expected to see the face of the most popular rapper alive, but it wasn't so. When the window rolled down I was staring at a middle-aged white man with a head full of gray hair and a pair of thick-ass bifocals on. A woman, who I guess was his wife, stared at me from the passenger seat through even thicker glasses.

If his jawns were coke bottles, then hers were two ice cubes held together by a piece of plastic. Both of them were blind as shit. I took a quick glance in the back of their vans and their kids, a boy and a girl who looked like they were both in high school, were staring at me too like they had never seen a stressed-out black man before. Of course they were rocking thick specs too.

"Do you work here?"

"No I don't."

"Then who do we pay to park our car?"

"You don't pay anybody you just get a ticket up there at that machine."

"All righty then. We'll just be on our way."

He rolled up his window and pulled into the garage. After the driver reached out to get his ticket he drove under the wooden arm after it went up. That brief distraction threw me off a little because for a second I just knew that the white couple was part of a Snatch-Back's game.

I started to jog again because I didn't want to lose sight of that van. I wasn't three good steps into the garage when the person that I had pure hatred for stepped out of the shadows. My jaw tightened and I stopped in my tracks as soon as he came out of the cut.

"Pussy!"

"So looka here, looka here. We meet again Akbar Schraudenbacher."

It was Darkman, the nigga from Chuck E. Cheese's who broke into my house and stood over top of Brie.

I knew right then and there that it was about to go down.

36. SATURDAY, NOVEMBER 29, 2003 (4:20 P.M.)

Darkman was staring at me with the sneakiest, cockiest grin I'd ever seen in my life.

That nigga was sitting at the back of the bank lobby like all the cheese back in the vault belonged to him. It was the first time that I really took a good look at his face. I knew what he looked like and all but it wasn't until then that I realized how butt-ugly that clown was.

He had real greasy skin and big-ass acne bumps that looked like they were about to bust at any given minute. It was like someone had dragged his face across a gravel parking lot when he was a baby. Of course he was cocky as hell. The monster boaws always had the most swagger. My insides were burning but I had to keep it cool. I looked over my shoulder at him one last time before the teller called me to her window. He was enjoying that shit way too much.

There was a damn good reason that Snatch-Back picked 38th and Walnut. He was in control of the situation since he had my daughter and he knew I would do whatever he said. That much was true but if Brie even had a scratch on her when I got to them,

I would guarantee his fifth cover on *Vibe* magazine. But just like Biggie Smalls, Aaliyah, and Left Eye, it would be a RIP cover.

When Darkman walked out of the garage and told me to follow him I had a gut feeling where we were going. He turned at Walnut and walked passed the UPS store toward the bank. He didn't really say anything to me until we walked through the first door where the ATM machines were.

"Lookahere beeyotch, Snatch-Back wants his fucking money back."

"What?"

"I ain't stutter. He wants you to get him a certified check for two hundred grand made out in his name. And of course you know he wants that tape. You got that in the car don't you?"

"Hold up, hold up, one thing at a time. He wants me to give him two hundred Gs?"

"Yeah nigga and you lucky because I told him to get back every single dime from your nut ass. You should look at it that he's being real nice. Much nicer than I would be after the stunt you pulled. You're lucky it ain't my money."

"Naw I ain't the lucky one."

"Forget all that, get the check so that we can be out."

It wasn't crowded at the Commerce at all. I was the third person in line behind a Chinese lady and another black dude. There were three tellers up front but the only one who seemed like she was working was this skinny dark-skinned chick.

When I handed her the withdrawal slip, she looked up at me with this expression like, "Where did he get this kind of loot?"

She got up from her chair and went to talk to her manager and then she pulled some forms out from a drawer and started to fill them out. It took about ten minutes for her to go through the process and it was the longest ten minutes of my life.

Every time I looked back to see what Darkman was doing he looked more irked and restless than the last time. I wasn't concerned about how he was feeling though.

The boaw probably thought that I was salty because I had to

give that much cash back to Snatch-Back but that's not what I was worried about the most. If he had a kid then he would know why I was really stressing.

"Now who am I making this out to?"

"Cephas Johnson. C-E-P-H-A-S."

"I know how to spell it. My uncle has the same name."

"Oh aight."

"You know that's the same name as the rapper Snatch-Back."

"Really?"

"Yeah. But I know you ain't giving him a check in this amount though. I read in *The Source* that he spends this type of money on one piece of jewelry. He got all them iced-out watches and chains."

"Word."

"Yeah. Must be nice."

After she finished crossing the Ts and dotting the Is, she stuffed the check into an envelope and slid it across the counter. When I reached out to grab it she put her hand on top of mine and leaned in close to me.

"Listen I have to ask this. Are you the guy who was fighting Eric Brockington on the news?"

"Naw, everybody keeps asking me that. I guess me and the boaw look alike."

"You look just alike. That's crazy."

"Oh well, that's life. OK, I have to go."

"See you later."

Darkman was already walking out of the lobby door when I turned around from the counter. Once I got outside he started talking a mile a minute.

"Yo, what the hell was you talking to that bank teller about?"

"Nigga what are you talking about I had to get the money."

"No, but that shit took longer than it should've and then she started whispering. What was she saying to you? What were y'all talking about?"

"Man I ain't trying to play a hundred questions with you. Where is my daughter?"

"You answer this first. Where is the tape?"

"I will hand the tape over to Snatch-Back when I get my daughter, simple as that."

"Nah man, that ain't gon' work. He instructed me to get the tape back before I took you to where they are."

"Well you need to get him on the phone right now and let him know that shit ain't happening."

"I ain't calling him—"

"Call that motherfucker right now or I will pluck your fucking eyeball out with a screwdriver! Do you understand that he has my motherfucking daughter? Do you understand that I don't give a fuck about his money or that fucking tape? Get that nigga on the horn right now or it's going to me and you again, and trust me you don't fucking want it with me right now."

Darkman paused for a few seconds and just stared at me like I was an escaped mental patient. He was far from a punk, but I knew that I had made him back down a little bit. The fire in my eyes alone would've incinerated his ass.

"Aight . . . give me a few minutes. I'm going to holla at him right quick."

I leaned against my car and let him handle his business. He called Snatch-Back from his cell and walked a few feet away from me. I could tell from his body language that Snatch-Back was giving him a hard way to go.

Snatch-Back probably told him not to cooperate with me but Darkman knew that there was no way in hell he could walk back over to me and tell me he wasn't taking me to where my baby was. It would've been easier for him to tear apart the Eiffel Tower with his bare hands.

Darkman hung up his cell after a few minutes of balling his fist up and screaming into the phone.

"Aight this is the deal nigga, I'm taking you to where your daughter is. Gimme the loot."

The boaw peeked inside of the envelope after I handed it to him to make sure all of the zeros were there. He then tucked it inside of the inside of his coat.

"OK, I'm going to get my truck from out of the garage and then we out. You're going to follow me and you better have that tape."

"Aight, bet. Let's get it."

He drove out of the garage in a shiny burgundy Yukon. If it wasn't brand-spanking-new then it was close. My heart started beating faster as soon as I put the car into drive. I was so nervous and hype at the same time.

My heart went from fast to warp speed when I went to pull out from the curb and Minerva pulled up beside me and blocked me in. Darkman didn't notice that I wasn't following him because he peeled off real fast and sped through the light at Chestnut Street.

That nigga rolled out with two hundred grand of my money and I was stuck to deal with a pissed-off baby momma.

37. SATURDAY, NOVEMBER 29, 2003 (4:50 P.M.)

Minerva hopped out her whip like she was about to pull out a burner and put five slugs in my chest. She was heated and I can't say that I blamed her. If I called looking for Brie and she acted shady and hung up on me, I would've came looking for her ass too.

She slammed the door of her cranberry Beamer so hard that it made a few people who were walking by stop and stare. I was sweating like a stuck hog at that point.

"What kind of games is you playing with me motherfucker?! Where is my baby at?"

"Minerva, listen, there is so much going on right now. It's too much for me to get into—"

"What the hell are you talking about? What is too much to get into and I'm trying to get my daughter? You are really trippin'. Are you on that shit?"

"What the hell are you talking about Minerva?"

"Are you fucking smoking crack nigga, because you are skitzin' like a fiend. I can't get a straight answer from you about Brie. First you told me your mom had her and when I called the house she said that she wasn't there. What the hell is up—"

"Yo listen, I'm on my way to scoop Brie right now. If you give me a half an hour I will bring her to your house."

"That's not going to work. I'm coming with you because I don't want you coming to my house and getting nowhere near my man."

"Minerva, on the real, I ain't thinking about you or him right now. All I want do is go and get Brie so that I can bring her to you. If you don't want me to come anywhere near your so-called man then you meet me at 39th and Market in the parking lot of Boston Market in like a half, and you'll be straight."

"What! Why can't I just go with you?"

"Minerva!"

"Oh I see, you got some chickenhead bitch watching my daughter and you don't want me to know who she is. Nigga I don't give a fuck who you mess with for real but if you gon' have bitches around my daughter then I need to now who the fuck they are."

Minerva folded her arms and just gritted on me real hard like she was about to sucka-punch me. She was on some ol' Catwoman shit with this black leather hookup. The pants and the jacket were skintight and her boots were black too but they were a different kind of leather. Her hair looked like she just stepped out of the salon. I could tell from how geared up she was that she ain't plan on taking Brie to Chuck E. Cheese's or the mall. They must've had plans to go out somewhere with Eric Brockington and I was throwing a monkey wrench in her shit.

It was time for me to start lying because the longer I stood there arguing with her, the further away Darkman was getting. I know he ain't notice that I wasn't driving behind him and truthfully I don't think he cared. It seemed like he was all about the money and he had plenty of that tucked away in that bank envelope. Snatch-Back on the other hand needed that tape if he was going to sleep at night so I was praying that his lackey would drive back to see where I was.

"OK Minerva, you got me. Brie is with a jawn that I mess with. You're right."

"What?"

"You're right she is with a chick and I ain't want it to be no kind of drama so I lied. I'm about to go and get her now, just work with me for a half an hour."

"Where do she live Deen?"

"She lives in Southwest."

"Southwest? And Brie is by herself with this girl?"

"Naw not at all. Kheli is with them."

"Oh I should've known that bitch had something to do with all of this. I don't trust her sneaky ass."

Her words made me feel sick in the stomach. I ain't never give Minerva much credit but at that moment I wanted to give her dap and just tell her, "If you only knew."

"Yeah, yeah Minerva . . . I don't want to get into all of that right now. Let me just go and get Brie so you can get her and be on your way."

She was getting her mouth ready to say something smart when my cellie started to vibrate. I hit the talk button and pressed it to my ear.

"Dude, what the fuck are you doing? I thought you were behind me."

"Yeah, yeah I know. I'm still at 38th and Walnut."

"What?"

I was trying my best not to give away too much to Minerva but the volume on my cell phone was loud as hell. She was standing so close to me that I know she could hear him talking. She turned her head for a split second because someone was honking for her to move her whip out of the street, and I turned down the volume on the sneak tip.

"Dawg, I'm trying to help you get your daughter back and you playing games. Wassup?"

"Naw I got set back a little bit when you pulled off and I ain't see which way you went. Where are you?"

"I'm at 40th and Market, are you still in the same spot?"

"Yeah."

"Aight I'll be back in like two minutes."

He banged on me before I could tell him that I'd meet him somewhere else. I ain't feel like explaining to Minerva who Darkman was and why I had to follow that nigga to go and pick up Brie. I knew right then that I had to get rid of her.

"OK, this is the deal. Move your car out of the street before you get a ticket Minerva and I'll meet you at Boston Market in a half. Is that cool?"

"Nigga don't play with me. You better be there in a half an hour."

"OK, bet."

"I ain't playing either—"

"Aight, bet Minerva. I'll be there."

She strutted her ass around to the driver's side of her BMW with enough attitude for ten women. I thought it would be much harder to get her to bounce, but thank God she went for my story.

Minerva drove off real slow at first like she was about to change her mind about leaving and then she just sped off. Her ear was glued to her cell phone.

A minute or so after she rolled, Darkman came speeding up to where I was parked. He drove up right beside my car and rolled down the passenger window of the Yukon.

"Yo, are you ready this time!"

"Yeah, let's get it."

"Aight motherfucker I ain't coming back if you lose me again."

After he said that he peeled off again, but that time I was right behind him. If that nigga would've drove into the Schuylkill River, the Honda would've been floating right behind him.

He went across Chestnut Street and banged a left onto Market. Of course he was driving like he ain't have nobody following him but it was all good to me. The faster and crazier he drove, I figured I was getting closer to my daughter.

We were underneath the El train for a block or so when Darkman banged a left onto 46th Street. After driving a few blocks I realized that we were headed right toward Nkosi's apartment.

It crossed my mind once that Snatch-Back might've been holding Brie there but that thought left my head when he sped right by Nkosi's apartment on Spruce Street. The light was yellow when he crossed the intersection and flat-out red once I got there so I had to honk my horn so I didn't cause a wreck. I wasn't trying to lose one inch on that nigga.

Darkman made a right onto Pine Street and I knew it was coming because it was one of the only times since I had started following him that he used his turn signal. He drove almost to the corner of 47th Street and then he just stopped the truck and put on his blinkers. He rolled down his window and waved for me to pull up beside him.

I did as instructed even though I would be blocking the traffic coming from the other direction.

"Yo, go find a parking spot and meet me at the gate right there."

We were in front of a place called Garden Court Condominiums, which almost took up that entire block of Pine Street. There were two gates but the one he pointed to was closer to the corner. Me and Brie had been by this building a million times when I took her for walks. I never really had any reason to pay it any attention though.

I sped to the corner and across the stop sign where a Lexus had just pulled out. I closed my eyes and let out a long sigh before I hopped out the Honda. When I got back to the building, Darkman had already parked and was standing there holding the black iron gate open. My heart was pumping again because I ain't know what to expect.

He pointed up the concrete walkway like I knew where the fuck I was going. I just walked but I was still looking all around trying to get hip to my surroundings. I remember it being really quiet while we were walking up the pathway past this little pool and fountain that ain't have no water in it.

He stepped in front of me as we were getting to the end of the pathway and made a sharp right in the cut. There was another skinny little walkway that was about three feet long and ended at a wooden door with like nine glass panels on it.

We didn't have to knock or ring the buzzer because the door flung open as soon s I got close. When I walked inside the dark, quiet building I was staring right at the grill of Jeffrey Stokes. Snatch-Back's manager seemed extremely irked with me but I ain't really give a fuck. I wanted all them niggas to imagine how I felt not knowing where the hell my daughter was at.

"Yo, did you make sure he wasn't packin'?"

"Naw. Turn around so I can check you for heat."

I held my hands out to the side and let Darkman do his job. He tried to be extra rough and extra, I guess to put on a fucking show for Jeffrey Stokes. When he was finished he tapped me on the shoulder and signaled for me to turn around.

"Yo, he don't have no gun but he ain't got that tape either. Wassup with that?"

They both looked at me with looks of disgust on their face. I paused for a minute and then I just spit it out.

"Yo, if Snatch-Back got my daughter then he already got that tape."

"What the fuck are you talking about?"

"Like I said if he has Brie with him then he already has the tape. I ain't talking no shit, take me to him and you'll see."

38. SATURDAY, NOVEMBER 29, 2003 (5:30 P.M.)

I really felt it the second time Snatch-Back kicked the horse shit out of me.

That bastard caught me off guard one time too many and my ribs was paying the price. Kheli was hysterical but I ain't give a fuck what she was going through. Right dead smack in the middle of all that shit was Brie and she was losing it too.

Kheli tried to leave a few times but Snatch-Back's goons wouldn't let her bounce. Every time she made a move for the glass door he would snap.

"Stay your ass right there! I want his daughter to see him get his ass whipped by the greatest emcee of all time!"

I was trying my best to keep all of my attention on Snatch-Back but it was hard as shit with Brie crying. That nigga knew that I would be distracted and it worked to his advantage for a little while.

I had never rumbled at the deep end of an empty twelve-foot swimming pool but it's a first time for everything. There were ladders and paint cans scattered inside the pool and on the side. He caught me with the kick after I backed up and tripped over one of them big-ass industrial cans of paint.

It was dark as hell down there but my eyes were starting to adjust. The little bit of light came from these lamps mounted on the walls on both sides of the pool. There was a big glass wall on the shallow end so that anybody walking down the hall could look right into the pool area.

I ain't expect nobody to come strolling down there anytime soon though. It was obvious that the jawn was under construction and that nobody probably came near that pool except for workers. It was a Saturday night, two days after turkey day, so there wasn't going to be no motherfucking interruptions.

It was all spooked out like the hotel in *The Shining* with Jack Nicholson. The fucking pool looked straight up haunted or some shit.

Kheli was standing at the shallow end, with Brie kicking and screaming in her arms. She kept trying to put my baby's head down on her shoulder and rub her back but Brie wasn't having it. She kept lifting her head and twisting her little body around to watch what was going on. Brie was going through it and that just made me more heated.

I couldn't believe that them pussies were sitting by and watching that shit go down. I know they were his boaws and all but they had to know that he was dead fucking wrong for putting my baby through that torture.

At that point in the game, Snatch-Back had his fucking tape back. Darkman had it safe and gripped up in his sweaty hands, but the boaw still wanted to throw me a rumble. I knew the deal though. I knew that even though I gave him back two hundred grand and the tape that he still would want to fight. I was cool with that because I wanted to knock his fucking head off just as much as he wanted to knock mine off.

I guess everything that I had put Snatch-Back through had him so pissed off that he wanted to handle me himself. He was heated but that nigga had played a very dangerous game with me too by bringing my baby into that situation.

Snatch-Back was extra salty because the fucking tape was with his nut ass all along. When my mom told me that Kheli took all of Brie's shit with her I knew right away.

Brie had this Dora the Explorer pocketbook that was big enough to hold her whole damn toy chest. I let her take with her when I ain't feel like carrying all the bullshit she wants to take out of the house. It was big enough to go over her shoulder but I never let her put so much stuff in there that it would be too heavy for her.

The infamous tape was zipped up in one of the inside pockets of the Dora bag. That's where it had always been because I figured it would be the last place anyone would go looking for a sex tape. I was right about that but I was dead wrong about trusting Kheli.

We were locking that shit up for a few minutes when I started to get over on him. His knuckle game was tight but the way I felt that day I could've knocked both Tyson and Ali out in their prime.

My daughter was being tortured. I know that her little brain was fried trying to figure out how and why her daddy was fighting while Kheli held her and just looked on.

Looking back, it was a no-win situation. Darkman, Jeffrey Stokes, and this short stocky boaw who I had never seen before were all standing on the side of the pool watching. They were quiet through most of the fight.

The only noise I could remember was Brie crying and Kheli begging for somebody to stop the fight. Both of their voices echoed in the empty pool area.

The next time I went down I fell pretty hard. That was when Snatch-Back kicked me in my ribs twice. What made it worse was that I fell down right on the bottom of one of those metal ladders that were scattered around the pool. The pain shot through my body like a bolt of lightning but I wasn't finished.

As soon as Snatch-Back went to jump on top of me I reached over and grabbed the handle of a half-empty can of paint and swung it with all my might. I clocked that nigga right on the side of his dome and he went down quick. A glob of the white paint got on his face but most of it landed on me.

It was all over my neck and face and a little bit of it got in my mouth. It was disgusting. I sat up and started to spit it out while Snatch-Back was still on his hands and knees trying to deal with that blow from the paint can. I had that motherfucker where I wanted him.

I hopped up real quick because I saw that he was about to do the same. Before he could react I scooped up another one of them cans and caught almost in the same spot. The second can was much lighter but it still did the job. That nigga dropped down to his knees and grabbed a handful of my shirt with one hand and started punching me in my chest with the other. I was drilling at his head trying to knock his brains loose.

Right after I caught him with a good-ass two-piece, I felt my knees give out underneath me. Darkman ran up on me and snuck the shit out of me. I ain't hear him coming. I hit the bottom of the pool on my side and when I looked up the stocky dude was on me like a fucking panther. This boaw, who I ain't even know, was fucking me up like I spit in his mom's face. Darkman was getting his licks in too.

At one point all three of them were on me and I was feeling every single blow.

I balled up into a fetal position and tried to protect my head the best I could but them niggas was throwing hammers at me and kicking me with their Timberlands. Kheli was screaming and cursing but I tuned her out because Brie was just as loud.

Darkman pulled me off the ground and put me in a full nelson hold. That's when the stocky dude just sucka-punched the shit out of me in my eye. I saw the brightest flash I'd ever seen in my life. I thought Snatch-Back was going to follow it up but he didn't.

He strolled in front of me real slow wiping the paint and blood from his face. I could smell what he had for lunch he was so close to me.

All I could think was, are these niggas about to kill me in front of my daughter? Is this the end? I was terrified but none of them niggas was going to break me so bad that I was leaving out of there without Brie.

"Motherfucker, if you ever come anywhere near me or I hear

that you even mentioned my name I'll make sure that your neck is snapped like a fucking twig."

Then he just spat the nastiest glob of hawk spit right in my face. Darkman let me go and shoved me to the ground. I looked up at all of their faces while I was laying there on my back. I would never forget.

They all hopped out of the pool and started to head for the door. I sat up and spun my body around to see what they were going to do next.

Snatch-Back walked over to Kheli and took Brie from out of her arms. Brie was kicking and screaming not to go to him. Just seeing that nigga touch my daughter gave me the strength to get up off my ass. My first thoughts was that he was going to head for the door.

As hard as it was for me to get up I managed to do it quick as shit. But instead of trying to roll out with Brie, Snatch-Back turned and walked back to the edge of the swimming pool. He lowered her down and then just as quick him and his boaws headed for the door.

Brie ran over to me as fast as she could with her arms wide open. I dropped back down to my knees and just hugged the air out of her. I ain't want to let her go. I could've stayed at the bottom of that pool forever, I was so damn happy that she wasn't hurt. She got paint all over her face too from me kissing her and squeezing her next to me.

I ain't notice at first but when I stood up to take Brie out of the pool, Kheli was still standing there. She looked salty as hell and it wasn't shit she could say.

As soon as she went to open up her mouth I heard Snatch-Back's voice from outside in the hall.

"Come the fuck on bitch, we're outta here!"

And just like that, she turned and walked away. It wasn't shit she could've said to me and Brie anyway at that point.

We made it back to the car pretty quick. As I was putting Brie into the car, a black dude walked by with his daughter who was about Brie's age. He looked at me with this disgusted look on his face and pulled his seed closer to him.

That's exactly how I felt too when I pulled up into the parking lot of Boston Market. Disgusted. Minerva didn't look at me first she just went straight to the back door to get Brie out of the car.

"What the fuck happened to my baby?!"

"Nothing, she cool. That's my blood and some paint got on her."

"Why the fuck are you bleeding? Where the hell you had her at Deen?"

She unstrapped Brie and snatched her out of the car like a rag doll. As soon as she slammed the door, I put the car into drive and turned to look at her.

"Minerva, I can't talk about it now. All you need to know is that Brie is fine. I'll call you later."

I peeled off and never looked back. For the time being, Brie was safer with her mother. I had to go and get my shit together.

39. WEDNESDAY, DECEMBER 3, 2003 (1 P.M.)

I don't know if I'll ever live to be as embarrassed or stressed out as the day I had to break it to my mother about Brie.

It was bad enough that she looked like she was about to break down crying because of how fucked up I was. My eye had started to come back to normal but I still rocked a pair of sunglasses that I borrowed from Shadeed.

I wasn't as stiff as a few days before then, but I was still pretty sore around my shoulders and ribs. It was nowhere near the pain I felt the first few days afterward. That was definitely the most lingering-ass whipping that I ever got.

My mom said I looked like an old man when I sat down on the couch in front of her and honestly that's what I felt like. I started to bitch up and not tell my mother what I came to say.

I ain't think she was ready for no more.

She already felt mad guilty since she was the reason I got my paws on the Snatch-Back sex tape in the first place. I kept telling her that it wasn't her fault and that there was no way in hell that she could've known what was on there.

If the label said *Teletubbies* then that's what it should've been. She had no way of knowing that a rapper and his boaws would be on there smutting out a chick.

She held my hand and scooted closer to me on the couch.

"Mom, I have something to tell you and I don't even know how to start."

"Jesus Christ. What happened?"

"It's about Brie."

My mom whipped her head around and looked at my baby who was humming along to a Barney song.

"Remember me and Minerva's new boyfriend, the football player was fighting at Chuck E. Cheese's?"

"How could I ever forget."

"Well . . . we weren't fighting over Minerva or nothing that, I rumbled him because of Brie."

"Huh, I don't get it. Why the hell did he want to fight you over your daughter? Oh my God, did he do something to her?"

Her body stiffened up real tight like she was about to explode. My mother was bracing herself for the worse.

"Naw mom, he ain't do nothing to her. It's just that—"

"What boy?!"

"Mom, Minerva told me that I ain't Brie's real father."

"What!?"

"Yeah."

"What do you mean you ain't her real father? What kind of games is that child playing?"

"Mom, it ain't a game."

"So wait a minute. If you ain't then who is?"

I just looked my mom dead in the eye and let her read it off my face because if I said another word, I think I would've broke down.

"So are you telling me that her new boyfriend, or fiancé, or whoever the hell he is, claims that he is the father?"

"Yeah mom."

"I don't believe it!"

"Mom, they got a blood test done and all. She was cheating on me with him back when we were together."

"No . . . no . . . no . . . I can't accept this. I can't believe that shit!"

My mom jumped up from the couch and ran into the dining room. Brie was so into the television that she ain't pay us no mind at all. I followed my mother into the dining room.

"How could she do this Deen? How long has she known?"

"Who knows. They told me that day and that's why we rumbled."

I ain't see the need to tell my mom that he was a homo-thug. That would've been too much information at that point. She was already crying and frustrated so that was where I drew the line.

She just sat there shaking her head crying. After a few minutes Brie got from in front of the TV and ran into the dining room with us. My mom scooped her up and just hugged her real tight.

"I love you grandma."

It felt like I was having a charley horse in my chest. Just as quick as Minerva had got on my good side, I was back to hating her guts. That bitch was the cause of all of this.

For the next hour or so we talked about the paternity situation. My mom really ain't have too much advice for me all like that. I think it was going to take some time for it to settle in a little more before she could tell me what she thought I should do.

But what a fucking difference a day makes.

For real.

If I would've waited twenty four hours more before I spilled the beans to my mom then I would've had a completely different story to tell. The more I think about it, I probably wouldn't have told her anything at all. It was going to take months, or possibly years, for me to wrap my own brain around what came next.

Just when I thought that the motherfucking plot couldn't get no thicker . . .

40. THURSDAY, DECEMBER 4, 2003 (9:30 A.M.)

It was what I expected and what I didn't at the same time.

With that being said it ain't make it no easier to open up the UPS package when it came to Nkosi's apartment a day early. When I looked through the peephole and saw the delivery guy's brown jacket I knew in my gut that it was going to be bad news.

I was so nervous that I almost asked him to open the envelope for me and read it. Nkosi was out and Brie was eating her breakfast and watching *Sesame Street*. Dude didn't give me a chance though, because once I signed he slapped the envelope in my hand and jetted down the hallway.

Even though Minerva and Eric Brockington had already dropped the bombshell on me I just wasn't ready. I can't even begin to put into words how low I felt after I read them results. You hear people say that the bottom fell out and I guess that's the closest way to break down how I felt. I didn't cry right away and I didn't scream or reach for the phone. If ever a time in my life I just needed to just chill with my own thoughts, it was then.

Brie was not my biological daughter and I had to deal with that shit.

Nothing seemed real to me. The only thing that I was sure of was that I loved her more than anything no matter what the blood test said. In fact, she was the only person that I loved from the gate without any strings attached. I think in some cases people even have to grow to love their moms and their pops but with me having a daughter it was instant and I decided that no blood test was going to take away from that.

The problem for me was that I know everybody else wasn't going to see things through my eyes. If the blood that ran through her veins wasn't mine that's all niggas would care about. And even worse, that's all any judge would care about when that day came.

I tried not to think about it too much though because the reality is, it would have drove me mad. The truth about me and Brie was staring me in the face and I ain't have the courage to look back in its direction.

Brie was humming along to Elmo and Zoe singing "Twinkle, Twinkle, Little Star" oblivious to what was going on. Her biggest priority at the time was dipping her fingers into a cup of milk to get the waffle syrup off her hands.

What the fuck was I going to do? What did it really mean in the scheme of things? Giving her up to Eric Brockington was not an option for me. I would sooner slit his throat and troop a life sentence or lethal injection. But even in my boiling rage I was sane enough to know that I couldn't get both of them.

If I was going to jail then I didn't want Brie to be a total orphan. Minerva would be spared but that bastard would not live to see her make it to kindergarten if he tried to slide in and act like Dr. Heathcliff Huxtable.

I hit the talk button on Nkosi's cordless a few times but I would hang up just as quick. At that point I think deep down that all my peeps believed Eric Brockington and Minerva from the gate so there was no need to call and tell them what they already knew. I wouldn't rest until I had my own test done though. I couldn't just take their word for it. I don't know a nigga alive who would have. Well, I didn't at least up until that point.

The next hour or so was very dark for me. It was a sad, low point that I'll never be able to describe. I didn't know if I would ever be able to get excited about anything else again. Trusting anyone wholeheartedly again was definitely out. The only thing that topped the anger was the embarrassment. I was salty as hell and the more I thought about it the worse it got. The reality of the situation was slowly eating me alive. But what came next nearly devoured me like a shark eating a goldfish.

Somewhere between the fifth or sixth murder scenario that I was planning in my head something there was a knock at Nkosi's door. At first, I had no intentions of answering it.

I figured that one of them reporters had found the apartment and they were coming to harass me. I lowered the volume on the television a little and listened for a few seconds. At first it sounded like the person had walked away and then it started back up again. And then I could hear a man's voice, low at first and then gradually getting louder.

"Saludeen, I really need to talk to you man. I know you're in there. This is important."

It was a definitely a dude but I ain't place the voice right away. I limped over to the door and looked through the peephole. Even with huge, dark sunglasses and fitted cap pulled real low, I knew who it was instantly. My blood started to boil.

If the whole IRS was on the other side of that door and they were there to audit me, they would have been more welcome then Eric Brockington. He had to have the worst fucking timing ever.

Nkosi had one of them African walking sticks next to his front door. Before I flung it open I grabbed it got a good grip on the handle. I was in no condition to be rumbling that boaw, being as I was standing on one good leg and working with a dislocated shoulder. He ain't have to know that though.

"Yo, what the fuck you want? Do you want me to whip your ass again pussy?"

"No, no, listen please listen man. I ain't coming with beef. Please, we need to talk man to man. Minerva don't even know I came here."

"So what's that supposed to mean to me?"

"It means I'm here so we can deal with this shit man. We can scrap every time we see each other, nah mean, but it ain't gone change nothing. We need to talk man to man, no bullshit. I ain't leaving until we rap."

"You talking shit?"

"I ain't talking shit, I'm just stepping to you like a man now."

"You should've stepped up to the plate three years ago dawg."

"You're right, I know that. You're right but I can't go back. We gotta just work this out now, nah mean?"

I looked that nigga up and down with a look of disgust on my face like he smelled like trash-truck juice. He looked pathetic and all but I knew that it had to take a lot for him to come to Nkosi's crib to talk to me. I stepped aside as smooth as I could without looking like I was crippled and motioned for him to come in.

Eric Brockington walked in real quick like he thought I was going to change my mind. I shut the door behind him and locked it. Of course with all of the obvious tension between us the first thing he did was turn his attention to Brie. At first she didn't notice that he walked in, but when she did she greeted him with a huge cheese grin on her face.

"Hello."

He paused for a few moments like he was in shock. He pulled the glasses and Yankees cap off and smiled back at her.

"Hello Brie."

"You see Elmo."

"Yeah Elmo. I see you're watching Elmo."

She turned her attention back to the television without saying another word. He walked over to the couch and stood there at first like he was scared to sit down.

"Do you mind if I have a seat?"

"Go 'head."

Eric Brockington sat on the edge of the seat. He ain't look comfortable at all and I'm not sure if I wanted him to. He sat his glasses and hat next to him and started to fidget his hands. I dropped the walking stick on the floor and sat back on the opposite end of the couch.

"So what's the deal? Did Minerva send you here?"

"Naw dude. I had to come and handle this on my own."

"I see."

"Have you made arrangements to take your own blood test yet?"

"Funny you should ask. I already got the results back."

"You got them back already?"

"Yeah and what Minerva said is true. I ain't Brie's real father. Does that make you feel good?"

"Dawg, I'm not getting a kick out of this at all. This shit is tearing me apart too because I know that all this is mostly my fault. I should've just looked into all of this back in 2001 when Brie was born."

"Listen, I ain't let you in here to run down the same ol' song and dance. What the deal?"

"OK, it's like this. I have been thinking that I want to look into signing my parental rights over to you. It's not that I don't want Brie and it's not that I don't think I can grow to love her and be a part of her life, it's just that I have been thinking about this a lot and it seems like the thing to do. I mean, you been putting in work for her since the beginning—"

"Hold up, hold up. You telling me you want to sign over your rights, whatever they may be, to me since I been here from jump?"

"Yeah, exactly."

"OK, so what does that mean for me when she turns nine or ten years old and you done already won two Super Bowl rings and you change your mind. If you give up your rights will it be a permanent deal?"

"I guess. I would have to ask my lawyers about that. I never had to go through no shit like this before. I been sued a few times for paternity and other bullshit but this is something new all together."

"So what did Minerva say about all this?"

"Dawg, like I said she don't even know I'm here. I came to this decision on my own. I ran from all of this before and I decided that this time out I was going to man up to what I did and handle this now. The only thing that mattered to me was football so I was pretty much out of it over these last few years."

"You still ain't answer my question. What about Minerva? I know she ain't down with this."

"Well it's like this and I hope that you can at least respect me enough to keep this between us for now but . . . our relationship is having problems and to be honest I don't know that we're going to make it. We been arguing, and shit has been tense and I know I'm gonna call off this engagement pretty soon, nah mean."

I ain't know how to feel about what Eric Brockington had said. What he was spitting sounded good but I had doubts about whether or not to trust him. I wanted to believe that it was just that simple. I wanted to believe that me and Brie could live the rest of our lives without no bullshit popping up when she was like thirteen and in the seventh grade.

I wasn't worried about Minerva too much because she always found a way to fuck up. The threat of her getting custody of Brie on her own didn't bother me at all. She was sexy as hell but that ain't mean she was fit to be a full-time mom.

She had more than two years to prove herself as a decent mother and she dropped the ball a few times. I know I'm not perfect, but I think I'm a damn good father. There's a lot I don't know, but as time goes on I get the hang of it more and more.

From what Eric Brockington was saying to me that day, he wasn't down for the challenge. It was ironic that this strong, grown-ass man who got tackled on the gridiron for a living was so intimidated by one little baby girl.

I lost respect for him, but I couldn't be all the way mad at him. A lot of niggas was in the same boat when it came to kids and I blame the way we're raised. Him being a millionaire ain't make no real difference.

Most of the black girls I grew up with could fry a whole chicken, feed and diaper a baby, and clean a three-bedroom house by the time they were twelve years old. Meanwhile the boys, like me, Nkosi, and Xavier spent most of our free time at that age playing video games or football in the street. We would've been considered weak or punk-ass bitches if we even knew how to boil water.

It was night and day the way people raised boys and girls, so I don't see why motherfuckers are surprised when niggas don't want nothing to do with kids. When Brie was born I had a million and one questions for my mom. Kheli ain't even have kids and she could tell me more about what I needed to do for Brie, even after she turned one.

Dudes don't give much thought to what it takes to raise a kid and what it really takes to be a decent father. Women read whole books on that shit.

I was the last one to make excuses for him, but like I said I couldn't be too mad at Eric Brockington for being pathetic and defeated at the thought of taking care of Brie. He looked like he would rather scale the outside of the Empire State building than wake up every morning with all of that responsibility. Out of nowhere he shifted the tone of the conversation real quick.

"And I want you to know Saludeen that my decision ain't got nothing to do with what went down at the pool tournament that night."

"Man I ain't thinking about that shit. When I found out you was going to be around my daughter I had to see what the deal was with you, period. I don't care what or who you're into for real."

It was awkward as shit referring to Brie as my daughter when I was sitting across from the motherfucker who was really behind the sperm that sealed the deal. That shit had me messed up.

"Are you going to tell people?"

"Man, like I said I don't care about all that. I don't care who you dick down when the lights go out, just don't come around me with that shit."

"Naw it ain't even like that . . ."

"We're cool then. I don't even want to talk about it no more. And I hope that you ain't decide to give up your rights as a dad just so I'll keep my mouth closed about you being a switch-hitter?"

"Naw, naw, that's not it at all. I told you, I'm not ready for this and you and Brie have a relationship already as father and daughter. It would be wrong for me to try and tear you two apart."

I just nodded and turned my attention back to Brie. She was cracking up laughing because Cookie Monster was wolfing down a cookie and spitting crumbs everywhere. We were having a conversation that was going to affect the rest of her life and she ain't have a clue what was going down.

"Do you mind if I hold her?"

"Hold her?"

"Yeah, if you don't mind. I just want to hold her again, nah mean."

The shit was too unreal. I thought, how in the hell did my life get to that point. Not even a month before that day, he was just another receiver on a NFL roster to me and now he was standing there asking to hold my daughter . . . his daughter.

I got up and wiped off Brie's face and hands with a baby wipe and hoisted her out of the high chair. Eric Brockington stood up too and walked toward us. He looked nervous as hell.

"Aight . . . this is where shit gets tricky."

"What do you mean?"

"What do you want her to call you?"

"I never even thought about that. I guess Uncle Eric."

"Uncle Eric?"

"Yeah and once she gets old enough to figure out that I ain't your brother or Minerva's brother then we can explain it to her."

"You think it's going to be that easy?"

"I don't know man. All of this shit is new to me the same way it is to you. We have to just deal with it."

When he first reached out his hands toward Brie she turned away and clung onto my neck with all her might. She didn't cry or whine, she just made it known that she wasn't down with him. But then she relaxed after I prodded her a little bit and made it seem like a game.

"Hey Ka-look-ee. You wanna go to your Uncle Eric?"

From the second he took her in his arms he looked a million times more relaxed. Eric Brockington was still uncomfortable as hell but he wasn't showing it as much. He rambled on about the characters on *Sesame Street* while she played with the platinum chain that was hanging around his neck. I found it hard to look at them myself because I ain't want to even think for one minute that they actually looked alike.

Weirdly enough, the conversation turned to his personal life while he was holding Brie.

"So, from what I've read this ain't your only child."

"Man, you can't believe everything that you read. I been to court so many damn times in the last three years with bitches who say I'm their baby daddy. Some of 'em I ain't even fucked. They might've gave me head and that's it and then the next thing I know they up in court trying to get paid."

"So you beat all of them paternity cases?"

"Yup. They all got played in the end."

"What about all them jawns who said you gave them diseases?"

"Same thing man. Believe it or not, I ain't never had a STD in my life. Well I caught crabs once in eleventh grade from this chick I boned but that's it. I ain't never had none of the major shit so I don't know where they got burned at."

"So why you ain't never sue *Sports Illustrated* or *ESPN* magazine for running them stories?"

"Man, it's not worth the trouble. My agent and my publicist told me that it would all blow over eventually so I just trust what they say. Besides I know the deal. I go to the doctor so damn much, it's off the hook. I'm probably the only dude on my squad whose constantly getting blood work done since my iron is so low. I know like the back of my hand that I ain't got no diseases, that I got the trait for sickle cell and that I'm B positive. Yeah so I know I ain't got shit."

"Well, when you and Minerva went for the paternity test did you think that she was trying to get paid too."

"Minerva got a private nurse to come out to my crib and draw our blood. I took her suggestion and did that shit on the low because that would've got out too quick. It would've been in the *Daily News* the next day if I would have went to the clinic with her or some shit."

"I can dig it. So you were nailing all these chicks raw and ain't never catch nothing?"

"Naw dude, I don't get down like that. I don't be hitting these chicks raw dog."

"Obviously you and Minerva did."

"Yeah . . . well . . . that was it. That's why I always had a feeling that Brie could be mine you know. I took the test because me and Minerva used to fuck raw all the time."

That shit made me cringe because me and her were together back then and this nigga was just blowing her back out. Even though I wasn't with her no more the wounds were still open. I was still salty as hell that this dude was smashing when we were still together.

At that Brie started reaching for me and I took her back from "Uncle Eric" real quick.

Brie ran straight over to the couch and grabbed his Yankees fitted hat.

"You like that hat? You can keep it OK?"

Brie put the hat on her head and started marching around in circles like a soldier.

"Aight man, listen I have to roll but I just wanted you to let you know what my plans were before I just had my lawyer write a letter or some shit."

"Cool."

"You'll be receiving something in the mail real soon and we'll have a more formal meeting."

"Aight, bet."

Eric Brockington left out I locked the door and made a beeline to Brie. She was in her own world, dancing and spinning around with the cap pulled so low that it almost covered her whole face. My heart was beating fast as hell because I knew that me and Eric Brockington would never make it to that formal meeting.

He had said one word too many before he left Nkosi's crib that day. No strike that. He had said one letter too many. It was like the first lesson you learn on *Sesame Street.*

If A is for apple then B is for blood. Yes, B positive, as in his blood type.

Not even an hour before he came I had just read with my own eyes that in no way in hell I could be Brie's real father. I picked the papers back up and my hands were shaking. Brie was running around the living room singing and playing and while my insides were grinding like crazy.

In a nutshell, Brie was type O negative. The only thing that was absolutely for certain is that Minerva was her mother. If I hadn't seen her come out of her pussy with my own eyes, I would've doubted that too. I had already believed that she was a lying whore but now I had it in front of me in black and white. She had a fucking A positive blood type which meant that in no fucking way possible on planet Earth was I the father. And to complicate my life even further there was no way in hell that Mr. Eric Brockington was Brie's dad either.

I would've bet my life on it, because we were both fucking B positive.

41. SATURDAY, APRIL 24, 2004 (2:15 P.M.)

There was tension in the air and for a motherfucking good reason.

Nkosi was putting his career on the line. It had been almost three months since he quit his job at the *Tribune* and ends were starting to get tight.

It was no better for me because he had convinced me back in December to withdraw almost every single dime of the two hundred grand that was left and return it to Snatch-Back. That shit was hard as hell for me to do, got-damn it was, but Nkosi convinced me that it would be worth it.

It was only a matter of time before Snatch-Back would tell the cops that I tried to blackmail him for the loot, especially if he was found guilty. I knew that he would try to take me down right along with him.

Nkosi figured it best if I just came up off the money so at least it could look like I ain't want no part in it. It was inevitable that I would have to testify at the trial so I just had to suck it up and send him his bread back. If I was ever asked why he put so much money in my account I planned on lying and just saying he was trying to bribe me not to tell what I knew.

Me and Nkosi had brainstormed for weeks until we came up with the perfect plan. We decided that he was going to do what he did best, write.

In less than a month, my man put together a book proposal that outlined the whole motherfucking story of what happened between me and Snatch-Back and how I got the tape in the first place. Of course we left out any little detail that would make us look like criminals.

By April, what went down at the mansion in Gladwyne was no secret. Snatch-Back was a household name even to people who ain't really give a fuck about hip-hop. A nigga couldn't ignore the hype around him if he tried.

The story about the rape and the delays in starting the trial was covered in every fucking newspaper and magazine on the racks. I was shocked to see his ass on *People* magazine because it wasn't that often that they put rappers on the cover.

You couldn't turn on VH1, MTV, BET, or Headline News without seeing some kind of update on the "Snatch-Back Sex Scandal." Every time Snatch-Back made a public appearance it was like a three-ring circus. News cameras would swarm around that nigga like he was the pope when on the real all he did was make club bangers.

My name came up a few times in some local articles but they ain't really know what part I played in the big picture. Most of the shit they printed was so off the meter that I ain't even sweat it. A few reporters were getting bits and pieces of the story from whoever their source was but they were still getting it all wrong.

The media was following every little detail closely but we had the advantage. There were a lot of reporters digging for big scoops but none of them had shit on Nkosi. That nigga was knee deep in that whole situation before any of those clowns knew anything. He was in it from jump, so he had the biggest scoop out of anybody.

Me and Nkosi had it all mapped out. If the publishing companies that we were pitching the book to gave us a deal, we would be set. Nkosi wasn't too familiar with the book biz, but he figured at the time that we could at least get two hundred grand advance. Especially since the story was so damn hot at the time.

Whatever happened next, would be all gravy.

I felt like I did the right thing and Nkosi backed me on it. I went back and forth with him for days before I finally broke down and handled my business. I probably knew what I should've done all along but the thought of getting paid out the ass made me ignore my gut instinct.

Me, Nkosi, and Xavier went over to Shadeed and Desiree's crib on a cold Sunday morning in December. It was the same day the U.S. troops pulled Saddam Hussein out of the ground over there in Iraq. Thank God Nkosi was on point. One of the first things he did when I let him see the tape was record an extra copy. He had it stashed away in his apartment.

He told me, "Man I just had a feeling that I should make a copy because you never know . . ."

Man was he right. When I pulled the tape out of my coat pocket and handed it over to them they just looked at us in shock. I told Desiree to do what she had to do with the tape. Snatch-Back was acting so cocky about what he had done and now a jury would get to see firsthand what Desiree Perry had been talking about for months.

Whatever the outcome, I knew I could sleep at night because I helped her out. She was a smut jawn and all, but I guess that really wasn't the point. If somewhere down the line a nigga had evidence that could help Brie out, I would hope that they came forward.

Shadeed and Desiree had the tape so if nothing else they were going to come up off a civil case against the boaw. Even if Snatch-Back was found not guilty they were still going to get some cheese one way or another. I knew they would break me off a little something when the day came but me and Nkosi wanted to get our own piece of the pie. After all that me and Brie had been through, I felt like I deserved it.

I heard that Kheli got suspended from her job without pay because her supervisors got word that she played a part in the infamous Snatch-Back sex scandal. From what I heard, someone had called her bosses and told them that Kheli put one of Snatch-Back's kids in danger. Of course, whoever called had their story a little screwed up but it ain't matter. Her bosses must've had good reason to suspend her. All I knew is that there was no way in hell I would ever come to her defense or help get Kheli's defense or help get her job back.

Nothing weighed harder on me than the fact that I ain't know who Brie's real father was. There were some days that I ain't even fucking want to know, and then others where it tore me apart on the inside. I ain't even tell Nkosi all like that how I would just break down and cry almost every night.

I needed to figure out a way to get some major cash for me and Brie before I even thought about trying to find out who her real father was. I never mentioned to Minerva that I knew Eric Brockington wasn't Brie's real dad.

A month or so after me and him spoke, I got a letter from his lawyer saying that he wanted to sign over full parental rights to me. In that same letter was a check for two grand. He wrote that I would get one every month just so long as the details never became public and I ain't say shit to Minerva. Ain't that some crazy shit. I was getting child support for Brie, who wasn't my real daughter, from a nigga who wasn't her real father either. That's crazy.

Eric Brockington kept to his word and broke up with Minerva but she ain't mourn for too long. Word on the street is that she moved on to a young boaw from Philly who plays for the Spurs.

It was burning up my insides to know the truth about who Brie's biological father was, but I realized that there was a chance that I would never know. I loved her to death no matter what so it didn't matter. I just knew that I had to limit who I told the truth to because I ain't really want a lot of people telling me what they would do if they were me. She was my daughter, period.

But first things first.

Me and Nkosi came up in a big way. We both met with an editor from Skye Larieux Publishing and man did he put it on us. Lionel Gruber called us back within a few days of receiving our proposal about the book.

During the meeting he said that he was confident about the book project since Nkosi was an accomplished journalist and a good writer. He ain't really talk to me as much during the meeting even though I was the one who found the tape and really went through all of the madness. I guess he figured Nkosi was the one who would be doing most of the writing, so that was cool with me.

Like I said we were expecting to get about two hundred grand, so when the words, "half a million," came out of dude's mouth I ain't hear too much after that. Nkosi had to tell me later that he also mentioned that he knew a film executive that was interested at looking at my life as a movie.

My head was spinning. Not only was Brie going to be able to get braces and go to private school, but I could move us to a house somewhere out in the cut that had trees out front and a swimming pool in the backyard.

Our meeting was sweet and to the point. Lionel Gruber was on his way less than half an hour after he got there. I was so fucking proud of Nkosi for pulling that shit off. He came up with a bangin'-ass idea and he took it and ran with it. I guess I can take some of the credit too because I got beat down over that bullshit and Brie had to live through it too.

It was unreal. Snatch-Back really came at my neck and tried to break me but I felt like I got the last laugh. I came up big-time and I ain't need none of his money to make it happen. We were about to come up off a legitimate hustle and that felt good.

Imagine that.

I was about to get rich from writing a book about a rapper whose videotaped sex scandal dropped into the hands of a nobody from South Philly who he never met a day in his life. The more I thought about it, it had so much drama and twists and turns that people would have to read it from cover to cover, and tell all their friends to cop one too.

Imagine that.

TURN THE PAGE FOR AN EXCERPT FROM
MISTER MANN FRISBY'S

BLINKINGREDLIGHT

PROLOGUE.

It felt like I was raping the second one.

She was with it at first, or at least she was acting like she was with it. But when I started to pull her panties off and grab her titties she was acting all tense like it was the worst thing in the world to be getting some dick. And from a fine-ass brotha like me at that.

I was thinking, what woman in her right mind would front on a chance to get with me? Especially since her husband is a shrivel-dicked little white man from Jersey who probably only can get it up twice a week at the most. He was the one who got her into that shit in the first place, so I figured it was him she should've been mad at. I was just doing my job.

Anyway, my cousin Dex was tripping me out because he was just sitting on the edge of the bed with a towel wrapped around him sweating like he just ran in a marathon. He was staring at us all hard like a kid watching cartoons on Saturday morning.

We had already nailed this Jewish chick from Willingboro, and he was just chilling. She was long gone but I still had to get it in with this bitch who was as stiff as an ironing board. She was acting like she wasn't with it, and to make shit worse Tony Salvatore was all up in her face with his camcorder. He was the coolest Italian cat that I ever met.

I remember there was a Lil' Kim song playing on the radio and that shit was getting me hype. It was the one where she be gruntin' and talking about giving head, so it had me mad horny. I guess Maria wasn't a hip-hop fan all like that, because it wasn't doing shit for her. She was just sitting there making me do all the work. I was doing my best to make it all right for her under the circumstances, but she was making me so pissed that I started getting mad.

I was like, "Look bitch, you better act like you know and get with the program," and she just rolled her eyes and looked the other way. That's when I grabbed her chin and made her look at me right in the eye. Now see, I wasn't going to make her suck my dick at first, because I think that's just something you should really wanna do, nah mean? Just because she was trippin' though, I had to do it.

Anyway, I told her I want head and she told me that she didn't do that and I told her, "What, you scared you gonna choke?" She just wrinkled up her face and folded her arms across her chest all tight like I was supposed to give a fuck. She was all right for a white girl. She had a small waist and a black-girl ass almost with some big-ass titties. I figure she was about a size six because she was a little bit bigger than my ex.

She had long blond hair and her perfume was off the hook. I didn't tell her though, because I wasn't in the habit of complimenting the jobs. Well, one thing led to another and before you know it I was standing in the middle of the bed getting my dick sucked by Maria. She was working my jawn like a champ when Dex got up and got in the action. I guess he couldn't take it no more.

So there we were, standing up on the king-size bed in a Double Tree Hotel suite with our hands up getting a BJ from Maria White, the wife of Harry White, the New Jersey accountant who should've stopped gambling when his ass was ahead.

After we got our shit off, I laid her down and nailed her like I was getting paid to do. Tony was loving every minute of it. He was maneuvering that camera so close to us that I thought his fat Italian ass was going to get butt-naked and jump on the bed with us.

It's funny now that I look back on it, but he was hooting and hollering and talking shit, rooting me on like I was Jerry Rice or some shit. Dex was cool with the BJ she gave him so he went and got in the shower.

I was tearing it up for about five minutes when she finally started to moan and show some kind of reaction to the work I was putting in. She was one of the weakest lays I'd ever had. I knew she was faking it but I didn't care. I mean, I know she was probably upset and all, but damn. I look at it like she should at least make the best of the situation. She tried to stroke my ego by saying I was too big for her and that she couldn't take it, but I know game when I see it. I mean, I ain't the smallest brotha, but I'm sure she could handle it. She should have been counting her lucky stars that Tony didn't make her fuck Dex. I think cuz they injected horse blood into his jawn when he was a teenager, but that's a whole different story.

Right when I was about to bust she tensed up real bad and it looked like she was holding her breath. I was gripping the back of her legs and could feel her tightening up every time I hit it. I was just smashing it like a superhero or some shit and thinking, damn, get this shit over with before she starts to cry or something. I busted again in the condom and stood up from the bed. I didn't have no more rubbers, and that was cool with me because Maria was the last job of the night before me and Dex were going to roll out to the club to crack on some honeys that we really wanted to get with.

She jumped up and grabbed her clothes and stormed into the bathroom all dramatic and shit like she was on the soap operas. I think she was crying but she turned her face away before I could really see.

When she was leaving the suite, Tony said some ol' ignorant shit to her like, "Tell your husband that dark meat tastes better," and me and Dex were just cracking the fuck up. Tony paid us in cash, as usual, and said that a copy of the tapes would be sent to their husbands, as usual.

The crazy thing about that night is that I think the first jawn was really into it. That was the first time a job ever gave me her number. She slipped me her cellie number after she got dressed and blew me a kiss on the low. I blew one back but I knew damn well that I wasn't going to holla back. She was a job, and I don't mix work and pleasure.